THE
UNVARNISHED
GARY PHILLIPS

THE UNVARNISHED GARY PHILLIPS

A MONDO PULP COLLECTION

THREE ROOMS PRESS
New York, NY

ISBN 978-1-953103-36-9 (trade paperback original)
ISBN 978-1-953103-37-6 (Epub)
Library of Congress Control Number: 2023934224

TRP-105

Publication Date: October 10, 2023
First Edition

BISAC category codes
FIC049050 FICTION / African American & Black / Mystery & Detective
FIC062000 FICTION / Noir
FIC028140 FICTION / Science Fiction / Crime & Mystery
FIC009100 FICTION / Fantasy / Action & Adventure

COVER TYPOGRAPHY AND INTERIOR DESIGN:
KG Design International, www.katgeorges.com

FRONT COVER PAINTING AND PHANTASMO ILLUSTRATIONS:
Adam Bennett Shaw; www.abshaw.com

DISTRIBUTED INTERNATIONALLY BY:
Publishers Group West: www.pgw.com

Three Rooms Press
New York, NY
www.threeroomspress.com
info@threeroomspress.com

To Rod Serling
who opened the third eye
of my imagination as a kid.

TABLE OF CONTENTS

INTRODUCTION

COMING OF AGE IN SOUTH CENTRAL, my baptism of fire as a community organizer was being part of CAPA, the Coalition Against Police Abuse. This was an organic undertaking for the infamous 77th Division of the Los Angeles Police Department that patrolled the area where I grew up. In barbershops and beauty parlors, you'd hear stories of the brutality befalling Black folk when encountering those officers.

These efforts evolved into working in the anti-apartheid movement. This internationalist perspective would eventually take me to Cuba as part of the Venceremos Brigade. Back home, my activism morphed into being a union rep. After that, there was my time as a printer and partner in a small union shop, 42nd Street Litho. The seed funding came from another partner, one of the founders of CAPA. He'd sued and won his claim against the Pasadena Police Department after they beat him so bad he lost an eye. There was also a stint as the outreach director of the Liberty Hill Foundation which today still funds social change community organizing. Then in the weeks after the LA civil unrest of '92, my path took me to an initiative as a co-director begun in *saigu*'s (the Korean term for the unrest) wake. The non-profit's goals were to better race relations at the grassroots level and affect policy.

Through all that, while participating in study groups and reading the likes of Karl Marx, C.L.R. James, and Angela Davis,

I was also clocking mysteries by Hammett and Chester Himes; sci-fi by Andre Norton and Asimov; Doc Savage and The Shadow reprints from '30s pulp magazines (often one of those paperbacks would be in my back pocket on my way to football practice in high school); crime fiction by Donald Goines and Donald E. Westlake; reading way too many comic books, and watching *Twilight Zone* reruns as well. The meld of socio-political analysis and noir was reflected in my first published mystery novel: *Violent Spring*, a story set in the uneasy aftermath of '92. The manuscript was penned in the wee hours of night while working for Liberty Hill. But to paraphrase bluesman John Lee Hooker, the pulp was in me, and it had to come out.

Presented then for your approval are stories ranging from a centuries old Aztec vampire, an astral projecting killer, celestial vigilantes, an undercover space ranger, a right-wing specter haunting the 'hood, and of course a mad scientist plotting world domination. In these pages is where grindhouse meets blaxploitation with strong doses of hardcore B movie drive-in fare.

Thank you Peter Carlaftes and Kat Georges of Three Rooms Press for championing this collection.

—*Gary Phillips*
Los Angeles

THE
UNVARNISHED
GARY PHILLIPS

DEMON OF THE TRACK

ADAM "DEACON" COLES TAPPED THE BRAKES and swung his '41 Willys coupe to the right, his high-beams illuminating the edge and the drop off. The green Mercury with a supercharger scoop sticking out of the hood brushed against the left side of his car. He didn't care about the body; it was full of dents, and the fenders and passenger door were mismatched colors obtained from the salvage yard. But he didn't want the Merc knocking him over the edge of the rise as they took the turn. The Mercury was on the inside of the curve, plumes of dirt and loose rocks clouding behind both cars as they sped, their rear ends bumping once, twice together, then apart again. Each car had big bore engines in them that were not stock; their mechanic-drivers had cut and welded and pounded to fit them into their respective vehicles. The roar of those engines filled the cabs of each car as their owners sought dominance.

The race crowd hooped and hollered and made other joyous noises down where the race started and would end. Behind the gathered rose a wide ramp of the Santa Monica Freeway under construction, a mass of concrete and rebar sticking out of the end as if the ramp had been sawed off by a storm giant, for this was as far as the work had taken the builders. The goal was to build a byway connecting downtown to the coast. In the process, the homes of working class Black folk, in what was called the Pico District—people who'd come west in the '30s and '40s to work the then-boom of oil fields and, later, aircraft—had been snatched up by eminent domain. Those same homes were rented back to them before they were kicked out and the houses torn down to make way for rivers of freeway cement.

The race took place primarily on a snake of land that had been bulldozed to gradually rise nearly a quarter mile up, then took a whip turn around to descend into a flattened, cleared area that once housed a park and an apartment complex. Now there were stands of unfinished pylons and piles of concrete and wood and glass debris from demolished houses to maneuver around, then another turn through a partially fenced-in area where several heavy duty trucks and tractors—and the crowd—were gathered, back to the rise of land again. To add to the difficulty, it was now dusk and the natural light fading, so a driver's vision and reflexes had to be sharp. The improvised racetrack was a rough oval the racers had to drive around ten times. This was the eighth lap.

They came out of the turn, the Merc taking the lead. Downhill the cars plowed, the Willys running over a chunk of concrete, which Coles prayed didn't blow out his tire. Reaching the flattened area, he swerved around a pylon, the Merc now on his right flank. The other car zigged and zagged between two interspaced pylons and veered back toward Coles's car. Traveling at more than 90 miles an hour, both were homing in on another pylon dead center, piled concrete on either side of the two vehicles. Coles went left and the other car gobbled distance opposite. But the Willys hit a sizable rut in the earth that would have snapped the front axle in half given the speed they were traveling.

Coles smiled ruefully. Fortunately he'd installed hydraulics taken from a junked WWII airplane wing in the front leaf springs connected to the straight axle. These helped absorb the impact. Good thing he'd run into a man he knew, Ron Aguirre, at a car show about a year ago, and Aguirre had shown him the hydraulics he'd installed on a custom car he called a *lowrider*. At the flick of a toggle switch, he could lift and lower the car's shell. Now as they reached the other turn, Coles pressed down again on the accelerator, then pulled up the handbrake in a maneuver he'd been practicing. He fishtailed through the turn, forcing the Merc to swing wider to avoid his car. In this way he gained the lead as he straightened out.

They whooshed past the crowd.

Coles kept in front but the Mercury was tight on his tail. As they got near the top again of the quarter mile dirt rise, the Merc attempted to gain an advantage by powering through the turn. But the driver miscalculated when to apply the gas and just as he was about to complete the turn, momentum caused the rear end to lose purchase, and the car skidded over the side of the dirt ramp. It rolled twice and landed upright down below. Coles completed the race, then ran from his car once he'd shut it off, to see about his opponent. Someone had already gotten the other driver free from his wrecked vehicle; fortunately both cars had roll bars installed on the interior.

"You okay, Sak?" Coles asked William Sakamoto. The other driver's face was cut and bruised.

"Looks like I'll live, Deac." He took a step but his knee buckled. Coles put a hand under his arm.

"Okay, maybe I'll sit down a minute," he grinned.

Bystanders laughed and clapped the two on their backs. Somebody had a folding beach chair and set it up for Sakamoto to sit. A few kerosene camping lanterns had been brought and these were lit against the oncoming night. Some of the people left and others milled around, talking about the race, or examining the Mercury while drinking beers. The smell of marijuana drifted about, and one beatnik sat on the crinkled fender of the Mercury, wailing on his bongos.

"Good race, Deac," said a blond in stripped pants and a sweater top. She handed him a can of Hamm's.

"You're the coolest, Dorrie."

"Ain't I?" she said, wandering away.

A tall man in a snap-brim hat and Hawaiian shirt stepped over to Coles. The night was warm.

"Mind if I have a word with you, Mr. Coles?"

They were near the Willys, and Coles leaned against the driver's door. "What can I do for you?" Coles was in rolled-up sleeves, tan chinos, and worn heavy work boots. His hair was close-cropped and a scar ran part of the length of his jawline.

"My name's Fred Warrens." He was in his late 40s, brown hair long at the nape of his neck, and with hazel eyes. He had a trim mustache and knobby knuckles.

Coles showed interest. "You manage the Centinela Speedway, don't you?"

"Yes, sir."

"What can I do for you, Mr. Warrens?"

"I want you to race at our track."

Coles chuckled harshly. "What, you going to have 'Bring a Negro to the Races' night?" He chuckled some more.

Uncomfortable, Warrens frowned. "That's a crude way of putting it, Mr. Coles, but we would like to offer you a featured spot. I know something of your record. Fighter pilot in Korea, flying Mustangs then the F-80 jets. Over seventy-five missions and ten confirmed kills in air combat. The Deacon of the Air they called you."

"Yeah, well," he said dismissively. "You read that old article on me in *Ebony* so I guess that makes you an all right sort of guy, huh?"

"What wasn't in that article is since the war you've been building and racing hot rods in pick-up contests all over town. A lot of people, Black and white, talk you up."

"Yeah, well, it still means me and mine is unwelcome at you all's precious racetracks . . . all over town."

Warrens looked off at a few people dancing and snapping their fingers as the bongo man beat out a frenzied rhythm. He looked back at Coles. "Let me put my cards on the table, okay?"

"Please do."

"It's no secret that Inglewood is changing and, well, we think we need to change with the times, too." Centinela Speedway was on a hill overlooking Centinela Avenue in Inglewood.

"Uh-huh." Coles folded his arms. "You mean them colored folk who've been buying homes near the plant since after the Big One has also meant they go to the races and have noticed the lack of shade down on the track."

Looking past Warrens's shoulder, Coles couldn't help but notice a Mexican-American woman he hadn't seen around before. She was dark-haired and copper-hued, wearing black jeans and a black top, lantern light glinting off gold hoop earrings. She was something. She glanced his way then smiled as a man in a T-shirt offered her a toke on the tea, the marijuana. The woman declined.

"The Inglewood chapter of the NAACP has threatened a boycott campaign," Warrens said. "They've been very active when it comes to jobs and promotions at North American Aviation."

Coles smiled bemusedly. "Didn't you tell 'em you had a couple of Black fellas working at your track already, Mr. Warrens? Both of them janitors I believe, now ain't that so?"

Warrens spread his hands. "As I said, we want to do things differently."

"Then bring some coloreds onto the pit crews," Coles countered.

"We can't demand that of a racer and his sponsors. That's their decisions to make."

"But you want me to shuck and jive at some kind of hopped-up show, that it? Make sure the cameras are there on me after the race and I got this big shit-eatin' grin on my mug thanking you and de Lawd for this special, special day. Maybe take a knee and break into Mammy while I'm at it?"

"You're looking at this all wrong, Mr. Coles."

"Sorry you wasted your time, Mr. Warrens." He took a pull of his beer.

Warrens lingered, taking in a deep breath and letting it out slow. He adjusted his hat and left.

Coles shook his head and finished his beer. Nearby was a mound of junk and, walking toward it, he tossed his can onto the pile. Turning, he encountered the woman in black.

"You are a skilled man," she said. Her accent was heavy but her words were clear. Like they were being tattooed on his spine.

"Maybe it's equal parts stupid sometimes," he countered, careful not to get lost in those depthless eyes of hers. "But winning is good for business."

"How so?"

"I build custom engines and cars so word gets around when you come in first."

"And coming in first matters to you?"

"Better than getting kicked in the teeth."

"Yes, I suppose that is so."

He made a sound. "I wasn't being that serious."

"I see."

"You're new around these parts."

"I'm Ymar, Ymar Montez." She put out her hand. There was a large jade-and-stone ring on her finger.

They shook hands. "Good to meet you."

"The pleasure's all mine, Deacon Coles." Those eyes.

"Deac," a voice called out.

He turned to see an inebriated Sakamoto holding out a beer to him. "Here you go, daddy-o."

"Yeah, cool, Sak, but I was just talking to Ymar here," hoping he'd get the hint and blow.

"Who?"

She'd slipped away and Coles couldn't spot her beyond the small circles of light the lanterns allowed.

"Never mind," he sighed, taking the beer.

His friend grinned, bobbing his head to the bongo beat.

Two afternoons later, Coles was sitting in the Gas House, a coffee, poetry, and jazz joint on Ocean Front Walk in Venice. The inhabitants of the beach community affectionately called the area the "Slum by the Sea" and was recently immortalized in Lawrence Lipton's book, *The Holy Barbarians*.

"Here you go, Deac," Dorrie Muldare said as she placed his burger and fries on the table. She waitressed at the coffee house part time while attending UCLA.

"Thanks," he said absently as he sketched and made notations on a pad of lined paper. Three other sheets of paper had been torn away and were on the table too, his cup of coffee having formed a brown-stained ring on one of them.

She turned her head to check out his work. "That for a new car you're putting together?"

He looked up at her. "Yeah. It's gonna be a killer." He tapped the eraser end of his pencil on the pad. "Well, of course I gotta get a backer first, but more races, more notches to my rep."

"Right. You know, maybe my dad could help."

"No offense, Dorrie, but those egghead buddies of his don't go in for no racing."

"But they're, you know, *with* it."

"Hip, you mean."

She smiled. "He just got back from another expedition, excited like a kid in a candy store. He's in a good mood, dig?"

"Where'd he go this time?"

"Some jungle deep in the Mexican interior. He found some Aztec artifacts he and his crew are still sorting through. But my point was, his friends at the university are all about equal rights, right? Some of them gave money to that bus boycott they had down south a couple of years ago. He just signed a petition recently about busting up the restrictive housing covenants here in LA."

She shrugged a shoulder. "I'll mention it to him. Who knows, maybe they'd sponsor you."

Maybe if Warrens had approached him several years ago, he might have gone along with the idea of a "Negro Night" at the racetrack, Coles reflected. Get some publicity for himself and do something for good intentions. But when he'd come back from Korea, no airplane manufacturer would hire him to pilot their prototype, or airline hire him to be in the cockpit. A couple had offered him a mechanic's spot. But he was vocal in telling them that if a white man showed up with his kind of record, they'd be bending over backwards to give him a job flying. And while car craft was all about skill and knowledge, color was still an intractable bar at raceways, where you could put your talents on bigger display than at a street race.

He smiled, spreading his hands wide. "I can see it now, 'The professors of archaeology present . . . the Black Speedster.' And the crowd goes wild." He let his voice echo off.

"Smart ass." They both laughed as she walked away, passing a bulletin board where numerous handbills were tacked up. These included announcements about upcoming events such as Lord Buckley, His Royal Hipness, reciting his ribald recitations with Art Pepper on sax, and one about details for the Miss Beatnik 1959 contest.

When Coles left the coffee house it was getting on in the afternoon. He walked back to his residence on Brooks Avenue, an apartment he rented in a fourplex in Ghost Town, the Oakwood section. There was a four-car garage on the side of the property that let out onto an alleyway. He took the stairs and let himself into his pad. Coles made a sandwich and, taking that and a bottle of beer back downstairs, put on his worn coveralls and got to work tuning up the Willys in his stall in the garage.

The day fell away to night and Coles was about done. He was on a creeper under the car, bolting the starter back in place. He heard her approach, then saw her feet. She wore leather sandals that laced up to her ankles, and around one of those ankles was a thick jade-and-stone bracelet. She spoke his name and gave him a thrill.

"Hello, Deacon Coles."

He rolled out to see Ymar Montez looking down at him. She had on a gathered skirt and beige cardigan. She put a foot on his floor jack, hands on her trim waist.

"Are you looking up my dress, Deacon?"

He hurriedly got to his feet, wiping his hand on a rag left on the car's fender. "Oh, no ma'am."

"Buy a girl a beer?"

"Sure, sure. Just let me get cleaned up and we can go over to Muldoon's. It's a pretty okay joint on Lincoln."

She jutted her head at the empty Schlitz bottle. "Don't you have more upstairs?"

"Ah, yeah, sure do."

"Go get me a bottle, why don't you?"

"On it."

He tried not to rush out of the garage. *Keep it casual,* he reminded himself. Just this knock-out chick right off the cover of *Stag* who stopped by. . . . Be cool, man, be cool.

He opened the fridge, thankful that two more beers were there. He took them by the necks with an opener back downstairs, figuring to pop their tops with flair to impress her.

She was gone; Ymar Montez no longer stood in the garage.

He regarded the two beers and muttered, "Guess I can drown my sorrows."

"Over here, darling," she said.

He came around to the driver's side of the Willys and gulped. There on the backseat, that A-1 gorgeous doll lounged against the passenger side door, her leg propped up on the seat. She'd discarded her skirt and top and shoes, and was in lacy black underwear. She'd hung the mechanic's light he'd been using in such a way that her form was partly illuminated. The light swayed slightly and it was as if she shimmered in and out of existence.

Coles wanted to pinch himself to make sure this was real. Talk about a wet dream out of the pages of a girlie mag.

"You going to keep me waiting?" She stretched languidly like a big cat, rubbing her hand between her legs.

Coles was deliriously light-headed. "Oh, hell no."

"Then come here and be with me, Deacon Coles. Be with me in your machine, your totem of power."

The two made hot, sweaty love. As Coles moaned her name and a rumble rent his shoulders, weird visions popped into his head, making him dizzy: images of blood running over a carved stone face; brown-skinned people in plumes and gold; a flash of silver symbols and something more within . . . He gasped as he climaxed, and she raked his shoulder with her teeth, nicking him slightly. He sat back trying to catch his breath.

"That was . . . " he began, his chest heaving like he'd just run five miles, " . . . amazing."

"Will you do something for me, my love." She playfully dug her foot on his slick chest.

"Anything."

"I need you to retrieve an item for me. A keepsake you might say."

"Sure, where is it?"

"A kind of bowl. It's at the home of Professor Edmund Muldare."

"Dorrie's father?"

"The same."

"I don't understand."

"He stole this container among other ancient belongings, you see. They call them *artifacts* and put them in museums for the public, as if that makes it all right. But they certainly make sure their names are associated with these supposed artifacts."

"I hear you," he said.

She leaned forward, her hand replacing the foot on his chest. "It's not his, it belongs to my people." She pressed her body to his and he wanted so bad to protect her. "You know what it means to be denied, Deacon. You know what it means to have strangers come into your land and pillage and take and destroy your history. Try to deny your existence and accomplishments. That you were a civilization while they were still in caves."

"Well, yeah, I guess. But Dorrie's dad isn't like that."

"Really? He took what is mine and seeks to profit from it. Is that right?" Her eyes seemed to fill the space in the backseat.

"No, of course not," he said robotically.

"Then help me."

He blinked hard, knowing this was off. Her argument made sense but he felt like he should talk to Professor Muldare about this, man to man. But he couldn't summon the willpower to say different. And anyway, she had his member in her hand, stroking it up and down, and damned if he wasn't rising to the occasion again. If she had asked him to slap the greens out of his grandma's mouth, he would have done it.

And he loved his grandma.

DORRIE AND HER FATHER, A WIDOWER, lived not far from Ghost Town. Nothing was that far from each other in Venice.

"He's away at some faculty function," she told him, head on his shoulders as they drove there in the Willys. "Dorrie is with him as he and his colleagues celebrate raping my land."

Getting through a side window of the Muldare's California Craftsman home wasn't hard after they'd parked and walked over a concrete footbridge. The house was along one of the remaining canals mimicking the original ones in Venice, Italy. Coles knew Black workers had helped dig those canals but were forbidden to buy here back then, though they could settle in nearby Oakwood.

Homes stretched on either side, where several other canals had been filled in as the automobile became more plentiful since the late 1940s. The sidewalks were in bad shape or nonexistent, quacking ducks brazenly walking or roosting about, more on land than in the water.

In the darkened study, Montez pointed to a bookshelf. "There. My prize is in there."

Coles had brought a flashlight, and he shined its beam at a shelf where she pointed. The cone of light revealed a glass-and-wood case about the size of a breadbox, and he walked to it. There were symbols and images in silver embedded in the case. *Like the ones in his vision when he'd made love to Ymar,* he noted, confused.

Taking a moment, he examined the rectangular case, then swung its dual doors open. "It wasn't locked."

"Give it to me," she whispered. Montez stood in the room but not near him.

He turned his head from her to what was inside. The object was gold, oval-shaped, and rested on three stubby legs, not unlike one of those Fabergé eggs he'd seen in a *Look* magazine once. He removed it.

"To me," she repeated sibilantly, her hand extended like a grasping claw. But she made no move to step closer.

He went to her and the lights came on.

"Deacon?" Dorrie Muldare said.

"Oh God, no, it can't be," her father said. "That witchy woman in the village spoke the truth."

He was an older man with a full head of white hair and horn-rimmed glasses, and he moved surprisingly fast for his age when he rushed forward. "We must stop her!"

"Imperious dolt," Montez said, backhanding the elder Muldare and knocking him across the room. He crashed into a wooden globe, sending it rolling off its stand and across the floor.

"Dad!" His daughter rushed to help him.

"Ymar, honey baby, what are you doing?" Coles said, disoriented as if in a dream.

"She's a vampire, Deacon," Professor Muldare said, having got himself up on an elbow.

"I am an Aztec queen," Montez said as she snatched the golden vessel from Coles's hand. "And you will lead my army of the undead, my good Deacon." She pulled the vessel apart, tossing the top half away, which, Coles saw, had acted as a lid. Without it, the bottom half, with its three legs, was a kind of chalice, and it held black fluid. "This life essence of Mictlantecuhtli, the lord of the underworld, will give me the power I've craved for centuries!"

She held the chalice aloft, sneering at the older man. "And to think I have a pirate like you to thank for finding that which had been shielded from me for so long."

"Stop her," the archeologist protested. "She will enslave us all!"

His daughter rose, but Coles was closer. Whatever spell Ymar held over him was snapped once he'd seen her treat the older man so harshly and heard him talk about slavery. He left his feet and dove at her as she started to drink from the container.

"No, you fool!" she bellowed as she was taken down. The dark viscous liquid was sloshed onto the drapes and carpet. She shoved Coles away, and he too was thrown back. He collided with the bookshelf, and the silver-inlaid case tumbled to the floor. Inadvertently, he stepped on it, splintering the wood and breaking the glass as he got back on his feet.

Montez was on her knees, bent over, her tongue lapping up as much of the ichor as she could from the carpet. She raised her head, fanged teeth now prominent. The thick black fluid dribbled from her mouth, down her chin. She wiped at it, licking the blood stuff off her fingers, eying Coles with evil intent.

The chalice was on the floor on its side. Part of its interior was coated in a tar-like goop that must have been the residue of Mictlantecuhtli's blood as Montez had claimed. Instantly, everyone understood this substance was the most potent distillation of the ancient Aztec deity. Montez strode toward this, her body twisting and reshaping itself. It was like watching a tree grow on a time-elapsed film.

"Not so fast, Vampira." Dorrie Muldare brought a heavy book down on the back of Montez's head; it was an edition of the King James Bible—said to have been in her family since the 1700s. The Aztec queen collapsed to the ground, groaning.

"Time to spilt," Coles said, scooping up the fancy cup.

The three ran from the house. They heard a screech and, looking back, watched in shock as a now airborne Ymar Montez ascended from the house into the moonlit night on large, leathery bat wings.

"Shit." Coles stared open-mouthed as did the others.

"We can't let her eat the . . . god's jelly," Professor Muldare sputtered.

"Right," Coles said, cradling the golden vessel like a halfback as he ran for the footbridge, leaving Dorrie and her father behind. The now-transformed Montez flew after him. She had clawed feet and hands, face elongated and distorted with bat-like features.

"Deacon," the creature cried at as she dive-bombed him. "I will have what is mine."

Before she could latch her claws into him, he turned and swung like Maury Wills at the plate, striking her with the chalice. She went end-over-end backwards and dropped into the canal, sending disturbed ducks into the air. Coles kept running and got to his car.

Having been parked facing west, he peeled off on Venice Boulevard, then made a right onto Speedway, which paralleled the ocean. It wasn't named that, as some believed, because racing took place along the street; it was narrow and two-way. He clipped the side of a Woodie station wagon coming from the opposite direction, the driver blaring his horn and cursing at him . . . until that driver saw a flying human-like creature whoosh down from above and chase the Willys.

Coles neared the Pen, the weight area where body builders worked out. His plan was to take a right off the thoroughfare and maybe lose the demon after him in the maze of streets called courts, only accessible by foot. He'd have to abandon the car, but he was too much of a target like this, he reasoned. He whizzed around the corner of the Lido Hotel, a rundown establishment, even by Venice standards. He nearly ran into two winos arguing in the middle of the street. There wasn't enough room to get by them, and his tires smoked as he braked hard.

"Move!" Coles yelled, sticking his head out of the driver's side window.

"Buzz off," one of the winos said.

Coles edged forward but it was too late. With a resounding thud, Montez landed on the roof on the car.

"The angel of death has arrived," one of the winos said. He prostrated himself before her.

Montez screeched and rammed her hand through the window on the driver's side as Coles tried to roll it up. But it was her clawed feet that grabbed at him instead and tore him from the car, the driver's side door ripped off its hinges as she did so. He was carried into the air, then let go to drop hard onto the ground. He landed, the breath knocked out of him. The Willys shuddered and died; the clutch had been engaged but no one was driving to give it gas. Wincing, he tried to rise.

"Oh, you little insignificant man," Montez said hovering, then dropping on him, all four of her clawed appendages digging into his flesh. Saliva dripped from her fanged mouth as she leaned her face close to his, her forked tongue flicking his nose. The chalice with its blood residue lay nearby.

"How would you like this tongue wrapped around your cock like I did earlier, Deacon?" She laughed at the horror on his face.

"What, you recoil at the sight of me, my sweet?" she taunted. Briefly she willed herself to take on her human guise, the naked woman of pin-up delight. Chuckling, she then reverted back to her monstrous form. "Soon, your ardor will be rekindled when I make you mine, now and forever." Her mouth opened wide, and she lunged forward to bite him and make him her vampire slave.

"It's endsville for us, baby," Coles said, burying a piece of jagged wood with silver inlay inscription into the large vein in her neck.

Her eyes went wide and she reared back in shock. Coles had picked up the piece after he'd stepped on the chalice's case, shattering it back at the house. He'd figured the hieroglyphs, or whatever they were in the silver, combined to create a barrier to her, which was why she couldn't open that case herself. During the fight, he'd wondered, *What would happen if he got the chance to stab her with a piece of the case?*

His answer now was an inhuman wail of anguish as she tried to fly away, but her wings disintegrated, her body self-immolating as she became earthbound.

The professor and Dorrie drove up in their car. Together with the two winos, who were sobered by fear, they witnessed the end of the Aztec queen of the vampires. Montez's charred skeleton caved in on itself as the fire lingered, and her ashes twinkled as they drifted skyward.

"Wow," Dorrie Muldare said.

"Yeah, crazy," Coles seconded.

"Indeed," her dad said.

When Deacon Coles walked into Fred Warren's office at the Centinela Speedway, he said, "I'll compete in your damn show race. But if I win, then you put pressure on them ofays to hire some colored folk in the pits."

"You got a deal, Mr. Coles."

And when Coles raced his souped-up Willys around the track—money to improve her having come from Professor Muldare and some of his colleagues—he could hear the gas churning through the fuel line and the syncopated whine of oil and metal as the pistons screamed in the cylinders.

As Ymar Montez had burned, he'd noticed a smidgen of the Aztec god's blood had gotten on his thumb. He'd licked it off and swallowed Mictlantecuhtli's essence.

His super-charged senses had become knife-edge sharp, and the smell of combustion inflamed him like a beautiful woman's perfume. He was now the demon of the track.

COMSTOCK'S ADVANTAGE

"WHO THE HELL?" THE SKINNY OLDER man said. A towel around his waist, his personal-trainer-taut skin was damp from his shower. Automatically, his eyes shifted to the bed but his boy toy had been rendered unconscious and hogtied. His eyes came back to the stranger and lost their surprise. Craftiness lurked behind them now. A lion in the boardroom he'd been dubbed by the business community.

"If it's money you want, I can help you out. And if you're a jilted lover, I can assure you the thing between me and Davey is purely professional." Davey was the man on the bed, various sex toys and a cat-o'-nine tails lay about.

"Sorry," Comstock said, "but those negotiations already happened without your participation." He then shot him once though the eye with his semi-auto equipped with a suppressor. The body crumpled to the floor as if it were made of broken balsa wood.

COMSTOCK HAD AN EDGE. IT WASN'T picking locks or master of disguise. Though he could be present yet unseen. His was a unique ability and in his line of work, eliminating human beings from this troubled world, such was not insignificant. Unlike the other skills he had an aptitude for and had honed over the years, this ability of his has been acquired quite by accident. It was while on his third tour of duty in Afghanistan as part of the Army's 17th Convoy Sustainment Support

Battalion that the incident happened that would, as the cliché goes, change his life forever.

Not three klicks out of Forward Operating Base Rushmore, having made a successful delivery of material including petroleum, food stuffs, and pallets of ammunition, the attack happened. The road was supposed to have been swept and cleared by the Afghan National Army, and confirmed by the U.S. brass less than a day before, but of course as was usual in the service, the information was not exactly accurate. By far.

Later they would calculate the IED that went off was at least 200 pounds of "going boom," as the soldier slang went. Their RG-31 armored vehicle was equipped with a roller extended in front of it, an attachment of metal and rubber wheels that looked like something workers would use smoothing out a slurry of asphalt on a highway. But this was designed to explode the device before the vehicle was harmed. The roller did its job but the power of the blast tore through the cab, the air going black from dirt and soot, and a sharp chemical smell searing Comstock's and the others' noses.

"We're hit, we're hit," yelled the corporal into the mic screwed into his helmet.

"The front wheels are jammed up," yelled the PFC driving the vehicle. "We need to get the hell out."

Spilling out of the halted vehicle to dash to one of the others in the convoy, the bullet that tagged Comstock, a one-time solar panel installer in Phoenix, was a ricochet off the side of the RG-31. Comstock went down and would vaguely recall his buddies carrying him low, his feet dragging across the ground to the relative safety of a companion armored vehicle. He was hauled in and dumped on his back in the thing. There was a jumble of voices above him, gunfire, and his vision blurry due to the blood seeping from his head wound, bathing his face in a red sheen. Then he passed out.

Due to battlefield medical advances, and that—it turned out—the round had creased his skull and brain but passed on without fragmenting, Comstock rated positive on all the tests they gave him when he was in recovery at Walter Reed. He didn't show evidence of brain damage and he was looking forward to being rotated out.

"You're one lucky man, soldier," winked his 40-something nurse with the crooked nose.

"Yes, ma'am," he agreed.

Comstock figured he'd try and get a job driving a truck for the civilian side of the military contractor who supplied some of the vehicles for the CSSB. He'd made friends with one of the company's managers and the outfit had been nice enough to send a basket of fruit to him at the hospital. Then one evening, after his physical therapy session, he was sitting in a chair in his hospital room. It was getting on late afternoon and the day had been overcast. Sitting there listening to a sports radio program, Comstock began to doze. Soon he was having a dream where he was floating along the hallway like a specter, unseen but he could see and hear everyone.

He wafted through walls as if they were movie special-effect greenscreen projections. Comstock found himself in a darkened room full of medical supplies. His friendly nurse was in there with a younger man, an orderly whose name tag read "Velasquez." It was obvious from the way there were buttoning up, they'd just been making love. The younger man fired up a joint and shared a toke with her, then after he had one more pull, extinguished the weed and put it back in his pocket.

"See you on Friday, Alice," Velasquez told her.

"Yes you will," she replied huskily, letting her hand travel south of his belt buckle giving him a lustful squeeze while she tongued him.

Comstock grinned crookedly and his eyes came open in his room. When the nurse made her rounds later, he mentioned offhandedly, "How you doing, Alice?" figuring it was a private joke and he'd tell her she was in his dream, but he'd keep it chaste.

"How'd you know my first name?" Only her last name was on her rectangle of a tag on her uniform.

"I, uh, guess I must have overheard it."

She smiled sweetly and finished up.

The next time his astral form left his body, he knew it wasn't a dream. For that time he followed one of his doctors home to a split level ranch house and noted the address. When he was released two weeks later, he had the cab driver take him there. The house matched what he'd seen as a wraith, his ghostly form not nude, but dressed as he was in actuality. He decided then that driving a truck or going back to installing solar panels was not in the cards.

Now several years on, Comstock was one of the highest paid pro button men. Whatever that enemy bullet had done to his brain, and in his astral form he couldn't carry physical objects or touch things, his ability gave him one hell of a way to reconnoiter. Over time he'd learned the limits of his power. He had to have been in physical proximity his target to be able to focus on them later. Generally, too, he found he could only project some 50 miles away. If he happened to see something shocking while tracking his prey, and this had occurred more than once given what people do behind closed doors, he would instantly snap back into his body. The same would happen if he suddenly lost focus.

THE COMMERCIAL JET TOUCHED DOWN IN Dallas and Comstock got off the plane in the heat and humidity with the rest of the passengers. He rented a car using a driver's license issued to one of the various false identities he'd cultivated over his years of experience and drove to his hotel. Along the way, he activated his GPS jammer to block the signal the rental was sending. Not that he'd purposely leave any evidence linking "Walter Monroe" to the killing that was going to go down soon, but he tried to be meticulous in erasing as much of his digital footprint as he could. That's why he'd memorize routes and byways in a city he was journeying to, as opposed to using any of those apps that told you in a nice lady's voice where to drive, even though he always used burners or encrypted phones.

His target was the CEO of some sort of oil and gas concern. Because he commanded a high-end fee, his targets were one percenters who invariably found themselves in the crosshairs of their fellow swells. All said and done about loosening regulations that strangled business or renegotiating foreign trade deals; when it came down to it, how business really got done proved crime in the suites was more brutal than crime in the streets.

"Here you go, Mr. Monroe," the pert desk clerk said as she slid his card key across the marble countertop. Her nails matched her emerald eyes.

"Thank you," he said. She smiled her practiced response back at him. Comstock reminded himself to not be a spectral creep and follow the pretty woman home later to get a thrill as she undressed.

In his suite Comstock opened the shades to let the afternoon light in and checked his watch adjusted to the correct local time. Pouring himself a glass of cranberry juice from a can liberated out of the minibar, he once again reviewed the information on 54-year-old Geoff Ralston, head of Sunridge Petroleum, headquartered here in Dallas, not too far from this hotel. Back at the window he could see Sunridge's gaudy orange and yellow logo on the side of its highrise. He threw the security lock on his hotel door and sat in a comfortable chair. His being able to astral project didn't require him to sleep so much as to go inward, to envision the neural connectors in his brain, and as he did this, as his heart rate decreased and his breathing got shallow, he could send himself out. At Hialeah horse racetrack in Miami a week ago, he'd positioned himself to briefly pass by the energy head.

Comstock sent his essence soaring, flying above the skyline, a sensation he never tired of experiencing. He entered one of the upper floors of the Sunridge building, watching the crisp men and women in their crisp suits go about their workday. He knew where the CEO's office was as he'd been supplied the floorplans. There he found Ralston in his corner office with the magnificent view on the phone joking with someone about a recent golf game. And so it went. Comstock sat cross-legged, floating in the room, watching. He knew from the past, the richer the man or woman, the more pressure they were under, the more they got their indulgences on. Married, divorced, whatever, none of them were celibate; they had to get their release some kind of way. It didn't have to be sex, but damned if the percentages didn't usually say it was.

Sure enough by the second day, the way in which he'd eliminate his target became clear to Comstock. No surprise but Ralston had a squeeze on the side, Debi Namaras, a blonde who couldn't be more than 25, he estimated. Ralston paid for her apartment on a street of leafy elms that ended in a cul-de-sac. From their conversations he understood she was a part-time bartender at a sports bar in the Bishop Arts District, but wanted more of her life. Of course, he promised the moon to her, particularly when she was giving him enthusiastic head. He'd already bought her a used Camry, which Comstock located in her numbered parking stall. At one point, while the two cavorted, the non-corporeal Comstock studied the lock on her apartment door and the one at the entrance security gate downstairs. No lock expert, more than once he'd lingered at an apartment entrance, walking back and forth gabbing on a cell phone, and when someone went in followed or disabled the lock with super glue.

Over the years, Comstock had observed various guys and gals of the upper crust who got some on the side had their drivers take them to their assignations. Ralston was old school and drove his black BMW 6 Series to her place. Okay, Comstock concluded after noting the man's pattern with the young lady over several days. The hit would have to go down in daylight with possible witnesses. But not on the girlfriend's street, he concluded. He withdrew his ghostly head from the engine compartment of the car, having scrutinized its electronic components. Comstock returned to his body and went down to the pool to have a swim and solidify his plan. Later he drove across town to a public library and reviewed the specs on Ralston's BMW utilizing a site for hardcore aficionados.

RALSTON WHISTLED A TUNE WHEN HE left the blonde's apartment two days later. He beeped the alarm off which also unlocked the car door of his Beemer. He got behind the wheel of the sleek machine, a satisfied grin on his face. The engine caught instantly and he drove away, the diffused rays of the sun filtering tendrils of light through the leafy trees. Comstock trailed him in his rental but not too close. He was pretty certain from his past observations of the route Ralston would take to get to the I-30 freeway and back into downtown and his office.

Just as the purring BMW cornered the commercial street that led to the on ramp, the car suddenly stopped functioning, the engine shutting off with the rapidity of snapping your fingers. It was times like these that Comstock reflected on the types of devices obtained via the so-called dark web. Gadgets like the one he'd just used to disable Ralston's car. New vehicles were built with a kind of black box that recorded accident data. His gizmo, which looked like a two-way radio, activated in close enough range, sent a false message to the black box that it was being tampered with—a code that told it thieves had stolen the car. This in turn meant the onboard computer would receive a signal from the black box and shut down the car's operating system.

Comstock wryly noted: good thing Ralston didn't favor rebuilt 1960s muscle cars whose electrical components were by, comparison, uncomplicated and immune to hacking. He stepped closer to the stalled out BMW, wearing his worn mechanic's clothes. He'd timed it so that Ralston would have just enough inertia to steer toward a curb, which he had. The steering wheel locked once the front wheels stopped moving. Comstock's heart rate quickened, hammering in his ears. The old excitement still stirred him but he'd long ago learned to channel the jangles through and out his body like sending forth his astral form. Hand cool around the weapon in his pocket, eyes scanning his terrain, he lessened the gap to the car

For surely a busy man like Ralston, with women to juggle and kickbacks to oversee, would be happy to ask this grease monkey could he take a look under the hood. And given nothing worked on the car, he might be standing outside, the interior stuffy as the power windows were up and there was no air conditioner. Or maybe Ralston was getting Triple A on the phone. But Ralston was unmoving behind the driver's wheel, Comstock saw. He had both hands in his pockets, his baseball-style cap pulled low on his forehead. He paused momentarily. Ralston's BMW was partially stopped in the driveway of an industrial store. Two men in clothes not dissimilar to Comstock's came out of the side of the store, guiding a large commercial refrigerator on a dolly toward a flatbed truck.

"Hey, mister," he said just loud enough, knuckle sounding on the driver's side window, "need a hand?"

Ralston lay back against the supple leather of the roadster's seat. His eyes were open, his mouth gapped slightly. Frowning, Comstock unlatched the door and swung it open some, stepping around it in the same motion so as to strike instantly and be gone. Pressing two of his fingers to the big vein in Ralston's neck, there was no pulse. He bent closer, detecting the smell of wine inside the recently deceased man's open mouth.

"Hey, we got a delivery to make," called out one of the workmen at the flatbed.

"I think this guy's had a heart attack," Comstock said. "Can you call 9-1-1, my phone is dead."

"Okay, hold on," the other one replied.

Comstock walked away briskly, not worried that he was leaving telltale fingerprints behind. Coated onto his hands was a clear plasticine-like material. He got back in his rental parked down the street and, making a U-turn, headed back toward the girlfriend's apartment. There was no such thing as a coincidence in his line of work. Ralston just up and croaked conveniently like that? Hell no, Comstock determined.

Namaras's Camry was still in its space when Comstock walked around to the rear of her complex and saw it there. He went to a side gate off the pool, having heard voices and splashing coming from there. He carried a tool box. Two women of a certain age were enjoying the water.

"Excuse me, would you mind letting me back in? I'm working on one of the forced air units."

"No problem," one of them said, a dark-haired forty-plus with big shades and an endearing muffin top. She made a thing of sashaying over in her too-small bikini.

"Thanks a lot."

"My pleasure," she flirted.

He touched the brim of his cap like a cowboy might. He heard the two chuckling and whispering at his back as he went in. Namaras's apartment was on the second floor and out of the line of sight of the pool. He knocked lightly on the door, unrushed, conveying nothing too much out of the ordinary.

"Yes?" came her voice.

"It's about the flooding, ma'am."

"What?"

"Apartment 29, pipe burst." That was the unit to the right of hers. The layout of the place had her kitchen mirrored against 29's. If she'd lived here any amount of time, she'd know that.

There was a pause, and was that murmuring Comstock detected? Was she on the phone?

Namaras cracked the door and examined him through the sliver. "Is this going to back up into my place?'

"I want to make sure it doesn't."

"Okay, fine." She opened the door more and he stepped in.

"You did a hell of a job on Ralston," he said, aware of the exposed doorway behind him.

Her alert face clouded momentarily then cleared. "I guess you're not the plumber."

"And I guess you're not just a part time bartender."

"Let's talk." She backed up some, her feet in sandals, wearing hip-hugger jeans and a crop top. What was seen of her exposed belly was toned muscle.

Facing her, he reached behind and pushed the door closed. It didn't click in the frame.

"I'm guessing you're working for the wife," Comstock said. He held the tool box before him, hand clasped on the other wrist.

"Who are you working for?"

There was a shuffling, shoe leather making a soft scuff over the apartment's carpeting, and Comstock looked from her to another woman appearing around the corner leading to the kitchenette. She must have been like a statue there, Comstock dimly recorded as the gun came up in her hand and she triggered off rounds at him.

He reeled sideways and went flat next to the small coffee table with a vase of flowers on it that exploded from a bullet. Another bullet grazed his shoulder blade and yet another clipped him in the back, in the posterior deltoid as he went prone. The lid of the tool box was rigged so that it flipped open on a spring release. The inner lid held another of Comstock's guns in a simple Velcro harness and the semi-auto was now in his hand. He shot the other woman from where he was down on the floor. His first bullet slammed into her chest staggering her backwards, crimson spraying across the beige carpet like an abstractionist throwing paint on a canvass. His second entered her forehead off-center and she dropped to the floor heavily.

Fighting disorienting pain, he was up and flicking the muzzle of his gun about. He waved Namaras off from going for the Beretta that belonged to the dead woman. The piece lay near her open curled hand.

Comstock judged the woman he just killed was forty or so, in heels and a designer dress ensemble. Her mussed hair was coiffed and the jade bead necklace she'd worn had broken when she fell, the balls laying everywhere as if an errant set of Tiffany marbles. She looked like a realtor who'd gone berserk. Or the late Ralston's once trophy wife.

Mouth agape, Comstock blinked at the other woman. "Fuckin' amateurs," he grumbled. Excited voices drifted up to him from outside. His blood, his DNA, was splattered over this crime scene and soon the police would arrive.

"Listen, I'll split the money with," she began but didn't finish as Comstock shot her too, once through the heart.

He started for the door but had to brace against the wall; a weakness like he'd felt when the bomb went off that time in Afghanistan wobbled his legs. He sucked air in deep, and out the door, and down the steps he went.

"Hey, man, you can't leave," a would-be Good Samaritan said to him, grabbing at his arm when he got downstairs. He had on a tank top emblazoned with "Wall of California" and reeking of skunky weed.

"Fuck off."

Comstock clubbed him viciously in the head and was past him as the man groaned, wilting to the ground. This being Texas, a state big on guns and self-defense, Comstock assumed the wife, partnered with Namaras, would have tearfully explained that this crazy man had broken in on them and what choice did they have but shoot him? They'd have witnesses attesting that he pretended to be some sort of repairman.

For the first time in his professional career, Comstock was in a slow panic as he drove away. That second bullet that struck him was lodged in his upper back. While he could concentrate and avoid an accident, he couldn't leave it there to fester and infect him, fever him up and maybe kill him off with who knew what internal toxins. The slug had to come out. But of the underground docs he knew, a few who'd lost their licenses due to drug habits or other such vices, none were in Dallas. The closest was in Fort Collins in Colorado.

He could make it, less than a thousand miles. That was like what, twelve, thirteen hours on the road? Less when he could gun it along sections of the highway. Like strolling to the corner grocery for a loaf of bread. Comstock psyched himself, steeling his mindset. Sweat salting his lips, he accelerated and tried for a few seconds to pretend the blinking lights in his rearview were just a hallucination. That chump he whacked must have seen him drive off. Now there were at least three cop cars behind him.

Shit.

Comstock wasn't going to be yet another moronic subject of breaking news, a hapless suspect no better than a liquor store stickup man, chased all over various freeways by vehicles and news copters for the enthrallment of reality show addicts munching on hot Cheetos. The object of conversation for maybe a half-hour to be replaced by the next titillation, be it the latest jaw-dropping tweet from the Oval Office to Bigfoot being spotted in the Walmart parking lot.

He pulled over and let the law swarm his car. Sidearms and shotguns pointing at him from every angle, he obeyed commands to "Show your hands . . . hands out the window now," and so on. He was roughly removed from his rental and thrown to the asphalt. A foot pressed on his back wound made him grimace and grit his teeth.

"Who the hell are you? You a Muslim, boy?"

"Why'd you kill those two women? Did you rape 'em?"

"You the boyfriend, asshole? Huh?"

On it went, Comstock remaining mum.

His fake ID was taken and, strapped and handcuffed to a gurney, he was finally hauled away. The beefy cop who rode with him in the back of the ambulance stared at him balefully.

"Just give me an excuse, son," he drawled.

At one point as they went along the vehicle humped over a substantial pothole. The ambulance lurched and the portable defibrillator crashed onto part of Comstock's head from its overhead rack. He wasn't sure, but he had an inkling the cop might have helped it slide off.

"Oops," the officer said, "you got a boo-boo."

"Your mama's got a boo-boo," a woozy Comstock croaked. Blood seeped into his eye from the fresh wound.

The EMT suppressed a grin while the cop smoldered.

This being Texas, they love them some executions, Comstock understood, so he was given tip-top treatment at Parkland Hospital and sent to the jail ward for recovery. In that way he'd be in good shape when they gave him the hot shot.

"You dropped off the radar after the Army, Comstock," the detective with the trim waistline and deep-set eyes said to him as he lay shackled after his operation. "Given the woman who shot you was the wife of Geoff Ralston, who just happened to have what looks so far like a heart attack less than an hour before, and the other a woman you shot who'd been seen in his company, why don't you set me straight on what went down, pardner?"

"Can't help you, slick." The dryness of his voice surprised him.

The detective studied him with a practiced detached interest. "Uh-huh."

He left, both knowing he'd be back once he got the toxicology results from Ralston's autopsy and looked further into Namaras's life. Comstock damn sure didn't plan to be around for that return visit. On the second day toward late afternoon, he felt strong enough and left his body. It took more effort than in the past but he chalked that up to his current condition. Spooking away, he looked back at his body and the stitched up wound on the side of his forehead.

Skulking about, he noted the cop assigned to guard his door was sweet on a curvy nurse. He would ease down the hall to chat with her at the nurses station. Good to know, Comstock catalogued, pleased. There up toward the ceiling, he lolled, happy to feel whole, free, even if it was in his unsolid form. Hands behind his head, he did the backstroke, careening across ghostly waves. Then as he came out of a loop, he saw an orderly at the door to his room. The cop, back at his post, and he exchanged a nod and in stepped the hospital worker. He was about to drift further along but ice was settling in Comstock's belly. He double-backed to his room.

The orderly's name tag read "Velasquez" but this wasn't the man he'd seen with Alice. This one now stood quietly inside the room, gazing at Comstock's inert form, the only noise the steady hum of the monitor. Comstock figured he must have been sent by his employers to tie up loose ends. Comstock made to re-enter his body and yell his head off. Only he couldn't seem to get back in. Like blowing your nose or scratching an itch, that's how easy it should have been. But his recent head wound, what had it done to him?

Only now he couldn't.

"Okay, be calm, you can do this," he said in his ethereal echo. The orderly stepped closer, a hypodermic in one hand while he extracted a fluid from a slim vial in his other.

"Shit," Comstock blared in his silent tone. "Shit, come on, this ain't no time for a vacation. Come on, get back in, get in," he yelled at himself.

The orderly raised the needle to inject its contents into the tube line from the saline solution into his arm.

"Now," Comstock screamed as he made a last dive toward his body, screaming all the way.

THE KWANZAA INITIATIVE

THE BLONDE GHOST DRIFTED INTO DR. Grayface's lab, phasing through an alloy wall. Her icy stare swept the interior. She saw Grayface, whose real name was Hans von Hanz, directing one of his assistants, both of them wearing welder's goggles. They were at a worktable upon which was a partially dismantled laser cannon. The assistant was welding a component in place, the flame thin, blue, and precise jetting from the nozzle of his acetylene torch.

The Ghost solidified her diaphanous form, her ability such that even garb, including the cape draped about her milky whiteness, became spectral-like as well. Some sort of limited engagement field, Grayface had concluded after several tests conducted on her at one point. She could extend the field to a degree and make say a book or dog intangible as well.

Once she did this to a tree hugger, freaking out the environmentalist's allies for several minutes that their friend's head had suddenly disappeared. The Blonde Ghost's boot-clad feet came down softly on the metal floor. The lab was part of the floating fortress of the Medusa Council, a not-so-secret cabal of right-wing corporate and business interests.

The craft was large enough to house some 200 personnel comfortably and designed to look like a flying saucer, though more disk shaped than bubbled in the middle and tapering to thin edges like a traditional UFO—at least one as imagined in 1950s films. There were four tank turrets equidistant around the top diameter of the airship. The craft was called the Sky Cutter. The cannon being repaired was usually mounted in one of those turrets.

Two days ago the Sky Cutter had swooped in over a massive rally in Cleveland protesting foreclosures. The protest had been given a boost due to a former governor and vice presidential candidate, Sally Mederici, who'd testified before Congress recently about how sorry she was the investment firm she was in charge of, Framken Ulbright Financials, somehow lost more than a billion dollars in assets.

The buzzing by the Sky Cutter had been an attempt by the Medusa Council's chairman—sometimes called Potato Head or, more often, Spud One—to put a scare into the gathered, more than 10,000 strong. Rather, salted among the protestors, in their gray and black, bandanas worn stagecoach robber style, were hardcore members of the 99 Brigade. They'd opened fire on the airship with a newly developed pulse wave device that blew the laser cannon apart. There was a cadre of techies among the 99ers who were about making the gadgets inspired by their beloved *Star Trek* reality. The Cutter flew away.

"Madam," Dr. Grayface said, putting his goggles around his neck. He nodded at the Blond Ghost who strode past him. He smiled thinly as she didn't acknowledge his greeting. He knew despite her practiced glacial countenance, her pulse was quickening given she'd spotted Perry Decaine in another part of the lab.

He was in fatigues and a tan T-shirt, its material stretched across his muscular chest. A few years ago on strikes against the 99 Brigade, he'd worn a black form-fitting suit and a domino mask he'd tie behind his head. The Blonde Ghost became smitten with that image of him. He'd still wear the mask now and then, for her. Toward the wall in back of him was a seven-foot-tall glass-like structure domed at its top. There was blinking machinery nearby, and wires and piping led from the machinery into the covering. There was a human form within, but obscured due to heavy gasses swirling about it.

"American Black," the Blonde Ghost said to Decaine, calling him by his operative identity.

"Clara," he said warmly, using her real name. He sat with one hip on a table and was assembling his handgun. Inspired by the Ghost's powers, the weapon's outer casing was composed of a blend of polymers such that its shell refracted light, making it nearly invisible. Decaine was so used to this procedure that he was looking at the Blonde Ghost as he reassembled the gun—machine-gray inner mechanisms visible one moment then gone the next as he finished its assembly.

Indeed this rock hard specimen of U.S. manliness was well-trained to do many tasks in the dark, the Ghost reflected pleasurably. "Are you ready?" she intoned, doing her best shadowy voice. It took concentration for her not to reach out and touch his arm.

"Naturally," he replied in that easy manner of his. "Everything is lining up as we've planned and plotted." He leveled his light brown eyes on her, and it was as if he could read her mind. There had been times she imagined he could.

Grayface walked over to the two, hands in his pristine lab coat. "The watch working okay, Perry?" Von Hanz had reluctantly earned his nickname due to an experiment going awry one time. It had left his face appearing immobile as his skin now had a concrete-like pallor to it.

There was a heavy silver chrome watch on American Black's wrist. "No worries, Doc. The adjustment you made was the thing. This bad boy works like a charm now."

"Are you seeing them today?" she asked unnecessarily. The Blonde Ghost momentarily phased from corporeal to phantom form then back to regular. It was an unconscious manifestation of hers when under stress. For by "them" she really meant *her.*

Decaine was standing, picking through several gadgets arrayed on the table—some familiar and some unknown to the Blonde Ghost. "Tonight's the night, eh, Blonde Ghost?" He paused, slightly shaking a gold plated Zippo in his hand. He smiled at her.

"The first blow in the war of the patriots is poised to strike at the damnable 99 Brigade. We will burn our place into history forever, won't we?" His words were both a challenge and a source of exhilaration to her. She almost got watery in the knees but maintained her stoicism.

"I will be in position," she said, hoping he interpreted her reply as the double entendre she intended.

"Good," a new voice boomed. A holographic monitor screen had suddenly appeared before them and on it was the spiky head of Spud One, their chairman. He was literally a blubbery head preserved in a chemical bath without a body. He had been, when he was a normal human, a conservative campaign strategist who'd guided many successful elections for the crusade. But he'd also had an oxycontin, Hillbilly heroin, habit and burned his body badly one night in a binge in a hotel room with two cross-dressing hookers. A side effect of the chemicals needed to be constantly circulated in his glass container caused the knotty growths to sprout—thus his appearance as an overripe potato with eyes and a mouth.

"The Kwanzaa Initiative commenced as a mere idle idea, and culminates with you as the mighty head of the spear we will drive in their raghead-lovin' heart, American Black," Spud One was saying. "You embody what we've always said: our Blacks are better than their Blacks."

The Blonde Ghost had first said those words but the three knew better than to correct him. The head laughed in that weird, chilling way like a villain in an old reeler tying the damsel to the train tracks. His voice was digitized through a squawk box, adding to its unearthliness. The trio nodded their assent. Thereafter, geared up and standing at the open hatch, Perry Decaine made an adjustment on his glide pac's control unit.

"Godspeed," The Ghost said. She gave him a chaste peck on his cheek, residue of her glistening black lipstick stark against his bronze skin. Tenderly, she wiped the evidence away with her fingertips.

There was a stone stare in his eyes as he put a hand around her waist, pulling her close. "Just in case it all goes south." They kissed passionately, and then American Black went onto the deck of the Sky Cutter as it momentarily hovered above the Watts area of Los Angeles. The craft was on radar stealth mode as it took position in the dark sky.

There were two crewmen on deck as well, their mag boots helping them cling to the airship's steel-titanium hull. The running lights were on, illuminating the figures. One of the crew saluted Decaine, and he saluted back as scuba-fashion, he did a back dive off the edge of the disk into the air. He was wearing a so-called flying squirrel suit of material that billowed under his arms and between the legs. He glided toward the earth, specifically the Flying Foxx auto junkyard off of Beach Street a few blocks north of the Watts Towers.

Dawn was ten minutes away as American Black zeroed in on his landing zone, his night vision goggles giving his field of vision a green glow. Rather than a parachute, the glide pac on his back employed a prototype anti-grav device Grayface had engineered— though the guts of the mechanism were derived from stolen tech. The instrument had a limited range, involving magnetic repulsion, so the wearer had to be less than 400 feet from a solid surface for it to work properly. But sure enough, as he zoomed in closer to smashing against a pile of junked cars, the glide pac kicked in and American Black's body suddenly, and jarringly, simply halted in mid-air.

"Grayface's gotta work on that," he muttered, teeth clenched. He dialed down the pac's power like lowering the volume on a radio and he touched down onto the ground. He was just outside the junkyard, his cover business for the last year.

"Say, home, you lost?"

Down on a knee, Decaine had just finished folding up his wing suit and turned to the voice. There, having come up behind him, were two members of the Rolling Daltons street gang. The outfit controlled this part of Watts, trafficking in the usual of drugs, but also having branched out into stolen cars and gun running. The gangbangers were in a tricked out Nissan 350Z. The aroma of marijuana drifted to American Black's nostrils.

He rose. "I'm right where I need to be."

"No shit." The Dalton in the passenger seat exchanged a quick look with the driver. His eyes were red and glassy. "Maybe we better show you the way out of this bad place."

"And here I was thinking I should try and get some gym time in today but you two will do for a tuneup."

"Fuck you talking about, bitch?" the passenger snarled.

Having already tired of the banter he knew was going to escalate anyway, Decaine charged forward.

"Hold up," the one on the passenger side said, reaching for a gun is his waistband.

But American Black had already covered the space and, as the Glock came free, he grabbed the man's wrist and shoved the muzzle into the cheek of the driver.

"Motherfuckah," the driver blared, reaching for the gun.

Decaine released the other man's wrist and with an edge strike of his hand to a cranial nerve in his neck, incapacitated him immediately. He'd done this so swiftly, the driver was still trying to comprehend what happened to his friend even as American Black used the handgrip of the Glock to club him unconscious too.

American Black smiled thinly at his handiwork. Yes, he was ready. Later, having deposited the trussed-up Rolling Daltons with an amount of weed and ecstasy pills in their pockets in back of the LAPD substation on 108th, he met with the rally committee at the Tabernacle of Zion church in South LA Rochelle "Roc"

Nyler was speaking. She was a lead organizer with Urban Advocacy, one of the groups putting on the rally.

The action happened to coincide with the first day of Kwanzaa. Spud One and Grayface got excited about the idea of being able to strike a blow not only against the 99 Brigade, but take on a made-up holiday by a professional Mau-Mau.

"Yet another move by the Left to destroy Christmas," Spud One had decried.

As far as American Black knew, Kwanzaa hadn't exactly become a household tradition in Black communities, but it was good for morale among the Council members. The two African Americans in the inner circle, Ragged Dick and Condor Connie the Cruel, were out-of-touch with the daily concerns and likes of ordinary Black folk.

"Okay, we've got our assignments and the Guild's legal observers will be stationed around in green caps." She held her hands apart. "Anything else?"

There were a few other last-minute matters then the meeting broke up and people began leaving to head downtown. There were several chartered buses in the parking lot, idling to take community residents to the area around City Hall.

Roc Nyler and Decaine stood near each other. His cover name to her was Sam Rogers.

"SEIU figures they'll have five- to seven-thousand members out," he enthused. He'd been the union liaison for the rally. Other unions such as AFSCME and the Teamsters would be in attendance, as well as segments of the building trades, historically more conservative than their sisters and brothers in other quarters of organized labor.

"You do good work, Rogers."

"Thanks, teach."

She smiled and took hold of his hand.

He smiled back.

"Guess we better get over there," Reverend Malcolm Stonehill said, stepping toward the doorway. He'd been talking to several of his parishioners who were among his church's contingent coming to the rally. He was a broad shouldered man in a charcoal gray pinstriped suit.

"On it," Nyler said, letting Decaine's hand loose.

"I'd do something sexist like pinch your butt but wouldn't want to you know, be all un-PC," he whispered to her as they walked out.

"That's right," she said, reaching back quickly and giving his crotch a squeeze.

"Oh my," he said.

AMONG THE MAIN THRUST OF THE year's end rally was the celebration of the generally successful occupation of more than 100 foreclosed homes in the Southland where the residents faced forcible evictions. This had gone on for a month and the rally was billed as the True 100. Renters rights groups, financial reform nonprofits, the faith sector, the unions, and more had not only pulled together to bring out the people, but they were also the ones who were occupying the homes. Estimates as high as 200,000 had been projected in terms of turnout.

But as Decaine stood on a set of steps, scanning the gathered, he estimated it was closer to nearly 300,000 who'd turned out. Large 16-wheelers driven by the Teamsters, maintenance trucks brought in by city and county including steamrollers and cherry-pickers, blocked the streets a half square mile around.

The plaza was at the apex of the freshly rehabbed section of three blocks of Grand Avenue redone in a kind of Champs-Élysées by way of Hollywood glitz. In the center of the plaza was the 65-story Prospect Tower, housing entities of international capital—including Framken Ulbright, F.U., Financials.

"I simply do not know where the money is, or why the accounts have not been reconciled as of today," the heretofore well-respected former governor had said under oath. She further stated, "I know only what I saw on the news," she'd said, her voice trembling with the proper amount of sorrowfulness. These were monies belonging to union pension funds, small farmers, teachers, firefighters, and so on. The ex-governor had to have armed guards attached to her, and the SEC promised an investigation to get to the bottom of this business.

What better symbol to stage the protest at—and what better day to sabotage the 99 Brigade—Spud One had chortled.

"SOON HERR DOCTOR, THE SWEET SOUND of freedom will ring loud and clear from down there." The Blonde Ghost stood next to Grayface at a monitor. They were afforded a view of the unfolding events inside the Sky Cutter.

He regarded her and, taking a dig, said, "Orgasmic you'd venture?"

She looked at him glacially. "My only regret with Timothy McVeigh is he did not go to *The New York Times* building."

Dr. Grayface would have laughed, but it hurt his near-frozen face to do so.

ON THE GROUND AT THE RALLY, Reverend Stonehill was before the podium's mic speaking about the need for a new Works Projects Administration. Thousands of placards shook and an echoing roar of approval went up from the masses. Checking his watch, Perry Decaine prepared for the bomb to go off.

After some discussion, it was agreed American Black would plant the bomb in the tower itself, this after putting it in the trunk of car and leaving it below in the underground parking structure had been dismissed. The thing was supposed to go off in the lobby of F.U. Financials, hidden in the soil of a potted plant.

F.U. was a particularly egregious example of postmodern wantonness. Not only had they "lost" a billion largely in working peoples' monies, but the outfit had benefitted from a bailout a few years ago. Already there were hundreds of cases of homelessness, impoverishment, and three suicides directly linked to this massive swindle in broad daylight. No one believed the money had simply disappeared and an investigation by the SEC had been launched.

Decaine had cloned copies of the magnetic pass cards used by the cleaning crew to gain access via service doors and the like to the inner stairwells and doors of the building.

The bomb's casing was to have the fingerprints of Nyler on it. She was suspected as being one of the leaders of the secretive 99 Brigade. American Black knew this was so from his months undercover and having gotten close to the woman. Very close.

The bomb went off and all eyes in the crowd looked upward toward the sound. But glass wasn't cascading down to them from blown out office windows—rather the Sky Cutter suddenly wobbled into view from hiding in the gray overcast clouds.

"That Black conniving bastard," Grayface hissed from inside the ship. He hurried toward the domed cylinder.

The Blonde Ghost was transfixed at the monitor as she watched gray and black clad members of the 99 Brigade jump from highrises onto the deck of the listing Sky Cutter. She did note those fucking tree hugging commies were wearing glide pacs. Doubtless American Black had snuck one of the devices to them to have it reverse engineered.

The laser cannons weren't normally manned until needed. But one of the Council's soldiers, called Centurions as a harkening back to the days of ancient Rome, who hadn't succumbed had gotten in a turret and was firing the weapon.

Two 99 Brigaders, a man and a woman, floating just to the left of American Black were seared in half by the sweep of the laser's ray, not even having time to scream as they died. American Black dialed his glide pac up just as another beam blast swept by where he'd just been.

"I'm going to kill you, traitor," the soldier in the turret vowed. He powered up the laser again, his shot going wide as the Sky Cutter listed once more. The ray seared off the tops off several of the large metal letters spelling *Prospect* at the top of the tower. Decaine had purposely set a secondary bomb in the craft's gyro systems so they wouldn't be able to make a speedy escape.

He suddenly cut the juice on his glide pac and as his body hurtled head first toward the Sky Cutter, the laser cannon swinging toward him, he threw a small frag grenade right through the opening in the turret where the gunner looked out over the barrel of the cannon. His aim was true and the grenade sent shrapnel into the centurion's neck and head, killing him. Freefalling, American Black then shot out a thin cable of titanium and platinum from his watch. On its end was a magnetized grappling hook and, as it took told, he grabbed his wrist with his free hand so the jerk of the line wouldn't pull his arm out of its socket. He arced back up over the Sky Cutter and let go over the deck, having to go into a roll as he landed to prevent breaking various bones.

On the outer shell of the ship, one of the 99 Brigaders screamed briefly as a blast from a Mac 10 ripped into her gut. She was blown off the decking from the impact of the rounds. Roc Nyler's expertly thrown butterfly knife penetrated the gunman's neck and he went over, dead. His mag boots held the corpse's legs in place, the torso folded over at the waist.

American Black had hidden sleeping gas canisters onboard. He hoped a majority of the crew would be slumbering by now. The gas fed into the air and heat ducts, knocked out immediately, and dissipated quickly.

"This way," Decaine commanded, his invisible gun sounding twice as he dropped a soldier exiting the access hatchway. By now the ship had righted itself and was heading west, out toward the Pacific. American Black hadn't rigged his gas to affect the pilots as he didn't want the Sky Cutter crashing into the protestors.

A computerized voice repeated over the PA system, "This is not a drill . . . this is not a drill . . ."

In the main corridor the 99ers battled with several centurions. The Sky Cutter was capable of high altitude flight, thus the ship could be pressurized. But as they were at low altitude, and not pressurized, firepower was employed by both sides, and holes were being punched through the ship.

"Watch out, baby," Decaine said, tackling Nyler as a burst from an assault rifle nearly vaporized her head. As he fell with the woman sideways into an alcove, even off-balance, he got off a shot, nailing the attacker dead-center in his forehead.

The 99ers made their way to Grayface's lab. This was where the Medusa Council's leadership would make their last stand. A brace of automatic fire blazed and two of the freedom fighters went down instantly. For a moment no one could pinpoint where the gunner was posted. But American Black, whose hearing had been heightened via nanotech, detected the scrape of cloth against burnished steel. He aimed at an air vent and let rip with a burst from a M4 one of the dead 99ers had wielded. That took care of the hidden assassin.

"Okay," he said as the assault crew rounded a corner and before them were the heavy double doors to the lab. Old-fashioned one inch in diameter rivet heads framed each door. "You two with Roc and me," Decaine continued, "the rest secure the flight bridge." The squad split up and the four advanced on their target.

"Where's that spooky girlfriend of yours?" Nyler whispered to Decaine. The Blonde Ghost had been conspicuously absent from the dust-up.

For an answer the Ghost's gloved hands suddenly emerged from the lab door and she grabbed one of the Brigadistas. Given she could dematerialize what she touched, she pulled him into the door but only part way. As metal melded with flesh, his scream was mercifully brief and muffled, his protruding lower half in the door ceasing to writhe in seconds.

"Bloodthirsty bitch," Nyler declared.

Absently, American Black reflected that Nyler's tone seemed odd. But he focused on setting the pulse wave mini-bomb. It was clamped on the door and triggered, blowing them inward. The three went in firing, having also tossed in a couple of what were called phaser grenades that blinded and disoriented their opponents. The smoke was still drifting from the heated barrels of their assault rifles as the remaining five centurions crumpled to the floor, dead.

The Blonde Ghost, who knew she couldn't sneak up on American Black, stood to one side. Dr. Grayface was next to his large domed glass cylinder. What was inside could be seen clearly now.

"Oh my," the 99er beside Nyler said.

"I present," Grayface began, "my greatest creation." With much effort he grinned slightly. "Maximum Black." The cylinder, which seemed seamless, suddenly parted at the top and each side descended into its base. Therein was a copy of Perry Decaine as imagined by the likes of Jack Kirby having drinks with Philip K. Dick, as Kirby sketched their idea on a flattened out cocktail napkin. The being was at least six-foot-eight, his frame seemingly twice the heft of the original. His forehead was disproportionately large and squarish.

"Cloned from my DNA," Decaine concluded.

"Cloned and improved," Hans von Hanz declared. "Whatever your abilities, he has them in . . . spades, shall we say."

Maximum Black, dressed in loose dark pants and a dark blue tunic with red piping, leaped and was on the 99 Brigader in a blink. He not only snapped the man's neck, but tore his head off and contemptuously tossed it aside. Blood spurted about from the torn neck like in a samurai historical drama.

Nyler yelled and started firing her gun. After a quick burst, which the doppelganger easily evaded, the weapon jammed. She glared at her Beretta M12 then American Black.

"Magnetic dampeners messing with the release mechanisms," he surmised. "Anyway, this is my fight."

"Yes, darling, it is," Roc Nyler said. She kissed him deeply.

He tossed the M4 aside. Decaine and his larger double circled one another, each with their fists raised as if squaring off for a bare knuckles contest of more than a century ago. A sneer on his face, Maximum Black swung, expecting to connect. Yet while the clone had superior strength and reflexes, he lacked American Black's combat experience. He came in under the blow and drove a palm heel strike into the other's chest, a move designed to stop the heart.

Maximum Black said in Perry Decaine's voice, "That all you got, little man?" A backhand swat sent Decaine reeling into a bank of machinery. The impact of his body busted up several panels, causing sparking and crackling of electricity. His larger version was airborne, a flying kick zeroing in on the downed man. Decaine rolled away and Maximum Black's foot went through more machinery.

Temporarily held in place, American Black struck and was counterstruck as the two used their kung fu skills on each other. But a switch up to Western-style boxing allowed American Black to slip an uppercut past the bigger one's defenses.

"Too bad I can't keep you alive, big brother," the larger man said, wiping the blood from the corner of his mouth. "You do have a thing or two to teach me." He pulled his foot loose, ripping wires and using his big hands to pull apart the bank of machinery, throwing it aside into a useless pile.

Again they hesitated as they stared down one another, each man seeking his opening. The ship hit an air pocket and lurched, American Black rearing backwards slightly. Maximum Black went down on his side and slid forward. With a leg sweep, he put American Black on his back. He responded with a quickness that would have been sufficient in any other situation. With a kick up and out of his legs, he brought this body upright again. Only Maximum Black had assumed he'd do this move. He lashed out with a double strike that broke American Black's right arm in two places.

The Blonde Ghost gasped. Roc Nyler was near her, reaching for the woman from behind.

With foot blows and blocking what he could with his left hand, American Black avoided being finished off by Maximum Black— but both knew their contest would soon be over. Breathing hard, Decaine had his back against one of the damaged panels, wiring loose like the tentacles of comatose squid about him. He noted that as Dr. Grayface addressed him.

"I know you think you'll be a martyr to the Cause, American Black." He did air quote marks. "Having died in a fight against the oppressor and all that rot," he went on condescendingly. "But once Maximum Black disposes of you, we'll of course engage the echo chamber among the so-called mainstream liberal media who will only be too happy to report on the newly revealed evidence, including videos, of you drugging and having your wicked, wicked way with female and male civil rights leaders and Democratic members of Congress. Hell, we'll throw in a few Teabaggers you'd call them who haven't been adhering to discipline as well. And," he added, "that you had a hand in stealing the supposed missing billion." In reality, the theft by strokes of a keyboard had been committed by the Medusa Council's financial black ops branch.

He snickered. "I think too I'll throw in that you practiced cannibalism with tender young girls. That would be exquisite." He hadn't looked that happy in years.

Grayface pointed at American Black. "You could have had it all, you sorry fool." Then to Maximum Black, "Finish him my supreme Negro warrior."

As the clone turned to destroy Perry Decaine he grimaced and clutched at his head. "What . . . what's happening to me?"

American Black had seen the loose wiring and realized the main trunk for the PA system was at his feet. As Grayface had gloated, he'd surreptitiously removed the power unit from one of the wave pulse mini-bombs in a side vent pocket of his pants. The unit emitted a signal at a certain frequency to activate the bomb. Maximum Black's hearing was more heightened than his, giving him a range like an animal, American Black surmised. He'd patched into the PA trunk and generated a sound only his larger double could hear—a high-pitched sound that was debilitating him.

Yet already the larger man was shaking off the effects, using his nanotech to shut down his hearing. But the distraction was all American Black needed. He came at the man who grabbed him in a bear hug, lifting him up.

"Ha," Maximum Black blared. He squeezed, cracking bone, soon to crush American Black's ribcage.

The magnetic dampeners would shut down his invisible gun, but only after the gun was engaged, after squeezing the trigger once. He only needed one shot and he took it, putting a bullet through the eye of Maximum Black. His arms went lax around Decaine who dropped to the decking, spent. Maximum Black staggered, his powerful body trying to go on despite the end of brain function.

He uttered forlornly, "The world won't be mine, Tony M," and he toppled over onto his face, dead.

"Oh, Perry," the Blonde Ghost said.

"Be strong," Roc Nyler commanded her. She had an arm around the other woman's waist. "We have the codes now." She referred to the bank accounts the stolen billion had been secreted away to in various countries.

"And each other." The Blonde Ghost kissed the leader of the 99 Brigade passionately.

Grayface and American Black exchanged a look of incredulity.

Nyler walked over to American Black, who'd managed to get to a knee, but he had nothing else left. He looked up at her and she put a hand to the top of his short cropped head. "You were turned on by my idealism while I was being turned on by money," and winking at the Blonde Ghost, "my bloodthirsty bitch and her pussy."

She laughed heartily and started to walk away. Grayface hollered, "I'll finish both of you defilers." He lunged at Nyler but she had her knife in his heart before he knew what had happened to him. He too staggered back and impotently clutched at the hilt of the blade. He did a half-pirouette of death then fell to the floor, forever still, grayer than ever.

Shooting out an observation window, the two women prepared to escape. Combined with her glide pac, the Blonde Ghost would be able to keep Roc Nyler aloft. The Sky Cutter was wobbling. The 99ers dispatched to the flight deck must have been ambushed by the two as American Black fought Maximum Black—the pilots having been killed too.

Roc Nyler and Clara "The Blonde Ghost" Rundgren looked affectionately at American Black as the ship plunged toward the calm, blue-green Pacific.

"Bye-bye, love," the Blonde Ghost said, blowing him a kiss.

Roc Nyler stitched Decaine with a chatter from the M4, the magnetic dampeners having shut down as the airship's control mechanisms failed. The two floated out like demonic angels as the Sky Cutter cleaved into the water.

"I know," Roc Nyler told the Blonde Ghost, whose eyes were moist. So were hers. They flew away as the Sky Cutter sank into the ocean.

CONSTRUCTED OF BROKEN METAL FROM THE Sky Cutter's hull, and the bloated dead bodies of Dr. Grayface and Maximum Black lashed underneath for ballast, American Black rowed his grim makeshift raft. He used a flat section of the downed aircraft's stabilizer as a paddle, heading back toward land.

What Nyler had shot was a projection, a holographic image captured of himself moments before while he kneeled behind a pile of the destroyed machinery. It was projected by the gold Zippo. Had Grayface, who had given him the new gadget this morning, and therefore it was unknown to the Blonde Ghost, been alive, he might have told the couple.

Despite his wounds and broken arm, American Black ignored the pain and rowed on. Not only did he have revenge to dispense, but he had the people's money to get back. Once more, he had purpose.

THUS STRIKES
THE BLACK PIMPERNEL

PRESIDENT TRUMP ONCE AGAIN BLAMED FORMER President Obama for leaks of classified information from the White House and for the continued vociferous protests against his administration. This in the wake of several of Trump's controversial executive orders and policies, such as when he halted immigration from seven, then six, predominantly Muslim countries to the US. Trump over time had doubled down on these comments in interviews with like-minded news outlets, during which he provided no evidence for his claims. Including that British intelligence had a hand in the surveillance.

"I think he's behind it," Trump said. "I also think it's just politics. That's just the way it is." He continued, "You never know what's exactly happening behind the scenes . . . I think that President Obama's behind it because his people are certainly behind it." He added, "Some of the leaks possibly come from that group. You know, some of the leaks—which are really very serious leaks because they're very bad in terms of national security—but I also understand that's politics and it will probably continue."

The man occupying one of the most powerful positions in the world reemphasized that Obama had engineered the bugging of the phones in Trump Tower prior to the presidential election. *"Terrible! Just found out that Obama had my 'wires tapped' in Trump Tower just before the victory. Nothing found. This is McCarthyism!"*

Trump had tweeted one morning in the early days of his administration.

Texas Agriculture Commissioner Juaquin Norcross, who most likely will be running for the Dems' nod to challenge Trump, recently spoke on this matter in an interview conducted with the *National Atlantic* magazine.

"Let's be clear, these ongoing fantasies of the president demonstrate how out of touch he is. He hasn't delivered on his campaign promises, notably attention to and repairing our infrastructure, let alone bringing jobs back in coal or steel. It's his patented tactic, when things go wrong he looks for others to blame when in fact the buck stops with him. Plain and simple."

@STATESMASHER—"That fool Norcross ain't nothin' but a gran pocho." #SellOutPocho

@ROLLON—"He's more legit than yer mama. You triflin' like the brothers and sisters say." #TriflinNig

@STATESMASHER—"That's not what your mama said last night, bitch ass. He need that big hard one like I give her, only a magnum enema." #BitchAssPunk

THE CAB OF THE SELF-DRIVING TRUCK had been retrofitted with nearly $50,000 worth of hardware and software. The 18-wheeler Kenworth was cruising comfortably down the highway at 55 miles per hour. Bill Collier, the human occupant in the passenger seat, technically the overseer of this test drive and a seasoned freight hauler, had many miles ago gotten bored with the amazed stares and gapes from other drivers. This since leaving the plant in Fort Collins with 50,000 cans of beers in the trailer. His destination was a warehouse some 11 hours away in Nevada.

Plenty of gawkers had taken photos with their smartphones of the empty driver's seat as the truck rumbled along. The vehicle was an automatic, as the tech that could handle shifting the dual clutch action of a big rig was—for the foreseeable future—nonexistent. But that was little comfort to the men and women Collier bent elbows with in taverns across this nation. Like global warming, no matter how hard some might deny its existence, the era of the autonomous truck was coming and jobs would be lost. Or rather, the idea seemed to be that the trucks would travel the highways where a jaywalking pedestrian or a kid running into the street to fetch her ball was less likely and therefore a sudden swerve or braking was not as much a factor. As they neared the city the trucks would pull into a designated facility and the human would climb aboard to drive it into the city handling trickier maneuvers. But what sort of wage would that be compared to truckers getting paid by the mile or the hour?

Collier was making another notation on his touchscreen iPad in his log for the engineers at GlobeStar, the Silicon Valley firm that had outfitted the truck. He felt a disturbance in his seat as the cab shook. He glanced up and saw that a family van had suddenly stopped less than half the length of a football field in front of them, despite the roadway being clear. Worse it was cocked sideways and this was a two-lane section of the highway leading to a rise. Acting fast but calmly as the sensors applied the air brakes and the rear tires of the trailer smoked, Collier pressed his palm on a large red button on the side console that would disengage the computers and return manual control to him. Akin to twin steering wheels in a driver's ed car, the wheel on his side of the cab dropped down into place as he got his hands on it.

At that exact moment zooming over the small hill outside the Kenworth's windshield, coming along in the opposite direction was a low-slung sports model ragtop Mercedes. A man and woman were in it, arguing, their mouths wide open, each gesticulating severely, their machine traveling at least 100 miles an hour. The man was driving but was glaring at the woman who was now giving him the finger. That way blocked, Collier had no choice but to twist the wheel to his right and take the 18-wheeler off the highway lest he crash into both cars. This took him across a span of gravel alongside a roadside café called the Duckblind—though this was the edge of the desert along I-515. Several cars were parked on the gravel and there was no space big enough between any of them to drive through unscathed. The truck's terminus was to have been in Henderson. But now it would be here as Collier fought for control of the truck, the rear trailer swinging to and fro as the tires sought purchase as gravel spewed from beneath the treads.

"Shit," Collier cursed, bringing the rig to a shuddering stop and shutting off the motor. He got out of the passenger side, the brakes hissing compressed air as the truck settled. Everything considered, he'd only clipped two cars and ruined a third. It was a black Lincoln and the front of the cab had crushed it between the right front fender and a cinder block building behind the restaurant, a separate toilet facility, Collier saw as he got out his phone. Others were already out of the Duckblind, taking their own snaps or heading toward him—no doubt the pissed-off owners of the vehicles he'd hit.

"What the hell, homes?" a 20-something Chicano in a Rams cap said as he walked over to Collier.

Among the small crowd of customers and staff ebbing out onto the lot were two middle-aged white men. One was in a sport coat and slacks, open collar, and his companion in short sleeves and rimless owlish glasses. The stern-faced men exchanged low words to one another and both got into a late-model Lexus and left the scene.

THE MAN OF MANY FACES WAS at his most centered when engaged in his daily regimen of exercises in his hidden lair underneath the Civil War-era Greenbriar Cemetery in a rugged part of town the hipsters would not be opening an artisanal grilled cheese sandwich shop in anytime soon, no matter the cheap rents. The entrance to his sanctum sanctorum, as it were, was via a secret entrance in a crumbling marble vault. The identification etched over its green patinated doors in marble read: The Obler Family. In his exercise area—past a computer console where he accessed the computers of the NSA and the Military Intelligence Agency through back doors created for him by a talented but quite paranoid hacker named Frag Lawson—the peoples's outlaw was finishing up as the sun rose over the broken and leaning headstones in the cemetery above him.

He was doing another set on the salmon ladder. This was a device where you started out as if doing a pull up. The bar you grabbed overhead was not fixed to its rungs and, utilizing upper body strength, you leaped up while holding the bar to the next-higher dual rungs and so on until you reached the top. His routine also included isolating certain muscle groups as well as overall development for motor control and power, which meant a combination of free weights weight training, yoga for flexibility and mobility, and a series of exercises in stealth and paralyzing hand strikes said to have been perfected by the mythical ninja Sarutobi Sasuke. Twice a week he altered this part of his workout with weapons practice, including kusarigama, chain and scythe, the bo staff, and of course nunchucks. There were also a set of wooden dummies with protruding "arms" and "legs" to practice kusarigama moves against. Added to that, he used electronic devices to push his vision and hearing to their natural limits while he would calculate the cube roots of various numerical formulas to hone his concentration skills.

By the end of this fast-paced hour-and-a-half, he was always sweating profusely, gulping in air, yet found himself fulfilled and ready. For he knew he would need all his skills as sharp as possible for what lay ahead.

CAMERA TWO CUT TO LINCOLN "LINC" Allard of the Hidalgo Foundation who was in-studio at CNN along with two more of the four panelists discussing the morning tweet by President Trump. In this one, he essentially repeated the fanciful notion advanced on a conspiracy site that the FDA, in collusion with Big Pharma, was suppressing the news that there was a cancer cure. That such a cure had been available for some ten years now. And, as per usual, no evidence was offered.

The normally taciturn Allard gestured vociferously. "Isn't it bad enough the leader of the most industrious nation on Earth hasn't anything better to do than repeat these wild lies, this poppycock that is forever being promulgated among the nutbags and disaffected? Worse, he encourages too many of the citizenry to believe such notions rather than actually adhere to fact. He and his cohorts can swallow their own Kool-Aid outlandishness, but science is science."

The view on television screens across the nation switched and camera one was a pulled-back shot of the three sitting at the rotunda with the bearded moderator. Margo Mayfair who was sitting next to Allard spoke. "Oh, Linc, when will you get off of that? The president knows exactly what he's doing. In this way he gets the people talking about a matter that in some way will touch all of us. He is a strategic thinker and is exciting folks to put pressure on the drug companies to stop being so greedy, and do their ethical duty to accelerate the research they've slowwalked all these years."

Mayfair was a registered Libertarian, the biracial daughter of old-line Civil Rights Movement icons. These bonafides grated on her parents' lefty friends but made the K Street political consultant a much sought-after twofer pundit darling among the right of center set.

Allard shook his head. "It's laughable how you Trumpsters contort yourselves like a Cirque du Soleil performer to lend credence to a man who is simply and clearly unfit for the office." That got a heated response from the beamed-in guest, his upper body displayed on a large monitor. "What Margo says was on the mark. You liberals just can't get over your envy of how this president connects with the common Jane and Joe."

"What I can't get over," the fourth guest, Helen Ruiz, a political science professor and columnist for the *Nation* said, "is how long will there be support for Trump given his string of broken campaign promises."

"If you want to talk about what's really troublesome, what about these attacks by the likes of so-called Latino activists calling for assassination?"

"What are you talking about?" Allard demanded.

Mayfair said, "There's been a lot of activity lately on what's called Brown Twitter about your precious Juaquin Norcross being a Trojan Horse. That he is nothing but a tool of whitey and should be dealt with accordingly."

That elicited groans from Ruiz and Allard. "I've seen some of those," Allard, who was Black, answered. "As has been exposed in the past, a lot of that's malicious activity by white supremacists, or as you prefer to euphemistically call them, the alt-right, pretending to be Black or brown."

Now it was the two others' turn to groan and guffaw. Then the director cut to commercial about a new miracle room duster.

"THANK YOU," TECH GURU ARTEMIS STOCKBRIDGE said to the waiter who'd brought him his bourbon on a shiny silver tray.

"My pleasure," the waiter, a stoop-shouldered balding Black man in his 60s, replied as the tech billionaire plucked the squat tumbler away in his long tapered fingers.

Stockbridge turned away and sipped his drink as the waiter slipped off to attend to another guest at the soirée. The gathered were in a brownstone in the Adams Morgan neighborhood of Washington, DC. The occasion was an informal yet nonetheless A-list-heavy informational fundraiser for a school voucher initiative aimed at the ballot in California backed by the Secretary of Education, who was working overtime to hobble and eventually dismantle the public education sector. Stockbridge was a tall man with coiffed longish blond hair streaked white and a trim goatee. He moved with a reassured casualness like the aging surfer bum image he cultivated.

"Good to see you, Margo," he said, kissing the cheek of the bronze-skinned, brown-haired woman with piercing gray eyes.

"Didn't think this would be your sort of thing, Artie." Margo Mayfair sampled some of her white wine.

"Whatever we can do to raise the education outcomes of our youth, particularly the disadvantaged ones, I'm willing to investigate."

"Even at the expense of choking the life out of the Department of Education?" Her eyes gleamed at him as she had more wine, the emotion in them uncertain. "Blue California is a ripe target for the forces of this administration."

"Yes, I know they're practically salivating at the possibility of pitting millennial hipsters who have made child rearing an artisanal undertaking against the poor and working class folks, many Black and brown, who are also frustrated by the far-too-bureaucratic, feather-bedded public school system."

She chuckled. "Now that's the tree huggin' billionaire I know."

He grunted and smiled. A white-haired man came over and addressed Mayfair.

"I hope you'll make it to the Cape this weekend."

"Wouldn't miss it, Marty," she said.

Soon their host, a friend of the secretary from their college days, had tapped her glass to get everyone's attention. She gave a short pitch to get the checkbooks open and toward the end of her spiel, after he'd handed his donation over, Stockbridge headed toward the first floor restroom that was past the well-appointed kitchen with its confectioner's oven and overhead pots and pans.

In the breakfast room next to the kitchen, the caterer's crew was preparing a last round of hors d'oeuvres. One of the young women who was assembling stuffed mushrooms had her earbuds in, bopping her head to YG's and Nipsey Hussle's "FDT."

Moments later, exiting the bathroom, Stockbridge didn't return to the main room where people were still conversing but went to a side door along the short hallway that let out into the garden area. A heady fragrance of transplanted jacaranda greeted him. There stood the balding waiter, an unlit cigarette in his hand as if he too had stepped out for a smoke break. It was a starry evening and the two were shadowy in the warm light of discreet ground-level lighting.

Without preamble, the Silicon Valley insider and founder of the Hidalgo Foundation began talking to the other man who in this guise was simply called Claude. "Two days ago there was an accident involving one of my subsidiaries, GlobeStar." He explained the driverless truck test, the family van having blown a tire, and the human driver having to make a quick decision given the circumstances. "The Lincoln the driver plowed into is leased to a company I know to be one of the many cut outs of Norman Bethune."

"You have my attention," the supposed waiter said. He'd dropped the voice he was using pretending to be an older man and reverted to his natural baritone.

"Bethune nor the man he was with hung around nor has there been any insurance claim made over the smashed-up car."

Claude hunched a shoulder. "So it was some sort of meeting he doesn't want attention over. But that could be any one of an assortment of wild-ass conspiracies up his butt he's getting the true believers worked up over. Like that time he was going around saying that Obama had planted secret nanny cams in the Oval Office to gather impeachable evidence against Trump."

"Which would have had its merits," Stockbridge said, blankfaced. "But speaking of nanny cams, for the purposes of covering our asses, the truck was equipped with such in case of an accident like what happened. Here's a little something captured at the incident." He took out his smartphone and tapped the screen several times to bring up the footage he wanted. He handed the device to the waiter.

"One of the cameras was doing an automatic scan and captured Bethune in the Lexus with—"

"Dirk Thane," the supposed waiter said. He stopped the video and replayed it. "I guess they weren't making plans for a Birther Reunion March on Washington."

"They could be," the billionaire deadpanned. His friend manifested a death's head grin.

"CHANTELLE, IT'S JERRY." THE MAN WHO'D stepped inside the compact mobile home was in jeans, a jean jacket over a buttoned-down shirt, and a baseball cap. He carried a fifth of gin in a paper bag. His eyes adjusted to the gloom.

"She had to step out," said another man in the room. He sat in a dilapidated BarcaLounger.

"Oh, hey, man," baseball cap said, "my bad. I didn't know she had company." He turned toward the door but this was a ruse. He dropped the plastic bottle of gin as a distraction to then use his opposite hand to unlimber the handgun he had in a holster on his belt under his jacket. He wheeled back around and was surprised the second man was standing there in front of him. He hadn't heard a rustle of clothing or his footfalls across the thin carpet. His face was a mass of scarring from fire.

"Who the hell are you?" Baseball Cap Jerry began, bringing the gun up to show he was a serious individual.

The other man was of a serious mindset as well. His hand flashed out and Jerry backed up, grabbing at his throat, letting his gun drop to the floor. The burned-faced man had jabbed him with stiffened fingers in a spot right beside his Adam's apple. Jerry struggled to breath. His gun, a semi-auto Browning, was now grasped by the other man—which he used to crack him against the skull.

"Ughh," he grunted, sinking to a knee, starbursts exploding behind his eyes.

"If you ever want to see your brown-sugar honey again, you will tell me what I want to know."

"If you've hurt her, you Black bastard, you and your illegitimate children will be skinned and gassed."

The burned-faced man chuckled and grabbing his quarry by the lapels, plucked him from the floor and threw him into the chair he'd been sitting in. "You talk tough for a guy who taps on a keyboard all damn day."

Jerry in the baseball cap glared at the other man, blinking.

The disfigured man knew a lot about Jerry Balis. He was a senior editor who worked for a fake news website that was part—albeit through several front companies—of Norman Bethune's empire. But Balis had a secret desire, some might argue fetish, for dark-skinned Black women. His current fling was Chantelle Wardlow who worked part-time at the local big-box store. Balis had told her he worked for a restaurant supply chain.

"I could make noise about blowing your thing with Chantelle to your masters," the burned-faced man said. "I suppose that would certainly embarrass you and make for some sideways glances, for who knows what you've said to this sister during pillow talk."

"You don't scare me."

"I should. This place is wired, Jer," he lied.

Balis's eyes went wide.

"And more than that, speaking of kids out of wedlock, what about those two cute rugrats you have with what's-her-name in Pittsburgh? Who you send money to on the regular."

"How do you know this? Is this some kind of test Norman set up? Well, I'm loyal."

"It's not going to be hard to spin the story that here you are, part of the chosen, yet cavorting around with 'loose' Negro women. It wouldn't be hard to paint the picture that they were actually undercover agents of a counter-espionage cadre Obama set up since leaving office."

"That's insane. No one would believe that." But his right cheek twitched.

The other man stood before him, arms crossed, holding the handgun. "Yeah, really? The Clintons sabotaged JFK Jr.'s airplane. John Podesta is a Satanist. Two or maybe it's three million undocumented voted in the past presidential election. Those followers of yours have swallowed a lot of poisonous pablum you've spoon-fed them. How long would they think you're still a true believer, huh, Jer? What would happen to you then?" He didn't need to elaborate, Balis knew the ferocity the ardent were capable of unleashing. Particularly on one they thought a turncoat—which, ironically, was what Balis was part of concocting against a public figure.

Silence ticked by, then, "What do you want?"

This time the burned-faced man didn't break into a smile like he had when he was Claude.

ONE OF THE GUARDS WAS IN modified camo and wore a watch cap with a logo on it. He was a member of a group called Blood of the Lamb Consecrated, so-called Christian gun enthusiasts dedicated to making America great again. He held his M4 assault rifle at rest but ready; diagonal across his chest, hand on the grip, finger extended over the trigger guard. A faint noise caused him to pivot. Two prongs of a modified Taser shot out of the dark, piercing his bullet-resistant vest and into his chest. The prongs were designed to penetrate as they were longer than usual and had screw-like tips that rotated, drawing current from the Taser. Voltage coursed through the wires the prongs were attached to, and the guard gritted his teeth and reared back. But he didn't go down.

"Take more than that, you motherless defiler," he wheezed at the masked man who stepped into view. Before he could bring the M4's barrel up, a suppressor on its end, twin throwing stars blurred through the air at their target. One sank into the guard's hand and the other snicked a wound alongside his neck as it twirled away.

"For the love of our savior," he declared, his finger reflexively jerking the trigger, spewing rounds into the earth.

The proletarian adventurer swiftly covered the distance between them. The blow of his heel to the guard's knee buckled him then he drove the sole of that same heavy boot into the man's face. Simultaneously, he wrested the rifle away from now lax hands, and used the butt to viciously render the other one unconscious. The intruder was dressed in black jeans, heavy black boots, and a dark zipped-up windbreaker and cowl-like mask. Like the unconscious guard's vest, the intruder's clothes were bullet-resistant, woven with Kevlar and a polyethylene blend. Various gadgets and tools were secreted about his person as well. Around the corner of the two-story cinder block building the second sentry lay on the ground, felled by the masked man's stiff finger strike to his carotid artery. The cinder block structure was supposedly the regional office of the restaurant supply business that Balis worked for, Industrial Kitchen Fixtures.

At a metal side door the vigilante produced what looked like a smartphone. Holding the device, he connected a wire leading from this to the electronic lock on the door. The screen of the phone-like gadget swam with numbers across its face as it hacked the lock for the correct passcode. Soon there was a satisfying click but the masked vigilante paused, paying attention to a disturbance of his chi. He turned his body away from the dark opening just as bullets raked the spot where he'd been standing.

Two members of the BLC rushed out of the building, firing their weapons. The masked man had sought cover behind a black SUV and he calmly cut these two down by shooting them in the shins. They were still alive and deadly and he rolled a mini flashbang grenade between them. It went off with a boom of heat and light.

"Dammit, the heathen has blinded me," one of them said, lying on his side on the ground. As his vision started to return to normal, he was knocked unconscious by three strategically placed blows of the attacker's fist to pressure points on his upper body. The other wounded man was already out, bleeding from his mouth and nose.

M4 in hand, the invader eschewed the front door the other two had exited. His lenses cycled from being dark like sunglasses, having altered when the flashbang went off, back to their normal green hue. He reached another metal door, in the rear of the building with a keyed lock, but not an electronic one. He bent and put his ear to its surface, listening for movement on the other side. Hearing none, he straightened up and extracted a small battery-powered, diamond-tipped drill to get him past the door's double lock.

Before he could get to work the door exploded outward, sending him and it flying in the opposite direction. He landed hard on his back—fortunately the door somewhere else instead of on top of him. His flexible armor had kept him alive but he estimated the three who came out of the building didn't know that. A beam from a light mounted on an assault rifle cut through the smoke of the explosion seeking his form.

"Where is that Son of Ham?" a voice demanded. "That ghetto-bred meddler's no damn ghost. He has to be here."

Two metal golf ball-sized spheres rolled into view, emitting green smoke. The three started coughing. Their eyes watering.

"Some kind of tear gas," one declared, running away, trying to clear his throat. An emerald pall hung about them as they sought to fan away the vapors.

"Wait, what," another gasped, a sudden weakness spreading through his limbs. "It's knock out—" He didn't finish for he collapsed to the ground unconscious.

The second Consecrated member was far enough out of the fumes that the inside of his head felt fuzzy but he was still upright. He spun in a half circle, shooting into the mist as he figured it was from that the masked man would attack.

"Die, you cut-rate commie tofu eatin' blackguard," he shouted over the rounds churning from his weapon. The firing stopped, a string of gray smoke drifting from his hot barrel. He turned. Before him a column of the velvety smoke seemed to be congealing around something solid in its opaque center.

"Got you, Pimpernel," he avowed, the assault rifle rattling its high velocity bullets again. The smoke separated but there was nothing within. "By Adam," he exclaimed.

"From me to you," a gruff voice said in his ear. The disguised man sank his butterfly knife in the other man's side and he gasped. A chop to his neck subdued him for the time being. Even as the wounded man dropped to the ground, the intruder was in motion. Now unfettered, the masked vigilante stepped into the facility's black interior. Calmly he put away his apparatus while tuning his senses outward for other presences.

Detecting no one else at least in his immediate vicinity, he then moved along rows of restaurant supplies from mobile pan racks, refrigeration compressors, to meat slicers. Though it was dark in here, aided by his goggles coated with a kind of night vision substance and his practiced light tread, the invader moved easily about, not disturbing any of the equipment. His goal was not pilfering a state-of-the-art countertop confectioner's oven but gaining entry to what lay beneath the supply house. So far, he hoped, no alarms had been raised. But he knew better than to be complacent. The Black Pimpernel reached what seemed like the door to the basement. He paused, his hand suspended above the latch.

From overhead there was a whoosh of air as a trapdoor in the ceiling banged open and dropping onto him were two massive anacondas. Worse, he could see the beasts had been genetically altered, proof of a rumor the Pimpernel had surfaced through dark web chatter. The Zelnoxx Corporation was a global agricultural enterprise that ran massive feed lots, manufactured pesticides, and owned the patents on numerous genetically modified seeds. The word was that Zelnoxx, at the behest of the current administration, had branched out into other sorts of research beyond vegetables, fruits, and livestock. Not surprisingly, the president owned stock in Zelnoxx. The mutated anacondas were thicker and more muscular than ones the masked man had encountered before. And like the long-gone stegosaurus, each had a ridge of small, hard pointy ridges lining their spines.

One of the prehistoric-sized snakes fell past onto the floor near his feet. The second creature wrapped part of its 30-foot-plus body about the masked man's torso, tightening about his body as it sought to squeeze him to death then devour him. The lights came on.

"Dammit," he grimaced, his hands latched onto the huge snake's girth. But already the breath was being drained from him and he heard a crack along his rib cage. The other snake slithered over to him and began coiling about his lower legs. Added to that he heard footfalls coming up from below through the door in front of him. The BLC guard intended to shoot him to make sure he no longer was a threat.

Blocking the numbing pain causing black spots to explode behind his eyes, he extracted a large silver capsule from a hidden pocket up toward his shoulder blade. The snake on his upper body reared its mammoth wedged-shaped head back and now, its mouth open and crag-like fangs poised, rushed toward him, intending to clamp onto his head.

Jamming his forearm under the creature's jaws to temporarily halt the snake's attack, he flicked the capsule into its maw and closed his eyes. Activated by the reptile's inner heat, the capsule released its contents instantaneously. The resulting explosion burst the anaconda apart, spraying the chrome cookware with its ichor, while hunks of reptile flesh flew everywhere. The masked man was knocked over, temporarily dazed. The first guard through the doorway was struck in the face by a section of snake and he was knocked backwards down the stairs, colliding with a man below him rushing up. The two tumbled over.

"What the damnation is going on?" a voice snarled from below. "Get your clumsy butts up."

Both hands on the second snake's throat, the dark intruder was back on his feet and charging forward, pulling the writhing anaconda with him.

"Figured I'd bring the party to you self-righteous bastards," he blared, leaping and descending on the regrouped guards ascending again. A burst from an M4 seared close but not into his form as the gunman couldn't get a clear shot given the marauder was now entangled with the other men. Like bowling pins, they fell back or off the sides of the stairs, taking out a flimsy wooden railing in the process. They all wound up on the concrete floor below, each scrambling to get to their feet, except one of them who'd landed on the side of his head with a thud and remained still.

"Got you, you slick sumbitch," one of the guard's declared, about to fire on the Pimpernel. But as he was still wrangling the snake, he gritted his teeth as he whipped the heavy mutant around. The enraged reptile sank its fangs onto the other man's arm, biting it clean off. As he cried out in terror, the snake got its body around him and went to work grinding his insides to mush while also wrapping its tail around another guard's lower legs.

A five-pointed throwing star sailed across the room and penetrated the side of the neck of another guard, severing a vital artery. Crimson sprayed from him as he fell to the ground dead. Two other Blood of the Lambs Consecrated were left but the intruder became a blur, delivering a combination of Jeet Kune Do strikes and old-fashioned fisticuffs blows. The two keeled over like cardboard cutouts onto the floor of the hidden computer center. It was from here, the invader knew, that the trolls and bots in service of the president and his minions generated the propaganda meant to pump up false stories, the alt facts, thus to mislead and misdirect while the real business of dismantling democracy went on. That the supposed tweets from POTUS, the more off-the-wall and seemingly unhinged, often came from this center, dictated by the likes of the Director of External Communication.

He reflected on the Ministry of Truth's slogan in *1984,* "ignorance is strength," as around him various writers, editors, and techs, male and female, either ran away or cowered near their cubicles.

Fists raised above his head, the avenger of justice yelled, "You've got a minute to get your asses out of here before I bring this place down around your ears." As they knew this man was ruthless, he was after all labeled the Most Dangerous Negro in America by right-wing talk-radio hosts and various alt-white sites, as one, the crew dashed for the stairs and the exits.

"Now if any of you are feeling frisky, thinking like you want to get your star on the wall in the Reagan Library or some such," he yelled, "try me." He was hefting one of the assault rifles, positioned in a way that he could cut down anyone coming at him. None of them took him up on his dare as they departed.

Free to explore and gather intel, the masked man used his electronic devices to access several databanks, gleaning useful information he stored away. Sitting at a console, watching a particular file download that contained financial records of the president's secret holdings in Russia, the back of his neck tingled. He swung around in the chair, snatching up the M4 he'd set close by as the wall near him exploded outward. Chunks of cinder block shot through the room like cannon fire, knocking over computers and pulverizing into other walls. The freedom fighter's finely tuned reflexes had kicked in, and in midair, he twirled his body so as to avoid two sections of cinder block. Still he was struck by a glancing blow that ruptured his protective gear.

"I'm going to stuff and mount your head on my wall, Pimpernel," declared the attacker.

The masked man regarded the new enemy before him. The man was encased in an exoskeleton suit that had been modified by the military from its original industrial use on oil platforms in deep water.

This master of disguise knew this from tech manuals he read for relaxation. He shot at the armored man with the assault rifle to no avail. Not that he figured his bullets would prevail, but he'd been curious. He was going to get a demonstration meant to be his last. The suit was a clunky assemblage of metal struts, servo units, molded sections like sides of freight cars removed and hammered into new shapes by a demi-god blacksmith, hydraulic lines, and a dome construct over his head. In the man-metal construct, he stood more than 10 feet tall.

"Are you done?" the suited man taunted when the firing stopped. Gripping a metal desk in a mechanized hand, he threw it at the disguised man. The Pimpernel went prone and slid on his belly as the desk flew mere inches over him, crashing onto a conference table, sending the laptops on it flying.

A hinged metal fist swung at him and only because he grabbed a piece of broken wall to absorb the blow, the administration's adversary survived. Still, the impact drove him off his feet and into the wall. He bounced off and fell to the floor. The armored man bounded over and the Black Pimpernel rolled away as a metal foot came down, cracking the floor instead of splitting his head open.

"You can't run forever, rabbit." Another swing and the fist missed, embedding itself momentarily in the cinder block. "Uggh," the suited man grunted as his micro-motors worked to free his hand.

This was the opportunity the dark intruder needed, and utilizing his parkour skills, he hopped on the listing desk, from there feet first to the wall, then recoiled upward and completing a somersault, landed on the back of the machine man.

"Get the hell off me." He tried to reach his hand back but his armor wasn't as flexible as human muscle and there was only so far the hand would go. "I'll get you," he yelled through the audio jack on the metal suit. Gyros whined as he twisted about to shake the Pimpernel off. He started to kick and otherwise move the desks and other obstructions from his path.

The unwelcomed rider knew the mechanized man's next move would be to head to a wall and try and scrape him off. Acting urgently but centered, calm in the storm, he had in hand two dull-plated tubes from his cache. The man in the exoskeleton was now at one of the walls and reared back into it, trying to crush the Pimpernel. His heavy body slammed against the cinder blocks but the masked man leaped free.

"Dammit," the armored man swore, thudding after the other one who bounded about. As the metal man moved forward grabbing at him, the Pimpernel, jumping up like a b-baller, twisted about in midair, and flung a broken a piece of a tabletop at those mechanized lower legs. His aim was true and the man in the exoskelton found himself tripping onto the floor face-first. The Black

Pimpernel acted hastily and applied the acid in his glass-lined containers to a specific hydraulic line—the one that went from the reservoir of the stuff on the back of the suit then t-offed to a main receptor on each leg. The connection severed, the legs would be unable to move.

"No, no," the now impotent attacker bellowed, banging the sides of his fists into the concrete floor, chunks of concrete being thrown up, dust rising about his form like a felled alloy baby having a tantrum.

Back outside, the Black Pimpernel was running. He knew from his reconnoitering there was a private airstrip that serviced the facility. There was also a Gulf Stream jet waiting on the tarmac in the dark. And Dirk Thane was a pilot.

There was open field between the office building and the airstrip. The masked man, sweat trickling down below his halfmask, paused, crouching down. The grass was tall enough in the field that the guard could easily be lying in it to pop up and gun down the invader. He could see a figure running toward the jet: Thane.

Reaching into his jacket he had only one play to make and it better work. He ran forward, thumbing a release lever free, then counting, tossed before him a grenade. He'd held it so that its fuse would burn some and in that way the grenade erupted in the air in bright reds and yellows. He too had dived into the grass but the brief pulse of light had revealed the top of the watch cap of the last guard. Knowing his cover was blown, he sprang up but was too late. Two shots echoed from the masked man's handgun from where he lay on the ground. His explosive shells ignited the assault rifle, which blew up in the other man's hands. He screamed, his hands and face on fire. He rolled around to extinguish the flames. Then he lay still, smoldering and groaning.

Thane was taxiing the jet. Dropping to a knee, bringing the burned guard's assault rifle up to his shoulder, the man in black shredded the jet's tires with well-aimed rifle fire. Thane was no doubt on his cell phone or radio calling in more troops. He had to act fast.

"I'll set the plane on fire and gladly roast you alive in it, snowflake," the Pimpernel called out. He was out of grenades, let alone hadn't brought along any thermite bombs, but he sounded convincing. "You have ten seconds." The hatch opened. "Get on the ground, face first."

"You don't know what you're messing with. This is so out of your league."

He shot over Thane's head to hasten compliance. Standing near the prone individual, he could see the metal attaché case just inside the door of the aircraft. "If you twitch, I'll kill you," he said, starting for the case. But he stopped, a fragment of information tickling at the edge of memory. He took aim and pumped rounds into the metal case. It was booby-trapped and exploded. He turned back to Thane, who tried not to look worried.

"Cute." As he'd done previously, he brought the butt of the assault rifle down on the other man's head and knocked him out. He searched his body and found the thumb drive he sought tucked in his sock. He left, flying the jet away as two black SUVs sped toward the field, shots flinging from them like runaway meteorites.

"DID YOU GET A JOB PLOWING that road to the private golf course?" The crowd, a mixture of races and ages, shouted "No," and "Hell no." The rally was across the highway to the Medgate golf course. The president had just been there golfing the past week, a facility he'd redeveloped in his real estate tycoon phase.

"But your congressman in step with this administration's supposed infrastructure recovery gave the private outfit that tax break to build it. Is that what you voted for? Is that what he promised here in Michigan? Well is it?"

There were more "no"s and cheers. Texas Agriculture Commissioner Juaquin Norcross walked back and forth across the small stage, holding the wireless mic, in black leather sport coat, designer jeans, and no tie. On he went, part of his barnstorming Red and Rust tour it was called. He used a handkerchief to wipe at the sweat on his face. Despite the admonishment from certain old-school handlers, particularly for a Latino candidate, even one with a "white" last name out stumping for a possible presidential bid, he wasn't shy about using weighted language.

"You can't call this mess draining the swamp, that's putting us in the swamp. What a *pendejo*."

The crowd gleefully echoed his last sentence. A man who'd been at the side of the crowd was moving behind several others as Norcross finished and was down among the people, shaking hands. This man did not look threatening in any way. Middleaged, heavy features, khaki pants, he looked exactly like the kind of working-class man who would come out to hear the maybe candidate. Better, he too was Latino. From his shirt pocket he extracted what appeared to be a normal ballpoint pen. He depressed the button and clicked into place the writing nib. One prick on Norcross's skin was all it would take. The symptoms would lay him up like dengue fever. Then he'd get the call that next time, it would be a bullet if he didn't quit—his poll numbers were looking too promising. He grinned, the bodyguards didn't even notice him.

A foot stuck out and the humble-looking man stumbled. Instantly, hands were on him but they weren't there to help him up. A bodyguard was on either side of him and one of them said in a low voice, "Come with us."

"Hey, you can't," he began but he was the one to get pricked. A quick jab into his arm and he went limp, disoriented and unable to speak.

"No problem, a little too excited is all," said one of the bodyguards to an onlooker. The man was hustled away.

Minutes later Norcross retreated to let a local band come out to finish off. He shook Linc Allard's hand.

"I might have to hire you full time as my speech writer, Linc. 'Course I can't match what Artemis pays you."

"I just give your words a bit of structure, you're the one that says them with conviction."

The candidate said, "We're fighting out of the corner, Linc. We ain't off the ropes yet. But we will be."

"Yes, sir."

"*Orale.*" He clapped him on the shoulder and walked off.

Allard winced, his two cracked ribs bothering him since that side door blew up on him. He'd have to talk to Artemis about enhancing his gear. Maybe micro server units would do the trick.

"RELEASED THIS MORNING IS WHAT MANY left and various mainstream organizations say is the smoking gun connecting this administration to the reported attempt on the health if not the life of Juaquin Norcross. Evidence has surfaced about small business owner Efrain Braga, a one-time youthful member of the contras in Nicaragua during the Reagan years, being used against Norcross. Further, computer records that are still being verified allege that the president's Director of External Operations Norman Bethune was involved, as was ex-military contractor and controversial figure Dirk Thane, the latter now having fled to parts unknown. Still to be determined is the involvement of the radical vigilante dubbed the Black Pimpernel. He's borrowed that name from the late freedom fighter Nelson Mandela who was referred to as that when he was public enemy number one in apartheid South Africa."

Margo Mayfair used the remote to click off the television. "Is this finally the beginning of the end?"

"His apologizers will have to twist themselves into Gordian Knots to make these new round of excuses," Linc Allard said.

"Including me, shit."

"We all must do our part."

Playing the conservative, Mayfair was able to gather intel from the rightest camp. It was she who told him she'd heard about the attaché case gimmick Thane had used in a tight spot in Afghanistan. She'd overheard the boast at some cocktail party.

"Don't you lay that selfless revolutionary shit on me, man." She leaned over and kissed him. When their lips and tongues parted, "As Juaquin's campaign heats up, how the hell are you going to keep up this crazy life of yours, Linc? The Pimpernel, Claude, the burned man, Ornett the janitor, and those other personas you put on."

"The good thing about all the deportations is the amount of menial work available for a brother these days, Margo. The return of the Invisible Man."

"Don't be cute. You know damn well you're burning the candle down quick from both ends." She looked away, wiping at her cheek. "Goddammit, Linc, what happens if you get found out?"

The raid on the Blood of the Lamb Consecrated headquarters had been a misdirection. Though the absconded files the Resistance knew would prove valuable. But since Mayfair had been invited to a confab on Cape Cod, she'd been tasked with discovering what Bethune and Thane had been meeting about at the Duckblind café in the desert. She was able to clone the smartphone of Martin Hallsworth, her host and confidant of Bethune. The leads gleaned from his phone led them to uncovering the plot against Norcross.

"Maybe it's time for a few more Pimpernels. For sure some women."

Mayfair raised an eyebrow.

"Yeah, I know. It's worse than heroin or booze, sex even. You tell yourself you're doing good, being righteous for the cause. You are. But God help you, when you slip on that mask and put it on the line, it's one crazy-ass rush."

"I tell you what else is a rush." She pulled him to her and they made love again. Later, Mayfair's double encrypted phone buzzed and, lifting her head off of Allard's chest, she retrieved it from the nightstand, noting the name that was on the screen, Druke Burbank. She grinned at the cover name and answered the call.

"Ah, Margo," drawled the familiar voice on the other end, "damn fine op you two pulled off."

"Thank you," she said.

"Looks like, I, ah, just gleaned some new . . . information from one of my taps on Trump. Significant and pertinent I'd say," he added in his clipped manner. The two discussed this some.

"Linc," she said in a loud whisper when they'd paused, waking her paramour and comrade-in-arms. His eyelids fluttered. "It's Big O, he wants us to come over tomorrow for a game of eight ball and a chat." She brightened. "Give me a chance to try out a new disguise."

"And a chance for me to win back the hundred he took off me last time, huh?"

"Double or nothing he says."

Linc Allard squinted at her with one eye. The following day, while being filled in on the latest intel gleaned from one of the various ways the current commander-in-chief was being surreptitiously surveilled, the former occupant of that office cleaned Allard's clock at the pool table—yet again.

FANGS OF THE FIRE SERPENT

"Uh-oh, folks, McCall has Smith on the ropes and is working his breadbasket. Suddenly an uppercut catches Smith on the side of his jaw but looks like he slipped most of that blow. Okay, okay, Smith counters with a combination hard right to McCall's chest and a left he ducked. But this gives Smith an opening and he moves sideways and now he's back on his bicycle, dancing and bobbing backwards, and this again flusters McCall.

"He's saying something to Smith but I dare not repeat such to you, our dear radio audience here on KNX. Ha, ha. Oh, wait, Smith abruptly stopped and pivoting more like a toreador than a pugilist sunk a straight hard right past McCall's guard and caught him flush under the left eye. I tell you folks, the speed at which Smith is able to deliver his shots, often off-balance, is truly amazing. It's no wonder this is a sold out crowd here at the Olympic Auditorium given McCall's Irish following and Smith's allure among our colored citizenry and the entertainers and musicians he hobnobs with.

"Referee Arthur Leibling breaks the contenders apart from a clench. Rocco Kaufman is yelling at his fighter to lower his shoulders and keep his head tucked in like he's supposed to. The fighters are back in the center of the ring, ladies and gentlemen, trading blows but nothing decisive. Oh, wait, McCall thought he had an opening as Smith has gone flat-footed, dropping his arms. He seemed to be running out of gas here in the eleventh round but I think it was a ploy. McCall looped in what looked to be a devastating left, I could feel the wind draft I tell you, folks. But Smith easily took the blow on his forearm and in rapid succession, his hands a veritable blur, peppered McCall's face and head with a series of fisticuffs. As my sweet, corn cob pipe smoking granny is want to say, he combed his hair back. McCall is woozy I tell you and the crowd, you can hear the men and women on their feet and demanding a knock out, boxing fans.

"McCall, his mouth guard red from blood, looks to rally with a jab, trying to open up that cut he put over Smith's brow early in the fifth. The punch lands solid but seemingly has no effect. Unfazed Smith moves in, crosses and overhands patterned in a dizzying display of ring generalship putting McCall on his back.

"Jimmy, Jimmy, turn up the volume so they can hear me over the roar. Referee Leibling is standing over McCall who is down on a knee, sweat and hope dripping off him like a wrung out wet sheet on the clothesline . . . six, seven, eight. . . McCall rises, he's back up I tell you, he's back up. Smith circles. McCall lashes out but his punches are weak, off-target. Smith gets in under a left and hammers McCall downstairs and upstairs and oh, mama, the punishment being meted out to Bruiser McCall. He stumbles and drops over on his side. The ref is giving him the count . . . and that's it, brother, the fight is over. Leibling raises Smith's arm as the crowd explodes. He gave them their knockout and then some. And let me tell you, if I hadn't just witnessed him going eleven grueling rounds of championship level boxing, you'd say he was just some fella who'd come in for in egg cream he looks so refreshed.

"And speaking of refreshing, this swell-looking colored dame in a silk getup with brocade stitching and a feathered hat has come into the ring and is all over the winner like a second skin much to the consternation of Rocco Kaufman. Ha, ha. Well, folks, I'm getting in there too so I can get a few words with the man who is more than likely to face Solly Krieger, the middleweight title holder. The man who for good reason demonstrated tonight why pound for pound, he's the best around. Why they call him Decimator."

IT FINALLY GOT QUIET IN THE dressing room. Achilles Smith had showered and was buttoning his shirt. Millard "Rocco" Kaufman returned from using the phone in the Olympic Auditorium's back office.

"How's it looking?" Smith asked, tucking in his shirt tail and zipping up and buckling his tweed slacks.

Absently Kaufman, an older man in baggy pants with a tangle of white hair, loosened then retightened the cap on a bottle of liniment as he talked. "Krieger's guy Shep is playing coy."

"Meaning they want to play me cheap for a match."

"Yeah, but I'm going to let him stew for a few days. He's not going to pin us as hungry. I was talking with Hildy from the *Herald-Ex* and what with his article that runs in the morning edition and figure some other noise that'll come from the boxing bunch, it'll seem like Krieger is ducking you if they don't make the fight."

"Sounds good to me, Rocco." Smith had been sitting on his haunches on the examination table and now stood up. "I gotta get going over to the Dunbar."

Kaufman rolled his tongue inside his mouth. "Seeing Rose?" She was the woman in silk who'd climbed into the ring to congratulate the fighter.

The middleweight smiled. "I'm'a find you a girlfriend to occupy your time other than that John Reed and Spinoza you're always reading, Rocco." He clapped his large hands together once, enthusiastically. "I know, what about Pig Iron Lil who hawks the news over on Broadway next to the Orpheum?"

"You're a regular Fred Allen, you know that?" Kaufman said. He shook a mashed up towel at Smith. "Just you don't go running off with that wild broad to Tijuana or parts unknown. The Krieger fight is going to be made and I want you on a regime now as we lead in to it. One that does not include chasing skirts."

Laughing, Smith was going to make another crack but there was a knock on the door and without pausing for an answer, in stepped a lanky Black man in a checked light gray box coat and dark slacks. He wore a hat and removed it while he identified himself.

"My name is Percy Kimbrough, I'm with the police."

Smith and Kaufman exchanged a look. "Ha, they let us spades work plainclothes, gate?" Smith chided. "I guess you get to chase colored robbers all over town."

Kimbrough, a light-skinned man with square good-natured features and a mustache like singer Billy Eckstine's, smiled wanly. "I'm afraid this is not good news, Mr. Smith."

"What is it?"

"It's about your sister, Helena. She's dead. Murdered."

Smith sagged against the padded examination table like being sucker punched. Kaufman put a hand on his boxer's shoulder. "When did this happen, Detective?"

"Her body washed up under the Lido pier earlier tonight. A couple of kids down there necking found her." He halted, watching the two.

"What else?" Smith asked. "Tell me all of it."

"She'd had relations recently is what I understand from the medical examiner but there was no tearing if you know what I mean. But there were bruises and her neck was broken."

Smith lowered his head and folded his arms as if to contain himself. "I'll make arrangements of course." He seemed to be saying it for the benefit of others not in the room.

"How long had she been in the water?" Kaufman asked.

"We figure no more than a day or two. Say, she was a nurse over at Queen of Angels, wasn't she?"

"Yeah," Smith answered.

"I need to ask, when was the last time you saw her? And she was a looker, she having any boyfriend troubles? Some mug you might have told to lay off and he took it out on her?"

Smith regarded the cop evenly. "I talked to her, must have been Wednesday afternoon. She told me she couldn't make it tonight 'cause she was going to be on duty. So, you know, I just figured I'd see her later like always. But I won't be seeing her again I guess." He was tearing up but got himself under control. "I know a couple of the guys Helena used to date. I doubt if any one of them could have done this, but I'll give you their names and where they stay."

"You know where they live, huh?" Kimbrough observed, taking a steno pad out of his inner breast pocket.

"I damn sure better know," Smith replied chillingly, already missing his big sister.

After giving the detective the information and his particulars like his address and phone number to his apartment on Maple, the plainclothesman left saying he'd be back in touch.

"Achilles, I don't know what to say," Kaufman began. "I'm sure sorry about this, it's a goddamn shame is what it is. She was awfully nice."

"She sure was." Smith put on his leather jacket. "That's why I'm going to find out who killed her and make that son of a bitch pay."

"You better leave this to the cops, son."

"Don't blow no gaskets, Rocco, you ain't an officer of the court anymore." In the Roaring '20s, a young Rocco Kaufman had been a criminal attorney until he was disbarred.

"Go over to the Dunbar and tell Rose, will you, Rocco? She'll be downstairs in the Zanzibar Room." The boxer headed for the door.

"Where you going?"

"Over to the hospital, see a friend who worked with Helena." Smith nodded curtly at his manager and left.

Kaufman was inclined to argue but hoped the younger man would cool down after tonight. Let him get this out of his system, this futile attempt, then he figured he'd get him out of town for a week or so to keep him away from the newshounds.

Descending the stairs to his car parked in back, Achilles "Decimator" Smith was glad what little talking he'd had to do to the papers had been done. Tomorrow the news of his sister's death and his win would be on the same pages and it made him ill inside just imagining that. The only cure was to set this right for Helena, he vowed. It would also be tomorrow when he'd make the call to their father Augustus in Galveston—at least to some cousins there. He would telephone in an effort to find his father, a professional gambler, sometimes vending machine mechanic, and full time womanizer.

Putting his Ford Cabriolet into gear, Decimator Smith hoped Detective Kimbrough would be busy with the names he'd given him for a day. Just maybe enough time to make a little headway. He wanted whoever did this to die by his hands. It wouldn't be the first time Smith had killed—though it would be the first time in California, he noted grimly. He got out to Queen of Angels Hospital in Echo Park and at this time of night, found a place to park almost in front on Bellevue.

Inside the main building he went to the unofficial colored ward. Segregation in Los Angeles was official in housing covenants and resulting neighborhood patterns, and unofficial in public accommodations like the hospital. It simply was that Black patients were on certain floors and in certain rooms. A Japanese-American doctor, Mark Kagawa, who knew Smith, was walking along a hallway he'd just turned onto. He'd been skimming through papers attached to a clipboard.

"Heard the last rounds of your fight tonight on the radio, Achilles, congratulations." The two shook hands.

"Thanks, Doc. Is Zora around?"

He hooked a thumb behind him. "I passed her at the nurses station on the corridor to the right."

"'Preciate that." Smith began walking briskly.

"I got my money on you if you fight Krieger," the doctor said, heading in the opposite direction.

He found Zora Montclair leaving a room with three patients in it. One was under a translucent oxygen tent, its sides moving in and out slightly like the membrane of a large sea creature.

"Des, hey," she said. "Helena didn't come in tonight. That girl must be staying out late these days gaycatting." She was a pretty copper-skinned woman of mixed heritage but considered herself, as society did, as Black. She had a captivating smile to go with a figure her plain nurse's uniform couldn't hide. She and Smith had been an item once until she fell for an insurance man with more money and future than him.

Smith gently took her by the elbow and guided her to a spot along a wall. "There's no easy way to say this so here it is: Helena was killed. Murdered."

"Oh God, Des," she said, gripping his arm, a hand to her mouth. She looked up at him with teary eyes. "Who could have done this?"

Decimator Smith was in ring attack mode, the only way he could function and not be frozen by the terrible fact of his sister's violent death. "Was she seeing some new boy-friend, Zora?"

Montclair wiped at her tears and looked into the middle distance, frowning. "No, not anybody you wouldn't have known about, Des."

"I need anything you can give me, Zora. This is very important to me, understand?" Not meaning to, he gripped her arm and tightened.

"Des," she said, referring to the pressure.

He released her. "I'm sorry. I'm just, you know . . . "

"Hey, wait," she said, snapping her fingers and lowering her voice as an orderly walked past. "Helena was making some extra money, off the books, see?"

"Yeah?"

She elevated her shoulders. "That's all I've got, Des. This has been going on for about a month. She mentioned to me last week the grown son of this woman she's been caring for had words with her about his mother's care." She looked at him hopefully.

"This son got a name?"

"I don't know his, but the elderly patient is named Harcourt."

"As in Harcourt Tire and Rubber? The ones outfitting the buses up and down the West Coast?"

"I don't know. But Helena said she had a big house in Los Feliz. Maids and the whole bit."

"Thanks for this, Zora." He started to leave.

"I gotta tell the girls," she murmured. "When's the funeral, Des?"

"Not sure yet," he called back, already at the end of the hallway. He didn't want to picture himself at his sister's coffin, looking down into it. He next drove to her place, two rented rooms and a bath all to herself in a good-sized two-story Craftsman on 68th Street near Hoover.

The widow Mrs. Gasparento greeted him at the door, the porch light on. "Oh my, Achilles, this is so awful," she commiserated.

"You know?"

"That policeman, Kimbrough called. Said for me to not let anyone in her rooms until he came here tomorrow morning." She put her muscular arms around him and squeezed his shoulders as he stood in the open doorway.

He squeezed her back then pulled away, his eyes steady on hers. "But I'm family, Mrs. Gasparento, and I need to see about some of her things tonight."

"I don't know, I can't have any trouble with the law," she said.

Her round face was framed by a full length of curly black hair, the gray in it hidden by hair dye. She was 40 or so pounds too heavy but even in her early 60s, there were reminders of the beauty she'd been back when—back when she and the late Mr. Gasparento ran a truck stop and bootleg whiskey operation in California's Central Valley.

"Won't be none," Smith said, "I'll be just like a little mouse."

"Sure you will, *carissima*, because I just got here off the squid boat." Smith was already heading to the stairs.

"You're tops, Mrs. Gasparento."

In his sister's main room Smith pulled down the Murphy bed and looked through her possessions, smiling at a picture of the two of them as kids in Galveston, Texas. There was their mother and father on either side of them, his sister squinting into the camera. She'd grown up to favor their deceased mother quite a bit, he reminded himself. Momentarily he sat, gripped by melancholy. The picture had been taken in front of their father's boat repair business on the water. About a year before he gave that up to give his full attention to the cards and little attention to his family.

He shook the past off and pressed on. He found Helena's address book and copied the address she'd written down of a Juliet Harcourt. He left the book, figuring if he was unsuccessful in finding his sister's killer, maybe Kimbrough would be. Though he doubted the cop's white bosses cared that much about a colored girl's murder, so how long would it be a priority? He continued searching and found a gold chain necklace in a dresser drawer. There was a small pendant on the chain and he assumed given its sparkle, it was the real McCoy. Now who gave her a diamond? None of the ones he knew she'd dated could afford that kind of ice. They were doing good to afford drinks and dinner for two at one of the jazz joints like the Club Alabam on Central. He briefly debated taking the item then pocketed the jewelry. He turned up nothing else of interest and left.

Descending the stairs, Smith saw entering the house a tall, reedy man dressed in a black suit and a white collarless shirt buttoned all the way up underneath. This was Elijah Morbilus, or so he called himself. He was of undetermined ethnicity and age. A dime store spiritualist hustler is what Smith had said to Helena about him. He rented a large room in the rear of the house off the service porch. Morbilus looked up, absently adjusting his rimless round spectacles on his shallow face.

"Brother Smith. The avenues are abuzz with your victory." He clasped his hands together as if in prayer, and bowed slightly.

"Thanks," he said, stepping past the dusky-colored man who smelled of incense and oils. Probably out giving a "reading" as he called them to some gullible old dame, Smith figured.

"Is there . . . something amiss?" Morbilus said. He'd stopped on his way to his room in the half-light of the hallway. Mrs. Gasparento came though the kitchen's swing door, worrying a dish towel in both of her hands.

A cold snake went across Smith's spine. He looked back at Morbilus. "Why do you ask?"

Slowly he waved a hand about as if sifting through vapor. "I, I don't know, but seems there is a disturbance around you, Achilles Smith. A great disturbance."

The boxer considered, then dismissed any notions that this hokum peddler could have harmed his sister. "I gotta get gone." With that he quit the rooming house.

Morbilus addressed the widow in a calm, reassuring tone. "Please Missus, tell me what's happened."

Mrs. Gasparento sighed audibly and told him what she knew.

Decimator Smith went to the Golden Bough Funeral Home on San Pedro, driving past the construction site of the new Coca-Cola bottling plant on Central Avenue. It was a Streamline Modem structure designed like a landlocked boat. Diagonally across the street was Engine Company Number 30, an all-Black fire fighting unit, one of two in the city. At the funeral home he talked with the night man on duty there, the semi-retired Reverend Milton Harshaw. The one thing Negroes had in common with white folks, the preacher was wont to say, was dying at peculiar hours.

Smith had interrupted his late night snack of a hogshead cheese sandwich with a side of brandy. After his condolences and a brief prayer the holy man insisted on doing for her soul, the middleweight made the various burial arrangements, including the pick-up of his sister's body at the coroner's lab. He paid with his winnings from that night's fight.

"I would be honored if you would let me speak at her send off, Decimator."

"That would be fine, Reverend." They shook hands.

Arriving at his apartment, Smith found Rocco Kaufman waiting for him on the street in his battered Plymouth coupe. His trainer joined him on the sidewalk. He carried a bottle wrapped in a paper bag.

"You didn't have to come here, Rocco."

"Sure I did," the older man said, clapping the younger man on the shoulder. He held aloft the bottle. "Let's have a few belts. Your trainer's orders."

They went inside and Kaufman poured whiskey in two water glasses the boxer retrieved from the cupboard. They clinked them together sitting angled to each other in two secondhand club chairs in the living room. There was a Zenith radio in a walnut cabinet in the corner, and a range of books from W. E. B. Du Bois to Roman history filling a built-in bookcase.

"You're not going to let this go, are you?" His trainer asked, after taking a sip.

"I can't, Rocco. I couldn't abide myself if I just sat around. You the one taught me to always take the fight to my opponent."

The older man nodded, looking off then back at the young pugilist. "Remind me to call Abe later, okay?"

Smith frowned. "Your brother? The kind of . . . out there one I met that time?"

Kaufman smiled thinly. "The one and only."

They drank and talked some more and wound up sleeping in their clothes in the chairs. The following morning Smith, bathed, hatted, shaven, and in the one suit he owned, wearing black wool socks with dark blue clocks on them, went up the drive of a tree shaded two-story castle-like mansion of stained glass windows and two turrets in Los Feliz. He parked in the roundabout and thumped the door with the lion headed knocker on the large front door.

"Yes?" said a Black maid in her uniform who opened the door. She eyed him suspiciously.

In a voice cold and flat he said, "I'm the brother of Helena Smith. I'd like to talk to Mrs. Harcourt about her. You see she was killed and I'm looking into her murder."

The maid gaped at him and stammered, "Hold on." She pushed the door to but not to catch and went to tell her employer. Momentarily she returned. "This way, please."

Smith took his hat off and followed her into a tiled hallway through a dark wood paneled dining room the size of his apartment and into a back yard, garden really, of various colorful flowers and plants. He expected to find a frail old woman possibly in a wheelchair, wrapped in layers of shawls. Instead he did find an elderly thin woman but she stood with the aid of a cane, while another maid, this one Mexican-American, stood close by. She too eyed Smith with wariness.

"Thank you, Garacella," Mrs. Harcourt said. "Please sit, young man. I believe you're a boxer. Helena was quite proud of you, said you were also taking classes over at the city college too."

"She made me, ma'am. She knew I couldn't box forever." Regret came and went behind his eyes. The maid drifted off but Smith had the impression she remained in earshot.

The old woman indicated a set of wicker chairs and each sat in one at a matching table. On it was an open pack of Home Run cigarettes, a crystal ashtray, and a fancy silver lighter. "Would you care for anything to drink?"

"No, I'm fine. I just wanted to ask you a few questions about my sister."

"And you say she was murdered?"

"Yes, Mrs. Harcourt." For the second time in less that 24 hours he retold what he knew of the details of her death.

"Oh, my, that's simply ghastly," the elderly woman said. "Poor girl. I would like to help you, really, but, I can't see how. Surely what happened to her has something to do with, well," she cast her gaze sideways momentarily, "with well, where you people live," she breathed. "One hears these stories on the radio I'm afraid." She looked at him for confirmation.

Decimator Smith almost snorted but kept a straight face. "I'm not ignoring that angle, ma'am. But did any man come around here bothering her or did she get a call maybe one of your maids overheard?"

She made a dismissive wave. "Oh, nothing like that, no. Helena came, attended to me, and that was that."

He gestured with his hat in his hand. "Maybe I could ask them, the maids I mean."

"I already said that didn't happen." She looked toward her cigarettes.

"How was it you hired my sister?"

Her solicitous faced slipped back into place. "Why that was because of my son, Van . . . Dr. Van Harcourt. He's a physicist at Cal Tech you see. He does very important work. He'd mentioned, given my recent operation, it might be a good idea to have a nurse on duty at certain times until I fully recovered."

"How did he find her?"

"Oh, I wouldn't know about such things. I'm sure through some registry or whatever it is nurses have." She jutted a chin in the direction of some gloves and pruning shears laying on the ground. "Now, I'm sorry, but I must get back to my flowers. They need me."

Smith was on his feet. "I'd like to talk to your son, Mrs. Harcourt."

She smiled. "He's quite busy. But leave your number with Ophelia and we'll see. Good day and again, I mourn your loss."

Suddenly both maids were there and he followed the Black one back to the front door. "I want to leave my number," he said.

The maid snickered. "Mr. Van ain't got no time to call regular white folks let alone a spook."

"Your missus said I could."

The woman all but rolled her eyes but went away, then returned with a fountain pen and folded envelope. He wrote his name and phone number on the envelope, then added a "regarding" and his sister's name. He blew on his handwriting to dry the ink, and handed it back to the maid. She pocketed the information and waved toward the door. Smith let himself out and drove away. The base of the driveway was blocked by a DeSoto parked sideways across it. Two white men stood near the car. The larger of the two had his foot on the bumper of the DeSoto. Shutting off the engine, Smith got out of his Ford.

"You lost, boy?" The larger one said, taking his foot off the bumper.

"I know where I'm going," the boxer said.

"You say Mister when you're talking to a white man," the second one said. He wore a black shirt under a dark brown jacket and gray tie.

Smith moved so as not to get pinned between the two.

The larger man advanced, jabbing a finger at him. "Whatchu doing around here bothering Mrs. Harcourt, snowflake? Huh? Get on back to your side of town, Smith."

The man outweighed him by at least 30 pounds and he wasn't flabby. There was no sense wasting time talking. Decimator Smith stepped right into him and unleashed two rapid punches at the man's mid-section, doubling him over.

"You Black bastard," he wheezed, scrambling forward, getting his arms around Smith's legs. The two fell back against his Ford and untangled. The other man charged forward, reaching into his inner coat pocket for his gun.

"I'll put my gat on him, Paul."

The big one, Paul, glared at his companion. "You telling me I can't take this dinge?"

"It ain't that, Paul, it's just we're supposed to, you know . . . "

"Nix, I said, nix. I got this bo." Paul came around swinging but Smith was too fast and easily ducked his first heavy blows. His assailant had assumed the pugilist would resort to ring tactics and therefore he'd have the advantage with street brawling techniques. But where Achilles Smith grew up in Galveston, running errands for his dad and Quill Lacouix's casino and sporting house at 12, he'd learned to be a scrapper.

Paul grazed him with a right but Smith wasn't about to get into a boxing match. Particularly not with the other man itching to use his gun. He kicked out with his heel and clipped the one called Paul in the center of his knee.

The big man yelled, stumbling forward. Smith brought an overhand right down on the side of his face and, just as quickly, followed with a right uppercut. Paul reeled as the gunman drew his .38.

Smith got his arms around the larger man and drove him toward his partner. The other man tried to move aside but got tangled up and all three went down.

"This goddamn jig," the gunman swore. He was on the bottom of the pile, pushing at his buddy Paul on top of him.

Smith clapped the larger man's ears and he cried out, gritting his teeth, grabbing at the middleweight. But Smith rolled and, up on his feet, punched at the gunman's face with a rain of blows, making him woozy. He grabbed the gun from his loosened grip and got to his feet.

"You better give me that roscoe," Paul demanded, also rising.

Calmly, Smith clubbed the large man on the head twice with the body of the revolver, sending him to the ground bleeding and senseless. He then grabbed the other man and threw him into the side of the DeSoto. He put fearful unfocused eyes on the contender.

"What are you going to do?"

"Who had you staking out the old lady?" Smith came closer, the gun leveled on the man. "Her son? How come?"

"I can't tell you that."

Smith slugged him and he wilted. "Keep away from me."

"Who?"

He tried to run and Smith yanked him back by the yoke of his jacket, twirling him around against the front of the DeSoto and onto the ground. Nearby, Paul groaned but didn't get up.

"I'm going to ask it one more time and you better give me some answers."

The man began to stammer and Smith jammed the hood's right arm in between the DeSoto's extended bumper and its grill. Smith put his foot on the elbow. "You want them to start calling you Lefty?" He put pressure on the arm.

The hood talked. He didn't know much, but he knew enough.

Smith then drove over to the *Eagle* on Central Avenue. Along with the *Sentinel*, it was one of two Black weeklies in town. He'd come to see a boxing fan and reporter he knew named Loren Miller. Miller was a graduate of Howard University. He was attending law school at night and traveled in various circles.

"He's an egghead," Miller told him in his closet of an office after Smith laid out what had happened during the last 24 hours. "Van Harcourt teaches physics at Cal Tech in Pasadena. Brilliant, he's big on Buck Rogers stuff, figuring out how to build space ships to the Moon and Mars."

His friend paused, worrying the stem of his lit pipe against his teeth.

"But he's supposed to be some kind of witchdoctor too. I've been sitting on a story for a year now from a colored gal, a maid who had to clean up after one of his occult sessions or some such at his house. But if we ran the story, given his family's rich, he'd sue and shut us down lickety-split."

"You talking about devil worship?" Smith asked.

His friend raised his eyebrows. "I don't rightly know, man, but I do know you better keep your country ass away from him."

Smith rose and put his hat back on. "I'll see you, Loren."

"I ain't foolin' Des."

"Neither am I."

Feeling edgy, Smith needed a tune up. He next went to the Broadway Gym where he trained between bouts. He greeted several of the fighters inside as he headed to his locker. There was a pay phone near the lockers and he used it to check in with Rocco Kaufman, telling him of his progress.

Kaufman said on the other end of the line when he told him about the thugs working for Van Harcourt, "Oh brother, like it or not, I guess you're in deep now, Des."

"Yep," the boxer opined.

He was an hour into his routine, sweating, skipping rope vigorously for coordination purposes, when Rocco Kaufman entered. With him was a lean balding man with owlish glasses hefting a large Gladstone luggage bag. Smith recognized his trainer's brother, Abe.

"Sorry about your sister, Decimator," the older Kaufman said, sticking out his hand. It was stained with various chemicals and burned in two spots.

"'Preciate that," Smith said, shaking the other man's hand.

"Let's go in the back," Kaufman said, jerking his head in that direction.

The three did so. There they gathered in an office that technically didn't belong to Kaufman, but due to his boxer's rising status, he was allowed to use unmolested. Rocco Kaufman closed the door as Abe Kaufman put the suitcase on a scarred wooden table and undid the latches.

Rocco Kaufman said, "As you know, Des, my brother is something of an inventor."

"Rocco figures you could use a few of my items."

Smith was fascinated by the odd-looking contents of the case, which included several handguns as well. "This is your hobby?"

"Not exactly," the older brother said. "When I was back east, I did some work for a few vigilante types you might say. I belonged to a kind of a loose association of scientists who helped out the best way we could."

"You heard of that bloodthirsty joker with the weird laugh and slouch hat in New York?" Rocco Kaufman said. "Abe designed a few gadgets for him through his operatives."

"I'll be," Smith said. He picked up a .45 in the case and began expertly disassembling it.

"Where'd you learn that?" his trainer said.

"In between carousing, Daddy managed to teach me a few things," Smith uttered offhandedly as he reassembled the gun.

Abe Kaufman rubbed his hands together. "Then let me show you a few other things, Mr. Smith."

THE NEXT DAY, DIGGING AROUND FOR as much information as he could glean about Van Harcourt, Decimator Smith stopped for a sandwich to-go at a cafe he frequented on Gage near Figueroa after a trip to the library. The counterman, nicknamed Toolie, handed him a folded slip of paper as he sat on a stool.

"Loren Miller's been looking for you, Champ."

"Thanks Toolie."

Smith read the note and whistled. Later, he went to the mortuary to view his sister's body in its coffin. Fresh gardenias and orchids scented the room.

"I don't have the right words, Helena," he said, standing over her. "I never would have made it out of Galveston but for you. Pushing me to not be like Dad, to imagine what life could bring for us." He teared up and wiped at his eyes with a handkerchief. He sat in a folding chair and remained still for some time. He wasn't sure what was ahead, but he was determined to see it through.

The smartly designed split-level house was partially built into the hill it crested. The house was of angular lines, plate glass windows and chrome flourishes. There were various cars parked about as there was a large irregularly shaped gravel area for this purpose adjacent to the home. There were also at least four men on guard duty, Decimator Smith counted. But he hadn't driven up the path to the house like the other visitors. He was crashing the party and had scouted the location by ascending on foot through the greenery decorating a side of the hill.

Smith wondered if Loren Miller, who'd done some recent legwork of his own looking into Harcourt's shenanigans, had been misinformed—that he'd come upon a house party the physicist was throwing. But he heard no laughter, no tinkling of glasses from within. Then he spotted four men in purple robes, two each carrying a nude woman, tied and gagged, down a less steep rise than the hill to a wooded area. The women, one blonde the other dark-haired, were terrified and the men smiling. He also saw a robed and masked figure handing a hip flask to a stocky man who drank from it. A light breeze flapped his coat open revealing a shoulder holster underneath. Smith concluded he was one among several guards.

Smith circled around. At this time of year, fortunately, there were not too many dry leaves on the ground so he could proceed noiselessly. Through a gap in some brush, he could also see the drivers of the cars, some in similar purple robes and some in their regular clothes, entering a cave. He recognized an LA city council member, a couple of movie actors and an actress among the gathered.

Scanning, he spotted a Japanese face and another colored man in the bunch, so he took the chance that even though these integrated idolaters, as his grandmother would've called them, probably knew each other, maybe some came and went in the group. In the center of the cave were two raised slabs carved from rock. There was also boxy equipment with gauges and dials about, including two large conical-shaped electrical coil towers, which struck Smith like something out of a Flash Gordon serial.

Smith had simply come in with the last of the 30-some-odd people traipsing into the cavern. Several were chanting and not paying him any attention anyway, as all eyes were on Harcourt in his black robe. Smith kept his hat low, watching.

"We are gathered because we believe," Harcourt was saying, "we will do what others have attempted but with no success for they were not given the light from the ancient one. For it is marrying science and the arcane that we will open the gateway and the lord above all lords will walk among us again. But first we must mark his way by the serpent of fire," he intoned.

Around Smith people began chanting, "Ze-uhl-co-tal, Zi-uhl-co-tal," along with other phrasings he didn't get, but he pretended to chant them too.

The women had been secured spread eagle with rope tied to iron rings in the raised slabs, the stone altars. A middle-aged man in a gray robe turned on the machinery and bolts of electricity surged between the coil towers. In between the towers was a row of tall oval beakers with various chemicals in them along a metal table. Copper tubing dipped in and out of these chemical baths and in turn, wire led from the tubing to the machinery. In the center was a large loop antenna some eight feet in diameter.

Van Harcourt produced a stone blade with an emerald handle. "And so it is wrought."

The people around Smith began to sway and act like they were possessed. He went along with this, working his way forward. The altars were each constructed with a channel next to the women's throats that let out on its side down below to wooden bowls.

Electricity crackled between the two towers. The crowd chanted and gesticulated, and the two sacrifices tried vainly to get free. Close now, Smith could see the sweat on Harcourt and the possessed look on his face as he cried out, "Oh, Master, oh Moyocoya, with blood as the catalyst, I will open the celestial gate for the arrival of your familiar and our supplication." Inside the loop of the antenna a blue haze materialized. Behind this was an indistinct shape.

He bent forward to cut the first throat and Smith shot off two rounds in the air from the .45 he'd brought under his leather jacket. Some of the people fled, others remained, unsure of what to do.

"Smith," Harcourt rasped.

The gray robed figure jumped the boxer from behind, knocking the gun out of his hand. But he broke free of his grasp and a combination sent the older man to the ground, down and out.

Harcourt dove for the gun as did Smith. They grappled, Harcourt stronger than Smith had anticipated. The knife flashed toward his body and he got a hold of the other man's wrist to stop it.

"We must kill this defiler," Harcourt yelled. Several of the followers, one of them in a mask, rushed forward but Smith got a jab in, disorienting Harcourt. One of the others pulled on Smith, inadvertently helping him up. The prizefighter easily blocked a punch from this man and hit him very hard in his solar plexus. As he gasped for breath, Smith shoved another man, an actor he'd seen in horse operas, who'd picked up the automatic.

"Let me show you what to do with that, Tex," Smith cracked. He punched him and snatched the gun loose and fired it into the machinery. There was a spewing cascade of sparks and bolts, and the chemicals in the beakers caught fire as the electricity short circuited. The blue haze evaporated inside the antenna's loop. For the briefest of moments, it seemed a reptilian face poked through but then that too was gone. A trick of the flickering light, Smith told himself.

He had several large capsules on him and he threw these all around. Abe Kaufman called them his electro grenades. They exploded in tight puffs of smoke and sparks. But the floating dark clouds the devices left behind gave off electrical charges of tiny lightning bolts that surged into and knocked out several participants.

"Interloper," Harcourt said, charging with the knife raised.

Smith shot him, dead center in the chest. He thudded onto the ground. What was left of the conscious demonists ran, except the robed figure in the mask. Smith shook his head in disbelief. Eccentric white physicist dead at the hands of crazed Negro was how the headlines would read, he foresaw.

"Good work, Des,"

Open-mouthed he stared at the masked figure who revealed herself. "Zora," he whispered.

"He killed Helena. He was quite taken with her after she came to work for his mother. They started dating." Zora Montclair came closer. "But because of the race mixing they both agreed to keep it quiet for awhile. Of course that was before I told her who he really was . . . who we all are."

Smith was trying to comprehend. "Just what the hell—"

Her knife had been in her sleeve. He hadn't seen it until she stabbed him. Fortunately it wasn't a long blade, but it was effective. She took it out slowly as he staggered back. He had enough strength left to squeeze the trigger but she was on him and a slice to his wrist sent the weapon skittering.

"Bye bye, Achilles. I always was fond of you."

She kissed him briefly and, with a hand to his torso, pushed him into the table of beakers and electrical wiring. He crashed into the chemicals and as he fell over, wires crackled in the solution that washed over him as he lay on his side. He was jolted with voltage and his body shook and smoked. Zora Montclair departed, whistling a tune.

Smoke and flame consumed the cavern. The two women remained bound to the altars. One of the towers had fallen on part of the slab holding the dark-haired one, discharging electrical current that threatened to strike her. Smith willed himself upright. Bleeding, unsteady on his feet, he nonetheless was able to pick up the stone blade, and used it to push the leaning tower away, snapping the upper portion of the blade.

But there was enough of its rough edge left for him to saw at the rope and get one hand free of the dark-haired captive. She looked worried but kept her head. The blonde screamed hysterically. He sagged against the altar, weakened and then he fell over, blacking out.

"YOU SEE, NO CAUSE FOR ALARM," he heard a familiar voice say. Decimator Smith opened his eyes.

"How do you feel?" It was the smiling face of the dark-haired woman he'd last seen tied to Harcourt's sacrificial altar. Next to her was Elijah Morbilus. He held an empty cylindrical glass bottle, smiling oddly.

Smith sat up. He was in pajamas in his bed. "I feel okay." He could tell his lower torso was wound with gauze over a bandage where the knife wound was. "Not that I'm complaining, but how did I get here?"

Rocco Kaufman said, "You can thank Anna for that." Smith looked at the dark-haired woman.

She said, "You got my hand free and I was able to use the stone knife to get me and the other woman fully loose."

"Who was she?"

She made a face. "Couldn't say really. She ran out of there in her birthday suit as soon as I cut her loose. She's probably still running."

"Only Miss Borsage didn't quit on you, Achilles," Kaufman said.

"You were out on your feet but she got you out of there and hid you in the bushes, doing her best to stop the bleeding."

Smith looked at the pretty woman, each holding their gaze on the other a beat or two longer than proper. "So what happened?"

For an answer, Morbilus showed him a copy of the morning's *Herald Examiner*. There was a front page picture of Van Harcourt's house with a picture of him and the burned out cave as inset shots. There was also an article about war news from Europe.

The faith healer said, "In the article, Councilman Mayfair, Judge Gainer, and a couple of others were rumored to be at the ceremony."

Smith asked, "Hey, what about those guards I saw? I wondered why they never rushed into the cave when the commotion started."

"They were doped," Borsage said.

"Right, I saw Zora in her mask giving a guard a drink." Smith got out of bed and put on his boxing robe, his ring name stenciled in an arc in big letters on his back.

"So Zora hips me to Harcourt because she wanted him out of the way to take over, right?"

"More like getting both of you out of the way at the same time we figure," Kaufman said.

Smith turned to Anna Borsage. "So you're one of those demon lovers?"

"Not hardly. I made the mistake of being sweet on Rex Stampton and he put a mickey in my coffee. Next thing I knew I was in my all-together about to be skewered."

Smith nodded. Stampton was the movie cowboy he'd slugged. "Good thing you had a membership card in your wallet from the Broadway Gym," Anna Borsage said. "I called over there and they got a hold of Mr. Kaufman."

Rocco Kaufman said, "I was scared to death last night, by the time me and the young lady managed to sneak you back here and not get nabbed by the cops." He had his hands in his back pockets, the way he talked when matters weighed on his mind. "I couldn't take a chance on taking you to a hospital, what with the fire, all that Boris Karloff business that went on up in the hills, not to mention a dead rich white man you might have to answer for."

The boxer and his trainer exchanged wan smiles. Kaufman continued, "So I sewed you up."

"And I administered certain medicines learned in the East," Morbilus said, bowing slightly.

Smith had to admit he didn't feel too bad, considering. "So what was all that hooey in the cave?" He remembered the reptile face but again dismissed it as a trick of the mind.

"Blackmail essentially," Borsage said, indicating the newspaper folded over on the bed. "The machinery were fancy props. Harcourt had cameras hidden around the cave to photograph the councilman, the judge, and a few others at the supposed summoning of the fire serpent. They'd be willing accomplices in murder."

"Why?" Smith said.

"Harcourt invested in various projects like housing developments and factories. He wanted strings pulled and favors met," Borsage illuminated.

Smith noted, "You sound like you know what you're talking about."

"Anna's something of a philanthropist," Kaufman offered.

She added, "Every once in awhile, I'd run into Harcourt at this or that dinner party. He was quite witty and charismatic when talking about the occult. Those in the cave had fallen under his sway."

Smith folded his arms. "But Zora got away and I bet that means there's more of these occult types she's going to use for what she wants."

There was silent agreement of his assessment.

AFTER HIS SISTER'S FUNERAL, THE MOURNERS gathered for a repast in the dining hall in the Mount Olive Methodist Church on Avalon. Plainclothes detective Percy Kimbrough talked to Smith.

"So this missing Zora Montclair twist was tied up in all this black magic mumbo-jumbo?"

"Seems so." Smith sipped his punch. "Heard this Harcourt had a nest egg of his dead daddy's money socked away and now it's gone too."

Kimbrough regarded him. "Stampton, that movie cowboy facing the chair for kidnapping, he swears he recognized you as shooting Van Harcourt."

"Only the woman he drugged swears it wasn't me," Smith mentioned. It helped too the .45 he used burned in the fire, destroying fingerprints.

Kimbrough added, "We also found that other dame who was trussed up and she says that you, or some colored fella, got stabbed."

Smith hunched a shoulder, "You know them ofays get us spades all mixed up, Detective. If I was there and got knifed, I'd be all sown up and sore wouldn't I?" He unbuttoned the lower part of his shirt to show there weren't wrappings around his abdomen. Whatever it was that Morbilus had given him had healed him fast.

Kimbrough pursed his lips. "Had to check, you know."

"No sweat. See you around, man." Smith buttoned his shirt as he walked off to compliment Reverend Harshaw on his eulogy. As Kimbrough left, passing him as he entered was Achilles's father, Gus

Smith. He wore a black suit with wide pinstripes and two-tone, black and white shoes. He carried a battered suitcase strapped closed and was unshaven. Father and son spotted each other.

"Sorry, I meant to get here sooner." He dropped the bag and put his arms around his son's shoulders. "I can't believe this happened to my baby girl."

The younger man returned the gesture. "It's been handled, Dad."

There were creases in the comers of Gus Smith's eyes but otherwise his handsome face remained unblemished. "Yeah?"

"He's thinking about getting out of the fight game and taking up a different line of work," Kaufman said.

"Hey, Rocco," the elder Smith said, shaking the trainer's hand.

"Could be," Decimator Smith said.

"What are you two going on about?"

"Come on," Decimator Smith said to his father. "Let's get something to eat and I'll tell you about it."

"Okay, son."

Walking to the table laid out with food, they passed Elijah Morbilus who nodded to the two men. "Father and son back together, excellent."

"Who's the junior grade Lugosi?" his father asked in a low voice as they went on.

"My spiritual advisor."

"Huh?"

Decimator Smith laughed for the first time in a week.

THE DARKLIGHT GIZMO MATTER

PASSALONG PETE'S REAL NAME WASN'T PETE. He'd been born 62 years ago in the Iberville Parish in Louisiana and came to Los Angeles with his family when he was 8 years old. He'd held various occupations since then from bootblack, that is shoe shine boy, sold the *California Eagle* and the *Herald Examiner* newspapers on street corners along Central Avenue, and even worked as a runner for the eastside bookie Carl "Straighthand" Newcomb until he died violently, rumored to have been slain on orders from the volatile Mickey Cohen.

But that seemed like a lifetime ago as Passalong Pete found himself scrambling for his life this starless night along a stretch of Main Street, identified as part of Skid Row in this part of downtown LA. As fast as he could, he ran past seamy adult bookstores. One such storefront had the lights on, its picture window grimy as if coated by delusions of wanton sex. Near the Tiger Pit Triple X theater at the end of the block, he considered ducking inside. But he knew this would be no sanctuary, he'd be trapped and easily picked out among the mouth breathers and the other pathetic old men in their stained raincoats. On he went, praying he'd spot a police prowl car, the first time in his life he wanted to see a cop. Sadly, there were none to be seen here among the threadbare traffic at half past one in the morning.

He did though spot a nearby phone booth. At the moment there were only a couple of bums passed out from cheap booze sleeping it off on flattened cardboard for bedding. He ought to know, he was one of them. This flash of self-revelation goaded him to get his feet moving again. He couldn't escape, but he could leave a warning. They were out there in the stillness and he knew they couldn't let him live. Not with what he knew.

Passalong crossed the street on leaden legs and pushed open the jointed door of the Pac Bell phone booth. He was out of breath and out of time. He couldn't run any more, too many years of abusing his body and mind. The light automatically came on and the hunted man stared at it as if it were a lover who'd betrayed him. Using his elbow, his other arm and hand protecting his face, he shattered the translucent glass cover and the bulb underneath, to darken the interior. He was near ecstatic to find a dime in his pocket and stuck that in the phone's slot. He dialed a Hollywood number he knew because he'd had to call it more than once from the drunk tank. He didn't have her home number but this would have to do. Sweat cooled on his warm face

The line connected. There was a whir and click, then a recorded feminine voice with a husky quality said, "This is Sable Reese. At the tone please leave your message and phone number. I will get back to you just as soon as I can."

After the beep the man said, "Sable it's Passalong. I did it this time, screwed up good. Yeah, well, so what's new, huh?" He swallowed dry. "Look, when you hear this, I'll be dead."

The dark colored Lincoln came out of nowhere and zoomed down the block, its big block V8 thrumming like caged panthers under the hood.

Passalong felt more than heard its presence and yelled toward the handset he'd dropped, "Get to the Crossmore Building, that's where he—" But he didn't finish his sentence as he tried to flee along the sidewalk. The big car, outfitted with armored sheeting, clipped the phone booth, blowing it apart in a spray of metal, plastic and projectile ribbons of glass. The stuff cut into Passalong and he stumbled onto the pavement. He just got his face turned around to stare horrified as the Lincoln smashed into and rolled over him. But the time it cleared his body, he was a corpse. Nonetheless its occupants stopped the car and got out to make sure their target was dead.

The two men in black suits, blue shirts, and black ties looked back. Each wore a kind of contour mask with slits for eyes and a mouth. Such precaution at hiding their identities seemed unnecessary. No police officer and no bold citizen showed themselves. One of the men walked over to the mangled broken remains of the man born Curtis Spicer. He bent, felt for the big pulse and was satisfied there was none. He got back in the car and drove off. In the backseat of the Lincoln was what looked like a large rectangular short wave set with all sort of knobs, toggle switches, and two oscilloscope-like screens. Incongruously, there was what looked like a short vacuum cleaner hose and plastic nozzle attached to this thing as well.

The one in the passenger seat removed his mask and said to the driver. "We didn't even get to use the whatzits."

"Don't you worry," his companion said, "you're gonna get to play with it again soon."

The two shared a disquieting laugh as they drove away. Back on the street where Passalong's Pete's cooling body lay sprawled across the real estate, the sleeping bums hadn't stirred once.

"RIGHT NOW THE FEELING AT PARKER Center is he was killed in a simple hit and run." Brad "Brix" Bradford hunched a shoulder and shook out a cigarette from a pack of Pall Malls. He didn't bother offering one to his friend, private eye Sable Reese as she didn't smoke. They were in her office overlooking the Sunset Strip. He lit up and sat back in the chair facing her desk, putting one leg at a right angle to the other.

"The cops run a check with the phone company?"

"Yep. They know he called you but there's no recording other than what you have."

"But I haven't been called or visited by the police and it's been two days."

The ex-cop smiled ruefully. "A wino buying it isn't much of a priority, Nef."

She frowned, shaking her head. "I can't make out his last words on the tape, Brix. But this was no drunken accident. I get that it's not a priority with the LAPD but it is with me. It wasn't just the ramblings of an alkie."

"Yeah," he nodded, "someone should care. Which is why I did a little digging yesterday. Knowing you'd want to bloodhound this matter."

Reese smiled and was about to speak but a scream from outside stopped her. She looked over at the window as Bradford was already there.

"Help me, somebody please help me." Three stories below a pretty woman in a mini skirt and go-go boots ran west along the sidewalk. Her shirt was nearly torn away. Bradford moved toward the door, unlimbering a snub nosed .38 Police Special on a belt holster beneath his sport coat. The two rapidly descended the stairs.

"There she goes," Bradford said, pointing across the street when they exited the building. The woman was running toward the Pioneer stereo store and bolted between a gap of that business and its next door neighbor, a freestanding Chicken Delight stand. The two took off and charged through the space between the buildings. They came out in a compact courtyard. A shot echoed and Bradford dropped to the concrete.

Crouched in the shadow of the gap, Reese quickly assessed where the shot had originated. Just as quickly and efficiently, she brought the Walther PPK she was handling into position and shot three times at an overhead sash window partly open where curtains fluttered. There was no breeze at the moment. A body fell through the pane, tearing the curtains loose from its rail as glass and wood rained to the ground. The dead ambusher hung in what was left of the window frame. His lax hand having let go of the hunting rifle he'd been holding. His rifle clattered to the ground as well.

"Find that broad," Bradford said, waving his friend off. "I'll live." His side was bloody where he clutched it with his hand.

Hearing an engine gun to life, she ran around out of the courtyard, exiting in time to see a Camaro with a lowered front end and fat racing slicks on the rear tear away. She ran into the street, firing her pistol at the retreating vehicle. The Camaro swerved 360 degrees and came full bore back at her. The woman who had been the decoy in the go-go boots was leaning out of the passenger side of the car, firing a Sten machine gun at the PI.

"Oh my God," a chunky woman decried. She was carrying shopping bags in both hands from the May Co. department store. The woman ran for cover, not dropping her purchases. Reese too sought safety.

Rapid fire ripped bullets into the asphalt and the Pontiac Catalina Reese dove behind. Several of the high velocity rounds punched through the steel and upholstery of one side of the vehicle and out the other. Luck was with her today and Reese wasn't hit. As the Camaro roared past, Reese was able to get off several shots through the now glassless car windows. One of her shots drilled though the Camaro's driver's side window like a point of a snow axe piercing ice. It created a spider-webbed hole. The bullet zeroed into the driver's collar bone and he lost control of the car. The Camaro twisted violently sideways and slammed against a delivery truck parked in a driveway. This meant the passenger side was pressed against the truck and the shooter scrambled over the wounded driver to get out of the car.

"Drop it," Reese ordered, her Walther steadied by both hands, the mini skirt machine gunner in her sights.

The other woman snarled a choice curse and attempted to trigger her weapon. But Reese was faster and shot her in the upper body. She went over backwards as if haymakered by Joe Frazier. The private investigator ran up and kicked the Sten gun away.

She demanded, "Who are you working for?"

"Screw you, baby," the wounded woman said. Blood leaked out from under her as she lay on the ground. Sirens approached.

Reese got a gleam in her golden brown eyes. "Too bad I don't have time to be polite." She ground the toe of one of her suede boots in the bleeding wound. "You better give me a name or I stomp you clean through to China, girl."

The gunner writhed and cried out in agony. "Colmaster, damn you, Colmaster." Blood gurgled frothily from the edges of her mouth. Her teeth ground into her lower lip, nearly breaking the skin. The gunner's smeared lipstick was called Passion Purple, Reese noted absently.

"Put the gun down now and get on your knees," a cop hollered from behind the private eye.

She voiced no argument and did as ordered. Four uniformed police officers surrounded her as she let her handgun go and complied, hands up. "Don't shoot, don't shoot," she said. Their questions came at her hot and heavy.

"You a Black Panther? This some kind of Black Power uprising?"

"You're gonna get the chair for this, missy."

"Where're your buddies? Huh? Where's the other Symbionese Liberation shits, huh?"

"Where's your Little Red Book, commie?"

"Back there behind that beige building my partner is wounded. He's ex-Rampart Division plainclothes Brix Bradford."

They couldn't quite process these words this afro sporting, Angela Davis lookin', obviously Ho Chi Minh spoutin' Black

Guerrilla Army charter member was saying as it related to the welfare of a cop, former or not. Collectively they simply wanted to ignore her though two of the uniforms, one was named Malloy she heard, did go check behind the building. Face down on the cracked asphalt, they handcuffed her and left a cop, his foot on her back, to guard her as the others—and more squad cars came on scene—secured the area. Eventually she was hauled over to Hollywood Station on Wilcox. She was put in a holding cell with several hag'ed out streetwalkers, junkies, and a possum-eyed woman who sat on the floor in the corner mumbling that the invisible tax collectors camping out at the waterbed store where she worked.

"Reese," A female uniform had come to the bars and called her name about two hours later.

"That's me."

"Come this way." She unlocked the cell door and waited, her face blank, not even registering boredom

The PI followed her down two hallways lit in sickly yellow light as if the officers were growing strange mushrooms. She was let into an interrogation room and sat at a small square metal table on a wooden chair. The set up was such that her interrogator could sit perpendicular to her and close. Bradford had told her this was the best way to question a suspect. You didn't want the barrier of a table between you and your prisoner. The officer wanted to gauge your body posture, what you did with your hands and so on as he purposely invaded your personal space.

Reese sat, turning in on herself, employing the meditation techniques she'd learned several years ago. The guru at the retreat in Oahu where she'd studied had been an older silver-haired gentleman who called himself Norvell Stockbridge. Reese would also learn this was not always the name he went by, nor had he always been in pursuit of inner peace and cosmic understanding. During the Great Depression he'd been a false fanged grim-visaged vigilante known for his ruthlessness and eagerness to spill gallons of villains' blood in his self-righteous war on evil.

When the beefy detective, tie loose around his unbuttoned collar, stepped inside three minutes later, Reese was calm and centered.

"My name is McAllister." He sat, lightly she noted for a man of his heft. He placed a manila file folder of papers on the desk, his elbow on it.

"How's Brix?' she asked.

He lifted an eyebrow with effort. "Surprisingly for a .30-30 high velocity bullet traveling through him, barely missing his stomach and vitals, and given he's no kid, he's in decent shape. He's over at Queen of Angels."

McAllister didn't say it but Reese knew he'd talked to Bradford who vouched for her. That meant a lot, the okay from one of their own. Too it wasn't as if she was an unknown quantity in law enforcement circles. "Good."

The LAPD detective folded his arms, his thick muscles straining the broadcloth of his dress shirt. "Who were the two that attacked you and Bradford in your office?"

No sense holding back as it would corroborate what he probably heard from Brix. "I don't know but it must be linked to the murder of Passalong Pete last night down on Skid Row. His real name was Curtis Spicer."

"And how did you know this individual? A down and outer it might be said."

"He swept up our building, where my office is I mean, twice a week."

"You arranged that, is that right?'

"I did."

"You used him as an informant?"

"Not as your tone suggests. It was a long time since he was in any kind of racket."

"Yet he provided useful information in that kidnap case you solved last year. Getting that kid back alive and in one piece."

"Yeah." Lafayette Templesmith was a Black millionaire whose only son had been kidnapped by neo-Nazis led by a wanted war criminal. They'd wanted money to finance the research on a chemical that would only react to specific concentrations of melanin.

McAllister, who'd been leaning back, sat forward some. "Why'd he call you?" His breath smelled of mouthwash.

"Brix and I were trying to find out."

The plainclothesman sat back again. He picked up the file folder and opening it, shuffled several top sheets aside and studied an entry. Reese didn't think he was doing this for effect as he genuinely seemed to be reading and considering something. He closed the folder, holding onto it in one of his large hands. "Just a second, Miss Reese." The cop left the room.

Several minutes later he returned. He opened the door but stayed in the doorframe, one hand on the knob, leaning into the room slightly. The file wasn't with him. "You can go."

Reese frowned. She'd shot a white man and woman on a street full of witnesses and now she could go?

"What the hell's going on, McAllister?"

"Bye bye, now." He walked away, the door remaining open.

Soon, in front of the desk sergeant, she collected her belongings, though her Walther was kept pending a clearance. As she made to leave, Reese noticed two uniformed cops booking a harried-looking older white woman in a pill box hat askew on her frazzled hair.

"Officer, please, I assure you, I'm not drunk or crazy."

One of them said, "Then how do you explain plowing into those people on the sidewalk, lady? Lucky no one was killed."

"I . . . I tell you, I suddenly couldn't see to handle my car. It's so horrible."

"But you can suddenly see fine now?" The other one cracked sarcastically.

"Yes, I told you. I was blind and now I can see again just fine."

"Then you'll be able to dial your lawyer. You're gonna need one." And with that they led her away.

The private eye walked back to her office. At one point she passed a wood fence. Super Bowl VII posters, the game had been played in town this past January, were mostly stripped away, replaced by placards for Tom Bradley, a Black man running for mayor. From the parking lot behind her building, she collected her burgundy colored '59 Stingray and drove to Queen of Angels hospital in Echo Park.

"I've always wanted a beautiful woman to bring me flowers. Though not laid up like that." Brix Bradford was propped up in bed in his semi-private room. He was hooked to an IV and his torso was bandaged.

Reese set the spring flowers on the rollaway table next to the bed. She leaned over and gave the older white man a peck on the cheek. A gray-faced wrinkled woman glared at them from the other bed.

"My daughter," Bradford beamed at her.

"Hmpphhh," the woman huffed. Grabbing the plastic privacy curtain, she pulled it around her bed.

"How you feeling, Brix?"

"Take more than a belly crawlin' bushwacker to put me down." He shook a finger at her. "Hey, how come you're out so soon? I talked you up good to McAllister but I figured they'd keep you overnight at least. You've had a busy morning, dear."

"Don't I know it." She looked around the room, wondering if the cops had bugged it. Bradford might have been out of the room or knocked out after surgery if they'd done so.

"You talk to your pal Jim?"

"Yeah, he's coming by. He had a client this morning so didn't get my message until he was back in the office." Jim Axelrod co-owned with Bradford a pool and Jacuzzi business. He and Bradford were also lovers. Not too many aside from Reese knew that. That the brawny, six-one-and-a-half, Korean War vet and ex-LAPD detective liked to swing for the other team, as he'd put it.

"Whoever sent those two after us had access to the phone company records," she said.

"Somebody with juice," Bradford added.

She made more chit-chat in case there was a listening device while finding a pen and a pad of paper with the hospital's logo on it. "Passalong had a sister, somewhere over in Compton I think. Guess I'll try and find her to see if she knows anything."

She wrote down her question: "You ever hear of a Colmaster?'

He took the pad and paper. "Can't say I do, Nef." He wrote down a different response and handed it over on the piece of paper.

The private eye nodded her head as she read the note. "Okay, check in with you later, Brix. Call me if you need anything." Rising, she patted his leg under the thin blanket.

"You step lightly, now, okay?"

"You know me."

He made a face. "That's what I'm sayin'."

Leaving the hospital in her Stingray, Reese picked up the handset of her radio-telephone and asked the mobile operator to make a call for her. She reached her party on the third ring. "Hi, Larry, it's Nefra. You around for the next hour or so? I need to bend your ear with a few question about a certain someone."

"Who's that, foxy lady?"

"Elton Colmaster."

A low whistle. "Heavy dude, Nef, heavy like getting Napalmed trapped in a coffin if you dig what I'm laying down."

"That's why I need to see you."

"Come on then. I'll brew us a cup."

Popping a Tower of Power tape into her newly installed aftermarket cassette deck, Reese took the 101 then 10 Freeway west out to the Venice area of Los Angeles. This was a Bohemian beach community of ramshackle apartment buildings, Craftsman single family bungalows, and an aura that had transitioned from beatnik to hippie to whatever it was now. Like the Italian city it was named for, this Venice had its own languid set of canals—there were even gondola rides back when but not now. Though there were still plenty of ducks.

She parked her car at a series of concrete archways in a diagonally designated slot in front of the Floating Eye coffee house Lawrence Radington owned and entered the establishment. Inside were a few patrons including a short-haired woman humming softly as she drank coffee while reading a Jacqueline Susann paperback. Bernard "Goldie" Hawes, a local jazz musician was in here too. He was noodling the keys on the old Steinway in the corner.

"Soul Sister Number One," Hawes called out to Reese.

"Hey now," she said warmly to him. The swishing of beads had her head turning to the newcomer who entered from the back.

"What it is, what it could be." The bespectacled Radington greeted her with a warm smile and open arms. He was in his 50s, lithe and sinewy with a tangle of white hair. He perpetually wore vintage Hawaiian shirts and smelled of Burma Shave.

They hugged. "Come to get on the good foot," she said.

"Step right on this way, Nef. Don't know if I'll blow your mind, but as the sages say, knowing is half the battle."

"Amen." She followed him toward the rear of the establishment, stepping through the beaded curtain. In his office there was an overflowing small bookcase and a surprisingly uncluttered desk. There was enough room for a Japanese tea set and they sat cross-legged at the squat table. He poured them steaming green tea into ceremonial cups from a brass teapot.

They tipped their cups to each other and sipped. Radington then said, "This cat Elton Colmaster is from unsavory money, Nef. All capitalism is dirty but his old man made money profiteering in

World War I. Then made even more on the black market dealing in much needed medicines in a post-war ravaged Europe. The son not only inherited all those rapacious qualities sitting on his daddy's knee, but he's refined them. Why you lurking around this old reprobate for?"

She told him of the morning's activities. "Brix's note said to ask you about him."

Radington sat back, resting on his hands flat on the floor. "That's 'cause I worked on a project that came to his attention when I was at Rocketgyn."

"I'm listening." Radington had once been an electrical engineer before tuning in and dropping out.

He smoothed the hair flat on the back of his head and stared for a moment into his not-so-distant past. "This project sought to create, well for lack of a better term, a way to cause blindness."

"What?" She recalled the woman in the pill box hat at Hollywood Station.

Radington made a funny face. "Yeah, but understand this was a time when the CIA was pumping LSD onto subway platforms of unsuspecting civilians. The idea was it could be used as a kind of fear inducer. Our optic nerves are connected to the brain and the brain operates on certain electrical impulses our bodies produce."

"This gadget could disrupt certain electrical impulses if you could isolate them," Reese conjectured.

"There you go. Imagine if, and this was designed to be a temporary effect, but what if enemy soldiers on the battlefield were suddenly not able to see. Not caused by a smoke screen or white hot light, but all of a sudden it's just black." He made a gesture with his hands like a stage magician does when they disappear a rabbit or pocket watch.

"You can't shoot, you stumble around completely disoriented, bumping into your fellow soldiers."

Reese added, "Easy pickin's to be killed or captured. Maybe even help in interrogation if with another pass of your devilish ray, they could see again."

"Right you are."

"Where does Colmaster come in?"

Radington sipped his tea slowly, then held the cup in both hands before setting it down. "It's not headline news that there's always been a . . . cordial relationship between the military and business interests."

"Rocketgyn is a private company but gets lots of contracts for the Army and what have you." She snapped a finger and shook it at him. "Colmaster is an investor in the outfit."

He nodded his assent. "The Darklight Project was the official name for this particular R and D."

The private eye absorbed this. "Was the project successful?"

He shook his head. "No, we gave some test subjects headaches and spots before their eyes but no blindness." He smiled wanly. "Five million in research and testing gone up in smoke."

"Our tax dollars at work." She looked off then back at her friend. "But Colmaster could have continued the research, paying for off-the-books work by scientists for hire?"

"Sure. Maybe he figures to sell his results back to the government or highest bidder. Or maybe use it for himself. Like he could blind the pilot of a private jet used by one of his business rivals."

"That's worth killing for," she stated solemnly.

"Nef, I don't need to tell you that Colmaster is a powerful and connected individual. He's got his hooks into the cops and having them stonewall this case."

"I need to see this through."

"Namaste."

"Namaste." She rose, trying not to let the enormity of the situation weigh her down. Back outside, she fired her Stingray to life. Given it was a sunny day, she decided to take the streets back to her office.

Now heading east on Venice Boulevard on this sunny day, she let her mind leap ahead, figuring out her next steps. She came to a red light and shifting out of gear, applied the brakes. The pedal felt slightly spongy and she realized she'd better get the car checked soon. Driving several more blocks, there seemed to be no further worry. But just as she was coming to a major intersection, the brakes failed completely. Reese clicked on her cool and downshifting, made the clutch groan. She maneuvered around a slowing station wagon and was heading right into the intersection, against the red light. She tried the parking brake and got no resistance. That cable had been cut. Drivers honked at her. Looking to her right, she saw a tanker fuel truck barreling at her even though the driver was standing on his brakes, creating a cloud of white smoke and ear-splitting screeching. This happened in milliseconds, signaling her sure demise.

Reese shifted out of gear. At the same time, she turned off the ignition and cut the wheel sharply. Her Stingray fishtailed violently and slid sideways along the sidewalk as she hoped it would. Pedestrians had scattered. The car slammed into a fire hydrant, ripping it free of its bolts. The hydrant's trajectory was like that of a runaway rocket. It arced upward then came down hard, right onto the hood of a Ford Falcon, bashing it in. The Stingray's momentum has been halted upon impact. Water geysered with force from the now exposed pipe and the intersection was flooded by the time the police and fire trucks arrived. Sable Reese had already been on her car phone to her attorney.

Finally released on a sizable bond and facing several lawsuits from disgruntled drivers, particularly the owner of the ruined Falcon, the private eye called a friend over at the *Herald Examiner* newspaper. He owed her more than one favor and he planted a false story, complete with an indistinct black and white photo from the archives of a woman covered up on an ambulance's gurney. The piece that ran in the late edition stated Reese had been injured in the crash and was recovering at an undisclosed location. This lie had been sanctioned by the reporter's editor on the promise from Reese that she'd have a juicy exclusive for the paper—or so she hoped.

ACCESS TO THE CROSSMORE BUILDING ON Olympic Boulevard in west Los Angeles during business hours was no big deal as it housed various offices including two optometrists and a talent agency specializing in juggling singers. Colmaster owned the building and had a penthouse on top. A disguised Sable Reese entered the lobby the following day. She was dressed in modest office clerk type clothing and wore a straight-hair wig over her large afro she'd tamped down under a tight cap. She also had on cat-eye glasses and flat heels.

There was a security desk with a bored looking older gentleman in a rent-a-cop uniform planted behind it. But far as she could tell, at least not during daytime, no one was required to sign in. She went about unmolested. Reese also reconnoitered the exterior, noting a metal door out back where the dumpsters were. Out front she spotted a Burger Land drive-thru across the wide expanse of Olympic from the office building. She walked over there then went back to see Radington.

Later, Reese returned that night. She'd discarded the disguise. The private eye was now dressed in a black form-fitting zippered jumpsuit and boots with composition soles. A stylish equipment bag was slung across her torso. She waited in the near gloom at the rear of the building. Sure enough, eventually one of the janitors came outside for a smoke break after dumping some trash. She slipped past him and through the door left slightly ajar. Crossing the lobby, a different security guard was in his cubby watching a portable TV. She crept unnoticed past him too and entered the stairwell. She went up steadily to the top, eighteen stories above. She was barely breathing hard when she got to the locked door leading to the penthouse level.

Looking up, she saw the wiring leading to an alarm on the door. From her equipment bag she extracted a device made by Radington about the size of a transistor radio. It had a heavy wire with an alligator clip and wire on the other end. This she attached to the alarm wiring, enabling her to bypass the alarm. Essentially fooling the circuitry that it was unbroken. She then picked the lock, a skill Bradford, the former robbery-homicide detective, taught her.

The exit didn't let out on a hallway but an open expanse. The penthouse was its own structure taking up a good portion of the flat rooftop area. It was glass-walled on one side but heavy curtains prevented a look inside. Stationed on a chair in front of a set of double doors into the penthouse, was a man in slacks and dress shirt with a gun in a shoulder holster. She wondered if he was the only guard. His legs were stretched out in front of him and he slumped, his snap-brim hat low on his forehead. From the angle she was at she came up behind him quickly and silently. Hand over his mouth, a specifically placed karate chop with the other hand sent him to slumber land. Behind her the door was unlocked and she stepped inside.

Reese found herself in a living room replete with a sunken conversation pit. A well-endowed woman wearing some sort of cave girl outfit like you'd see on a *Flintstones* cartoon wiggled and gyrated her body in the pit area. A Les Baxter lounge music LP played on a stereo. A man in an expensive suit, sans tie, sat on the couch. He was in his 50s, thickset with workman's hands, and smoking a stubby black cigar. He clapped and guffawed, animated by the woman's grindhouse performance.

"Oh, baby, you're the greatest there ever was," he said excitedly. "Dimitri and his buddies are gonna dig you."

The cave dancer, gyrating her head about, noticed the intruder. The man turned his large square head, following her gaze.

"You," Elton Colmaster said. He gaped, barely catching the cigar as it fell from his hanger of a mouth. "What does it take to stop you!?"

"I guess this chick ain't here to party," the cave dancer concluded. She seemed sad about that.

"Marty, Francois, get your asses in here," Colmaster yelled. He was off the couch quick for a man of his size.

Rushing through a doorway at the side of this area came two of his henchmen. One of them had a partially-eaten sandwich in his hand. He threw this aside and reached for the .45 in his shoulder rig. The other one had a revolver already barking bullets in his hand.

The private eye had dived behind the stacked stereo system that included a receiver, tuner, dual cassette tape deck, and turntable. Rounds tore into the works, sending shards of metal, plastic, and glass everywhere. On her belly, Reese shot from underneath the table the stereo was on, blasting open the guts of the gunman. Cave girl screamed in horror as pieces of entrails and blood splattered her. She cursed and ran toward the side doorway. Her action momentarily put her between the other hood and Reese who was in motion as well.

"Stupid broad, get the hell out of my way," the one with the .45 bellowed. He clotheslined her and she went down hard on the carpet on her backside. Simultaneously he cranked off shots from his cannon and the reverberation boomed in the enclosed space.

But Sable Reese had gotten to relative safety behind one of the couches in the conversation pit. Not that the furniture stopped the bullets, it was just he wasn't sure where she was as the couch was over six-feet long. Then the lights went out. No, not the lights, she understood. She was blind, the Darklight gizmo at work, she concluded. That must have been what Colmaster had run to operate.

"What the hell?" she heard the hood proclaim.

"That's okay, Marty," Colmaster said. "I've got my mask on, I can see. I'll come to you and get your gun and deal harshly with this nosy bitch."

Reese quieted the panic bubbling in her. Calling again on what sensei Stockbridge had taught her, she visualized the layout of the room in her mind. She channeled energy into the four senses left to her. The lighting had been subdued to better set the mood for the woman's sexy dance. There were two table lamps on and she pinpointed them in her mental schematic. She looked to the left, sightless but not defeated. She detected Colmaster's shuffles as he trod mouse-like over the thick carpet. She shot with her replacement Beretta and he laughed scornfully.

"Dumb dame," he jibbed.

She shot again and was rewarded with the tinkling of glass and plaster breaking as the struck lamp fell over.

"How the fuck . . . " Colmaster growled, now running to where his henchman was before she could shoot out the other light and put him in darkness too.

She blasted two more shots, locking in on his heavy breathing. He was not a man who had salads for lunch. Years of thick steaks and martinis and little exercise had its effects on his constitution and corresponding girth. She brought him down like a charging bear. His wheezing, dying body crashed hard onto an end table, splintering it apart as he exhaled a death rattle.

"Boss, boss?" the one called Marty hollered as he stumbled about, knocking into all manner of furniture. "When the whatzit's blindness wears off, you're gonna get yours, girly." He wanted to sound defiant, but it came out as hollow bravado.

It wasn't hard for Reese to locate him and ducking his punch, put the muzzle of her weapon to his chest, silencing him for good when she pressed the trigger.

"Ughhh," the hood sighed as he expired.

He sagged against her and she eased him to the floor. She then sat down cross-legged as if meditating and waited. In less than an hour her vision returned. She was alone with the two dead men. Colmaster's protective mask of mouth and eye slits was comically askew on his face set in surprise. The one she'd knocked out she'd bound with his climbing line. Reese studied the Darklight machine, a low rectangular metal box that used what looked like a short vacuum cleaner hose to aim its invisible beam at the intended target, she surmised.

She called her lawyer first who in turn called a contact in the Defense Department, getting him out of bed back in D.C. What followed was a lot of back and forth, Reese being threatened with legal action from Colmaster's board of directors. Eventually it was uncovered that Colmaster had made overtures to certain foreign powers to sell his prototype—foreign powers considered the Cold War enemies of America—all that went away. She wasn't officially thanked nor was she sued.

"I guess Passalong must have seen something about what Colmaster was up to one night cleaning up at Burger Land." She'd found out he worked there a couple days a week in addition to cleaning her building. Reese discussed her recent case with a recovered Brix Bradford. "He'd gotten that second job and was looking forward to getting a decent place to live the burger joint owner told me." She shook her head sympathetically.

"That louse Colmaster had his henchmen out on the streets using the device randomly to test the results," Bradford added. "Though the scientist who worked on the device, we haven't identified who that was yet."

"Whoever it is, I'm betting he's going to make himself known." Reese paused, then, "Real soon I'm thinking."

"Yep," Bradford agreed.

NO ROOM! NO ROOM!

MY GOD. WHEN WAS THE LAST time she was on a bus, hanging by the strap and not overpowered by someone else's body order or worse, someone trying to mask their funk with way too much perfume or cologne? Six months ago? Could that be? Had it only been six months since becoming the way things were now? How much longer? Sailors on a carrier or submarine got shore leave. There was no leave from this—at least none was forthcoming. Trials to develop a vaccine had yielded little and estimates for the creation of such were in the years not months.

Katie Claremont had to pause to remember a time when it was safe to bathe and it was fine, even preferred, to have one's own space, as they used to say. Huh, when was that phrase last uttered? Probably every damn hour of every damn day, she figured as she scanned the faces of the other miserable passengers.

The disembodied voice of the self-driving vehicle announced her stop. Claremont reached past an older woman to pull the signal cord. The woman hacked into her face and smiled sheepishly at the younger woman as several more phlegmy coughs escaped her infected torso.

"Sorry," she said.

"No worries. At least I got it for free."

There were many who subscribed to the theory the more you exposed your body to germs, the better off you were in preventing the onslaught of the virus nicknamed Crowdus. Thus the laxness in washing. There were even cough parties where guests drank or got high and, laughing uproariously, coughed on each other. Needless to say, mud wrestling had come back big, for both men and woman and mixed matches as well. Televised events of eight or more tag teaming in the muck had gone through the roof ratings-wise.

Unlike any other time in the history of humankind and pandemics, this particular virus demanded a kind of ongoing herd immunity as opposed to social distancing. As far as the scientists could discern, it was part of delaying the body's natural adaptive immune response that was a factor in preventing the disease. At first the translation of that for people meant they could go about their daily lives, eat in a restaurant, go to the movies or a concert, and what have you. You'd be around people. But the virus mutated and as deaths of those in rural areas or families of less than six in an apartment or house mounted, the idea took hold that the more you were around others, the better your chances of not contracting the invisible killer. Not that everyone died from getting the disease. But the effects of having Crowdus were so excruciating, often leaving the patient with various chronic illnesses, folks of course wanted to avoid the risk as much as possible.

Claremont stopped at her neighborhood market to buy a few items. This time of the afternoon, the line was only halfway down the block. As was the new normal, people tended to push together a bit more than what would have been acceptable in the past. You might peel away because you wanted semi-privacy while talking on your phone, but the fear was such that arguments and fist fights sometimes broke out if you did this.

"You too good for the rest of us?" would go a typical refrain. "Get your ass back here."

There were too many documented cases when a loner was away from others for more than 20 minutes and when they came back, they had become asymptomatic carriers. The constant pressure was to not be 6 feet away from other warm bodies. There were some who took to living in isolation gear, essentially modified hazmat suits, but you had to develop a certain mindset to essentially be enclosed in cumbersome attire pretty much 24/7. As to being intimate, well the word quickie never meant so much as it did now. Orgy clubs had taken on a weird respectability as never before. The open stall, with only a cubicle-type wall between the toilets, had become quite the feature. Sleeping arrangements had taken on similar design, with a row of futons separated by a wall a typical layout in mandatory communal living.

The need of keeping others around you constantly had an effect on personal conveyances. Public transportation was way up. For those in their own vehicles, ride-sharing took place in autonomous vans. Deliveries were mostly by drone and long-haul trucks had for some time been driverless. Warehouses where orders were filled were always bustling and burnout was common. But there were plenty willing to replace the ones who quit as fulfillment jobs paid well given the necessity of the work. The internet billionaires weren't willingly paying these salaries. But the fact that workers were always huddled together led to so many instances of sabotage, a living wage and humane conditions were the obvious solutions to labor strife. Claremont worked in one such facility.

"Hey, Bill," she said to a lanky man with sad eyes who stepped out the door of her apartment building.

"Right on time," he said as he gave her a half-wave and walked off down the street, surrounded by strangers.

Bill was one of her roommates and timing was everything. If one of them had to leave for work, then one of the other seven better be stepping back in. Various staggered and stacked work schedules had to be rigorously maintained. If an accident happened or a bus broke down, then you had to call to tell all concerned.

Entering her apartment, Claremont involuntarily did a quick head count, noting only four of her roommates were in their shared living space. Two of them were watching or listening on their phones, earbuds in, another watching TV with his headphones on, and the fourth reading in the corner. None were more than 4 feet apart.

"Is Meredith here?" she asked, putting away the groceries. Then before anyone could answer, she heard the comforting flush coming from the bathroom. As this was an old building, the john had been designed with a shower, sink, and toilet. On the wall was a countdown device and each time an occupant was in there, the timer had an electronic voice warning the user of 5 minutes left . . . 3 minutes and so on.

One time one of them had come back drunk from a co-worker's going away party and passed out on the toilet. Fortunately the timer operated manually or by sensor. Claremont had rushed in there as the robot voice boomed "Alert, alert, alert," and shook her roommate awake and dragged the woozy woman to bed to sleep it off.

Meredith came into the room. "Hi, Katie." She plopped down on her usual spot and opened her laptop.

"Hey," she said, trying to sound amiable.

Standing there, the familiar ambiance of being around people who were doing their best to tune out the need to be as close to others as was necessary, made the skin on the back of her neck itch. What was it about the last few days that had gotten to her? Why was it now she so longed to be on top of a snowy mountain staring at clouds? Hyper-cabin fever they called it. Lately every damn burp, yawn, and fart had stretched her nerves to the snapping point. Barefoot Brad picking his Cro-Magnon toes, Lindsey's finger twirling her ponytail over and over and over again, and Karen and her gum chewing to relieve stress. Was it any wonder the murder rate had skyrocketed?

She went into the bathroom, unable to catch her breath. Shortness of breath was not one of the symptoms of this virus.

She started at her reflection in the mirror and for a moment wondered who the hell that haggard-looking woman was staring back at her. She wasn't yet 30 but she looked like her Aunt Jean who was 25 years older than she was.

"Shit," she muttered. Claremont resisted the urge to grab a knife form the kitchen and chop off a couple of Brad's prehistoric toes. She did though gather her clean clothes and take a shower, letting the alarm go of as she unhurriedly toweled off. She yelled out to assure her roommates she was stepping out. She got dressed in the hallway, out of sight but in proximity to the others. Thereafter she had little choice but to join the others though beneath her calm facade, she was screaming to be alone.

That evening she slept in her clothes. Her cubicle was the last toward the rear and no one noticed. If they had, they would have known what she was going to do. She was about to "go country," as it was called.

Early in the dark of morning, Claremont slipped on her moccasins and eased out the back door. She'd greased the hinges a week ago in preparation for this time. Bill was back from work so there were six left in the room. Even at this time of the day there were plenty of people out on the streets. No one paid any attention to her as she walked until the pedestrians began to thin. She wound her way into the industrial area where the robot trucks moved about. There were clusters of humans here but they were in control towers overlooking this vast expanse of asphalt as the 18-wheelers, bobtails, pilotless forklifts, and logistics drones hummed. A lone figure she knew would show up on their sensors but she wasn't going to be deterred. On she went. High intensity lights snapped on, illuminating her form as two drones buzzed her.

"Miz, please enter the door to your left and come into the control tower." The voice boomed from one of the drones. "You will be immediately tested and monitored to make sure you are not infected. Please this is for your safety and ours."

She continued.

"Madam, I implore you to gather with your fellow citizens. Or we will be forced to ask for police assistance."

Her destination was the old 7th Street bridge, a holdover from not only a bygone era, but a bygone century, the 20th. Another warning was issued. She could hear the approach of a police van at her back. She started running. Claremont could see in the near distant mist the snowy peak. She quickened as the van's brakes screeched to a halt behind her and officers alighted from the vehicle. Orders were barked as footfalls got closer. Goddamn LAPD was always in shape.

From over her shoulder a voice said, "Okay, lady, you had your chance."

Electric current shot through her when they blitzed her with a non-lethal compliance weapon. Stars burst behind her eyes and her legs refused to obey. Claremont sank to the ground and was swarmed by bodies in dual protective gear—against germs and bullets. Offering little resistance, she felt the sting of a hypodermic needle piercing her arm. The last thing she saw was that snowy mountaintop. It brought a smile to her face.

THE HYPODERMIC WAS WITHDRAWN, MOMENTARILY HELD upright at the end of the care android's arm. It was then placed back upon a tray that slid back into the control booth where the medical techs looked on. Katie Claremont's withered body lay on the hospital bed in the comforting quarantine room. The drug in her veins did its work and she soon succumbed, fading away like smoke. The plague had ravaged the world, killing tens of millions even though all the precautions had been taken. The result was economic upheaval that resulted in full employment for those left and a green terrain resplendent with animal life and pollinating bees. Katie Claremont's nude body, the brain harvested and a permanent smile on her wrinkled features, was gently carried by the asexual android and placed in a sort of open wicker casket.

These organic coffins were part of a series of conveyor belts at different levels in a vast room where other women and men, also dead and also unclothed, were carried away. The dead were transported to a large brass double door that swung outward allowing them into a processing plant tended by robots overseen by humans. This was where they were ground up in enormous geared teeth. The human mulch would eventually be added to a nitrogen rich mixture and used to fertilize this verdant world, dispensed in industrial-sized bags under the brand called Nature's Gold. Projections were the planet would be down three and a half to four billion before this particular virus was done with destroying the flesh. The remaining population would be heirs to an Earth of incredible colors and smells and a lushness not envisioned since the Garden of Eden.

IN THE OVERCROWDED HOLDING CELL, KATIE Claremont awoke, the other narrative already eluding her. A palpable funk assailed her as the women jammed in there tried to assume a comfortable position as there was no room to even sit on the floor. Some managed to sleep standing up. She wished she could do that. At various intervals a voice would announce over the PA system last names first. Those persons would wade through the sea of the arrested and be taken out by the guards as the gate swung open. Claremont was eventually summoned and she went out, escorted along with several others toward the large brass double doors.

SHADEROC THE SOUL SHAKER

OH FOR THE DAYS WHEN HE could snort him a line of flake while some groupie was down on her knees, her head buried between his spread leather-clad legs pleasuring him like he was a visiting pharaoh. Goddamn, that time in his room backstage at the Forum . . . the two big titty blondes. Sheeet, the top of his head damn near blew off that night as they sexed him up, down, and sideways. Churchill "Church" Gibson shook his head, regretfully cycling away from the glorious past into the stone-cold reality of now. He glared at the screen of his laptop as if it were an adversary. He put aside his coffee and tapped the keyboard and the music app replayed his most troubling track through external speakers. The green audio readout traveling from left to right as the music filled his compact home studio space.

He tapped a key again mid-way through to bring silence. The track was all right, but it wasn't killer. It merely filled space. None of the tracks so far were killer. No, that wasn't quite right, two of them he was happy with . . . not in love with, but their shine only highlighted how lackluster the others were.

"Motherfuck," he muttered. There came a momentary gurgle in the middle of his chest, and he closed his eyes, centering his chi, breathing in and out slowly, summoning his mindfulness. He took hold of his crutch, sliding his arm through the bracket, latching onto the T-handle and rose from his seat with a grunt. He walked over to his wet bar that no longer was stocked with

Johnnie Walker Black, Majesté XO cognac, and blunts thick as a big mama's clit and tré potent as if laced with jet fuel. Now it was an assortment of bottled green and red concoctions of blended fruits and vegetables, vitamins, and his various pills for blood pressure and what have you. He sighed and checking his TAG Heuer Carrera watch, a gift from Quincy Jones, took his meds. He swigged it down with some kind of kale and berry smoothie that while he would never actually like the taste, at least his tolerance for it had grown.

"Those were the days, weren't they, Church?"

Licking green foam from over his top lip, Gibson turned and gaped. There in his studio stood Shirley King. She'd been one of his backup singers once upon a time, one of the few who managed to make it across that 20-foot expanse to the spotlight. He'd produced her first hit album. Then it got messy when they got involved. But, he frowned, hadn't she died in that car crash in Paris? Higher than a 707 in '02?

"Shirley," he muttered.

She always had a body to make a sissy hard and she was rockin' it in a lavender dress with a slit up her shapely thigh. She sat before his laptop, swiveling toward him on the chair's ball bearings.

"I must be trippin'" he said. After the stroke four years ago, these days he barely had imbibed any booze or what they called controlled substances. Okay, sure there was a blast of Macallan 25 he'd had last Christmas, alone, but it was only one drink and that was months ago.

"Maybe I'm your subconscious talking to you, baby," she said. King crossed those magnificent legs. "Maybe the Mother Ship beamed you up and deposited you in the Cosmic Slop you could be swimming in, or could be I'm the constipation you got sneaking that bacon cheeseburger yesterday."

He grinned. "I'm weak."

"That was your excuse when I caught you wiggling your finger in Jeanie on the tour bus."

"Yeah," he agreed.

She smiled sweetly, crooking a finger at him. "Come here."

He did, feeling more spryness in his steps than in some time. She turned back to his laptop and after a few taps, brought up on the clips from Shaderoc the Soul Shaker. This was a new version of the Stagolee-inspired, "super bad" brother persona created by a comedian friend of Gibson's named Renaldo Redd. Redd had parlayed the character into a couple of low budget actioners in the '80s—*Shaderoc vs. Dr. Funkenstein* and *Shaderoc: Seekers of the Pimp Cane*. Both had done well at the box office. Enough so that Redd had been preparing a third outing, the bigger budget *Shaolin Shaderoc*. But he died of a heart attack as he panted while peeling off the panties of a percussionist named Sheila Ramirez.

Even before Redd's body was interned at Inglewood Cemetery, complete with six Amazon honeys in gold hotpants and matching top hats as honorary dancing pallbearers, Gibson had made his bid for the character. He'd recalled coming up with the Shaderoc moniker as he and Redd drove up the coast one day, passing a bottle of Jack back and forth while Redd told him about his idea. But through various legal and who knew what all else twists and turns, Ramirez eventually secured the rights to the character.

"Wasn't there a Shaderoc graphic novel out in the early oughts?" the King apparition said. They both watched the actor playing Shaderoc as *Crouching Tiger, Hidden Dragon*-like, he sailed through the air delivering a devastating kung fu kick to three bad guy ninjas, scattering them like bowling pins.

"There was. There was also a talk of a limited series on cable but that didn't happen. Until,"

"Until Thomlinson."

She meant the cult director/writer Nic Thomlinson known for giving grindhouse the A-picture treatment. He worked out the rights with Ramirez the flick was scheduled to drop on Netflix.

Going full bore on the retro vibe, brought Gibson out of semi-retirement to do the soundtrack.

"But it's not flowing like it used to, huh, Church? Like the notes were singing their song in your head."

"I felt it when I worked out the title song and recorded with Marie and Sylvia," he answered, the two old friends of both of them.

"Meaning they knew where to fill in where you left holes."

"True," he admitted. For the big love scene between Shaderoc and Xtal, the Queen of the Aztecs, he'd scrapped the dopey lyrics he'd written and went with an instrumental version which had come out pretty good, he'd concluded. But since then, he was running on fumes and Thomlinson and the suits would know it.

"I've already pushed back the deadline," he said. Knowing such increased expectations or dampened them in some quarters.

Elbows on the desk, King leaned forward, her fingers with their gold twinkling nails pressed before her face as she looped the scene again. This time with the lackluster track Gibson had been listening to underneath. "Speaking of fingers, stud, yours still work, right?"

"About the only damn thing that does."

"Figures. Get your guitar."

He shrugged, and turning, reached for his Fender Telecaster. He pulled a stool close and turned on the amp as King swung the mics attached to adjustable arms into position. She smelled good, Gibson noted as he plucked the strings while he tuned it. How could a ghost have a scent? But then again, how the hell did a ghost have solid form?

If a gun was pressed to Gibson's head, later he couldn't recount how it all went down. How Shirley King dusted off the Yamaha keyboard in the closet and played the thing like when he first heard her in that night spot on Florence in the 'hood. He worked his fingers and thumbs on the strings like he too was in his 20s again, standing before thousands in the Sports Arena, his licks moving through them like current. He was sweating and rasping the songs that used to make the honeys swoon and the men bop their heads. The music like a cocoon around him as he and his band, Rhythm Pulse, did their thing and there was no one who could touch them.

Head back, the Telecaster a blood-pumping part of his body, was a thing alive that didn't make music, but rather the music channeled through it from the Source. He was plugged in and the crowd was with him. Looking across the sea of faces he saw his ex-manager Sandy Igar. Smiling, into it. What the hell . . . ?

Head back in the gloom, Gibson's eyes came open. "About time, ya goddamn lazy bastard."

Igar was standing over him in Haggar flared slacks, that porno actor mustache, and those two-tone aviator shades—a look he sported well past its prime.

"Dreaming about pussy your sorry self ain't never gonna get you can do any time. Right now, we got to lay down some sound, son."

With effort, given his left leg was the one with the strength, he sat up on the couch in his studio. "I'm in purgatory, is that it? I have to earn my way out by completing this soundtrack?" The real Igar was still alive but had been ensconced, some said entombed, in his Bel Air mansion for years. He was said to be suffering from a short list of long-suffering ailments.

The fit Igar before him had his hands on his hips like an NFL coach judging his new prospect, a sour look on his face. "Look, crip, you gonna sit there and wallow in self-pity or you going to earn?"

"Carrot and stick, I see," Gibson muttered, slipping on his crutch. He must have sued Igar at least three times during his music career. "Or better," he huffed, getting to his feet. "that stick up your ass."

"My job is not to stroke your fragile ego," Igar began. "That's what groupies and your hangers-on are for."

"My job is to get the best out of you, and that takes sweat and blood," Gibson finished. He knew all the Igarisms. The two settled in, trading insults and verbal jabs back and forth, Gibson re-worked two other tracks. As had happened to him in the past, he was annoyed and envious that Igar knew his shit all too well. He couldn't sight-read like Gibson and at best could keep time banging a cowbell, but the sumabitch knew how to pace, where to empha-size this riff over that one, what to bring up and what to bring down. More in the role of engineer than musician, Gibson worked the mixing board cutting and remixing tracks at Igar's direction.

"I'm going to grow tulips out of the shit you spread," Igar said.

"I'm'a put my two lips on ya mama tonight," Gibson replied, but followed the other man's cue.

Finally, as dawn approached, they took stock. "Okay, that's not too bad," the Igar simulacrum allowed, sitting on the stool, his ear turned toward the playback monitor speakers.

A spent Gibson was back sitting on the couch. "It's great. The best I've done in I don't know how long." His said in a whispery tone as if his vocal cords were made of some gossamer material.

Igar turned his head toward him. It was a stuttering, mechan-ical motion, as if there were gears in his neck and they slipped slightly with the effort. He removed his glasses revealing all-white eyes with red glowing outlines. This did not rattle Gibson.

"About my end," the Igar thing said.

"I got your end, bitch." Gibson grabbed his crotch, managing a chuckle.

Igar returned the insult but Gibson's attention was on a framed original artwork print on a near wall. It was the cover for his *Dominoes with Selassie* album. The more he stared the more he was drawn into the scene, that of a man and woman warrior, back-to-back, with futuristic-looking weapons in their hands, battling half-monster reptile and half-machine creatures. He blinked and it was if he were floating away.

"About time you go here, brother man."

Gibson blinked again. Before him was Shaderoc the Deifier, the Demolisher, the Defender, the Soul Shaker. He was a big cat as Gibson had always imagined him. Six-four or five and built like Mike Strahan back when or J. J. Watt now.

"Sheeet," he muttered.

Shaderoc wasn't real. That is, Gibson looked down at his hands and they looked like . . . his hands. But this construct before him was hyper-idealized, like a live pencil drawing by comic book artist Jack Kirby, inked with fluidity by Gil Kane and colored in a combination of a bold primary palate.

"We've got our back up against it, Church," said Shaderoc in his, of course, bass voice. He was hefting a retro kind of space rifle like what Dr. Funkenstein's minions used in that movie. The weapon looked like it was made of tin and plastic. In a scabbard attached to his belt was a sword.

Gibson realized they were in a good-sized cave and a group of people were crowded in here too. There was the fine muscled sister from the album cover in a kind of modified tiger skin bikini with breechcloth, heavy gravity boots slinging a large, curved knife weapon like the Klingon's bat'leth. There was Miles Davis in his Kind of Blue phase, sharp in a sharkskin suit, shades and wielding a onyx samurai sword, the blade phasing in and out of solidity. Near him was a hunched over Chet Baker who worked the valves of his horn and out of the music-end swirled color tendrils that snapped as they lashed and licked the thick air. Big Mama Thornton was in a svelte aquamarine space suit while she expertly loaded a magazine into a World War II-era Thompson sub-machine gun. Like a character in a Sam Fuller movie, she rolled the dead cigar stump around her mouth.

"Are you ready?" Shaderoc asked Gibson.

Given he was unarmed and unprepared, he said, "What can I do?"

Shaderoc looked bemused. "Bring it home, baby, bring it home."

"I want you bad," the wet dream woman said as she threw her body roughly against Shaderoc's. She kissed him with lustful ferocity as he kneaded a handful of her incredible backside.

Looking away, Gibson was handed his Telecaster by Stevie Ray Vaughan. Charlie Christian sparked a cheroot behind him, Gibson heard a screech and turning around, flying into the cave were musical notes the size of greyhounds. They undulated as they spread about, the strains of Muzak and smooth jazz. Miles was visibly shaken but rallied as an F note rushed at him, a jaw full of razor-like teeth opening in the note head. Those teeth closed in on Miles's face but he executed a spinning move, his sword cleanly severing the note head from the stem.

"Take that, motherfuckah," he rasped.

All about him Shaderoc, the Tiger Woman and the musicians did battle against the invading notes. Invaders and defenders experienced losses. A ravenous note dove for him and a panicked Gibson strummed his axe on reflex. To his surprise, the sonic waves the guitar released burst the demon note into tiny pieces. A hand clamped in his shoulder. It was Shaderoc.

"With me," the big man said, already in motion.

Down a dark tributary to the cave they went. Gibson still was on his crutch, but he somehow kept up with Shaderoc's long strides. From up head in the half-light came a blast of sound that sent Gibson on his back and Shaderoc to his knees. Growling, venal notes swarmed about them, their teeth lunging for them, and a jumble of off-key singing assailing their ears.

Gibson had managed to sit up, but he was nauseous.

"Come on, follow me, Church." Shaderoc was back on his feet, aiming and firing his rifle, disrupting some of the notes which died screaming. More of them filled the tunnel. The soul shaker went prone and started belly crawling forward. Gibson imitated him, using his arms to propel himself forward. He was glad he'd been diligent in his workouts.

"We got to get to the Source," Shaderoc said over the cacophony.

Apparently, they were heading toward the origination point of the attacking notes. They began to travel down an incline and soon found themselves sliding through dirt and loose rocks into another chamber.

"Shit," Gibson swore as they came to a halt.

Before them was a giant pulsing entity, sort of like a gigantic cocoon or hive from which knobby exoskeleton-like shell material protruded. There were also thousands of undulating feelers wiggling from the mass. The hive construct was lit from within and the demon notes squirted into life from the ends of the feelers. A rhythmic drone beat pounded at their bodies as well. Shaderoc crawled over to Gibson.

"We got one chance," he said. "I'm going to rip open a seam in that mutha and in that moment she'll be vulnerable.

"Shaderoc, I—"

"No, this is how it must be. I told you, only you can bring it home."

Before he could object again, the big man was up and seeking handholds invisible to normal men, scaling the rock wall. Hundreds, thousands of notes swirled about him. He unlimbered his rifle strapped across his back and blasted the notes to hell. Others he wrung their stems in his bare hands. But they were overwhelming him, their racket and jagged teeth opening countless wounds and gashes on his mighty body. His clothing was ripped to shreds and his rifle had been torn away from his hands. But Shaderoc kept on.

Then in position, he looked over his shoulder at Gibson and winked. The notes battering him, he unsheathed his sword, but it wasn't a saber. It was the fabled pimp cane and was resplendent, made of dark burnished wood with a jeweled head in the image of a pitbull's skull. He jumped from the small ledge he'd gained.

The pimp cane was arched high over his head, held in both hands as he yelled. "Die nasty, mothersucker, die." Shaderoc came down at the Hive Mother, his body engulfed in her musical killer note children.

But the beasts couldn't halt Shaderoc's momentum. Out blazed a laser blade from the end of the cane, crackling with cosmic gravitas. The white-hot beam opened a deep gash in the rutted hide. "Now, man, now," he yelled as the notes engulfed him, stilling his words forever as he fell away.

"Shaderoc," Gibson yelled. Getting upright, the fizz and pop like toxic carbonated water flooded his chest again. But he rallied and his fingers worked the strings feverishly, his thumb thumping a ferocious funk attack. His fingertips bled, sweat blinded his eyes. He sent his sound spears at the opening even as it healed itself shut. The wound closed, most of his sonic javelins bouncing away impotently. But hadn't one or two gotten through? Hadn't he been able to pull it off? Agonizing moments crawled by and Gibson could see no change as the notes zoomed around his body like a cyclone, those hungry teeth nipping at and sampling his flesh.

But as he sunk down, as his consciousness left his torn body, even as he watched his arm ripped off and eaten, the hive burned brighter from within. Its pulsations increased and as if too much water was being streamed into a balloon, its sides stretched beyond tolerance and burst. In one collective ear-splitting wail, the notes died. Some of their bodies slammed into each other, the cavern walls, or simply fell to the earth, writing in their death agonies.

ONE-ARMED, GIBSON, HIS STUB MIRACULOUSLY CAUTERIZED, crawled to Shaderoc. His form was getting soft, his hard, distinct Kirby-lines dissolving. In his outstretched hand with the squared off fingers was a squarish block with miniature tubes and knobs all over the surface of it—a gadget straight out of the *Fantastic Four.*

"Take it, you earned it."

"What," he stammered.

"Make me proud," Shaderoc said and died.

Gibson rolled onto his back. He held tightly onto the gizmo which was warm and hummed in his hand. Overhead was black, yet in that void he could see the distant twinkling stars. The dark vault got lighter and lighter; Gibson's face placid in satisfaction.

"Oh, jeez, hey, Mom, Dad, better come here."

"What is it, Cory?" called the middle schooler's father anxiously.

"Is he dead?" said Cory, not sure what he should feel.

"Tell your mom to call 9-1-1, okay, buddy?" Nic Thomlinson bent down to the body splayed across his doorstep. "Tell them we need an ambulance." He felt for a pulse in Church Gibson's neck but could detect none. Looking about for a clue as to how long the musician might have been out here, Thomlinson saw something sticking out of the dead man's fist. He knew from those *Forensic Squad* episodes he helmed a decade ago he shouldn't remove evidence, but he did. It was a thumb drive.

"Huh," he said, pocketing the item.

SEVEN MONTHS LATER, THE SOUNDTRACK ALBUM of *Shaderoc the Soul Shaker* would be the number one download for three weeks running. Church Gibson would be nominated for a posthumous Oscar, and there was interest of a biopic about him. While different people had their favorite track from the film, the complete score on the thumb drive recovered from his stiff fist, was a track of what was presumed Gibson yelling "Shaderoc" over and over, with a haunting, evocative guitar instrumental underneath. Thomlinson used it on the ending credits.

GRAG'S LAST ESCAPE

"YOU'RE NOT AUTHORIZED TO BE IN here," the senior Talusian engineer said upon entering the power core room. He gaped, fully realizing what the imposter was doing. "By the seven veils," he muttered, advancing.

Undercover agent Grag stood from having been hunched down while she'd uncoupled the phasing device. She held this in one hand and in the other, the disguised cutter beam she'd just used.

"You must be a spy," the engineer declared, reaching for the com to alert security. "Are you from the D'Noths? The Requan-Na's? No matter, our interrogators will get the truth out of you."

Grag sliced off the Talusian's extended arm with her cutter beam. He wailed pitifully, his copper-based green blood spurting onto control panels and slicking the deck. Fortunately for her, the thrum of the scout ship's engines muffled his cries. As he panicked and shook, she covered the distance between them and clubbed him unconscious with the phasing unit. Grag knew his name, Sisstran. She cauterized his wound with an adjustment to her tool's beam. She dragged the alien across the deck behind the thruster reactor console where she'd bound the other two of the engineering crew on duty that evening. She exited via the main hatch which irised open then closed after she stepped through.

Grag, a lieutenant in the Solar Rangers military wing of the United Galaxy Alliance, hurried along the corridor, tucking the prototype she'd been sent in to steal in a tool bag, its strap slung across her torso. Her goal had been to pull off the theft undetected but it wasn't the first time a plan had gone south on her. Rangers didn't whine, they improvised or so the hooah went. At least, she reflected, she still blended in with the other Talusians with their ridged foreheads, highly arched eyebrows, and pointed ears. The surgically-altered soldier took a right at a particular juncture then down an access ladder to the lower conduits and ducts.

Expertly snaking through the river of tubes, she made her way to the landing craft bay, the visual of the ship's schematic committed to her prodigious memory. A nano-tech enhanced memory that served her well over numerous espionage missions, taking on the persona of various humanoid alien life forms over the years.

Reaching the end of the deck, she took several more turns, ascending at one point, then got to the desired grate. She eased the panel open slightly, looking down in the bay. The air in there was rich with the aroma of machine oil and afterburner fumes. That smell was ever so inviting as she—

WOOGA! WOOGA! WOOGA! an alarm blared, everything suddenly bathed in red.

"Intruder alert, intruder alert," declared a voice over the ship's communication system. "Security to the landing craft bay. Medical triage to engineering," the voice said.

"Shit," Grag said as she kicked the grate free. It clattered on the deck below as she too dropped to the floor. Ahead of her the main hatch opened and armed personnel rushed in, firing their plasma pistols. A ray blast nearly severed Grag's head but she was diving and got behind the stubby nacelle of a lander as the beam sizzled over her. She blasted back, the crossfire searing the bay in a lethal light show.

"Set on stun," the captain of the guard ordered. "We need her alive to get answers out of her."

Grag belly crawled between the skids of a lander. She took aim and used her cutter to slice through several particle module canisters stacked in a corner. The containers exploded violently, jagged energy bolts flaring in all directions. A nearby lander exploded when it was struck.

Several security members were sent flying due to the concussive force, while the rest scattered for cover. A lander was struck with a white-blue shaft and exploded, its solid star fuel supply liquefying and spilling across the deck on fire. Grag was knocked against a bulkhead, but she was only dazed and got her feet under her quickly. Yellow and orange flames clawed upward from the burning fuel, curling into black smoke that rolled through the bay. The automatic extinguishers came on, dousing everything in chemical retardant. Some of this got in Grag's eyes and she had to blink hard to try and see.

A stun blast doubled her over and she stumbled backwards, falling to the deck.

"Got you." A Talusian declared as he tried to wrench Grag to her feet. But the Ranger shook off the effects of the blast, its power attenuated by her uniform's armored weave.

Not as weakened as she pretended, she jabbed her stiffened fingers under the Talusian's ear right on his nerve point. He withered to the floor as two others fired at her. Breathing hard, she scrambled for his sidearm, its range much greater than her cutter beam and more precise. She took out one of the aliens shooting at her and the other ran behind one of the ships for cover.

Grag needed to be gone before more security swarmed through the hatch. Ducking behind a lander, she withdrew from her tool bag a large oblong egg—a darkling bomb. Underneath its translucent plasticine gray sheath was movement, a diaphanous life form flitting about in the viscous liquid.

This was an artificially grown construct that mimicked a sea creature known as a kadju, a cross between an Earth bat and a squid. She threw the egg at the Talusians and it burst open as one of them shot it. Now exposed to oxygen, the lab produced kadju swelled in size ten-fold. It floated in the air, its numerous tentacles interconnected by bat-like membrane. When the Talusians shot through the creature's spongy body, the thing released through its wounds a velvety blackness that engulfed the area like reverse light. Grag's attackers groped blindly in the opaque darkness.

"Goddammit," a member of the detail swore. The epithet a rough translation from the Talusian as interpreted by the translator chip in Grag's neck. He managed to get his hands on Grag and tried to get an arm around her neck to choke her out. She flipped him over her shoulder and karate chopped his neck. With him out of the way, she hurried inside a lander and powered it up. Like her brain, her eyes had been altered some time ago and Grag could see in the dark.

The computer-generated alarm echoed, "Warning, cargo bay doors opening. Warning, cargo bay doors opening."

Security had to abandon the bay or die from suffocation. Some of them blazed their weapons set to full strength, trying to cripple the ship Grag had just highjacked. The secret agent stayed calm, her hands steady on the controls as she pulled back on the manual yoke and headed the ship for space.

A few blasts got close, one even nicking the hull, but she zoomed the craft out of the bay, only then allowing herself a moment of relief. But Grag knew she had to remain alert. She hadn't had a high success rate by being over-confident. Escape was never certain. The Talusian scout ship was well-equipped to shoot her down. But as the ship turned her way, no plasma beams or pulse missiles came at her. She allowed a grim smile. Grag had planted a virus two days prior in the onboard computer affecting the weapons array. She soared away.

It wouldn't take long for the bridge detail to override the sabotage so she knew she couldn't be in flight too long. Grag inputted the override codes to hack the sub-space radio and tuned it in to find a specific frequency. "This is Solar Ranger Grag," she said over the radio, also relaying the correct password. "I have the phasing unit but I'm on the run. Need to ditch my getaway ship. I'll be making landing on Gastor-7 and engaging my homing beacon."

Grag increased her speed, burning up the lander's fuel supply at a faster rate than normal. This was going to be a one-way trip to Gastor-7, a jungle planetoid at the far edge of this quadrant. It was Type R which meant a breathable atmosphere for humanoid-like life, water, plant life, and carbon-based life forms. In Gastor-7's case, this was represented by animals and insects of the prehistoric size variety. It was not hospitable and the average temperature was 40.5 Celsius, 105 degrees Fahrenheit in Old World reckoning. The planetoid came into view and Grag activated her homing beacon as she brought up a topographical 3D holo-image projected above the ship's navigation panel. Her attention on the image, trying to determine a good place to land, she looked up through the plexi-shield in time to see a flying dragon-like reptile heading straight at her. Landers weren't generally outfitted with proximity sensors, given that you flew by sight. And to her surprise, like the dragon of fables, it screeched a funnel of fire at Grag's ship.

"Holy Shit," she cursed, steering away from the beast, part of the tail section of the craft on fire. Apparently its saliva was what burned and as this coated part of the lander, the fire would continue.

"Where's that chemical retardant when I need it?" Grag quipped, seeing the flames through a side oval window. Digital readouts on several of her panels blinked on and off and the lander rattled. Grag swallowed hard and focusing, seared the dragon with a plasma blast. Wounded, it veered off. But sure enough, having swooped in from starboard, another dragon rammed the ship then latched its feet onto the hull to tear into the ship with its claws.

"Great," Grag muttered. "It just keeps getting better."

There was a way to surge an electrical charge through the hull but that took a few moments to rig and Grag figured her time would be better spent abandoning the ship. The one thing the lander did have was a parafloater. As she got the rig out of a locker near the hatch, she could hear the flapping of the air creature's massive leathery wings. The beast bellowed at this impudent intruder to its world, using its claws to rend the lander's alloy and carbon fiber casing. Damned if the thing didn't rip a seam open in the hull and spewing in its fire, alighted the interior.

"Time to go." Gritting her teeth, Grag blew the hatch and tumbled backwards out of the destroyed landing craft. The dragon was still interested in the lander and held on to it as it burned. Rather than engage her para-floater too close to the ship and become the creature's appetizer, she let herself freefall toward the surface. The dragon then tired of its toy and threw the ship away. Above Grag, the lander trailed black smoke and slammed against a hill and exploded.

Her face grimly set, Grag crashed through a canopy of tree-tops, turning on the device. She came down faster than anticipated, branches tearing at her as the stabilizer initiated and fifteen feet from bashing her body against the ground, the anti-gravity buffer kicked in. She alighted on her feet.

Grag had to take a knee to gather herself. That was closer than she would have liked but she was still upright. She had a mission to complete. Rising, she unlatched the para-floater from her back and set it aside. She made an assessment of her surroundings. She was sweating from the tension and the humidity. It would at least be a day before help arrived and she hoped the Talusians didn't find her by then. Grag had disabled the automatic tracker in the lander. There were several planets and moons in this quadrant she could have escaped to and the aliens would have to conduct a systematic search for her. She set about looking for food and water.

There were smaller animals she spotted that her handheld personal computer identified as edible. But she was a vegetarian and was glad to find several exotic fruits that would sustain her as well as water. She also came upon the skinned carcass of an amphibious reptile about the size of an alligator on Earth.

"Hunters," she murmured, staring at their handiwork. Gastor-7 was on the United Galaxy Alliance's no hunt list due to several of its animals being unique. Her being on the run would be deemed an exception if she did eat meat. There were on and off-world sensor devices for detecting the use of pulse rays and the like but she knew there were ways to circumvent such things. She sniffed the air and recognized the whiff of refined oil—gasoline. These kind of hunters were known to use old-style gunpowder, guns, and primitive hand-built vehicles which wouldn't leave a digital footprint. They would also be using a liquid fuel ship to get them and their equipment to and from the surface, a regular pulse ship in higher orbit. Such an operation meant this was a costly enterprise, no doubt a trophy hunt for a wealthy dilettante. That meant these would take extreme measures not to be found out by the law.

She moved through the brush more carefully and soon found their camp. She wanted to observe them and figure out how best to deal with these beings. They must have been otherwise engaged when she'd arrived, she concluded. Two men and a woman were in the camp, talking. One of the males was human, the other two hairless, red-hued, four-armed Maldorans. Several carcasses were in freeze pods, the animals' frozen and astonished expressions evident behind the frosted plasti-shields. There were two tents and assorted other outdoor gear including three gas-powered vehicles swarming with pipes and fat tires, the metal cobbled together from the scrap heap with big-bore gasoline engines mounted on their tubular frames.

Too late she sensed a fourth one moving in behind her.

"Who the hell are you?" said the human woman. Her antique .30/06 bolt-action rifle aimed at Grag.

Grag had shot that type of long gun at the range. But she knew it was foolish to try and establish rapport with her over their familiarity with old guns. "I'm a Solar Ranger."

"You're not in uniform and you're a Talusian." While several alien races were in the corps, the Talusians were not part of the UGA.

"I'm a human on undercover assignment."

The others heard them talking. "What's going on, Valmarr?" one of them said.

Valmarr jerked with the barrel of the gun toward the camp site. Grag complied. "She says she's law."

The human male roughly patted Grag down, relieving her of her tool bag. Given how they acted, she surmised Valmarr and this other human were the guides. The couple didn't seem to want to drift far from one another.

He dumped the contents of her bag on the ground. He picked up the phasing device. "I'm fairly updated on astro tech, but haven't seen this before." He held it up to Grag's face. "What is this?"

"That's classified."

The female Maldoran was trying to hack into Grag's comm-computer. "This thing has a sophisticated lock on it."

"What do you think, Rodrigo?" Valmarr said to the human male.

He regarded Grag then motioned for Valmarr to step away. This was the time the two would decide her fate. They might tie her up and continue the hunt. But the Talusians might show up or, more likely, her fellow Rangers. Either way, they'd be in the shit. Disabling her might be an option as they packed up. But she could ID them. The Maldoran couple faced a stiff fine. It was the guides that had the most to lose. Judging by the way they carried themselves, this wasn't their first poaching excursion and if they were arrested and their activities looked into, who knew what would be divulged, Grag evaluated grimly.

She was a liability and liabilities had to be dealt with, she coldly concluded. Fear didn't well in her, only anger. They would try and take her life and she wasn't going to let that happen.

"I guess you've figured how this would go," Valmarr said, coming back toward Grag after her discussion with Rodrigo.

"Wait, what are you saying?" the Maldoran male asked, worried.

"You're going to be an accessory to murder," Grag said matter-of-factly.

An uncomfortable Valmarr chewed her bottom lip.

Rodrigo addressed the couple. "We told you there were risks."

The Maldoran woman gestured with her four arms. "From the wild life, but not this."

Grag said, "Your guides have much to hide." She was sure their past included hunting exotic protected life forms up and down the evolutionary ladder. She shifted toward her tool bag on the ground.

"Let's get this over with. We're going to have unwanted visitors way too soon," Rodrigo stated.

The Maldorans moved in front of Rodrigo to protest and Valmarr was momentarily distracted. Grag went low, extending her leg in a sweep, knocking Valmarr off her feet. Rodrigo lunged for his rifle leaning against one of the freeze pods. Prone on her stomach Valmarr rolled, also reaching for her rifle. The hunters weren't the only ones with an old style weapon. In a tear away section on the exterior of the tool bag, Grag pulled a knife free and stabbed Valmarr through the hand, momentarily pinning her to the ground.

As her cry of pain and defiance had the red-hued Maldorans going redder with panic, Grag had the rifle and shot at Rodrigo, who dove for safety behind one of the freeze pods. Valmarr pulled the knife free and charged at Grag, trying to gut her.

The ranger blocked the attack with the rifle and swung the stock alongside Valmarr's head, stunning her. Another blow to her temple sent her to the ground unconscious. Stepping in front of him, the Maldorans sought to interfere with Rodrigo again. Grag scooped up the phasing unit and ran to one of the motorized contraptions. She jumped into the driver's seat and mashed what she guessed was the ignition button. The big engine coughed. The retort of Rodrigo's rifle shots were gobbled up as the big block hemi with the double-barreled carburetor roared to life and Grag drove off.

With the open air engine behind her seat roaring and belching an odor of fuel in the exhaust, Grag had never piloted this kind of vehicle. She had virtually in a few holo-video games, so she had a kind of abstract knowledge of the throttle, brake, and steering wheel. Pressing on the pedal, she zoomed forward. She wondered if her teeth were going to rattle out of her head as she nearly smashed against a tree but got the machine under semi-control and tore off. Rodrigo shoved the female Maldoran aside and shot at the fleeing Grag. His bullet whined past her ear.

Still, driving one in reality was a much more challenging experience and she wasn't adept. Rodrigo was coming up from behind fast in one of the others and handled his vehicle expertly over the rough terrain. Grag plowed through bramble, getting snagged by thorns and bushes, which cut her face and ripped her clothes. She heard an electronic sputtering noise and saw that the bullet had struck and damaged the phasing unit.

She bounced over a rocky patch of ground. A dog-like lizard creature bolted in front of her. She swerved to avoid colliding with the animal and skidded through a copse of giant mushrooms. As she side-swiped the plants, a dust rose from them and enveloped her. She sneezed several times. Getting clear, her eyes widened.

"Aw, fuck," she swore as she went airborne off a cliff, water and rocks below her. The slapdash vehicle bounced once, twice off the sloping cliff face and landed with a jarring suddenness, pieces breaking loose. What was left of the vehicle was a mangled ball of metal.

Rodrigo, who knew this cliff was here, came to a stop near the edge. He got out of his idling machine, looked down at the wreckage, smirked victoriously, then climbed back into his vehicle and drove off.

Down below Grag's sternum was caved in, a leg broken on one side, a hip on the other side of her body, and she was bleeding out from the second big artery in her thigh. What air she could take in wheezed out immediately. So this is what failure felt like, she thought; she was going to die alone and her mission a bust. That bothered her more than anything else.

Her hand felt around some and came upon the phasing device, which fizzed and crackled. What the prototype was designed to do was allow a solid object to phase, to become invisible and un-solid, thereby untouchable, yet able to fire its weapons on the enemy. It would surely shift the precarious balance of power in the galaxy.

Grag's hand got hot as the phasing unit began to hum, throwing off a yellow light that grew in intensity. This didn't panic her. Oddly she found the pulsations comforting, bracing her for the end to come. She gripped it tighter as if it were a life raft. The heat radiated up her arm and she would have cried out but her vocal chords could only manage a dry croak. The heat covered the rest of her, the phasing unit seemingly melting into her skin, mother-boards and data chips stretching into the thinness of wires crawling up her arm like kudzu. Grag had the sensation of a ghost-like version of herself rising from the wreckage, looking down on what had been her corporeal form. Then that too blinked out of existence as her mind shut down . . . or so she believed.

Rodrigo calmed the husband and wife down by convincing them that the Ranger died in an accident. Yes, there were the tracks of his vehicle too but they'd be long gone and no record of them being here when others arrived. Packed up, he ushered them onboard the surface-to space craft. He turned at the sound of a footfall. He was on edge and had kept his rifle strapped on him. It was in his hand as he stared at a changed Grag.

"The hell," he said.

Grag was partly coated in metal. Not as in an exoskeleton, but pieces of the ATV and the phasing unit warped and re-molded into attachments to parts of her body and her remaining torso.

Rodrigo shot and the bullet passed through her. He looked shocked and she amused. He quickly re-loaded but as he brought the rifle up again his throat was now in her fingers and she crushed his windpipe. He crumpled to her feet and died gasping.

Valmarr and the couple were in the ship's doorway. The human woman had a med patch on her temple. They remained mute when Grag drove her metallic covered fist into the side of the ship, ripping out its guidance mechanism. Stoically she looked back at them then walked into the jungle. When the Solar Rangers arrived they arrested the three and listened to their story. They searched for Grag but didn't find her. They did find the downloaded data about the phasing unit and so the precarious balance of mutually assured destruction was maintained, until the next means to threaten the fragile peace came along.

From the jungle, Grag watched them depart. In her transformed state, part machine and part flesh, her consciousness could reach out to the higher-level animals, phasing with them. It wasn't as if she could communicate with them, but could experience Gastor-7 from their point of view. She felt protective of them. In this, her final act as a chameleon, a human who'd never truly been at home in her own skin and was thereby able to always disappear under-cover, she was in a role she wouldn't be abandoning.

She had a mission. She was home.

BRET KHODO, AGENT OF C.O.D.E.

THE SCUBA DIVER IN NYLON TRUNKS and flippers swam as fast as he could, pursued by two mermen. One of the sea creatures had a spear gun and the other a good-sized knife. A spear hit the tank of the scuba diver but only dinged its surface. He descended toward a rusting hulk of a freighter partially buried in the ocean floor below. He shot through undulating seaweed and into the ship.

The two mermen, gray-blue scaly bodies, with gills on the sides on their necks and large, bubbly slit eyeballs, slowed as they got closer to the ship. They signaled to each other and one went in through the opening to the cargo hold, the other through a jagged hole in the side where the long useless ballast tanks were located.

There was an oily gloom pervading the interior of the freighter. The two pursuers proceeded cautiously from opposite ends, essentially trying to box in their quarry. The one with the knife came to a bend in a passageway, on the lookout for telltale air bubbles. But the scuba diver had been holding his breath and he jumped on the merman's back as he swam past. They thrashed and twisted as the scuba diver held the wrist of the merman's knife hand. He had his other arm around the merman's neck. But rather than try and pull his grip tighter, the scuba diver relaxed his hold. Like an underwater Fred Astaire, he let him go, spinning him away from his body and into the bulkhead.

The merman with the spear gun had arrived and, having reloaded his weapon, shot a spear again at the scuba diver. The diver reacted fast enough that the spear didn't impale him dead center. Still his bicep was nicked by the tip and blood eddied from the wound. The spear gunner moved in. But the scuba diver struck with the stiffened ends of his fingers, right into the area of the merman's Adam's apple.

The merman gagged, a wreath of air bubbles escaping his open mouth. He tried to clear his head but the scuba diver struck him again and then ripped off the combination mask and regulator, also tearing lose the hose to the oxygen tank hidden underneath the ribbed rubber dorsal fin on his back. He broke for the surface as the other pretend merman attacked the scuba diver anew.

The two fought with their knives, the scuba diver having unsheathed his as well. As they engaged in their underwater ballet of parry and thrust, a great white shark suddenly shot into the passageway, attracted by the blood in the water. The combatants went still at the sight of nature's near-perfect killing machine. The scuba diver went horizontal, stomach up, and kicked the merman in the chest. This sent him toward the shark and it did what sharks do, and promptly clamped his jagged teeth on the merman's thigh. He screamed a burst of air bubbles as the shark shook him like a poodle's chew toy and began devouring him.

While the great white was busy rending and biting his disguised human prize, the scuba diver cut the other merman's mask into strips. Swimming away, he tied them around his wound to prevent trailing blood. Up toward the light, he could see the remaining merman swimming across the water's surface. The scuba diver increased his speed . . .

The beachgoers lazing or playing on the warm white sand stared at the scuba diver coming out of the ocean. He took off his mask to reveal a chiseled handsome six-foot Asian man, stark eyes, tawny-skinned, and muscular in a lithe way with high cheekbones and black hair, a bit long over his ears. That's not why he attracted attention, other than turning the heads of a few pretty women. It was the man in the sea creature costume he dragged with him by the collar of his rubber suit that was the grabber. Some looked around for movie cameras but saw none. A pretty brunette in a turquoise bikini listened to a transistor radio laying on a blanket. Playing was "Midnight Confessions" by the Grass Roots. She stared slack-jawed at the newcomers.

The scuba diver let go of the unconscious man who plopped onto the sand as something buzzed. He unhooked a square compass from his weight belt and clicked a hidden button on the side of its casing. The compass was a disguised two-way radio.

"Agent 77?" a query sounded over the radio-compass. It was a whispery, ethereal voice. It was as if a specter had materialized on the other end of the connection, and was experimenting in how to speak to humans via their artificial devices.

"Yes, sir," the scuba diver said to the head of CODE, Confidential Operations for Defense and Enforcement.

"Have you had success dealing with the saboteurs?"

"I have, Zero-One," Bret Khodo, Agent 77 of CODE answered. Zero-One's true identity and even what he looked like were known only to a select few. His office in CODE's headquarters was sealed and guarded, and he communicated with his personnel via radio speakers. If it was necessary for him to be in person, he wore gloves and a silken hood with reflective material behind the eye slits.

"Good man. As you're already on the West Coast, I'm sending you in to rendezvous with Agent 82 in Los Angeles."

"What's the situation?"

"Briefly it's this."

KHODO SETTLED THE '68 DARK GREEN Mustang Fastback at the curb on the Sunset Strip. He didn't bother to put a dime in the meter as he got out and jaywalked across the street to the high-rise housing Maltese Magazine Distributors.

On the sidewalk, coming past him was a brunette in granny glasses, fringe vest, and a flower print dress. She had a folded over copy of the *Free Press* newspaper in one hand and she put a coin in for him saying, "I dig your vibe, man."

Khodo looked back at her and grinned. "Right on." He continued into the building.

Inside, he took off his sunglasses, like the kind Mastroianni sported in Fellini's *8-1/2*. He tucked them away inside his dark Bill Blass blazer as he got on the elevator. He also wore bell bottom slacks, an emerald colored paisley shirt, and scruffy dingo boots. A pretty Black woman with a large afro and a short skirt gave him the twice over as the car stopped at various floors. He returned the look. Khodo reached his floor and touching the edge of his snap-brim to her, he got off.

"Yes, can I help you?' the red-headed receptionist asked him when he stepped to where she sat behind a rotunda. Off to one side was a rack of the various magazines the company distributed, including *Buckhorn*, the leading men's magazine in the nation.

Khodo had pushed his hat back on his head. "Is Tony Barabos in?"

"Do you have an appointment?"

"No." He turned from her and headed toward an open doorway.

"Sir," she said, rising from her seat, "you can't just barge in there." She rushed from around the rotunda.

Khodo was in an inner hallway and marched toward Barabos's office, head of the company. The redhead was at his heels.

"Don't make me call security on you, sir," she said testily.

Khodo whirled and smiling serenely, gave her a nerve pinch like Spock wielded on Star Trek. She wilted unconscious in his arms and he gently eased her onto a molded plastic chair in a cubicle. A twice-divorced accounts rep, cigarette dangling from his mouth, his afternoon blast of scotch in hand, witnessed this.

"Can you teach me that? There's a couple of chicks I'd like to try that on."

Khodo chuckled dryly and opened the door to Barabos's office. He entered unannounced.

The exec looked up startled from the line of coke he was snorting from his glass-topped desk. A tawny-skinned surf bunny in a polka dot bikini and sandals was off to one side of the room. She had on Pioneer headphones, plugged into the stereo system, and was doing the Frug to a playback from the Teac tape recorder.

"Who the hell are you?" Barabos demanded.

"You're going to tell me where Rodar will be tonight."

Barabos, in a pointed collar shirt opened to reveal his thick chest hair and gold medallion astrological sign, absently wiped away a residue of powder from his mustache. "I don't know what the hell you're talking about, man."

Just then two bruisers entered the office, both several inches taller and heavier than the wiry Khodo.

"Time to go, Charlie Chan," one of the goons said. He wore a sharkskin suit sans tie. He had a bent nose and one of his ears was cauliflowered from various fights. He put a beefy hand on Khodo's arm intending to turn him around and Spanish walk him out. But the larger man suddenly found himself airborne after being easily flipped. He landed heavily on his butt on the shag carpet.

The other one had a blackjack handy and swung it at Khodo's head, who ducked and sidestepped away. Khodo countered with striking his heel into the man's knee, which caused him to buckle. Then a combination left-right also put him on the floor, dazed.

The man in the sharkskin suit was upright and had a Luger in his hand. That is, he'd barely cleared the weapon from his shoulder holster when Khodo charged him, chopping the gun from his grip, cracking his wrist in the process.

"Hey," the other man grimaced.

Khodo finished him off with several blurred blows to the man's upper body and head. He flopped over, done.

As this was happening the other thug again came at Khodo, but a roundhouse kick connecting with his jaw halted his hostilities.

At the desk, gathering Barabos's shirt front in his hands, Khodo, his hat having left his head, talked calmly and forcibly to the executive.

"Now I know you front for Solango. That this outfit moves cocaine and H in its trucks, a revenue stream for him."

"I, I can't tell you anything, he'll kill me."

"CODE will protect you, Barabos."

"No, you're lying. You'll feed me to the wolves."

Khodo sighed and let the man go. He looked over at the gorgeous woman in the bikini who was coming over to the desk. She started to say something but just then three men in coveralls dropped down outside of the picture window on a window washer platform.

"Get down, Agent 82," Khodo yelled.

He tried to shove Barabos out of the way as one of the men squeezed rounds from a Sten machine gun. Slugs tore into the walls as the window burst into tinkling multishaped shards.

Barabos was hit and screamed in pain as he toppled over. From where he'd thrown himself on the floor, Bret Khodo extended his arm, bending his wrist downward. His watch stem shot from his wristwatch in a puff and the projectile exploded a few inches in front of the man raking the machine gun. The stem was a miniature grenade devised by CODE's tactical weapon's unit, the X-9 section.

His face partially destroyed, the machine gunner lost control of his weapon and accidentally ripped bullets into one of his fellows. The third gunsel, a tough-looking individual with thick brows, manhandled the other two—the dead and the dying—over the platform's railing given they were no longer useful. Their bodies broke and released crimson when they struck the pavement 34 stories below.

The last man on the platform only had a handgun and wasn't keen on seeing what other gadgets the secret agent might put into play. He pushed the lever on the rig's motor to draw the platform upward.

"Get back here," Khodo growled. He dove out of the window. Agent 82 stared at his hurtling form open-mouthed.

Khodo clutched a portion of the bottom of the platform. The man standing on it was shooting into the flooring trying to kill him.

"Die you lousy rat fink chink," the henchman said.

Two of his bullets whizzed very close to Khodo, one of them singing past his brow. But the athletic agent, hanging from the platform, got to the edge of it and swung his legs out and up. This caused the platform to tilt, upsetting the man's balance on the thing. Those few seconds of distraction allowed Khodo to hook his feet on the platform's railing. Just then one side gave way, the twin cables snapping—the exploding stem grenade having weakened them. Khodo was in the process of doing a sit up, hanging by his feet but it all went haywire as the damaged platform banged against the building.

His feet lost their hold and Khodo fell away. But like a trapeze artist, he flipped his body over in midair and was able to get a hand hold on the damaged platform. The other man was at the top end of the platform, the end still held by cables. He'd dropped his gun when, in a panic, he'd reached out with both of his hands to hold on.

The hoodlum could do little but swear at Khodo who got himself up and around, and onto the platform. The rigging was stuck in place.

"You're through," Khodo said. "You're going to tell me about your boss Andor Solango."

"Go to hell," the other man yelled. "My old man fought you Japs in the Big One and I'll be damned if I'd tell you the time of day if I was wearing an armful of Timexes."

The Hawaiian-born Khodo sighed. "I'm part Chinese too as if that makes a difference to you, haole."

The angry hood gritted his teeth. "You aren't gonna make fun of me." He let go of the cable and, partly sliding and charging, got his arms around Khodo. The two went over backwards, falling from the tilted platform. Khodo was able to latch onto the end of the platform, the hood holding onto his legs.

The dangling man began hitting Khodo about the legs and gut with a fist.

"You idiot," Khodo yelled. "You'll kill us both."

"If that's the way it has to be," he replied nihilistically. "Remember the Alamo," he yelled, renewing his xenophobic attack.

The two were struggling outside the large window of an architectural firm. Several personnel were at their draft tables, watching the struggle. A handsome older woman in pearls was talking into a phone to the police. The dark-haired, bikini-wearing surf bunny marched purposefully through the office to the window. She was barely noticed.

"Excuse me," she told a heavyset man in rolled-up shirt sleeves at the window. She gently touched him on the shoulder to move him aside. He ogled her, complying.

Calmly the woman aimed a pistol she'd taken off one of the goons at the window and shot the glass out. Tucking the gun back into the bikini's waistband, she then used both hands to simultaneously chop at either side of the hood's knees.

"Ugghh," he moaned as this action caused several nerve endings in his body to go to sleep. He let go of Khodo and was caught by the woman, who falling backwards, got him inside the office. Then one of the other two cables broke lose from the platform. It began to twist around.

"Bret," she said, concerned.

Khodo swung back and forth holding the platform. As he competed his third arc, gauging his momentum would be enough, he let go, propelling himself feet-first inside as well. The platform completely gave way and fell to the earth. He and the woman left the office unmolested. Using a fireman's carry, Khodo transported the unconscious thug as well.

"You okay, Ida?" Khodo asked the supposed surf bunny.

Dr. Ida Canaris Pradesh, PhD in quantum physics and Agent 82 of CODE smiled casually at him. "I'm good to go, Tarzan."

She'd been sent in undercover a week before as Barabos's personal secretary. He had a thing for exotic women. The doctor, of East Asian Indian and German descent, had passed for a Mexican jet-setter from Guadalajara as per the dictates of her cover. They re-entered the shot up office. Khodo dumped the unconscious man on the floor.

"In fact I think we can find out where they'll be bringing Professor Rodar tonight." She stepped over one of the goons, who'd been killed in the barrage. A wall safe hidden behind a Buckhorn Buck Girl of the month calendar had been exposed and she began dialing the combination.

"It was only this morning that I was able to finally surreptitiously watch Barabos when he opened this safe earlier today and discerned its combination. I intended once I had a minute alone to go through the contents."

Standing behind her, Khodo breathed onto her neck. "You're a gas, Doc."

"Flattery will get you everywhere, Agent 77." While she worked the safe's dial, Khodo searched Barabos's body. Pradesh got the door open. Inside were packets of money, a tin of cocaine, and some folded papers. She took the documents and the two hurried from the office at the sound of approaching sirens. Pradesh also took an oversized woven beach bag from the side of the bullet drilled couch. In the stairwell Pradesh removed a miniskirt from the bag and put it on.

'I'm trying not to drool," Khodo cracked as she also buttoned a cotton shirt into place.

"Isn't getting me out of these clothes your objective?" she teased.

"Our duty comes first, Dr. Pradesh."

She patted his cheek, smiling. "Indeed."

The two managed to get out of the building and blend in with the crowd that had gathered in front looking up at the shot up office. Police cars blocked the Strip as armed officers rushed into the building.

"We better drift," Khodo whispered in Pradesh's ear.

"Right."

The two spies walked along and found a googie-style coffee shop called the Tik-Tok two blocks away. There Khodo had coffee, her tea, and they went over the papers.

Ida Pradesh had on her reading glasses and was perusing an insurance document. "Solango must have had Barabos lease various properties around town for various reasons. But," she continued, "unless we're going to check each address out, how do we narrow down where they'll be bringing Rodar tonight?"

Khodo, sitting opposite her in the booth, smiled and slid an ornate gold key across the table. It was topped with a ram's head.

Pradesh picked up the key, frowning at it. "What is this?"

"They give those to members of the Buckhorn Den, also on the Strip by the way."

"This is what you took from Barabos's pocket?"

"Yep."

She put the key down. "And . . . ?"

"And," he added, tapping the table, "We know Solango owns a piece of the *Buckhorn* magazines and clubs. The club here in LA includes a hotel, and just happens to have a helipad on its roof.

This has to be where they'll bring our kidnapped big brain tonight for the auction."

She nodded. "Makes sense. They sell off Rodar in a private room there, and the winning bidder can leave with their prize via helicopter. But this assumes, given Solango now knows we're on the hunt for him, he doesn't postpone the auction."

"I don't think he has a choice, Ida. That conniving bastard Malachinko, head of the Soviet space command was spotted sneaking through Canada. We also have to figure a Red Chinese representative is in town and possibly an oil-rich sheik as well. They won't be hanging around cooling their heels and risking exposure. Solango will double the guards but the sale has to go on.

"Okay, so what's the plan?"

He smiled crookedly and said, "My dancing prawn is to die for."

"Hmmm?" she murmured.

"Would you mind getting HQ on the line? Operations desk."

"No problem," she said, taking a compact out of her bag. She opened it and pressing a hidden button, the powder puff and such flipped over. Revealed on the underside of a metal disk were several tiny knobs, switches, and a speaker grill. She turned a dial and fiddled with the knobs. The disguised two-way communicator hummed. The mirror of the compact fuzzed over like a TV screen with electronic snow on it. The video link cleared, showing a handsome 40-plus woman with a beehive on the other end. She wore a leopard spotted eye patch.

Khodo was now sitting next to Pradesh. "Miss Beauclair, how's the weather in DC?"

"Agents 77 and 82. What shenanigans are you two up to today?"

"I need what only you can give, my dear," Khodo cracked.

Miss Beauclair touched her beehive, smiling wryly. "He's quite the charmer, isn't he?"

"He thinks he is," Pradesh said, grinning broadly. She gave his thigh a squeeze under the table.

Khodo said, "Miss Beauclair, would you please work your magic, and get me any leverage you can over one of the managers at the Buckhorn club out here. I need an in."

Eyebrow raised, she said, "Is this just an excuse for you to ogle scantily-clad women?"

"Probably," Pradesh interjected.

"Nonetheless, do get back to me with all possible speed."

"Of course. Beauclair out." The screen went to gray fuzz then back to its mirrored surface. It was believed among CODE personnel that the one-eyed woman was one of the few who knew Zero-One's true identity. Some had even speculated the two were married.

Khodo and the doctor were soon in his Mustang heading toward her cover apartment in Hollywood.

"I think we have a tail," she said, looking from the side view mirror. "The cream and tan Chrysler Imperial two cars back."

"Yes. Seems there was a backup to the men who stormed Barabos's office."

"Car has a whip antenna on it,"" Khodo added.

"Meaning it's probably outfitted with a radio-telephone and he's been in contact with Solango."

"No doubt." Khodo was cruising along Highland, having intended to go east on Hollywood Boulevard. Instead he kept heading north, passing his intended turn. Giving the big block Fastback some pedal, he revved forward and sped through a red light at Franklin. Drivers honked and cursed. A TV repair panel truck had to screech the brakes, its back tires smoking to avoid slamming into the hurtling car. As the Chrysler came up it was slowed from running the light due to the tangle in the intersection. Ahead, Khodo zoomed past one of the parking lots to the Hollywood Bowl and, taking the slight rise of road to the left of the entrance onto the 101 freeway, he kept going.

Pradesh unlimbered her sidearm, a small and efficient Beretta.

Khodo reached where Mulholland Drive began on its eastern end. He took the shifter out of gear and put the vehicle into a drift as he turned the body sideways, making his left, screeching through another red light and reengaging the clutch. This time a car traveling in the opposite direction didn't stop and clipped the rear bumper of the Mustang. The Mustang wobbled but Khodo got the car back under control and headed west on the two lane road that ringed the Santa Monica Mountains.

The Chrysler was behind them now and looking to close the gap. On the passenger side a man in sunglasses stuck his head out of the window and let loose with a shotgun. Buckshot tore into the side panel and destroyed the right side mirror, but Khodo and Pradesh were unhurt. There was armor plating beneath the machine's hull.

Pradesh reached over to the radio dial and, twisting it one way then rotating it back to a specific point, engaged one of the custom features of the CODE-issued sports car. The rear lights flipped down and out popped twin machine gun spouts that ripped a fusillade at the oncoming vehicle. The spouts were swivel mounted and they went side-to-side, up and down laying down their fire. The windshield of the oncoming car was spider-webbed from the onslaught but neither hood in the car was killed.

"Get their front end," Khodo advised as he veered around a station wagon and hurried to get back in the proper lane to dodge a bobtail truck descending Mulholland.

Pradesh adjusted the machine guns and stitched a rapid burst across the Chrysler's grill despite the other driver's attempts at evasive maneuvers. But his vision was partially obscured by the condition of his windshield and over compensating, he sideswiped the car along the guard rail. Khodo took a right onto a residential street, the Chrysler bearing down. Steam sputtered from his shot up radiator, the temperature gauge's indicator steadily moving into the red.

"You do know this is a cul-de-sac, don't you, darling," Pradesh said evenly. "Then let's hope this works." Khodo bore the Mustang toward a Gregory Ain-type low-slung house at the apex of the cul-de-sac. The shotgunner was shooting at them again and a grenade hit the roof and blew off part of the top. Only the armor kept the two from being ripped apart by shrapnel. Still some got through and cut Pradesh on her shoulder, Khodo on his neck.

A grim-faced Khodo flipped open the top of the stick shift exposing a button that he pushed while it looked as if he was going to drive the Mustang through the front of the house. Jetting out the Mustang's exhaust pipe was a chemical compound with a silicone base. This super slick solution coated the roadway.

At the last possible moment, Khodo cranked the wheel viciously. The Mustang's body shuddered but its racing struts and heavy duty ball joints did their job and, churning up the well-manicured lawn underneath his tires, the car turned away. Behind him the front tires of the Chrysler contacted the slick stuff on the asphalt and it was evident there was no stopping the hurtling two tons of steel, cloth, glass, and rubber. The car kept going and its trajectory took it past the side of the house, through shrubbery and wooden fencing, into a backyard pool below street level. The large pool was shaped like a grand piano. The tiered house was constructed partially into a hillside. The Chrysler soared headfirst into the pool, causing a huge geyser of water.

The driver was knocked unconscious, his head poking out of what remained of the damaged windshield. The shotgun man had gotten out and swam toward the side of the pool. Soaked and hauling himself out, he was met by Dr. Pradesh who in three swift karate chops had him subdued. Khodo rescued the driver and flopped him onto his stomach on the wet tile deck, coughing water. The owner of the house came out. It was the famed pianist Liberace and he gaped wide-eyed at his visitors. He was dressed in an off-white robe of luminescent quality embroidered with musical keys as if they'd been spilled all over the material.

"Sorry about the mess, Lee," Khodo said. "Your Uncle will get the damages repaired." The secret agent hadn't picked this street by accident.

The other man chuckled. "There's always such delicious excitement with you, Bret." Behind Liberace through the glass doors, a man with dark, long hair and a broad chest, like a denizen from a paperback cover about a barbarian, could be seen in swimming trunks.

"When you're done, come on in for some mimosas and crepes. Looks like you two could use a bracer." The piano man traipsed back into his home.

"How do you—" Pradesh began.

"Lee's done contract work for us. He gets invited to a lot of interesting places." Khodo put the gasping gangster on his back and, bending, placed the muzzle of Pradesh's handgun under his jaw. "You're going to call your boss and tell him you were successful. That me and Ida are dead."

Any objections he was going to raise died in his throat as he looked from the set features of Khodo and Pradesh. "Sure, whatever you say," he replied.

THAT EVENING AT THE BUCKHORN DEN, less than a mile west of where the shooting had happened that afternoon, a new hibachi chef entered the busy kitchen. It was Khodo wearing an orange conical hat and matching apron over his white pants and shirt. He had several types of kitchen knives from tapers to a saw and raker combination tucked into pockets of the apron and his waistband. He was introduced by the manager, Mike Yoshida.

"Everybody, this is Chen. He'll be filling in for Ayoki tonight on table two," Yoshida said to the staff.

There were brief acknowledgements and everyone got back to their tasks of chopping, mixing, baking, and what have you. The dinner crowd would soon descend in full force. Yoshida pulled Khodo aside.

"I hope this squares me with the IRS," he whispered.

Straight-faced Khodo said, "I'll put in the good word as promised, my man," the agent said. When Pradesh and Khodo radioed into headquarters for background information on key personnel at the club, the manager's troubles with back taxes and hints of hiding money from the tax man had been reported by Miss Beauclair.

"Good evening." Khodo bowed slightly in his outfit as people sat around the large flat hot steel griddle of table number two. Part of the establishment's attraction was watching your steak, vegetables, noodles, fish, and so forth being cooked on the grill in an entertaining fashion by the chef expertly wielding his various knives to chop and slice the ingredients.

A greater attraction was the Ramettes, the scantily-clad wait-resses with their little furry tails and little furry lamb ears that poked out of their hair.

"Here we go," Khodo said, "a pretty garnish for the pretty lady." He cut a radish into the shape of a rose and added it next to a piece of properly seared tuna on a customer's plate. He continued his patter as diners sipped their cocktails and murmured, dazzled by the speed and preciseness of his hands and blades. He received brief applause now and then after particular flourishes.

"Hey, you chop-chop pretty good, Hop Sing." Khodo sought to ignore the drunk bigot.

The patron, a red-faced middle-aged white man in a loud plaid jacket kept it up. "You no sloppy-sloppy with brades," he joked in a movie Chinese accent, laughing and flailing his hands about.

His companions giggled some but a couple of them gave Khodo a chagrined look.

Khodo calmly reached over, took hold of the man's tie, and sliced it neatly into sections he flung on his board, knife away from the hot grill. Somebody gulped audibly.

He said quietly, "I'm very precise when I cut."

The drunk dipped his head slightly and remained quiet.

Khodo cooked and entertained for more than an hour, expertly preparing food for the patrons while engaging in fast banter. He finally spotted a face he was familiar with from past surveillance footage. Doctor General Xiang Lin-Wu of the People's Liberation Army was moving through the restaurant on the far end. He wore a tailored Savile Row suit and three body guards were in step with him—one of them a striking-looking woman in a slit dress. Ida Pradesh, who'd commandeered a stool in the bar, fending off passes from several men, had also seen the Doctor General. She trailed him and his entourage through an archway.

Khodo motioned for the manager roaming about to come over. "Taking a break, folks. See you soon." There were groans of disappointment as he handed over his knives, apron, and hat to a sour-faced Yoshida.

"I'm rusty," he complained

"It's just like riding a bike, brudda," Khodo replied. He moved off, the more inebriated patrons clapping loudly as he left and joined Pradesh.

"I put a tracer on one of his guards," she said. "One of the men who I was able to get close to." She batted her eyes.

"Solid, doll baby."

They entered the kitchen where Khodo had left a leather, deep-bodied attache case between the industrial-sized refrigerator and a metal table. He retrieved this and the two went through a side door into a service hallway that led to a small room used by the staff for smoke breaks. The smell of tobacco was heavy. There was no desk or table but there was a built-in ledge that Khodo put the case on and opened it.

Among grenades, a grappling hook attached to a knotted nylon line, and other items in the case, was a built-in metal panel that resembled the face of Pradesh's compact-radio. But when he switched it on, a blueprint of the high rise the Buckhorn Club was located in was displayed. A red blip was ascending on the blueprint. They both watched the red dot intently. It soon stopped.

They looked at each other, nodding.

ANDOR SOLANGO WAS DISPLEASED THAT ONE of his fingernails had been trimmed unevenly. He'd have to reprimand his manicurist. He was six-four, muscular, prematurely white-haired, and bronze-skinned. An accident years before had left his face immobile, emotionless. His pale eyes were like looking into an arctic abyss. He wore a tan colored Nehru jacket and matching slacks.

Solango refocused. His guests had been served refreshments and were chatting about various geopolitical matters from Vietnam to the Congo. Among the gathered was the five-foot, one inch hunchbacked Major Vitally Malachinko, his brilliance the reason the Soviet's got into space first with Sputnik. Solango held up a hand.

"Ladies and gentlemen, please take your seats and we'll get the auction underway." Double doors to his left opened and escorted in by one of his leg breakers was rocket scientist Victor Rodar. Previously he'd been secreted away by the Defense Department, working on a hush-hush project involving satellites capable of shooting laser rays with pinpoint accuracy as the key to a sophisticated anti-nuclear missile defense system. The Defense Department had dubbed it the Flash Gordon Initiative.

Rodar was a compact aging man with thinning hair in a rumpled tweed jacket. The muscle indicated for him to sit in a comfortable chair positioned before the gathered. He looked nervous, but not frightened. He was a man, who, since childhood had come to accept the vagaries of fate. One had to maintain a certain determined pragmatism about such things, he'd long ago concluded.

"Care for a chardonnay, Professor?" Solango asked.

"Why not," Rodar said in his Austrian accent. A glass of white wine was brought to him.

Solango began as this was done. "I don't have to give you an overview of this man's accomplishments. You know what he was working on and you also know if he were to perfect his system for your respective country, what sort of nuclear superiority that would grant you in this madcap world of ours.

"To underscore what Dr. Rodar has to offer," Solango continued, "I give you one simple demonstration for your edification." He turned his head and said, "Krieg."

In stepped Krieg, a large-muscled bald-headed man in fatigues and a tank top wearing what looked like a large flat battery on his broad back. This was connected by a thick cable and wires to a futuristic-looking rifle in his hands. He aimed the weapon at a five-inch square of steel wheeled into the room on a cart. The yellow-white concentrated beam released from the rifle sliced off a corner of the slab. The severed piece fell to the floor, making a dent in it beneath the carpet. A din arose and subsided.

If Solango was capable of smiling, he would have. "You'll notice the ray's length was pre-adjusted such that it cut through the steel but didn't extend to the wall beyond. The prototype is based on the good professor's schematics. I'll throw the ray rifle in with the purchase price."

The West Coast's Marquis of Crime surveyed the eager faces in the room. Then, "The bidding begins at six million." Several hands went up as dollar or pound sterling amounts, each topping the other, were shouted out.

The eventual winning bid for the scientist was thirteen million and was made by the hunchbacked, dwarfish Malachinko of the Soviet Union. The room began to empty by the main door. That was when the side double doors burst inward, a henchman stumbling backwards through the opening. He fell over, arms outstretched, eyes rolled up in his head.

"Krieg," Solango yelled.

The big man turned his laser rifle in the direction of the door. Two smoke grenades rolled in from that direction, emitting their gray pall. At the same time, the air duct covering in a wall up toward the ceiling was kicked out and feet-first, Agent 77 dropped into the room. He was wearing special goggles that allowed him to see forms in the smoke and a mini-oxygen breather.

Dr. Ida Pradesh seemingly sprang from nowhere and jumped on Krieg's back, attacking him. They went at it in the ante room on the other side of the double doors.

Crouching low and pivoting around in the main room, Khodo dropped two of Solango's guards with shots from his field-issued .45. He rolled and the strike of his hand made another one tumble and he put a bullet in his skull. But a kick to the side of his face knocked him over though he recovered quickly. He was on his feet and in his Wing Chun stance. He kicked his gun laying on the floor aside.

As he suspected, his opponent was the woman who'd accompanied Doctor General Xiang. She too was in a kung fu stance. The smoke dissipated as the remaining people hurried from the room.

A slight bow and fist-to-palm salute from each, the two then engaged in fierce, close quarters combat. There was a succession of blows and kicks, Khodo delivering hammer strikes that would fell a man twice her size but not stopping her. The woman partially ran up a wall to do a back flip and nearly cold-cocked him with a foot sweep. Their hurtling bodies and chops at one another turned chairs into kindling.

Krieg had thrown off Agent 82, slamming her into a wall, dazing her. He rushed back into the main room and shot his weapon at Khodo. But the man from CODE had heard the whine of the apparatus as it powered up and dove out of the way. The ray blast meant for him cleaved the Doctor General's woman in two—the horror of her predicament forever etched on her face.

Fortunately for Khodo it took several seconds for the rifle to recharge between bursts. He was across the room lunging for the big man as Krieg clicked dry on the trigger. Their fight was brief and intense, a showcase of hand-to-hand combat of various styles including American boxing, kung fu, and even footwork involving capoeira. Each breathed heavily and had bloodied the other's face. Krieg then stepped in, feinting like he was going to throw a right cross, but actually intending to land a left flush to Khodo's chin.

But the man from CODE had sensed this. He slipped the punch and countered with a heel strike of his palm to the big man's jaw that made him blurry eyed. From his standing position, Khodo launched himself straight up in the air and whipped his leg around. His foot connected with the side of Krieg's face. There was an audible crack as the bone broke. The bruiser's body spun about on impact and went down hard. As he sought to rise, Khodo finished him with a fury of pummeling fists to his head that broke the nose and drove him to the floor, still and spent.

Khodo quickly stripped him of the weapon and running, lashed the battery pack on, heading for the roof. He didn't even take a moment to check on his colleague. There wasn't time. Too much hung in the balance.

Solango, Malachinko, and two henchmen were herding Victor Rodar toward a flying craft of a modernistic design Khodo hadn't encountered before. It was a saucer-shaped craft of silver-gray metal and glass. Clearly the Marquis of Crime was putting his ill gotten gains into R&D to further his criminal enterprises.

One of the hoods heard Khodo's footfalls on the roof and fired at him. The spy sought cover behind the two-story-tall Buckhorn Den neon sign supported on struts and angled on the roof. The gunfire exploded several letters that sparked and sprayed fissions of electricity in all directions. Khodo returned fire with the ray rifle, searing a hole clean through the gunman's chest. Solango, Rodar, and Malachinko were at the flying craft. It was splayed out like a metal jellyfish, sloping upward to a plexiglass canopy over a cockpit in the center of the circular fuselage. It sat four.

The remaining goon made to also get in but Solango pushed him back and before the man could object, he shot him dead. The criminal mastermind was counting on Khodo having orders to bring Rodar back alive—which he'd been instructed to do. The craft began to lift off, a central turbine engine underneath providing lift.

"Dammit," Pradesh said, now beside him. "Now what do we do?"

He turned to her, smiling. "Lisbon."

"Lisbon," she agreed.

Solango was at the controls. He didn't give a damn about the Russkie Malachinko, only he hadn't been able to make a call to have his money transferred, so there it was. The ship was hovering about 20 feet above the roof and Solango was about to switch over to forward motion.

The deformed Malachinko was leering as he glared out the clear canopy. "Glorious," he said happily.

Solango and Rodar looked at what he saw. It was the voluptuous and brainy Dr. Ida Pradesh bearing her wonderfully developed breasts. Reflexively, Solango dipped the aircraft toward the woman for a better view. But just as he did that, he realized this was a diversion a fraction too late.

Khodo had climbed up the metal sign and from the angle he was now, he could shoot into the craft. As Solango pulled back on the yoke, Khodo put a ray blast through the canopy, boring into the control panel. The airship spun around in the air and crashed into the roof at an angle, partly embedded in the roof's shingles and wood underneath. The occupants were shook up but alive. While Pradesh held a handgun on the two, Khodo roughly hauled Solango and Malachinko out of the aircraft and trussed them up.

"You haven't seen the last of me, Khodo," Solango vowed.

Ignoring him, he said to Pradesh, "Good work, Agent 82."

"You too, 77," she replied.

They stared at each other and kissed, pumped on the excitement of the recent events. By the time the CODE cleanup crew arrived, Professor Rodar had a gun on the imprisoned brigands, feigning ignorance as to the whereabouts of the two agents. When in actuality they were several floors down in a suite getting it on to the strains of Dean Martin on the stereo.

Dino sang, "Ain't That a Kick in the Head," as Agent 82 murmured, "Oh, Bret."

For unlike the speed he'd displayed earlier pretending to be a hibachi chef, he was slow and deliberate with his hands now—very deliberate.

ENTER THE SILENCER

BOOKER ESSEX, NOW KNOWN AS THE SILENCER, grabbed the hood in the fedora with an arm around his neck just as the second hood let loose with a burst from his Thompson machine gun.

"You goddamn moulie," were the hood's last words before bullets from the chopper ripped a diagonal up from his stomach across his chest—his body jerking at the impact of the high speed .45 rounds.

As those rounds tore through the crook's body, Essex was already moving. Crimson spread like ink blots on the dead man's custom-made dress shirt as his corpse collapsed onto the floor. Returning fire to drive the other two torpedoes back, Essex had shoved the body aside and dove through the swing door into the kitchen.

"Hold on," the machine gunner said to the third hood next to him who began to advance. "Looks like this fuckin' jay-bo ain't gonna be easy pickin's like we figured."

The third member of Laugher Graziano's gang nodded briefly. He carried a snub-nosed .38 revolver in a hand with a diamond pinky ring in a gold setting. The two separated some, each slowly approaching the kitchen door of the Fuzzy Feather Gentlemen's club. The metal rear door was locked and they heard no gunfire indicating their quarry was trying to exit. But they figured he wouldn't leave as they had the bait.

"We'll deal with you after we take care of this mook," the one with the handgun whispered. He shook the barrel briefly at a woman in a short robe tied-up on the stage. She was a stripper in the club, on her side, bound and gagged, a colorful silk tie around her mouth. Her eyes were wide not with fear, but with defiance. Her blonde hair was tangled and unruly. To the side of the stage, a staircase led to the VIP section on the second floor. A steam room and curtained alcoves were available there.

Now the gunmen were on either side of the swing door, the Thompson man looking through the portal-style window. The lights were on inside but Essex wasn't visible. There was a long counter with stainless steel pots and pans suspended above on hooks, and they assumed he was low behind that.

"You'd think it being all white in there the jungle bunny would stand out," the other hood cracked nervously.

The stripper, who did the bump and grind as Ginger Strawberry, swore at them but it came out muffled.

The machine gunner eased the swing door open with the muzzle of his magazine-fed Tommy gun, hoping the Silencer would show himself to take a shot. Nothing happened. He reared back and looked at his partner. They reached a silent decision. Together they both crashed into the kitchen. The Thompson handler laid down a barrage to keep the Silencer crouching, while the other hood's goal was to round the counter and blast him.

But a step away from the counter, the lights went out and there was a hiss like the quick release of air from a truck's power brakes. Then cold silence. Diffused spill-light came in through the portal window illuminating little.

"Tony," the snub-nosed man ventured. Tony was the now deceased Thompson gunner. "Tony," he repeated. Again no answer and he backtracked out of the kitchen in a hurry. He took hold of the trussed up woman and sliding her off the stage, got her to her bare feet. He dug the business end of the gun into her cheek.

"Okay, hotshot, better show yourself or your girlfriend here gets got," he called out. There was no movement from the kitchen and he repeated his threat. He undid the tie over Ginger Strawberry's mouth.

She began, "Why you lousy low life, scum—" He struck her in the face with the pistol. This elicited a groan as he intended.

"That's enough," Essex said from the kitchen doorway. He had one hand holding the swing door open, the other one out of sight. His voice was sibilant, shadowy, as if talking was an effort. It was not the voice he'd always had.

"Throw your piece out," the remaining hood demanded.

"Don't do it, Book," the woman advised.

He did as ordered. The gun was a modified .32 semi-auto machine pistol with a 20-round magazine and was fitted with a stubby sound suppressor on the muzzle. Twin tubes lead from the suppressor back into the body of the weapon.

"That's something," the hood said admiringly of the gun. He gestured with his revolver, using the woman as his shield as Essex had done with the first hood. "Now come all the way out with your hands up."

The Silencer did as ordered again. He wore a jean jacket over a ribbed turtleneck and flared slacks that broke just so on his Nunn Bush boots. His Fu Manchu mustache glistened with sweat. Though unlike the current style, he didn't sport an afro, rather he kept his hair boot camp short.

The gunsel wore a checkered leisure suit, his shirt open to expose his hairy chest and a heavy gold chain over the thicket. He smiled. "The boss is gonna be happy to have your magic gat," he said, referring to the specialized weapon. So-called silencers really weren't silent like in the movies. It muffled a gun's retort, but you could still hear it, just quieter. Essex's weapons were truly mere whispers when they went off.

In a flash the thug took the gun from the side of the

woman's face and as he squeezed the trigger to kill Booker Essex, he was quite surprised to feel a sting at his temple. He hadn't heard a thing.

"What the fu— . . ." he muttered then fell face-first onto the plush carpeting of the Fuzzy Feather—the body dying as his brain ceased function.

Essex crossed the distance and set the wobbly Ginger Strawberry in a chair.

"How'd you do that, Book?" she asked.

"Ever see the show, the *Wild, Wild West*? How ol' Jim West had this derringer on a slide mechanism up his sleeve?" He held his arm such so she could see the end of what looked like a small rectangular box with four holes in the end of his sleeve.

"Your version of that," she said. "Always cooking up a gadget."

"Better get your stuff and let's get out of here before the fuzz come pounding through the doors."

"Good idea. I've got the cassettes too." She stood and the robe flapped open, revealing her sculpted nude torso and sequined G-string. Essex looked away, his face warm.

Strawberry, whose real name was Marcia Mathers, noted this with a wry smile. She came over to him, pressing herself against his back. The blonde put a hand on his shoulder. "I know women don't scare you, Book."

He looked sideways at her. "It's not that, Marsh. But you're Bobby's sister."

"I'm also my own woman. And we're not kids anymore."

"Ain't that the truth," he agreed.

She kissed him on the cheek and went into the dressing room to get her clothes on and retrieve her purse and items. Thereafter the two left the club by a side door to Essex's three-year-old 1972 Ford LTD. The vehicle had a pristine Landau top and mag wheels, with a big block 460 Brougham engine under the hood. There were special items Essex had also built into the car besides further souping up the motor. He brought the machine to life and Mathers wasn't surprised she could barely hear the thing running.

"Living up to your name, huh?"

"Guess so." He turned on the heater and a police scanner hidden behind a fake grill in the dash.

Tires crunched over gravel as he drove off in the dark of post-three A.M. from the strip club. The place was a few miles out of town off the highway, mostly industrial facilities around, large structures made of metal sidings and low roofs. The trees were bare, their limbs pointing up to the wintery sky as if accusing the weather of indifference.

PAUL "LAUGHER" GRAZIANO, SOMETIMES CALLED THE Laughing Man by friends and enemies, wore slacks and slippers, and an athletic undershirt underneath the silk robe he'd tied around his trim waist. He was pushing 60 but maintained a regime of racquetball, swimming, and athletic sex with young women his daughter's age. His nickname was derived from a childhood incident when he was 11.

He and a friend were running from a copper after robbing a blind newshawker at his sidewalk stand. They ran into the street and Graziano was struck by a street car, causing nerve damage in his face. He was caught and sent to reform school. The other kid, Benny "Bean Pole" Mathers, got away. Thereafter the left side of Graziano's face drooped, and he learned to talk out of the other side of his mouth. His melancholy appearance earned him his opposite sobriquet.

He prided himself that he pretty much weighed the same as he did when he played basketball at Theodore Roosevelt High. They were the Rough Riders. That was before he was kicked out of school for taking bets on the games. The same school some years later that Booker Essex, Marcia Mathers, and her now deceased brother Robert had attended as well. Less than a year after they graduated, Essex was drafted and Bobby Mathers volunteered for Vietnam.

Laugher Graziano puffed on his thin cigar, looking out the window from the study to his backyard and the pool he better cover soon. A few ducks swam about in the water, quacking happily. What did it mean to be happy, he pondered as he turned back to Loomis Kassel, his Bill Blass-dressing, Yale-educated, half-German, half-Italian consigliere.

The time was just past dawn and both men were aware of what had gone down at the Fuzzy Feather a few hours before. Indeed Kassel had already dispatched a crew to clean up the mess. Due to having a homicide cop named Bert Chastain on the pad, he'd gotten a call from the detective and with his help, was keeping a lid on the matter—for the moment.

"I know," Graziano began unprompted. "I should have listened to you and not given in to my weakness. But who the fuck checks on the background of these broads? They all use a made up name strippin' and hookin' on the side." He shook his head. "Who could figure that chick would be undercover snatch?" He laughed sourly at his joke.

"We not only need to deal with her, but this colored gentleman."

"I need to color him red."

Kassel adjusted his Yves St. Laurent-designed frames. "I have a solution, only it's going to cost."

The Laughing Man spread his arms wide. "Doesn't it always, Loomis? Doesn't it always?"

EVER SINCE PHYSICALLY RECOVERING FROM THE fire resulting from the bomb, the Silencer had gone underground. With Chastain, Graziano's gang, and the self-styled revolutionary Rahim Katanga and his bunch all crowding him about making deadly inventions for them, he had little choice. But before it all changed, he and Bobby Mathers had managed to make it back to the world from 'Nam and opened their auto garage. It didn't hurt that both men had earned a few medals and were welcomed back as hometown heroes.

At their Danang Drag Motor Specialists shop, they repaired everyday cars and customized those who could afford something special. Life was good then.

He looked toward the sound of water coming from what had been the boss's office and the private bathroom and shower within.

In there Marcia Mathers was finishing up and turned off the hot and cold facets. Leave it to Booker, she noted appreciatively, to be able to bootleg electricity and running water into a place that went belly up months ago.

She pushed the pebbled glass door open and stepped out of the shower, taking off the rack one of the large towel Essex had provided. Drying off next to the portable heater, she stood in the compact office area he'd converted to a kind of bedroom with a cot, lamp sans shade, and numerous technical books on a makeshift shelf. There was a photo taped to the wall of Essex and her brother as soldiers in a jungle clearing in Vietnam. Both had vacant smiles on their faces—the smiles of men who had seen and done too much over there.

There were no pictures of Charlotte Sumlin about. There was though a charred piece of what had been the hand painted sign over their garage. The fragment leaned atop some of the books and Mathers picked it up, looking at it wistfully. She vividly remembered that terrible day. She'd just gotten off the phone with her brother and it would turn out to be the last time she'd speak to him.

Mathers learned later that afternoon about how a bomb had gone off in the garage. Her brother, the police surmised, must have been talking to Charlotte Sumlin who'd stopped by to see

Essex. Essex had been away to pick up a part and was just driving up when the blast went off. From his eye witness report, Sumlin had been in the open bay of the garage, waving at Essex. Bobby Mathers was behind her, wiping his hands on a shop towel. Then there was the orange-red flare that filled his vision and the boom of the exploding sticks of dynamite. His windshield shattered into his face from the concussive force.

She put the fragment down and taking the towel from around her and unwrapping the other one from her wet hair, she got dressed. Marcia Mathers came into the kitchen area—mostly a jury-rigged stove that had been thrown out and a coffee maker—where he was preparing breakfast for both of them. Her hair was wet from her recent shower and she smoked an unfiltered Marlboro. She wore tennis shoes, jeans, and a sweater top.

"Hash and eggs," she said, chuckling. "Some things don't change."

"I've added paprika," he said, turning off the fire as he stirred the concoction in a skillet.

There were two plates on the one small table and she picked them up so he could spoon out food onto them. There was toast and fresh coffee, too. Essex had turned this corner of the once-thriving refrigerant coil factory into living quarters and more. There was a work bench nearby with parts and tools strewn on it, a blueprint tacked to the wall above it, as well. Also hanging on the wall were three different shoulder holster rigs with specialized silent handguns in each.

Sitting and eating, Essex said, "I got a wig for you and some padding to make you look less, you know."

"What?"

"Voluptuous," he got out. "Recognizable I mean."

"No, I meant what the heck are you talking about?"

"So I can get you out of town," he said.

"I'm not leaving."

"But Graziano's on to you, Marsh."

"He's on to you, too."

"I'm prepared."

"Then prepare me. We both loved him, Book. I want to get his killers, too."

He was going to argue but could see she was in no mood for the hassle. He allowed too that a smart sexy woman who on her own did a gutsy thing like infiltrate the strip club, knowing it was owned by the Laughing Man, then making sure to insinuate herself to him to learn a few of his secrets, well that was certainly not someone you sent packing given the firefight was about to light shit up.

"So what's our next move, sarge?" she said, chewing on the hash and eggs.

"You know that waiting ain't my bag, but they'll make a move. Soon. That smart boy of Graziano's, Kassel, he's like those West Point greenhorn lieutenants we had to suffer in 'Nam. He's read up on his Alexander the Great and von Clausewitz. He's going to bring in the heavy hitter and draw us out to trap us."

She regarded him. "Always thinking and always prepared."

"Let's hope so," he said dourly. "But in any battle, there's always the unexpected factor, that turn of bad luck or roll of capricious fate you didn't account for."

"Seems we're both pessimists." She got up from her seat and picked up her plate and his even though neither had finished breakfast. She put them on the stove as there was no sink.

She turned back to him and her intent was clear in her eyes as she took off her shoes using her feet.

"Look, maybe this isn't such a good idea," he hedged. Because of vocal cord damage from the fire, his voice was coarse and whispery. And at the moment, he was so caught up in conflicting emotions, he could barely talk at all.

"Maybe," she said, unzipping her jeans and stepping out of them. "Most times you've thought of me as a sister. And me, you're my other brother. We've known each other since junior high, Book. The two white trash kids, miserable thief for a father, and that goofy Black kid who always had his nose, appropriately, in a book. We've known too that we've gone back and forth in our feelings for each other." She paused, a solemn look settling on her face, then added. "Charlotte isn't coming back. But don't misunderstand, I'm not pretending I'm her. I'm not trying to take her place."

"I know."

She was close on him now and he leaned forward and gently kissed her mound encased in her lacy black panties. She caressed the top of his head. He looked up at her, his hands on her thighs.

"This might be our one and only time. We might not come out of this whole or alive," she said, her voice as hoarse as his. She touched a tear at the corner of his eye, the scars from the fire on his face. She undid his zipper and straddled him. They made love as the Laughing Man and Kassel planned their executions.

"HOW IS IT YOU CALL YOURSELF a cop, Chastain?" former petty street thug Ronnie Brownlee, who now went by Rahim Katanga, growled. As leader of the Ministers of Praxis, names were everything.

The beefy cop spread his arms wide. "Hey, I'm doing my job here, Ronnie boy."

There was bristling from the other members of the Ministers of Praxis, MPs for short. The two uniformed officers with Chastain, one Black the other white, reacted too. Their hands went toward the hilts of their tethered nightsticks.

The plainclothesman continued. "It's a known fact your little troop here has had run-ins with them Reds," he gestured with his hand as if conjuring up the name. "The Luxembourg League," he finally said, snapping his fingers. "Them."

"They wouldn't kidnap our youth, Chastain," a woman with a bubble afro said.

Chastain gave her an up-and-down, like sizing up a double cheeseburger slathered with bacon and onions. "Y'all say four kids went missing after they attended your propaganda class."

"After school program, policeman," a tall MP emphasized. "We help them with their math and reading skills."

Chastain pursed his lips, biting back a sarcastic comment. "So anyway, these four don't make it home afterward." He consulted his notepad. "But these are teenagers, between 13 and 16 you said." He looked up, a sincere expression on his face. "They could be off smoking reefer or grabbed a car to go joy-riding, doing who knows what they get into at that age."

"Jesus," the woman exploded. "We're calling your boss, Chastain."

He laughed hollowly. "You call on us oinkers only when this kind of shit allegedly happens and you expect the department to be at your beck and call. But any other time you're spitting on us and cursing us out."

"How about you just do your job, man?" Katanga said.

"We're on this," the Black officer answered.

Chastain shot him a withering look. "This matter will be dutifully investigated. Starting with me grilling their parents, a couple of whom, single mothers and all, have records." He and Katanga glared at one another then Chastain exited the storefront office. He was followed by the two uniforms who looked embarrassed.

"I'm calling Councilman Ricks," the woman with the large afro said, stalking toward a dial phone.

Katanga had a different idea.

As a youngster, Graveheart, not a family name, was fascinated by TV western shows like *Have Gun Will Travel* and *The Rifleman*. This was not unusual for a red-blooded American male of that generation as kids were given cap guns modeled on their favorite lawman's six-shooter or bounty hunter Josh Randall's tricked out sawed-off rifle from *Wanted Dead or Alive*. It wasn't the delivery of frontier justice that fascinated him but the power those masters of the gun wielded on such shows. Seems whatever bit of folksy wisdom they dispensed had more import given their handling of shootin' irons.

Of course the fact that these actors were the leads and therefore the script was tailored to show them as infallible and stalwart, seemed lost on Graveheart. Or more likely he'd long ago learned to ignore such realities. Ever since he was big enough to hold a gun he had. Not only learned to hold them, but use them quite well.

THE LIMESTONE QUARRY WAS AT THE opposite outskirts of town from where the Fuzzy Feather strip club was located, though both off the same highway. The facility was owned by a middle-aged, country-club-going, married church deacon who, in cliché fashion, had tumbled hard, for one of the big-breasted strippers at the Fuzzy Feather. Laugher Graziano had some compromising photos and thus he had no choice but to let his facility be used for the nefarious undertaking underway there this weekend.

The trap was simple. The kidnapped teens were in a van wired with dynamite in the quarry pit. The instructions were relayed by several dope fiends and other such riff-raff along the underworld grapevine. The Silencer was to appear at dawn or the youngsters would be sent to Kingdom Come.

His LTD drove up on schedule and he exited the vehicle. It was cold and he was wearing a full length Super Fly-style patterned coat and broad, flat-brimmed hat with a buckle headband. He had on shades too.

"HOW DO YOU KNOW YOU WON'T be cut down as soon as you step out of your car?" Mathers had asked. "Somebody with a rifle and a scope. What do you call 'em—a sniper?"

He was cleaning one of his guns and looked over at her. "You've read Ralph Ellison's *Invisible Man*?"

She had a hand on her hip. "At your urging, yes," she answered sharply.

"There's a few soul brothers and sisters, skycaps at the airport, housekeepers at a couple of the swank hotels and what have you that I make sure to put a few extra twenties in their Christmas funds each month."

Essex derived income from several patents he owned or had sold for goodly amounts. One of his innovations had been a prototype for a miniaturized walkie-talkie, a kind of phone the size of a cigarette case you could put in your jacket pocket—inspired by those episodes of *Star Trek* he watched as a kid. He started to reassemble his weapon. Essex had invested his monies in such enterprises as a childhood buddy's Black hair care products line and an auto parts chain.

"Yeah?" she said, interested.

"So white folks see them as part of the furniture. They're there, but not there, dig?"

"What're you getting at, Book?"

He smiled. "Figuring some newcomers might be coming to town, I spread extra green around and got the lowdown."

"Yeah?" she said.

"Yeah," he answered.

"You know what they say, Silencer," Graveheart was talking, "I thought you'd be taller." He stepped out from the girders of the elevated office shed made of corrugated metal. Several massive dirt haulers and crane trucks were parked about as well.

"Ain't no stress." The other man was unbuttoning his coat. A slight breeze came up, exposing the shoulder holster underneath, strapped over his black turtleneck. Sweat dappled below the edges of his sunglasses.

The two were about 25 feet apart. They stood down each other on the edge of the main pit, the van with the captured teens at the bottom. The wind ceased. Graveheart, all in black including his Stetson, a six-shooter strapped around his waist gunslinger fashion, spread his boots a bit further apart. He was in his shooting stance.

"This is how it works, hombre," he said. "You live, the kids go free. You die, they die."

"Let's get to it . . . honky."

The Silencer took a step to the right and time slowed as the two readied themselves for the showdown. It was only seconds that went by but each worked to keep their heart from thudding too loudly in their ears. Each took the measure of the other, each with eyes on the opponent's hands and then in the time it took a dog to flick its tail, the guns came out. Both men fired, the Silencer's round zinging past Graveheart's torso.

Conversely, the Silencer dropped his modified gun, clutching his chest as he went over onto his back. Graveheart had grouped two dead center mass.

The out-of-town hitter had assumed he'd feel more elated but it was what it was—killing was becoming as blasé to him as going to the corner store for a carton of milk. How sad. He raised his hand to signal for the toggle switch to be flipped, transmitting a radio signal to the dynamiter to blow up the teens. But nothing happened. He looked over to where two of Laugher Graziano's men were supposed to be crouched down beside the huge tires of one of the big haulers.

He couldn't see them from where he was, but why hadn't they stood up once the Silencer was put down? Smith & Wesson in hand, he advanced. Both hoods were proned out, dead. The remote control device was gone. The Silencer had struck.

"Holster your piece and let's settle this for real, Graveheart," Booker Essex called out. He wore no fancy coat or hat, but was in sans-a-belt slacks and a similar black turtleneck Rahim Katanga, as his stand-in, wore. His gun in its shoulder holster.

Graveheart knew better than to try and spin around, firing. He was fast but not inhumanly so. He'd be dropped in a blink. From above he heard a sound, and glancing up, saw a female head with a puffy afro atop the raised office. In the clean light of morning, he could easily see the glint off her rifle. She'd slept up there through the night.

"I'll be more fair than you," Essex continued as the gunman stepped away from the truck. "You win, you walk away."

Graveheart didn't waste energy or risk distraction with a response or gesture. His hand trembled slightly from excitement. Every sense was breathlessly on edge in him. It was as if each millimeter of his skin were receptors for all the atoms swirling about him. He'd never felt this alive before. This was a challenge.

Nothing happened, then simultaneously both men drew their guns and each fired a single bullet. The bang of Graveheart's pistol was the only one audible. They gaped at one another and Graveheart worked up a crooked smile as he wheeled about and fell over, exhaling one last time.

The teenagers were freed and Katanga and his Ministers of Praxis started to leave. The militant paused and looked back at the Silencer. "You did good, brother."

Essex nodded and they went their separate ways. He still didn't know which of the three had been responsible for the bomb. He wouldn't rest until he found out.

BERT CHASTAIN HAD A BIG GRIN on his mustachioed face as the foxy blonde lead him by his erect penis to one of the happy alcoves after his steam. After the deaths here at the Fuzzy Feather and the subsequent newspaper investigation, Laugher Graziano had been forced to sell the establishment. Not much was known about the buyer but he'd retained a number of the girls who'd worked their under the old management—and re-opened the upstairs VIP section as well. One of those chicks was this knock-out called Ginger Strawberry who had his stiff johnson in hand leading him.

"Baby, I can't wait to get down with you."

"Me either," she grinned, looking back at him.

In the alcove the blonde sat him down on a built-in bench. He now sat on the towel he'd had around his waist. She kneeled before him, Chastain's erect member quivering. That feeling and his hard-on faded fast as an arm went around his neck and the cold muzzle of a modified .32 pressed against his temple.

"Essex," he wheezed.

"Listen to me, asshole," the Silencer said to the suddenly uncomfortable and vulnerable nude man. "I knew sooner or later you'd come around for your usual taste," he began.

"I'm a cop, Essex, if you kill me they'll hang your Black ass for sure."

The Silencer squeezed harder, choking his captive. "Don't kid yourself, Chastain. As shitty as you are, won't too many of your fellow blue on blues get too worked up about your demise."

"Look, I already told you," Chastain said, his voice cracking some. "I had nothing to do with planting that bomb."

"Shut up. For now you're of value to me. Make sure you let the other scumbags like you, the vice cops on the make, the robbery-homicide boys getting their cut, that the Fuzzy Feather is open for business. Let the word go out to the crooked city council members, judges, all of them, got me Chastain? Tell 'em they get a discount."

"What the fuck are you up to?"

"What my lot in country would have called reconnoitering."

Chastain understood. "You want dirt on them. You got this joint bugged."

Essex released his hold and tapped the bent cop twice, hard, on the cheek. "Now you're getting smart. And just in case that rat brain you call a mind is thinking of crossing me, you should know I'm just taking over what the Laughing Man started."

If it was possible, Chastain's eyes got wider. He'd done all sorts of activities and had certain conversations over the years at the Fuzzy Feather—activities that could get him fired and conversations that would get him federally indicted.

"Looks like I got no choice. I'll be your Huckleberry . . . for now."

"Good boy," Essex said, disappearing into the passage behind the trick panel in the wall he'd come out of to surprise the cop.

Marcia Mathers had stood before the two in her short robe and heels, though she'd tied the robe shut. "I'm the manager here now, so you'll report to me. We clear?"

An uppity, devious colored and a broad had him by the short and curlies. What had he done to deserve this? "We're clear."

She walked out and after getting dressed and back outside in the wintery evening, Chastain pulled his coat close. Despite being a stone killer, the idea of not knowing when the Silencer would strike next made him uneasy—very uneasy.

TOBIN AND GAGARIN

TOBIN TOSSED ASIDE HIS HALF-EATEN PASTRAMI on a Kaiser roll. He had sliced onion in his sandwich and had plopped a swath of mustard on his food as well. The paper plate the sandwich and some potato chips were on slid across the small table and fell to the floor. He shot to his feet in the small eating area of the Pear Tree sandwich shop on Kearney, and picked up the soft metal napkin dispenser in a knotted hand. He used this to club about the shoulders of Gagarin who'd covered the distance from the doorway to him in several long strides—silent as he did so, his eyes hard and bright.

The two men grappled and grunted, punched and jabbed. Gagarin backhanded the napkin dispenser out of Tobin's hand. The dented item clattered onto the counter fronting the grill. Tobin was slammed against the soda dispensing machine in the narrow passageway leading to the unisex bathroom and rear exit. The two other patrons in the establishment, a construction worker and a pretty blonde listening to the pre-game banter at Candlestick Park on her Walkman, gaped at the two fighting.

The owner of the eatery, Li Chin Wa, also known as Suzy Li, swore at the two from behind the counter. "You two motherfuckahs need to take this shit outside. Get the fuck out of my place."

Tobin kneed Gagarin in the gut and smashed him in the side of the head with an elbow. But the other man wasn't dazed. Lowering his shoulder, he rammed Tobin into the nearby opposite wall. At that moment re-entering the place was Jorge Vallensuala, Li's boyfriend and the cook. He'd been on a smoke break as Li didn't like to stink up her tidy restaurant with cigarette odor.

"Jorge, no," Li yelled as her man, seven years younger than her and still fit from a regime begun during his stint in San Quentin, charged at the two combatants.

But he wasn't looking to get into the fray and snaking past the two, used his foot on the crash bar to kick open the rear door. He then spun around and, grabbing Tobin by the shoulders of his charcoal gray suit, backed out with him. Gagarin got separated but followed them out as Vallensuala hoped. They were now in a brick-lined alley that slanted behind the shop.

"Have at it," Vallensuala said and went back inside, pulling the door shut behind him.

Tobin and Gagarin, the latter spitting out a clot of blood, stared at one another for a few beats, each sucking in air. Gagarin started forward just as a motorcycle came down the far end toward them. Tobin suddenly stuck out an arm, clotheslining the helmeted rider who was upended from his bike. The 750 cc Yamaha skidded along the asphalt and stopped against the side of a Dumpster, motor running.

The rider, a thin individual, tried to sit up. "The fuck is wrong with you, man?" he said, his helmet askew on his head.

Tobin took hold of him and rolled him into Gagarin's legs, entangling the two for the time it took him to reach the Yamaha.

"What the hell is wrong with you guys?" the rider exclaimed as Gagarin, down on his palms, worked to get himself back on his feet.

But Tobin had got the bike upright and straddling it, revved the handle's accelerator while simultaneously clicking it in gear with his foot. He roared off, the rider and Gagarin chasing him.

"That's my brother's bike, you bastard," the rider said as he ran. He took off his helmet and threw it at the thief. The helmet hit

Tobin in the back but didn't upset his balance. He got to the opposite end of the alley and made a left onto Market, heading east. Seconds behind him came the other two.

"You know that dude, don't you?" The rider clamped a hand on the arm of Gagarin's light windbreaker. He also had on jeans, a cotton patterned shirt and steel-toed work shoes that showed a lot of scuffing.

Gagarin smiled thinly at the rider and at four inches taller and at least 40 pounds of muscle larger, shook off his hand casually. Gagarin stalked about and saw a delivery van across the street, the kind with a sliding side door. It pulled up and double-parked in front of an office building. The rider was also looking around, for a cop. A trolley car heading west clanged along its tracks in the middle of Market Street.

Gagarin got in the delivery van while its driver wheeled his packages on a dolly toward the office building, the entrance facing Market. He looked back wide-eyed and open-mouthed as Gagarin sped off in his van, which had been pointed west. The radio was on and Johnny Bench was making a quip to his co-broadcaster Jack Buck as the players warmed up on the field at Candlestick. It was the third game in the "Battle of the Bay" World Series, the Oakland A's versus the San Francisco Giants.

Gagarin goosed the pedal and, tires screeching, crashed through the wooden barrier arm seconds ahead of the clanging streetcar. He could hear passengers gasp and shout as he sped past. The front of the trolley clipped the rear edge of the van, knocking Gagarin sideways, causing him to fishtail into a Toyota. The driver of that car stomped on the brakes, trying to avoid a collision with another vehicle. Tires smoked as brakes squealed and the delivery van zoomed off, the Toyota finally skidding to a stop.

Up ahead Gagarin spotted Tobin on the motorcycle. As he'd hoped, the man hadn't heard the commotion behind him or if he had, was concentrating on getting away and had ignored the disturbance. He was also obeying the traffic laws so as not to be noticed for excessive speed. Conversely, Gagarin ran a red light, causing a produce truck driver barreling through the intersection to bleat its horn—he barely avoided a collision. Suddenly the wheel jerked in Gagarin's hands and at first he assumed he had a flat. But a glance to his side saw a lowrider Monte Carlo, Big Daddy Kane blasting from the interior, swerve into the side of the van and both vehicles swayed and shook. He swore.

An earthquake was roiling the landscape. Buildings shook and several pedestrians fell to the cracking sidewalks. Drivers pulled their cars to the curb or slowed considerably. Gagarin, his mouth clamped tight in determination, kept driving, even though he was sliding back and forth on the roadway. He fought the steering wheel for control of his stolen vehicle, nearly clipping another car. But he was past the tangle of congealed cars and trucks behind him at the intersection of Market and Van Ness. Bench and Buck weren't on the radio now; only static filled the airwaves.

Almost to Gough, the quake continued rumbling and somewhere nearby Gagarin heard concrete and steel rending and tearing. Inwardly he counted less than 20 seconds and then the upheaval seemed to subside. An older driver trying to motor his preserved 1966 Mustang seemingly had experienced a heart attack and lost control of his car. The Ford skipped onto the sidewalk, frozen pedestrians re-animated and diving for safety. The Mustang sheared a water hydrant from its base and his car plowed into the front of a trendy dress shop, destroying the plate glass window and the posed mannequins therein. Car alarms went off and dogs barked. A geyser of water cascaded from the hole left by the absent hydrant, splashing good Samaritans attending to the injured driver. A mannequin in a sequenced dress was splayed across the now convex shaped hood of the Mustang, steam from the ruined radiator rising over the tableau as if this were a part of a post apocalyptic photo shoot.

Tobin had managed to remain upright on the motorcycle but a refrigerated produce truck jackknifed in the roadway, avoiding an accident with cars that had stopped due to the dead traffic lights. Tobin glanced behind him to see vehicles oncoming, but slowly. Noticeably, there was a van moving faster and it didn't matter he couldn't yet make out the driver. He knew who it was.

Tobin revved the motorcycle and took off, intending to get around the end of the truck, through the gap between its rear and the curb. But before he could reach the opening, a cracked lamppost fell over onto the top of the truck. A severed power line crackled and sparked. There was still a large enough area to get through though he'd have to walk his bike as now some people were out of their cars and walking around in the street, relieved and disoriented.

"Hey, stop that thing," a motorcycle cop ordered Tobin. He'd roared up on his service-issued Kawasaki as if from nowhere. "Can't you see we have an emergency situation here?" he said indignantly. He maneuvered close to Tobin, glaring at him, and pointing at the ground.

Tobin nodded, straddling the idling motorcycle. So did the officer, blocking his path.

"Let me see your license," he demanded.

Tobin smiled, clicking the clutch into first gear. Simultaneously, he twisted the accelerator while also holding down the brake lever.

The officer glared at him and reached for his holstered .357 Magnum.

He released the brakes and the Yamaha whooshed out from under him, rearing back yet gunning forward nearly vertically upright. The machine struck the motorcycle cop. The bike bowled him off his own motorcycle before the Yamaha's engine quit. The bike fell over too. The officer began to sit up, intending to level his gun at Tobin. But the other man was moving fast and kicked the downed cop full in the face. Tobin went back over again, and another kick to the side of his helmeted head had him moaning and reeling.

The officer's revolver in his hand, Tobin turned and fired two rounds into the windshield of the van that was honing in on him less than 200 feet away. The windshield blowing out from the gunfire, Gagarin ducked and veered off. The delivery van's rear ties smoked as he braked, then he stalled the engine as he hadn't taken the clutch out of gear. Somehow Gagarin had not hit any other vehicle or object, though the van was now cocked sideways on Market Street, the front end less than three inches from the passenger door of a Camaro.

Tobin ran north and Gagarin abandoned the van to pursue him. A knot of pedestrians clotted before him as someone fainted and civic-minded pedestrians fluttered about seeking to help. Gagarin moved quickly around them, nearly knocking a heavyset woman to the ground.

"Asshole," she yelled, flashing the finger at him.

He barely noticed his nicked collarbone where one of the bullets had grazed him. His blood stained his shirt collar. But there were other pedestrians dazed or comforting one another, some with injuries, so he didn't stick out as he went on. Several people had witnessed Gagarin assaulting the cop, but given there were more immediate needs in the aftermath of the earthquake, Gagarin calculated it might take an hour before an APB was issued for Tobin. Time enough for him to find the man and finally settle this after all these years.

He walked on, knowing he had to conserve his energy. It wouldn't do to run. There was also the reality his quarry was armed, and should he jog past some recessed doorway he could get his head blown clean off.

Several blocks ahead Tobin rushed down a side street looking first into a hair salon. The mostly female clientele and staff were standing about talking about the quake while one staffer swept up the broken bottles that had fallen from their shelves. A few of the women had on plastic aprons, and some in curlers having been under the hair dryers. The Magnum tucked uncomfortably in his side waistband under his buttoned coat, Tobin attempted to hide the bulge with his hand over the area as if he'd hurt his hip. He moved past the women and two doors down saw the man he'd been after.

He was a forty-plus individual in a brown suit carrying a slim attaché case. Tobin had spotted him half a block back, and watched when he'd turned off on the street they were on now. The man apparently had been looking for a pay phone as he now stood before a shell-type model attached to a pole set in a space between two buildings. His attaché case rested against his lower leg as he spoke into the handset.

"Hello, hello," he repeated. "Is there an operator there? Hello?" He turned at the presence of Tobin, the handset a few inches from his ear. "I got a dial tone but now all I hear are other voices on the line." He held the instrument toward Tobin for him to hear. Tobin brought the pistol up and clubbed the man into unconsciousness. He put the gun into the attaché case and using a fireman's carry, took the man to an overgrown grassy area behind the salon.

Tobin got the brown suit off the man and having stripped out of his gray one, got in the pilfered clothes. He'd picked this individual as they had, he'd estimated, roughly the same build. The sleeves were a bit short on the coat but he wasn't looking to make the cover of GQ. A woman in a tight skirt and dark stockings came out of the back door of the shop, talking into a mobile phone the size of a walkie-talkie.

"Brad, have you reached the daycare?" She was intent in her conversation and it was several moments before she glanced around. She gasped at seeing the man with the bloodied head lying on his back in his briefs and T-shirt, his shoes beside him.

The woman frowned, wondering if he'd had a stroke or nervous breakdown due to the quake as she could also see the charcoal gray suit near him on the ground as well. She continued talking to her husband over the phone as she bent down to assist the man in his underwear.

Tobin made his way down to the end of the side street and began walking diagonally across an empty lot of weeds, dirt and trash that on its far end would put him on Fillmore. He looked around and didn't see Gagarin among the people behind him, but he knew better than to become complacent. Residents and business owners were out of their apartments and shops as they discussed the quake and inspected exteriors for damages. Fire truck and ambulance sirens filled the air as Tobin stepped onto Fillmore and continued in a northern direction.

He walked past a small market and could hear the restored broadcast over the radio coming from within.

"Chuck, we're getting reports that part of the Bay Bridge has collapsed. And there may be a fatality as a result."

"That's terrible news, Angela," Chuck said.

Tobin continued past and was coming to a storefront that was partially caved in, yet on either side of it the structures were undisturbed. Two men of differing ethnicities in orange and saffron-colored robes and wrappings were trying to leverage a good-sized statue of the Buddha through the opening of what had been the picture glass in the store front. One was bareheaded and bald and the other wore a Giants baseball cap. In the door-frame of the entranceway, a load-bearing beam had fallen and was lodged there, blocking access and egress.

"Brother, could you help us, please?" the man with the baseball cap asked Tobin.

He was going to ignore the request and walk on but a patrol car was rolling slowly from the opposite direction down the street. He didn't think the man he'd robbed for his suit had gotten to the police yet, but he best look like a concerned citizen to blend in, he reasoned. He told the monk or adept or whatever the hell he was he'd give them a hand.

Tobin put the attaché case against the building and helped the men get the plaster statue out of the wrecked shop. It wasn't so much heavy as awkward. This was a custom-made Buddha. Part of the sculpture included an open book in the cross of the spiritual teacher's legs. The Buddha's right arm was raised at a right angle to its body, flashing a two-fingered peace sign. There was a drift of rubble and glass cluttering the front of the shop.

"That's it, my good brother," the baseball fan said.

Sweating, the three managed to wrangle the statue through the opening and rested it on the pile of debris. Inside the shop, various spiritual and self-help books were scattered about the checkered linoleum from where they'd exploded off the shelves during the quake. The reading Buddha had sat facing out in the window on a pedestal with a marble top. Putting a hand on the Buddha's head for support, Tobin climbed back out of the shop to stand for a moment next to the statue, which was about five feet tall. He glanced down the street and could see a man approach on a bicycle. The form looked familiar. Sure enough the rider was Gagarin.

The SFPD officers had halted their car and were idling the vehicle in the middle of the street. A man was talking to the cop on the driver's side. Gagarin came to a stop several yards south of the shop. There were people out in the street so he didn't seem out of place.

"I think we can take it from here, brother," the robed man in the baseball cap said, sticking out his hand.

Tobin exchanged shallow pleasantries with the two, shaking their hands. He started off, carrying the attaché case with the stolen police gun in it. He didn't need to look around to know that Gagarin was plodding, slowly no doubt, after him as the street ascended gradually. He heard the crackle of the radio in the patrolmen's car and wondered if that was about the attack on the motorcycle officer. He maintained a steady pace even as the street got steeper. *One foot in front of the other*, he told himself, taking in air through his mouth.

End of the first block, then another, then a bend in the street and now he wasn't in the line of sight of the cops. But gunshots carried. Maybe he'd get lucky and there would be another siren to mask the sound should he get a chance to turn around and blast Gagarin. More distance was covered. Maybe by now they'd moved on, called away to help where the cornice of some building fell away, crushing some hapless senior citizen splat on the sidewalk. A quick over his shoulder glance told him Gagarin was peddling not more than four yards behind him—like Tobin waiting for his opportunity to pounce, but needing to be far enough away from the law.

At a small intersection with stop signs for the east and west directions, a car came along with its turn signal blinking. Tobin was close and he ran toward the vehicle, removing the Magnum from the attaché case, papers and file folders spewing from it as he let the case drop away. He rushed to the side of the car, startling the driver, a woman with wild, bushy hair. He leveled the gun on her.

"Oh shit," she screamed, the driver's side window partially down.

Seeing the gun, Gagarin had already veered off, peddling furiously for the far sidewalk and a few trashcans in case Tobin was reckless enough to shoot at him—authorities in earshot or not.

Tobin gestured with the gun and told the woman to get out of the car. She did. Only she was so frightened she hadn't set the brake and the car, a stick, began to drift backwards in neutral

He swore and began running after it. But he was suddenly struck from behind by an object and he tumbled onto the street, barely getting his arm up in time to prevent landing on his face. He skinned his forearm raw beneath his now torn coat and shirtsleeve.

Tobin still held the gun but as he got himself turned around on the ground, Gagarin was already airborne. He came down like a pro wrestler, planting an elbow in his gut as hard as he could.

"Ughh," Tobin exhaled as the wind was knocked out of him. Momentarily he went weak in his limbs and Gagarin wrestled him for the Magnum. The trash can he'd thrown at Tobin rolled away, its contents spilling all about. The rolling car same to a stop, the rear end softly smacking into a parked Hyundai Excel.

Gagarin tried to gouge out Tobin's eye and the other man struck him on the side of his head with the barrel of the gun.

"Police, police, hey, I need assistance," the woman was yelling as she ran back the way they'd come.

Neither man could afford to be arrested. They stopped pummeling each other and got off the ground. Tobin was still holding the Magnum. He rushed forward and jamming the barrel in Gagarin's side to muffle the retort, pulled the trigger. Only Gagarin had put his hand on the gun to deflect it and as the hammer fell, it clamped on the fatty part of the side of his hand. He screamed and punched Tobin in the face, wrenching the gun loose at the same time, the thing hanging from his hand.

Gagarin got his other thumb on the hammer, pulling it back and releasing his hand. But Tobin grabbed at the gun while wrapping his other arm around Gagarin's shoulders. That's when the dog attacked. It was a Doberman pinscher and the animal bit down on Gagarin's hand holding the .357.

Gagarin grimaced, involuntarily letting the gun go as the dog chewed on his meat and muscle. The weapon clattered as it hit the asphalt.

Tobin laughed, running away as fast as he could though he limped now.

"Come, Brucie, come," a woman commanded.

Brucie the dog did as ordered, returning to the side of a voluptuous woman in a school girl's short pleated plaid dress, thigh high fishnet stockings, and heavy boots. Her starched white shirt was immodestly unbuttoned revealing the top of a lacy black bra. Her dog collar matched Brucie's.

A siren cut through to Gagarirn despite the pain of his bleeding, pulsing hand.

"That'll teach you, you gun-loving fascist extra Y chromosome swine," the woman shouted, pointing an accusatory black nailed finger at him.

He stared at her open-mouthed and briefly considered picking up the gun and shooting her dog. He was a good shot with either hand but the image of being cut down in a fusillade of gunfire by the police overrode his desire for retribution—at least so far as Brucie was concerned. Fatal injury to Tobin was another matter altogether. He also ran away.

The two took parallel paths partly along residential streets heading further north, toward the water. Soon back on a commercial street, Tobin went into a record shop when he spotted another patrol car on the thoroughfare. He busied himself looking through used rock LPs in a bin as the car drove past. He paused once, staring at an album of a cartoonish fox face in a top hat looking out at the viewer. The fox was winking at him. Over the shop's speakers the news played about the aftermath of the earthquake. The shop itself seemed to have suffered little damage save for hundreds of spilled cassette tapes and a large crack in one wall.

"All right, Chuck," a woman announcer was saying, her voice grave. "Not only do we have the tragedy of the collapse of the Cypress section of the Nimitz Freeway in Oakland, we can also confirm several buildings in the San Francisco Marina District have been badly affected."

The newscaster continued. Tobin exited the shop, the patrol car having gone past

Gagarin got his hand cleaned and bandaged by a paramedic who motioned him over as she was helping carry an elderly woman on a stretcher out of a Victorian-style fourplex. He told her a dog was loose and had attacked him. He thanked her when she was finished and went on. On part of a block he could see diners at tables through intact restaurant picture windows and two or three doors away, glass and wood and concrete could be scattered about from damaged structures.

Walking on Tobin saw trendy shops and eateries that seemed to evidence no sign of the quake, though he could hear snatches of conversation about the event spilling into the street. Coming out of a narrow street onto the Marina District, damage to buildings and the sidewalk was apparent. He faced an old-fashioned diner set back on at an angle on a gravel lot. The neon sign on metal stilts atop the establishment declared the name MARTY in large lit red neon Gothic letters. Seen beyond the sign in the middle distance was the Golden Gate Bridge. Behind the diner was a wharf.

There were several police, fire, and paramedic personnel and their vehicles around as the injured or shaken were tended to by the professionals. There were also rescue personnel searching and for anyone trapped beneath rubble, dealing with distraught people over their lost pets, and the like. In the near distance firefighters were putting out a blaze from what was left of a two-story warehouse. Tobin scanned the area, smiling, figuring out his next moves.

A WIND KICKED UP BUT GAGARIN ignored the chill as he walked closer to Marty's, his thin windbreaker flapping about his sturdy frame. He stopped, his head jerking around, inhaling and tasting the air. He knew the other one was close. Suddenly Tobin sprung from a thatch of shrubbery and tackled him.

Tobin wrapped his forearm around Gagarin's neck, and snagged Gagarin's wrist and twisted it behind his back with his other hand, and started dragging him backwards. But Gagarin swiveled his hips and bent forward, trying to throw Tobin over his shoulder. This didn't work but with him on his back the two fell to the earth, continuing their scrapping.

"Hey, hey you two," an officer called out. He ran forward, unholstering his .357. Another cop was not far behind him. He was with the K-9 squad and had a muscular German shepherd galloping easily on a leash ahead of him as he'd been using the dog to sniff for survivors.

The combatants broke apart. Gagarin couldn't believe the bad luck he was having with dogs.

"Go get 'em, Bear," the officer told the animal as he released the restraint.

Bear the dog leapt forward and into the brush in a shot, the two members of the SFPD running behind the canine.

Ahead of them was the dock and Tobin and Gagarin, running side-by-side, made for it. A shot from one of the cop's pistols tore into planking at their heels.

"Be careful," the K-9 officer yelled. "You'll hit Bear."

Bear's sharp teeth almost took a chunk out of Gagarin's lower leg. The dog did tear his pants, exposing a tattoo on Gagarin's calf, the head of a red-eyed crow. Arms pumping like Olympic runners, as one the two dove off the dock and into the cold, dark water. Bear was well-trained and stopped at the edge of the dock. The two cops arrived, guns pointing as both shined their Department-issued flashlights onto the Bay.

"See them?" one said

"No. And why don't we hear any splashing around?"

"Hell if I know."

Bear too looked out on the water, panting.

The patrolmen moved their lights back and forth on the surface of the calm water. The officers were convinced that somehow the two men must have swam under the dock without making noise. A while later a patrol boat prowled about without spotting any sign of them either. Hours later there was a report of two wet, bruised men, one in workingman's clothes running about a half block ahead of the one in a torn suit. The man in the suit was chasing the other man across the Golden Gate Bridge, through the nighttime traffic on the span. The bridge had apparently not suffered structural damage and hadn't been closed post-quake. They were heading toward the Marin County side of the world-renowned bridge. Eyewitnesses reported the man in the torn suit was carrying a hatchet.

MATTHEW HENSON
AND THE TREASURE OF
THE QUEEN OF SHEBA

ETHIOPIA, 1928.

Italian Infantry Sergeant Piero Labreza cleared the thicket carrying a World War I era Beretta submachine gun. Finger on the trigger, he scanned the terrain before advancing into the open, walking across the hardpacked ground toward a raised platform hewn from basalt on top of which stood a series of obelisks of varying heights, one of them as tall as a four story building. On these stelae were carvings of images and words which, even this peasant's son understood bore import. Behind the obelisks was a terraced pyramid which sat in a shallow depression in the earth.

"The captain was right," he uttered, awed at his surroundings.

Shifting his attention back to the task at hand, he proceeded in search of the stranger who'd taken out two of his patrol. Originally, the orders had come down to travel from their outpost in Eritrea and cross the border into this sector of Ethiopia. Given the precarious relationship between the two countries—fascist led Italy being a colonial occupier in the Horn of Africa—this was supposed to be a secret retrieval expedition. So, a stranger aware of their presence was not a good thing on several levels.

A figure darted out from behind an obelisk and ran toward the pyramid. Instinctively the soldier sergeant rattled off a several rounds from his weapon, but the man was gone. Yet, where? He hadn't seen him go up the steps to the pyramid's doors. Warily he went onward, realizing the captain would have him skinned him alive for disobeying orders of not killing the man. But what was he supposed to do? How the hell was he going to bring him back alive? At least, alive enough to answer questions.

The sergeant licked parched lips. The captain had ordered his platoon to split off to find and capture this man. All they knew was he was Black, his nationality undetermined, though the consensus was—from brief glimpses of the big shouldered mustached man— he was not Ethiopian. Kenyan, maybe? But something about him suggested he wasn't that, either. Whatever. The plan was to bring him back to camp, torture the bastard, find out who he worked for, then kill him and leave the body out to be eaten by nature's four-legged predators.

"We mean you no harm! Surrender now, you know you're outnumbered."

"Really?" came the distant reply also in Italian, though not as fluid. "You don't want revenge for the death of your comrade? I certainly would."

Smart man, the sergeant reflected as he looked up at the pyramid. From what the captain had told them, this pyramid wasn't used for burials like in Egypt. And unlike churches in his homeland—ornate, with Rococo flourishes reflecting their Baroque roots—this red stone ziggurat was composed of several tiers, rising some four stories then leveled off to a flat area. Here and there were also window openings. Atop the flat area was a sort of miniature three-sided pyramid that maybe was a story and a half.

Taking a deep breath, he mustered confidence. What with his sub-machine gun, extra magazines and the two grenades, he'd bring this buck back and earn the admiration of his commanding officer. It was about time he was awarded a better rank, wasn't it? This place was called Alexum and had remained long hidden from outsiders' eyes according to his captain. Up the flight of steps to the wooden double doors he paused, listening. He then used the barrel of his rifle to open the already ajar door and, crouching low, stepped quickly into the dark interior.

Inside the vaulted chamber, he could discern shapes, some sunken, others in relief, carved into the floors and walls. Easing forward, he passed through a shaft of light streaming in from a high window. Then a whistling and before he even fully registered the sound, his hand was impaled by a knife.

"Dammit," he swore, lifting his gun hand to see it wasn't a knife, but some sort of five-pointed star, each triangular segment a sharp-edged blade. His hand throbbed. But there was no time to deal with that. Footfalls had him whirling around. Orders be damned, he let loose another burst of bullets. But, again, his target disappeared. He cautiously stepped forward, and was struck hard in the face by the bottom of a boot.

The assault bowled him over and the owner of that boot, Matthew Henson, one of the first men to reach the North Pole, landed upright after his flying kick. Henson smashed his fist into the bridge of the soldier's nose as he tried to aim his gun. This staggered him, blood staining the man's lower face. In a blur of Henson's hands, the firearm went clattering and briefly airborne, the soldier wound up on his back on the floor.

"Don't worry," Henson said in English, smiling down at him, "you won't be in pain long."

"The hell are you—" the sergeant began, but wasn't able to finish as again Henson's foot lashed out. This time it was two vicious blows to the downed soldier's head, knocking him out. Dressed in worn khakis and a blue sweat-stained cotton work shirt, sleeves rolled up past his elbow, Henson hefted the unconscious man over his shoulder in a fireman's carry and off he went.

THE BASE CAMP OF THE ONCE seven—now six—man patrol consisted of a few tents, their armaments, rations, water, and the vehicles they'd driven: an armored car outfitted with tank turret, and an Opel Blitz light truck. The other three sent out to locate Henson had returned more than forty minutes ago. They were now certain Sergeant Labreza must have been fallen at the hands of the mystery man.

"Could be he's hiding in that lost pyramid of yours," suggested the corporal.

Captain Enzo Moretti nodded slightly. When the patrol entered the country, Moretti had told his men their goal was to ascertain the Alexum's existence and once that was done, attempt to secure a specific artifact. The men believed they were doing this on behalf of their superiors or maybe even Il Duce himself. Moretti didn't disabuse them of that notion.

"Hey, you guys! Help me, huh?" a voice cried out.

"Labreza," the corporal said, taking out his holstered Beretta.

"Hold on," the captain advised, hand raised. "Our enemy is clever and might not be alone." He, too, had his sidearm out. "Cautiously, eh? Fan out."

In a clearing, they spotted the sergeant tied to a cross of wood beams splayed on the ground. Deep gouges in the ground indicated he'd been trussed up elsewhere and dragged here. He didn't appear to be hurt beyond his obviously-broken nose. He was clad only in his underwear.

"I got slapped awake and here I was," he explained. "The sonofabitch broke my fingers on both hands." He wiggled his thumbs.

"Oh my, Labreza," one of the men joked, "did you and your dusky companion's lovemaking get out of hand?"

The men cracked up.

"Ha, ha, very funny," Labreza said. "And for your information, that sprite we're chasing is an American."

That shut them up.

Labreza told them what little he'd learned while they got him loose. Meanwhile, Henson was sneaking into camp from another angle. Using one of the grenades he'd taken off the noncom, he pulled the pin and was just about to stick it down the barrel of the turret on the armored car when the soldier's whose leg he'd broken hobbled out of his tent to relive himself.

"He's here, he's over here," he yelled. Fortunately for Henson, the man's pistol was back in his tent. He fell down trying to race back into the tent to retrieve it.

Inside the armored car, several artillery shells ignited when the grenade went off. There was a big boom and a hail of shredded pieces of metal and rubber. A table-sized piece of makeshift shrapnel pirouetting through the air severed one of the soldiers in half as he double-timed back to camp.

Henson was already gone.

Ears ringing, the captain glared at the dead man. Grimly he addressed his other men. "We must hunt him down and finish this. If we can take the American alive, fine. If we have to kill this . . . whatever he is, so be it."

Wordlessly, the remaining four mobile members of the patrol checked their weapons and set off on foot. The one with the broken leg said a prayer for them as he buried the other soldier. The sergeant, still in his skivvies, looked on helplessly.

"This way," Captain Moretti said after he'd consulted a hand-drawn map. He'd paid an Arab trader handsomely for it back at their military outpost in what the Italians called the First Born Colony. The trader claimed he'd drawn it from memory a year before when he'd last come though this area. He'd held onto it until finding a buyer who knew its worth.

By late afternoon the soldiers arrived at the Pyramid of Alexum—said to have been one of several palaces built for Makeda, better known as the Queen of Sheba.

"Magnificent." As if it were an attractive woman, the captain's fingers caressed the symbols on one of the obelisks. He marveled at the significance of this find, lost in visions of glory back in Italy.

"Captain?" the corporal said.

"Right. Look, men, I better tell you the truth. We're not here on orders."

"What?" one asked.

"But, we take care of this impertinent Negro, we will all be rich men, I wager."

The other three traded looks.

"Come, let us be bold." Captain Moretti marched off, his machine gun at the ready.

One of the men shrugged, and followed the captain. The remaining two did as well—if only to exact revenge for the deaths of their mates.

"Looks to be only this one way in," the corporal remarked, hoisting his rifle and fingering his holstered sidearm. They stood in front of the still-open double doors of the pyramid.

"Don't forget, the sergeant had two grenades," Captain Moretti said. At the doors, he crouched down looking for a trip wire across the opening. Satisfied there wasn't one, he rose and went inside.

Looking around, Moretti pointed at one of the privates, "You and I take this floor, you two take the second. There may be hidden chambers, even traps, so be careful."

"You mean traps installed by the ones who built this?" The corporal said, sweeping his hand around.

"Yes," Moretti admitted.

"What were they guarding?'

The captain smiled. "We shall see."

There were stairs leading up, and the corporal and a private named Calabrese ascended them to find themselves on a kind of mezzanine. It appeared there was no way beyond. On one wall was inscribed a large disk that repeated some of the symbols and text found on the obelisks. With the sound of stone scraping against stone, the outer ring began to rotate. An inner ring also started spinning in the opposite direction.

"What should we do?" Calabrese gaped.

"Hold," the corporal said, his rifle held low but aimed at the disk. The rotating stopped. Some of the inscriptions had aligned, but neither man knew what that meant.

"Look," Calabrese said, pointing. A section of the far wall had opened. "Well, do we go in?"

"We don't have much choice." The corporal paused at the opening, looked inside, then stepped through. He turned back to signal the private. "Come on, it's okay."

The private started to follow the path the corporal had taken. Halfway there, the floor dropped beneath his feet and he fell through, swearing then wailed once.

The stones slid back into place.

The corporal gulped and considered running back to the stairs but wondered if he'd make it without falling as well. And if he did, the others would surely brand him a coward.

"Damn." He turned back. There were more inscriptions along the walls. There was also a conference-like stone table built into the floor with modern portable chairs around it. The pyramid was in current use he concluded.

"Hey," he called out in English. "We just want the American. Give him to us and we'll be on our way." A bird landed on the window, chirping merrily. He glanced at it.

"No need to shout, I'm right here."

The corporal wheeled about, firing his rifle, even though he knew he would be too slow. Rounds from the sergeant's confiscated machine gun blistered a ragged diagonal across his torso. The corporal fell forward onto the stone table, a wide-eyed look on his face, then rolled off onto the floor. Henson was on the other side of the table, smoke rising from the barrel of the machine gun he held.

Downstairs, the two heard the commotion and rushed to the stairs.

"Corporal!" the captain called out. He called out again, then ascended, followed by the private. Upstairs, they saw the corpse of the corporal, staring dead-eyed at the ceiling. The captain closed the man's eyelids.

"You think Calabrese went after him?" The private said hopefully, indicating an opening in the wall beyond the table. An opening that hadn't been there moments before.

The captain didn't answer. Ducking his head inside the next chamber, he walked on through. The private shook his head and once again trailed his commanding officer. The two were now in a passageway that somehow allowed sunlight in though neither could detect the source.

"Doesn't look like a way out of here," the nervous private whispered.

"We're coming to another hallway," the captain said, whispering as well. "Be ready."

At the corner they paused. Goaded by his desire to plunder the pyramid's perceived riches, he stepped into the new hallway, his machine gun leveled before him. The two went along until an unfamiliar sound greeted them.

"What is that?"

"Quiet," the captain ordered.

There was a humming beneath their feet. What sounded like gears meshing became evident and a vibration thrummed up through their boots into the legs.

"The hell?" The private panicked, trying to run back the way he'd come, only now the floor went sideways and loomed upward, causing him to fall into the captain. Both men crashed to the floor which continued to slope up, then tilted to one side then the other, keeping them off-balance.

"We have to crawl," Captain Moretti yelled, using his elbows to move forward, pistol pointed ahead. On he went in the gloom, the indirect light having ceased. Seconds later the floor stopped moving. As the two got to their feet, there was a new sound, stone scraping on stone. A hidden door slid open, harsh light causing them to squint. Moretti put a hand up until his eyes adjusted. In that revealed doorway a figure appeared, backlit and unmoving.

"Devil," Moretti hollered as he churned off rounds at the figure. His bullets didn't affect the shadowed man who remained standing and unharmed. Again, he fired, but the panel in the wall slid back in place. Moretti ran to the spot but could detect no creases in the solid surface.

"Let's get out of here, leave this cursed place," the private said.

Moretti dropped his machine gun and grabbed the man, screaming in his face. "You fool. There's a treasure worth millions in this pyramid and I mean to have them."

"*Them?*"

"The three crowns of the Queen of Sheba. Each was said to have been imbued with wondrous properties. One was to have been forged from a rare element extracted from the center of the earth, the second made from an unknown gemstone mined from the Nile, and the third from a glowing rock from space itself."

"That's a fairy tale, Captain."

Moretti backhanded him. "It's true, and they and whatever else this pyramid holds will be *mine*. And mine alone you grape-stomping peasant."

"No, they won't," Henson said.

The captain and the private were again bathed in bright light, this time from the end of the hall. And again, Henson's figure dominated the doorway. Both men fired at him with the same impotent results.

"Mirrors, it has to be," the private declared. Yet no glass had shattered.

The captain was no longer interested in logic. He ran at Henson, emptying his gun until it clicked dry, screaming profanities at the top of his lungs. He went through the image which evaporated into ethereal wisps around him. He found himself in a large space, the walls here rough and unfinished. He looked over his shoulder, but the opening was gone—that wall solid once more. He tossed aside his now-useless machine gun and unholstered his handgun, moving along. His boot stepped on something that yielded and, taking another step, he felt something slither over his boot. He looked down, snakes covered the floor.

But the floor had been barren seconds ago.

Given his background, he absently identified some as Kenyan carpet vipers and African puff adders. Both species were venomous. He started to laugh at the joke of it all as he pumped bullets into the beasts with his pistol until it, too, was emptied. A puff adder coiled around his leg and he snatched it off. But it struck like a bolt and sank its fangs into his forearm.

"Dear God, he is the Devil, he's commanded all the snakes in the world to come *here!*" More of the serpents twined about him, and withering down into the pile of the hissing creatures, numerous sets of fangs latched onto him, filling him with so much more venom. Captain Moretti soon gratefully succumbed to the eternal blackness.

Uncontested, the private was allowed to stumble out of the Queen's pyramid. An armed Matthew Henson was there to greet him. The private dropped his gun and held up his hands.

"When you get back to your base," Henson began in Italian, "that is, if you can find your way back, tell them your captain went mad with greed and killed the others when you found out he'd lied to you. Or make up whatever story you three want to, I don't care as long as none of you try and come back *here*."

"I don't—" he began.

"If you think your superiors will believe the truth, go ahead. If you don't get court martialed or shot for desertion."

Finished, Henson left the bewildered soldier and picking up the man's gun, was soon swallowed in the shadows of the pyramid. Thereafter he ascended stone steps at the back of the ancient edifice to the flat area and the smaller pyramid there. A sweep of wind and dust kicked up, though the air had been still moments before. The wind soon subsided, and standing before Henson were three figures in ceremonial garb.

They spoke to him in Amharic which he didn't understand, but their import was clear. One of them handed Henson a wooden chest the size of a desktop radio. He made to refuse the gift but the three insisted. He dipped his head in thanks, and departed.

Eventually, he got back to Addis Ababa and the hotel where he'd first received the message from his buddy, decorated WWI aviator, jazzman, and boxer Eugene Bullard. Somehow at his club in Paris, Bullard got word about the trader and the sale of his map to the captain. Knowing it would take him too long to get there himself, he cast about and found out Henson was in this part of the continent on another matter and had reached out.

"This arrived for you while you were away, Mr. Henson," the desk clerk said in his crisp English.

"Thank you." He took the telegram and, unfolding it, read the brief message.

Matthew Henson—needed immediately back in Harlem, USA—matter of life and death—money no object.

He cocked an eyebrow reading the name of the sender. Henson refolded the message and asked the clerk to charter a flight back to the States.

TACOS DE CAZUELA
CON SMITH & WESSON

Augustina "Gus" Blanchard, M.D. passed under a stand of trees with drooping limbs into the plaza area. It was past eleven p.m. and remained hot and humid, the air still like a rundown watch. At least there wasn't the intense whiteness of sunlight bouncing off the sparkling concrete, only the warm yellow circles of overhead sodium lighting. Momentarily she had to focus to retain her bearings, reminding herself why she was here and steel her will on what was yet to be done. What *had* to be done. She removed her earbuds, looping the thin cord around her neck. Her cotton shirt clung to her damp back, the coolness of the cloth against her skin keeping her centered. Before her there was a 20-something couple at the taco truck, the man with a Cubs cap on backwards. Both wore baggy cargo shorts and limited-edition sneakers. The young woman scrolled through her smartphone while she half-listened to her boyfriend rattle on about how the start-up he was part of was going to establish a recognized niche in the gaming industry.

"It's all about the IP, babe. We've got some iconic characters populating our shit. Disney won't have anything on us," he chuckled.

"For sure," she muttered, amused at something on her screen with its harsh light detailing her pronounced cheekbones.

Their order was called and the two walked off to a clutch of nearby illuminated lunch benches. Other people clustered there too as the free concert in the adjacent park had ended not long ago. Their food had been deposited on cheap paper plates that required them to hold the goods with two hands.

Blanchard stepped up to the order window. As she understood it, it didn't matter whether or not she used the name "Jesse" with this older man looking down at her through the opening in the plexiglass, a glow from inside illuminating the vehicle's interior fluorescents along the ceiling. Though that was the name in flowing script alongside the mobile kitchen, "Jesse's Tacos." He didn't look like a "Jesse," but then, she wasn't here about the name that may or may not be on his business license. This individual was balding and pleasant-faced. He reminded her of a younger version of that actor she saw now and then when, after any one of her demanding shifts, she zoned out binge watching *The Big Bang Theory*. Bob Newhart, that was the guy she concluded. Jesse in his short-sleeved white shirt and old school black frame glasses looked like an accountant, not a man who dealt in . . . well, what it was he dealt in.

"What can I do for you, ma'am?"

"I'd like the special," she said self-consciously though no one else except the cook, his broad back to her as he was cleaning the grill, was within earshot. At least she hoped that was the case. Was this an elaborate sting? Was she willingly putting her career and freedom in jeopardy as some division of the Chicago Police Department listened in on one of those too-damn-small and too-damn-clear digital devices? There had been these exposes in the past about secret groupings with the department such as off the books interrogation locations. How well could a trauma surgeon take trauma she wondered.

"What special would that be?" The placid demeanor didn't change but there was a brief flintiness in those eyes. There was a tattoo on the back on one of his hands. It was a ship's wheel, like something from a schooner two centuries back.

"The tacos de cazuela," she answered as she'd been previously instructed.

His head dipped slightly with a nod and he turned it sideways to address the cook. "You get that?"

"Yeah," came a grunt as a thick hand reached for the ingredients along with a comal-style pan. "Chicken livers with that?" were the only other words from him.

The supposed Jesse had turned back and raised a questioning eyebrow at her.

This flummoxed her for a few seconds. What was the right response? Was this a test to see if she was a cop? "Sure," she settled on.

"Okay. That'll be a hundred and fifty even."

She handed over twenties and fives. As she waited for her order, Blanchard couldn't help but continually scan her surroundings, nerves prickly. She was used to all manner of gore and carnage in the ER—faces blasted full of glass from auto accidents, gunshot victims bleeding out into a towel pressed on the wound, knives in the head, hell, even an ax buried in a poor bastard's groin. Images and conditions she'd come to grips with as part of the job, part of her duty to set right if she could and, sometimes, accept that their fates were out of her hands as the breath of life left their body forever. A doctor had to learn to compartmentalize or could easily fall into the trap of self-medication various colleagues of hers had succumbed to over the years. Not just losing their license but their sense of purpose. Tonight, though, her gnawing worry had a different origin.

"Tacos de cazuela," the bespectacled man announced, breaking the silence.

"Thank you." With steady hands she took the special, which was passed to her through the opening in a white paper bag, grease staining the bottom.

"Hope you find the order satisfactory," he said.

She didn't know what to say to that so didn't say anything. She walked away briskly, keenly aware of moving from the light into the gloom of night. At a city trashcan she opened the bag and removed a handgun she recognized, a Smith & Wesson 9mm M&P. She crumpled the top of the bag but then hesitated in tossing the contents away. Rather, reaching the perimeter of this section of Millennium Park, she left the bag next to the homeless individual she'd seen on her way in. He was asleep in a fetal position in dirty clothes on some flattened cardboard, a shopping cart of oddball possessions next to him. She paused to assess him, feeling the regular pulse in the big vein of his neck. She moved on, putting the earbud back in place and removing her smartphone from the back pocket of her jeans. She tapped a familiar number on redial and made sure the mic on the coated wiring was unobstructed.

"Any problems at the truck?" said the voice on the other end of the line.

"No. So far, so good," she said, as she continued to walk and talk. "I'm heading back home." She'd stuck the nine into her waistband at the small of her back under the tail of her untucked shirt.

"Nervous?" asked the woman on the other end. "'Cause I sure as hell am."

"Some," she admitted, "but I know how to use that to my advantage."

"Who you talkin' to, Gus? You've long since figured out how to use that kind of energy to deal with all sorts of obstacles. No second-guessing on the operating table. Isn't that one of your favorite sayings?"

"Am I that vain . . . and predictable?"

"Assured, you cutters would say. Of course I'd say you is who you is, baby." There was only a trace of sarcasm in her voice. "Wish I didn't have to work tonight."

"Me too. But at least no getting that good thing of yours means I'll be rested and ready tomorrow."

"Gus, I . . ." began the other woman.

"I know. Love you."

"Me too."

Blanchard ended the call and continued to where she'd parked her car. While downtown Chicago wasn't the hyped and mischaracterized South Side, which did suffer from an inordinate amount of gun violence, a woman alone—and a Black woman of a certain age at that—night or day better be aware of her surroundings no matter what part of the city she was in. But she made it back to her several-years-old Lexus without incident and beeped the car unlocked. Maybe a part of her hoped she'd have been challenged. For what a surprise a would-be mugger would have to shockingly discover the older chick he'd eyeballed as an easy mark had come strapped. Could fill her hand in a whisk like a gunslinger of the Wild, Wild West like the tag line to that rap song by Kool Moe Dee popular when she was a kid back in the day. Comfy on her leather seat and starting the car, she drove off to her apartment, Sarah Vaughan rhapsodizing over the car's speakers.

Morning and she awoke early. Automatically she checked her phone and saw that she hadn't missed any emergency calls. That didn't mean there wouldn't be some reason to summon her to the hospital later, but for now she could pretend she had a day off and it was best to get herself in gear. After a shower and a shave of her legs, she had some orange juice and a piece of seven-grain wheat toast with a single smear of margarine. She packed her exercise bag with her workout clothes and fetched her yoga mat. Blanchard left the gun, slid under the stacked washer-dryer combination. But being the kind of person she was, she'd done her trimming just in case this plan of hers went south. Okay, maybe she was a little vain she admitted. But she sure as hell didn't want to get laid out on the mortician's table and have them do a quick job leaving her corpse with razor burns and cuts.

"Heh," she chuckled mirthlessly at that, setting her alarm and heading out of the door. Getting behind the wheel of her car, earbuds in place, she talked on the phone.

"Anything else you want me to see to before we make our plays?" the woman said.

"I think we've prepared as best we could," she answered, guiding her vehicle away from her building and out into traffic. "Just knowing you're, you know, around is terrific comfort."

"You smooth talker you."

"Later, gator."

"Be safe."

She set the instrument aside. After her workout at the rec center, she checked the time and made her way over to the Wicker Park area. She parked at a pay facility and walked the three blocks to her destination. Her disguise was minimal, an afro wig over her naturally frizzed-out 'do, sunglasses, and bland clothing. Not that she figured her target would recognize her if they passed in the street, but this wasn't a time for any slip-ups. Having prowled this neighborhood previously, she went into the hipster coffee shop named the Queen Bean and, after getting her coffee, was able to get a seat at one of the windows. This afforded her a view of the rehabbed apartment building across the street. Around 11 a.m., out came a youngish brown-hued Latinx in the company of an older white man with silvery hair brushed just so. He was over six feet and was a fit 63-year-old. It could have been a father visiting his daughter but Blanchard knew the deal. They chatted and smiled as they walked along the street, disappearing around a corner. The man was Dr. Broderick Freslan, an oncologist of some renown and chair of her hospital board at Becker Memorial. The woman—Teri Baldwin nee Theresa Ortega—was his girlfriend some 28 years his junior. She was a part-time pharmacist at a

Walgreens and, on her own, could not afford the rent in this building. This and other pertinent facts hadn't been learned from expending shoe leather or perusing public documents, but was the product of gossip from the staff —the charge nurses in particular, especially if you had an insider and bought a round or two at the watering holes they frequented after their shifts.

She crossed the street and waited until the gate to the underground parking swung open to let a car out, she went through and descended the ramp. The disguise too would help given there were surveillance cameras down here aided by the half-light from several regularly dispersed wall scones. She walked confidently along, parking slots marked on the concrete with parallel white lines and numbered to the corresponding apartment overhead. She came to Baldwin's car, a few-years-vintage Camry with a bonded front fender. Freslan might be springing for the rent, but he wasn't so gone he was outlaying money for his squeeze to tool around in a shiny new sports car. Surely, he still had financial responsibilities at home, even though his children were grown and his wife had her own income as a senior exec of a home furnishings company. According to what Blanchard had learned from those drinks she'd bought on more than one occasion, this wasn't the first time the old horndog had squired a younger woman he'd met at a soirée.

Standing close to the car, surgical gloves on, Blanchard took out a prybar a little more than a foot long she'd put in her messenger bag and inserted it under the middle of the bottom of the trunk's lid where the latch was. She wasn't trying to be subtle and, sure enough, having watched a couple of instructive videos on YouTube, she muscled the trunk open. This set off the car's alarm, but she expected the whoop-whooping. No one else was here at the moment and it's not like alarms didn't go off all the time all over the city. People didn't come running like the Lone Ranger as the usual response was to be irritated at the jackass whose car was making the racket. And anyway, she wasn't stealing anything from the junky trunk. She finished and, pushing the lid down, Blanchard was surprised when the lock caught. The alarm ceased.

"Huh, looks like I have a knack," she muttered sardonically. Walking away, she calmly removed the gloves and stuffed them in her bag with the prybar.

"Oh my god, there ought to be a law against those damn things wailing." A woman with green eyeshadow and ostentatious bracelets declared as she went past the moonlighting doctor and head deeper into the garage.

"I know," Blanchard commiserated. She went through the door the complaining woman had come through, before it closed. Blanchard exited the apartment building by the front glass double doors. The sun was now up high and hot, and she was glad to be shorn of the wig back in her car.

"Mr. Raleigh, what day is it?"

"Thursday," the older man replied.

"Day or night?"

He paused, but then answered, "Night. 'Round midnight I reckon."

"Good," Blanchard said, examining the head wound further and taking another look into his eyes with her penlight. She concluded the septuagenarian wasn't suffering from a concussion after his fall at home. "I admire you, Mr. Raleigh. Having the wherewithal to make it here under your own steam. Particularly in the early hours."

"I didn't make it this long by sitting around and fretting."

"I heard that." The doctor applied some antiseptic, and rather than use sutures, she explained to him she was going to use liquid stitches.

"Is that glue you're putting on me, young lady?"

"Yes, sir. Believe me, it's as good as regular stitches but less worry for you. But no showering or getting it wet for two days, okay? Okay?"

"Yes, ma'am."

She kept working. "Now I'm going to write down when I want you back and nurse, ah, what's your name again?"

She leaned toward Blanchard's ear. "Marsh, doctor."

"Nurse Marsh will see to it that we get you home."

"I got here with a hole in my head, didn't I?" he chuckled.

"I know, but I'll feel better if we get you a ride back to your place."

"Dr. Blanchard is always on top of things, Mr. Raleigh," the nurse said.

Given her coloring, it wasn't evident that Blanchard was blushing. Two hours later, after she and the nurse attended to a 10-year-old with a hundred and one temperature and a drunk woman who'd passed out on a ride share driver, the two had gone into the supply closet. Back to the quietly closed door, Marsh, a dark-skinned Black woman with hazel eyes, pushed in the button lock on the knob. As she did this, Blanchard put an arm around her and, tight on her, the two kissed. Marsh took Blanchard's other hand and guided it between her legs. Soon that hand was inside those scrubs.

"Gus, you sure you want to go through with this?" Marsh said between gasps.

"Girl, you know the thrill turns you on."

"Don't be such a smartass."

"I can't help it when I'm with you."

Marsh was nuzzling the other woman's neck. "Losing your license is the least that can happen to you."

"I'm not stopping now. I can't." She paused, eyes intent on her lover. "You can back out, Ursula, you know I wouldn't hold it against you."

"Shut the fuck up." She kissed her again, closing her eyes to hide them tearing up.

BLANCHARD WANTED TO BE FAMILIAR WITH the gun. When she'd first began working the ER, she'd been warned. Not about the horrific wounds and complications bullets caused to the human body she'd encounter. That you could get used to, her seasoned colleagues had advised. Given time, a doctor worth their salt would become inured to the blood making the floor slick and soaking into your garb like spray-painted camouflage. What really got to you was explaining to families who'd brought their loved one in that they didn't make it off the operating table, they were brain dead or they'd be impaired in some way for the rest of their lives. How the wails of anguish often turned to stares of recrimination, that clearly you weren't a good enough surgeon, that your incompetence was what had let them down. That as much as you wanted to offer comforting words to them at any stage of your interacting with the gunshot victim, you best be circumspect. Not only did this help you focus on your task she'd been reminded as a possible saver of life, you didn't want your attempts at kindness coming back to bite you when, and it was when and not if, you got sued.

She'd been interviewed as part of the research the American Medical Association had commissioned on the nature of gun violence. The results of which, along with other such articles, had been published in the Annals of Internal Medicine. Yet as the debate raged on between the NRA pro-types and anti-gun forces, and those who found themselves somewhere along the continuum of being okay with guns in qualified hands but also wanting more stringent gun control laws, Blanchard had become fascinated by the mechanism itself. Like a scalpel, it could aid or take away life. She'd signed up for a class that included "lab" time at a run range. Then she had no other agenda than to alleviate her fear of this mechanical device. To understand it the way she understood setting a broken arm or recognizing the effects of a teenager tripping on ecstasy. Now her desire to familiarize herself with this illicit weapon was for a whole other purpose.

"Wow, that's what they call center mass, right?" She was a dishwater blonde with freckles. Late 40s was Blanchard's estimation.

"I guess," she answered, referring to the target sheet with the concentric ovals and numbers inside the body outline. Blanchard had brought it in from the other end of the indoor range.

"Are you in law enforcement?"

"No," was all she said. She removed the ear muffs she'd put around her neck.

"You have any tips for me? You can see from how I shot I'm new to this."

"Bend your knees slightly. It helps to absorb the impact of the recoil. Why are you here?"

Her lip quavered at the edge as she said, "Us girls have to be prepared, right? It's a big bad world out there."

"For sure. Good luck."

"Same to you."

"It seems this might be a good place to adjourn," Dr. Freslan said, palm tapping the pump top of the hand sanitizer and then rubbing the stuff over his long tapered fingers. "We've had yet another productive meeting."

"Second that," another board member said.

"Bob, you were ready to hit the back nine before you got here," a tallish board member joked.

"You know me too well, Joan."

The people around the conference table scooted chairs back on the industrial carpeting and rose, most gathering up pens and note pads.

"I'll follow up with Richmond on the Treestone inquiry," a bearded man said to Freslan as they exited.

"Great, Randy, let me know."

Freslan and several others made their way downstairs while a few lingered to talk to colleagues on duty or return to their offices there in Becker Memorial. In the parking garage he pointed his electronic fob at his late model Jaguar XJ and got behind the wheel. He'd started sniffling, wondering if a cold was coming on. He considered passing up his pool time at the club but decided he'd chance getting sicker and do his workout anyway. When a man romances a younger woman, he shouldn't just rely on those little yellow pills to do all the work he mused humorously. But God bless the bastard who invented it.

After his session and a steam, as Freslan toweled off, a form appeared in his peripheral vision. He turned staring at the visage of his deceased older brother. That broad smile of his on display, he waved at him from the end of the bench.

"Wallis?" he stammered.

"I'm sorry, what did you say, Brody?"

"Wha—. . . ?" Freslan started, blinking and looking over at Denny Huang, a partner in a white-shoe law firm. He had a foot up on the fixed bench, untying one of his wingtips.

Freslan looked back around but the apparition of his brother was gone. "Nothing, thought I saw somebody I knew but I was mistaken." He chuckled to make it seem light.

"Yeah, that happens," a distracted Huang said as he straightened and began unbuttoning his shirt.

Freslan shook his head as he continued getting dressed. He'd had dreams where his brother was in them, even ones recalling themselves as kids, but imagining him in a waking moment, that was distinctly new. He chalked it up to his age and some form of latent wish fulfillment and drove to his home on the Near North Side. It was a rehabbed mansion dating back to the Gilded Age. His wife was out of town on a business trip and Freslan envisaged an afternoon of smoking a cigar indoors and watching the title fight he'd TiVo'd from the previous week. He'd already exchanged several sexually loaded texts with his girlfriend and planned to be over at her place later. Being an experienced cheater, he'd some time ago began using burner phones with whatever current younger thing had captured his ardor.

By the time he parked in his driveway, he had to dab the back of his fingers against his runny nose.

"God damn it," he muttered as he walked to his door. At least his throat didn't feel hoarse, he reflected. A yellowing splotch on his lawn momentarily was yet another thing raising his ire. Freslan made a mental note to have a talk with his gardener.

"Well, about time," said a voice as he stood on his flagstone walkway.

From his portico, Freslan saw a voluptuous blonde in a see-through negligee and high heels in the doorway. She had a martini glass in her hand and, given her amazing build and beehive hairdo, looked as if she'd stepped off the cover of a paperback novel like the kind he and his buddies would buy from the drugstore in his youth.

"Who the hell are you?" he stammered, more aroused than suspicious. Could this be a trap by his wife to see if he'd bite? Because he hoped to nibble on this babe.

"I'm the girl that's gonna fuck your brains out, honey . . . after I suck you off."

Oh my God, she had a southern accent. Freslan was well-aware he was stuck in place, keys in hand and raging hard-on tenting the front of his pants. This had to be a set-up, he dimly acknowledged. How else could she have gotten past the alarm system? But he knew what he was going to do as he followed the scent of her heady perfume and the heavenly backside barely contained in those lacy panties into the confines of his home. But just that quick he didn't see her once he was inside. He had a more immediate problem. What the hell was he inside of exactly or was he even in anything?

The floor had disappeared, and he now stood in a space between worlds or, at least, that was his impression. He was on a sphere that was connected to other spheres by strut-like formations of varying thicknesses. These spheres were a deep yellow hue and their tentacles tending toward orange. Their surfaces were fissured with black lines, some of which were circular in nature and others zig-zagging every which way. All about him were revolving planetoids and, as a flaming meteorite went past him, he didn't panic. The hurtling rock made a 90 degree turn and started ascending in a space where the laws of perspective seemed not to function. The meteorite exploded in a shower of violet marigolds that, at the center of each, were mouths. Some of these phantasmagoric apparitions were talking in Russian, German, Spanish and Yoruba, which he recognized from a past trip to Nigeria. A bewitched Freslan watched as a particular flower mouth floated sideways to meet a coiling twist of a diamond-like substance. The sparkling coil took on a more recognizable formation, that of a giant, eyeless worm. The creature wound around him, and he was lifted off the sphere. His heart thudded in his throat, yet this was tempered by his curiosity.

"Where am I? What's happened to me?"

"More to the point, what will happen to you?" the worm said via not an oval mouth, but a more human-like one with sparkly teeth.

It was a female voice, but he didn't conclude it was the dream blonde from the porch. This was a voice he knew but he wasn't sure and at the moment couldn't place. "What do you mean?"

"You can make amends," the thing said, its slit eyes boring into him.

"Isn't it a little late for that?" He was surprised he was so straightforward with this being. "And anyway, I balance the scales. I give back in money and volunteering. I do my part."

"How concerned citizen of you."

"Am I to justify my existence to you? A frightener clearly of my imagination?"

"Shit," Blanchard swore softly, the psychoactive was wearing off quicker than she'd wanted. Well that's what you got for concocting a formula with a recipe obtained off the dark web. Blanchard stepped closer to Freslan and took his head in her hands. He shuddered and she couldn't help but smile, hoping that however he was hallucinating what was happening, he was scared. She spoke, "Where's the Ostrander file?

From his drug-affected perspective, the older physician felt the bands of the worm tighten around his rib cage as the head of the thing swiveled about as the mouth became a maw to engulf him. He prayed that his death would be quick. But the beast did not clamp its dripping fangs on his head to feast but rather asked him a question.

"Why do you want to know that?" he asked, his apprehension of the monster fading, though he wasn't sure why.

"Because I asked you, asshole."

"That doesn't sound otherworldly. In fact, just what the hell is going on here?"

The worm's head moved even closer to him, turning so that baleful eye took him in. It said, "I will keep you here for all eternity. Consuming you little by little but you will not die. Indeed you will regenerate, and you will only know endless suffering but no release."

"Bullshit."

Like a bolt, the head was a blur as it latched onto his hand which stuck out between its coiled body. Blood spurted in an arc as his hand was bitten off. A shaft of pain lanced his arm and informed his brain that he'd been horribly violated.

"Now do you understand?" the copperhead said.

"Yes," he stammered. Small orbs of translucence floated in from somewhere and attached themselves to his bloody stump. They pulsed there in place and he saw his veins and muscle tissue in them as that part of his body was regrown.

"The Ostrander file," his tormentor repeated.

"In the warden's office," he breathed harshly, shallowly.

"What?"

"The school on Dearborn. One of the abandoned ones on the South Side."

"Austin Dabney?' the creature said incredulously. "You're lying."

"No, please, I'm not. It's there. Beneath the school is a new structure, an underground facility that's nearing completion."

"A secret testing lab."

"Well, yes," Dr. Freslan said, his lips dry and throat arid. The orb beneath his feet began to shift and, like a radio transmission not coming in clearly, the pavers in his kitchen appeared under his feet then just that quick went away again. "What's been done to me? Have I been drugged?

"You have access to this facility," the worm declared.

Freslan looked about. His surroundings blinked in and out of existence, from the unknown to the familiar and back again. He smacked his lips, wetting them. "Who's done this to me?"

He watched as the giant worm withdrew from him and took root on his kitchen floor—and he understood now he was in his chef-designed kitchen. The magical monster hadn't had him in its grip but he was tied to a chair by duct tape and nylon cord. His hand hadn't been eaten but there was a canvas sack on it, one of the ones he and his wife used for grocery shopping. He looked up and the insect had taken on human form.

"Have you lost your mind., Blanchard?" He snarled. "Not only will I have your license for this, but your freedom too."

She put a gun under his chin and pressed it upward. "Where's your card key, combination or whatever the hell you use to get into the Dabney location?

"Blanchard, you need to stop now, and maybe you'll live past this evening."

"You think you will?"

"Oh, come now, doctor," he scoffed. "You've played your cards. Though I will admit, that was clever. You spiked my hand cleanser, that it? Knowing from past observation I tended to keep the dispenser close, the other one in the center of the table. A mild case of OCD I'll grant you. A psychoactive absorbed through the skin was that it? The girl at the door and all that, imagery implanted through photos and such, I gather."

"Correct. All to get you to talk freely. Which you did."

"But you are done."

"I'm just getting started, doctor." She then shot him in the foot.

"My God, you are mad," he yelled. "The police are probably on their way right now."

"As you've no doubt felt, I've shot you in the fleshy part of your foot. Given the caliber and close proximity, it's fair to surmise the round exited. There's little doubt you'll make a full recovery, barring infection."

Freslan's mouth was a grim line.

"I might not be so accommodating in my next shot."

AUSTIN DABNEY PREP WAS ONE AMONG several closed and boarded up campuses on the South Side. The reasons why were varied and ranged from the official line about the campuses being underutilized and under-resourced to accusations of administrative racism given a majority of the targeted schools were in Black and brown communities. When Blanchard and her brother Matty had attended the high school, the place had a rep for a powerhouse basketball team and a fierce chess club. Over the years she'd gone back to talk to various classes, particularly recalling the bright young faces in the Girls in Science program.

There was sagging cyclone fencing around the series of buildings, which included a three-story main structure, some bungalows and an auditorium—the permanent buildings circa the 1940s. It was in the auditorium where Blanchard performed in a few school plays like "Our Town" and "Cherry Orchard." She'd also helped build sets for some others. She hadn't taken acting as an avenue to be a professional actor but to build up her confidence and to train her memory. Though she did realize the experience on the stage had also been a boon to accessing the proper emotions and demeanor when talking about difficult matters with patients or their family.

IN SEVERAL SECTIONS THE CHAIN LINKS had been severed and graffiti had been strewn over the surface of the former school. Years of tagging had resulted in layers of colors and styles one upon the other. As the sun was still in the sky, Blanchard had parked on the side of the campus and entered onto the cracked asphalt that way. The locks to the auditorium had been breached some time ago and she let herself in, her messenger bag slung across her torso. According to the information she'd obtained from a reluctant Freslan, there was a hidden elevator behind the stage that led down to the facility.

"How the hell was it built under everyone's nose?" she'd asked him, pressing.

"There was a series of old sewer tunnels that ran beneath the school," he'd begun. Blanchard remembering unlike other aging schools on the South Side, the toilets at Dabney never clogged and or backed up.

"Once the clay pipes were jackhammered out from below," he'd continued, "An access point was disguised at an overgrown dirt lot less than two blocks away. That site was fenced in by high, solid walls and workers, tools, and material trucked back and forth on electric flatbed utility carts."

"You know you can't trust Freslan," Marsh said over her earbuds.

"Who you talkin' to? You damn well know I've come prepared."

"Still, that m-f hasn't lasted this long by not being crafty and shifty as shit. Don't get over-confident."

"I appreciate your concern as always. How about you, you good?"

"I got this, girl."

"You better smartass."

"Talk soon."

"Yes, we will."

She touched the red phone icon on the screen, took the earbuds out, and replaced the whole of it in her messenger bag. Blanchard picked her way through the gloom. Remains of numerous sets were piled around haphazardly. She tapped the flashlight app on her phone to life as she prowled about. Sure enough, as Freslan had said, once moving aside some sheets of plywood paneling, there was a metal door and a swipe card lock on it. Freslan had a magnetic strip card for it and she used it. The split door parted, and she stepped inside the car. She pressed the only button on the panel and, after the door closed silently, she began her descent.

This didn't take long, and Blanchard hadn't quite centered herself as the doors came open again. But there was no turning back now. She didn't know what exactly to expect. The physician had asked Freslan about anyone here and he'd answered in the negative, but that didn't mean he was telling the truth. She'd considered he would withhold such information hoping his allies got the drop on her and kept her from getting to the file. Still, Blanchard reflected as she walked along the gloomy hallway, there was a reason Freslan had put the file here. Making her way along another passageway that had T'd off from the first one, a panel slid open along one of the walls. She then heard an electric whine. Rolling into the hallway was a small conveyance the size of a kid's wagon on four rubber tires. It looked like one of those robots she'd seen bomb squads use on the news. But this was mounted with two compact conical shapes with gleaming metal balls on each. The balls spun rapidly and whipping around from them were multiple strands of various lengths that crackled and sizzled. As the machine advanced, the electrified whip ends sparked against the walls and floor. Maybe the charge in them would only stun her or maybe if she were stung enough times, her heart would overload and she'd be a goner.

Blanchard ran into the other hallway to get back to the elevator, but a series of parallel steel slats slid into place from one wall to the next, blocking her path. Though wearing Kevlar woven material, she knew her armor wouldn't long hold up against the oncoming possible high voltage assault. She then rushed forward toward the one side door she'd seen. The electric shock 'bot was almost to the end of the other hallway and would soon be upon her. The ends of several of the electrified strands struck her, sending surges through her upraised arms. She gritted her teeth against the pain as the god damn thing advanced on her at steady pace.

Blanchard had her back against the door, which was in a recess, but that hardly offered safety. Her face and upper body stinging, she had her hand in the messenger bag and out it came with a small canister she knew by feel. She dove, sliding across the floor away from the robot. She also thumbed the release valve free and, twisting around, rolled the canister onto the floor as her head buzzed and vision got bleary. The robot passed through a glistening white cloud hissing from the defensive weapon she'd used. Parts of the machine were now coated in a white frost as it exited. This was the effects of the pressurized liquid nitrogen contained in the canister. The revolution of the ball was slowing down, the lashes going limp. But the stuff did the trick and froze several internal mechanisms of the robot. It still had some forward motion, albeit even slower than before, but was no longer a danger to her.

She was on her knees and rising, kicked the machine over on its side. She looked up toward the ceiling and walked back toward the door. There was an electronic combination lock on it. She regarded it for a moment and took out her mini pry bar. Utilizing brute strength, she pounded on the lock instrument with the burglar's tool, not worrying about stealth. She got the punch pad loose enough to get the end of the pry bar in the gap between it and the door and popped it free. She paused, a gloomy maw before her, cool air caressing her sweating face. Blanchard took a step inside, sensors bringing to life overhead lighting that dully hummed.

She stood in a chamber primarily of chrome, steel, and more than one cluster of apparatuses like out of one of those Marvel Comics her brother used to drool over when they were kids. To her right were three human-sized cylinders in a row of clear material she took to be a polycarbonate of some grade. Two of those cylinders were occupied, one by a man and the other by a woman. He was an older Black man and the woman, she wasn't sure as to her race. They were nude and held standing in place by brackets and couplings around their arms and wrists. Closer to them, the cat burglar doctor estimated both were past 55 but the years of hard living evident in their otherwise calm faces, eyes closed, also suggested to her they might be younger. The scars and old sores on their skin told her that they'd been in and out of shelters, and on the streets for years.

Wiring and cables sprouted from machined attachments on the cylinders, which had gauges, dials and blinking lights embedded in the housings. These cables led to the high-tech equipment and, for a few beats, she watched a live monitor screen indicating heart rate, respiration and so forth. The two were in a kind stasis she figured— possibly a chemically-induced coma state. The third individual, dead, lay on a necropsy table. He was an older Black man rummaging in his late sixties. His chest plate had been cracked and spread, the lungs extracted. Rubber gloves on, she prodded the pink lungs that lay off to one side in one of the larger trays. Near a corner to this stood a drug storage cabinet Blanchard also noted. It had inset glass panels that allowed viewing of its contents.

Several steel knives, dissection scissors, and such lay near the body, blood and body fluid coating their sharp ends. As she suspected, there must be cameras hidden about the not-quite-finished complex. The fact the instruments hadn't been cleaned indicated the dissection had been interrupted at her arrival. Maybe an alarm signal when she activated the elevator. Whatever, Freslan had gambled that whoever was present, would be able to either take her prisoner, as she had him, or silence her for good. But they as of yet hadn't come at her directly so what did that tell her Blanchard wondered. She turned from the body, tempted to examine it further but knew she better be on guard. There was a door toward the rear of this room, and she headed toward it. But having covered less than half the distance to it, that door swung open on hydraulic hinges and in flew a drone. Blanchard stared at it, not sure of what to do. The four rotor helicopter-like craft dove at her and a liquid jetted from it, striking the side of her face as she reflexively turned away.

"Shit," she blurted, realizing the drone was squirting pepper spray at her. Though not a direct hit, some of the chemical had gotten into a corner of her eye and Blanchard's eyes teared up and reddened. Nonetheless she had the wherewithal to duck behind a desk, the drone buzzing and dive-bombing her. It spat more of the fluid at her as it did so. But this time she was ready and snatched up an instrument tray to block the spray. She hurled the tray at the aircraft, but the remote controlled device zipped out of the way. The drone hovered near the ceiling and Blanchard made a dash for the side door, the drone zipping down from above. The door had shut, and she rammed her shoulder against it to no effect. She turned, running across the lab back to the door she'd entered that remained ajar. The drone hummed at her back and then flew up and over her, directly in her face.

Sure enough it shot more of its pepper spray but Blanchard had crossed her hands in front of her face for protection. Still some of the stuff had gotten past and inflamed her eyes. They burned and Blanchard was having a hard time seeing. She bumped into a three-legged stool, knocking it over. Her feet got tangled up in the upset stool and she also went down onto the floor. But this was a good thing as it kept her face away from the drone and she started belly crawling toward the door. That's when a dog started barking.

"Are you fucking kidding me?" she hollered.

URSULA MARSH ENTERED THROUGH THE FRENCH doors off the patio, the rectangular-shaped pool behind her. As planned, Blanchard had left them unlocked. The house was quiet, and she could hear the soft hum of the refrigerator in the kitchen. Freslan was tied and duct-taped to a chair in the den, also as planned, his eyes covered by a bandanna.

"Who's there?" he said, hearing the approach of Marsh's footfalls. "That you, Montcreef? You take care of that trouble-some bitch?"

"Who the hell is Montcreef?" Marsh said. She'd been tasked to check up on Freslan as Blanchard didn't want to be the cause of his death if such could be avoided. Her girlfriend had pointed out she'd get enough time for kidnapping anyway. She wanted to text Blanchard to see if she was all right but knew better than to send an incriminating message that could be traced later.

Freslan cocked his head at the new voice. "Ah, the accomplice. Come to make sure I hadn't gotten loose and called the authori-ties is that it?"

"Doubtful you'd be calling the law, given what's about to be exposed of your extra-curricular activities." She and Blanchard weren't too worried that he'd be able to identify her by her voice later. The two kept their relationship low key at the hospital.

"You're here to do me harm?"

"That's not your concern why I'm here."

"What if I made it worth your while?"

"You want some water?" She instantly regretted saying this. Did it make her sound like a nurse?

If Freslan noticed, he didn't let on. "I'm serious, young lady. If you stick with Blanchard, where do you think that's going to take you? Do you honestly believe beyond a round or two of obligatory outrage on the usual suspect cable shows, that anything but ruin will befall her and those who help her? You do understand the way this country operates, don't you?"

"Your kind won't always be calling the shots."

The older man chuckled. "Oh, please, spare me. You might very well lean to the left side of the aisle, but I can assure you my kind are always calling the shots."

"Well, I must be going."

"No, wait, really you must listen to me. I have money."

"No shit, like this place is an SRO."

"I mean money on the premises, my dear. Cash."

"Yeah," she said, sounding interested. "Your mad money is it?"

"Mad to the tune of two million dollars."

"Bullshit."

Confidently, he said, "Oh, no, this is not a flight of fancy on my part. You have me at a disadvantage. Why would I do anything to anger you? When the reality is I want to recruit you to my side?"

"Does money solve all problems, Dr. Freslan?"

He cocked his head again as if a distant note were being played. "You tell me."

BLANCHARD WAS KEEPING THE SNARLING BULL mastiff back with the three-legged stool. As he—and it was male—charged at her, she'd poke it with the end of the stool's legs. More than once the animal tried to clamp those big teeth of his on the wood, but she'd been able to keep that from happening. She was now pressed back against the table and so far she'd been able to hold the dog off from snacking on her leg. Then, staring into the beast's snapping jaws, it hit her. All this was a delaying tactic. Whoever was here must have called in reinforcements. That only made sense Blanchard glumly concluded. And though loath to hurt the dog, and she liked dogs, Blanchard had to put herself in motion and get what she came for.

The dog backed up and stopped barking and snarling. Blanchard regarded the predatory intuition in those eyes as the large canine growled low in its throat. The damn creature was processing how best to attack her. As it stood still on its sturdy legs, she slid to one side and tensed her forearms. The muscles in the dog's rear flanks bunched and, momentarily rearing back, it then sprang at Blanchard. She caught it alongside its body with a quick swing of the stool. The dog was knocked away, but it was far from out. The animal's nails scraped on the tile floor as it renewed its attack on Blanchard. She swung the stool again and this time only caught a glancing blow against the dog. Worse, the mastiff got a bite on one of the legs and wrested the stool out of her hands. The stool then clattered free from its mouth.

Blanchard hopped onto the desk, the dog's hot breath on her calf. It leapt up, getting its forepaws on the desk, barking vociferously. She looked around, trying to think clearly with her heart thudding in her throat. The dog tried to clamber up to her. She jumped off, running with a destination in mind. She got to the medicine cabinet, the dog just about on her. She tipped the cabinet over, getting it between her and the dog. Given this was in a corner, the only way to come at her was for the beast to leap onto the cabinet. But Blanchard threw one of the double doors open and got her hand on the tumbled-over glass container she'd guessed would be in the cabinet as it was standard fare for this sort of lab. With her other hand she held the door up as a makeshift barrier. But her exposed hand paid the price as the dog nipped at her fingers,

"Sorry about this, Spike," she said lowering the door and, using both hands, opened the container of diethyl ether as the big dog leapt at her across the expanse. He wasn't instantly affected, and his momentum carried her over as he landed on her chest. But now the liquid, which vaporized on contact with the air, had gotten in his nose and he was panting and salivating but not tearing at her flesh. She rolled him off of her. The canine wasn't quite unconscious but had been rendered lethargic and disoriented. He lay on his side, drooling. Crazy, she reflected, but druggies liked to ingest the chemical for the same effect. Off she went through the now-unobstructed side door.

Blanchard was in another hallway similar to the first two— gloomy, sterile and gray. Though there were no doors along this stretch. She'd slung her messenger bag back on and had the S&W in hand. Making her way along, her senses were prickly and her throat dry. There was a set of double doors at the end of this hall and she concluded this would be where her quest would end one way or another. Her grip tightened on the gun as she edged closer. Silently, a panel slid open in part of the wall and twin bright lights blasted her in the face. She reacted, shooting the gun but her wrist was struck, throwing off the shot. She was then clubbed with one of those flashlights and her gun and messenger bag were grabbed from her.

"Take her back to the lab," an accented voice said.

"Yes, Professor Montcreef," one of the others said.

A groggy Blanchard was dragged back to the lab she'd just been in and deposited on a stool. The dog was elsewhere. Blanchard's head began to clear and before her was a somewhat hunched over individual regarding her. "Declan Montcreef," she said, bitter ash in her mouth. On one of the built-in lab tables, they'd deposited her messenger bag. Her gun was nowhere in sight. On either side of her stood not hired muscle but lab assistants, Blanchard estimated, a man who looked nervous and a woman with freckles.

The older man dipped his head slightly. "Interesting to see you again under these circumstances, Dr. Blanchard."

"Would that our positions were reversed," she replied.

Laughing slightly, Montcreef said, "Funny how fate works out."

He'd been imposing in his youth but now as the years had taken him past 70, various ailments had him using a cane. It was made of dark wood with a silver orb for a head. His eyes were as keen and questioning behind owlish lenses centered on a prow of a nose as Blanchard remembered. He still had an untamed head of hair, white with silvery ends like caterpillar's legs. The lab coat he wore was crisp and white, a cruel visual irony given the blood she knew was on his hands. The freckled woman also wore a spotless lab coat and struck Blanchard as all business. There was an object in her coat's pocket, heavier that a smartphone Blanchard clocked.

"You're quite the hustler, I'll give you that."

Montcreef shook the end of his cane at her. "I know you said that to get a rise out of me and it does. But I can attest that after the many years of my exile from the bosom of the medical community, which you among others playing your part in denigrating me I clearly recall, I am close to triumph."

"Bullshit," she spat.

One end of his mouth twitched, and his smile revealed canine-like teeth. "The proof, my dear, is in the doing." He indicated the third currently empty cylinder. "And with your fortuitous arrival, you'll play your part in bringing my decades of effort to fruition."

"You've been drinking your own Kool-Aid too damn long, Montcreef."

He'd walked over to the partially dissected cadaver, this time using his free hand to point at the body. "This unfortunate fellow suffered from a variety of medical conditions after so many years of drug use, insufficient diet, homelessness and so forth. When he came to me—"

"You mean when you snatched him out of the shelter," Blanchard interrupted. Freslan sat on the board of a clinic serving the working poor and homeless population. A friend of Ursula's who volunteered there had first raised suspicion when several of the patients went missing.

Montcreef's exasperated expression was as if he'd been upstaged by a student during a lecture. "Continuing, this unfortunate's array of problems included a rather advanced stage of respiratory illness." He turned his big round glasses on her, his eyes momentarily obscured by streaks of light reflected in the lenses. "And yet your no-doubt cursory examination of his lungs indicated what to you?"

She reluctantly said, "Based on just visual observation and an initial probe, I would regard the lung tissue as healthy and stable."

"Indeed those lungs are that of a twenty-two year old, doctor. I reversed not only the ravages but some forty years of wear and tear through my cellular regeneration process."

Blanchard slow clapped. "Hooray, the rich and self-absorbed get to live even longer as they fret about which personal jet to upgrade to and should they shell out even extra for the gold-plated toilets in that bird."

He shook his head. "I suppose it's your parents who are to blame for you and your brother's militant views."

"You need to take his name out of your mouth, charlatan."

The freckled woman tensed but Montcreef waved her off.

"Dr. Blanchard is a product of our hard-pressed inner city. Through dint of will and a . . . native intelligence, she is the woman she is today, warts and all."

Blanchard turned to the freckled woman. "And your boss has long gussied up his belief in eugenics with various permutations and obfuscations." She then glared at Montcreef. "But a Nazi is an asshole, et cetera, et cetera."

Montcreef tapped the end of his cane on the concrete floor. "You of all people should understand what it is to be misunderstood, Dr. Blanchard. But I must admit it does bring me joy to know you will play a part in the furthering of my experimentations."

Blanchard came off the stool in a lunge, intending to get her hands around the old bastard's throat. The freckled woman tased her, once on the neck and then in the chest. She crashed to her knees, dazed.

Montcreef stood over her, keeping more than an arm's length back. "I so want you to appreciate what is to be done with your body before I harvest it."

"Fuck you," she managed, spittle on her lips.

"Is that any way for a scientist to talk? One who is as fascinated by the mind as by the limitations of our physical existence?" In his hand he held her phone and attached earbuds. He dropped them to the floor and stamped on the instrument, destroying it.

"We gonna get the show on the road or what?"

Montcreef huffed. "We shall, doctor, we shall." He nodded to his assistants and they got her to her feet. Taser pressed to her spine, Blanchard was marched into another room that was a distinct contrast to the lab. It was a well-appointed office in modern furnishings that included a large flatscreen monitor on one wall.

"What have you done with Freslan?" Montcreef asked Blanchard.

She smiled at him as Montcreef sat behind the desk that commanded the room. She stood before it, flanked by the two assistants. "Wouldn't you like to know?"

"I don't want to be unduly rough, doctor, but matters are at a critical juncture. While any degree of exposure has much less of a sting in this era of all manner of hogwash proliferating what you young folks call social media, I cannot have the market unduly influenced if a premature announcement were to get out."

"It occurred to me," Blanchard began, "that your breakthrough, stellar though it may be, is a one-time thing, isn't it?"

Montcreef inclined his head and the younger man next to her glanced at Blanchard sideways.

"That's what you're up against, isn't it? Through your organ regeneration you can extend life thirty, maybe forty years beyond the actuary tables, but that's not what you've sold your far-too-interested investors. Those greedy bastards want a zero or two more on that prognosis."

Blanchard put her hands on her hips, causing the freckled woman to flinch. "But when you attempt to renew the process, there's cellular failure and tissue decomposition."

"What makes you so sure?" the other woman said.

Blanchard pointed at Montcreef. "It's what he didn't say when we were in the lab. He talked about reversing the effects but not about prolonging life, well, really prolonging it. And I know your precious professor better than you know him and that would have been the first thing he would have crowed about."

Montcreef spread his hands. "You have me, Dr. Blanchard. But you see I have been preparing for the next phase of my work. The phase where I use relatively younger and healthy organs. Revitalize those and once transplanted in the host, my estimate is seventy to eighty years extension of life."

"That's still not immortality."

He smiled his mongoose smile at her. "But I will be a vociferous ambassador."

"Getting the sucker to pay in big," Blanchard said. "But won't they be disappointed when the clock finally does run out?"

He hunched a shoulder. "Possibly. But they'll be the outright rulers of this planet. And by then, I'll surely have made many improvements on my methods."

"You plan to be around for that?"

He bowed slightly. "Oh yes."

"And this is where you tell me where I come in. You plan to harvest my organs, regenerate them and have them put in you."

"You are quite perceptive, my dear."

"Right," she said and slugged the freckled woman across her forehead with a sap. The woman cursed and stumbled back, hurting. Blanchard had previously slipped the blackjack up her sleeve in case her messenger bag was taken from her. The man lunged at her, but Blanchard had anticipated his attack. She dodged aside and simultaneously kicked him in the stomach, making him gasp. Given her years of Muay Thai classes, she figured she could handle this guy who wasn't a leg-breaker but a put-upon lab assistant. Problem was, Montcreef had the gun and was rising, firing it. Fortunately for Blanchard, he wasn't proficient, and several shots went wild as she scrambled for safety. Unfortunately for the male assistant, a bullet entered his eye and exited the back of his head, spraying brain matter.

As another round blasted through the room, shattering a lamp, Blanchard locked into the other woman who hadn't yet fully recovered from the previous blow. Blanchard used her as a shield, driving both of them at Montcreef, who'd come around to the side of the desk trying to get a clear shot.

"Let go of me, bitch." The freckled woman struggled to get free.

"My pleasure." Blanchard shoved her into Montcreef. They got tangled up and Blanchard planned to hit the freckled woman again and grab the gun. But the other woman acted faster and had her hand on the weapon's slide, taking it from Montcreef.

"I'm going to fix you good," she said as her other hand closed on the gun's grip.

Blanchard stepped, pivoted, and elbowed the woman in the mouth, which rocked her. The two then grappled, Blanchard holding onto the wrist of her gun hand as the two wound up partially on the desk.

"You are nothing if not troublesome," Montcreef said as he cracked his cane's orb on the back of Blanchard's skull.

"Shit," she wailed, gritting her teeth. The other woman punched her on the jaw and Blanchard found herself sitting on the floor, her back against the heavy desk.

The freckled woman had the gun aimed at her. "Get up so I can hit you again."

"I'm going to shove that gat up your ass sideways."

"I wish you'd try."

"Ladies," Montcreef said, "please." He stood over the one he'd accidentally killed. "This is a problem. Stefan has a significant other, I think he'd be called."

Blanchard said, "Killing the homeless doesn't give you pause, but this you give a damn about. Typical."

"I am no butcher, Dr. Blanchard. These," he went on, gesturing toward the lab, "are the detritus of society. Castoffs who already have one foot in the grave and, if anything, in death I have given their life meaning."

"You know the sad thing is, you actually believe that horseshit."

The freckled woman poked Blanchard hard with the handgun. "I can't wait until you're on the table, sweetie."

"Well, let's secure our guest and then we'll need to do something about our associate's body. It's so unseemly to just leave him lying here drawing flies." He sounded genuinely saddened.

"Make her dispose of the corpse." The freckled woman flicked the gun toward Blanchard. "That way maybe some trace evidence gets left on him and she gets the blame for his death."

"Good thinking, Marva."

Marva smiled and said, pointing the M&P at Blanchard, "Go on."

"You expect me to carry him?"

"However you do it, you're getting him out of here."

"Yeah, where would that be?"

"We have a kind of crematorium," Montcreef answered.

"Of course you would." Blanchard got her hands under the dead man's armpits and lifted his top half off the floor. Some of his blood stained her clothes.

"There's a handcart you can use." Montcreef sat behind his desk again, staring off into the near distance.

"That's damn white of you." Blanchard backed out, dragging the corpse.

"Keep being funny," Marva said, following her out.

"I need to compose myself."

"Very good, professor," Marva said to him.

"About that cart," Blanchard said, sweating and stopping to rest in the hallway.

"You're doing just fine. Down that way and then to the left."

Blanchard resumed her efforts. Near the juncture the scratchy interplay of claws on the polished floor interrupted the syncopation of a corpse being dragged along a corridor. The scratchy interplay intensified.

"Oh shit, slow down, Rebus," Marva said to the mastiff as it sped from around the corner, eager to renew its match with Blanchard. The dog barked and snarled at her and only the body of Stefan kept it from attacking her.

Marva yelled, "Come on, boy, get back now. It's okay. Get down, get down."

The dog was momentarily stymied but also blocked the way they needed to go. Blanchard didn't dare let go of the body.

Marva was behind and to the side of Blanchard but had to step out and forward to assert herself with the dog. "Take it easy, Rebus. It's me."

The dog had its front paws on the corpse's lower limbs and looked from her to Blanchard. Marva bent forward and the look in the dog's eyes softened. She patted the beast's squarish head and as he nuzzled her hand, calming down. Now was the best time to make her play, Blanchard determined, while the other woman was distracted.

"Here's a snack for you, Rebus."

She rolled Stefan's body onto the dog, riling him up again. Marva swung toward Blanchard with the handgun, but Blanchard had already closed the small distance between them and punched her in the gut. A follow-up right cross to her face staggered her. The dog, of course, reacted to this and charged at Blanchard. But putting her hand on the dog's muscular back, she vaulted over him and ran down the shorter hallway that led to a metal door inset with a rectangle of glass. The oncoming canine galloped after her and Blanchard couldn't help but imagine what it was going to feel like once those teeth got a hold of her. But her rubber soles were better for traction as Rebus lost his footing on the slick floor and slid into a side wall before he righted himself. This allowed Blanchard a few seconds of relief and she reached the door, snatched it open, and went in. She closed the door behind her but could see no way to lock it. There was though a small metal table, and she got that lodged underneath the latch, the length of it inclined against the floor. Then she sat in between the legs to better weight it against the door.

The room was mostly unadorned and contained essentially the cremation furnace and conveyor belt to feed the deceased into it. There was something odd about the chamber, but Blanchard didn't understand what was that had registered in part of her brain. The dog snarled and flung itself at the door but couldn't get in. A quiet descended, then a shot echoed, Blanchard instinctively ducking. But by the ping she heard, the round must have ricocheted off the door. Marva pounded on the door from the other side.

"We got all the time in the world, Blanchard. We'll starve you out."

"You think I won't be missed? You figure I came here without leaving a trail?"

"You're lying."

Rebus chimed in as if he too didn't believe her.

"Okay."

Blanchard couldn't tell if Marva went away but she knew she couldn't just sit here. She got up and went closer to the rectangular furnace, realizing what it was that struck her strange about the device. This version wasn't powered by gas but was electrical.

"Advances in death disposal," she muttered.

A pounding against the door had her turning her head. The table was sliding back and momentarily would be dislodged. She figured Marva would send Rebus in first and she'd be behind him gun blazing. She had to upset that equation. Blanchard tore back to the furnace just as the door was struck again and the table came out from under the latch. It swung open and in loped Rebus followed by Marva, who'd been ramming a flat hand cart at the door.

FRESLAN MOVED FAST FOR A MAN of his years. He whipped around from the wall safe, the gun firing. It was fitted with a suppressor. As he cranked off two rounds, sounds like hornets buzzing in a closed glass jar followed suit. Stuffing puffed out of a throw pillow on the couch and the second bullet chipped wood off the door jamb. But Ursula Marsh had been wary and had shifted her position from where she'd been standing behind the aging physician. He gaped as he realized he hadn't been effective in eliminating his threat. Adjusting, twisting his torso to his left where she now stood, he looked to correct his mistake. Instead the shaft of Marsh's extended collapsible baton cracked against his wrist and while he didn't drop the gun, his third shot was impotent.

"Bitch," he howled.

Marsh struck again with the baton, this time across his face. He remained on his firmly planted feet, his head weaving about as if there was a damaged spring in his neck. She easily took the gun from him. She pressed the suppressor's muzzle against his temple.

"Now unload that cash from the safe, ya scuzzy, bitch," Marsh told him.

"What's going on here?" a new voice said from behind Marsh.

BLANCHARD USED HER SHOULDER TO KNOCK the door into Marva. When she saw it was coming open, she'd managed to get in place. She came from around the door and, knocking aside the other's gun hand, punched her in the gut, doubling her over. Rebus was charging at Blanchard and she kicked the hand cart into him. Returning her attention to Marva, she was too slow, and a bullet slammed into her upper body, the impact sending her over.

"That's what you get," Marva snarled, "dead. I'm going to enjoy helping the professor carve your ass up like a Christmas goose."

Rebus the unwavering cocked his head as he approached the downed woman and began sniffing Blanchard's lower legs. Her foot lashed out and clocked the animal under the jaw, stunning him. Even as Marva reacted, Blanchard whipped her legs around and got them entangled with the other's ankles. Over she also went, and Blanchard was on her in a heartbeat.

"You goddamn—" Marva started but didn't finish due to the double tap of Blanchard's fist loosening her front tooth.

Rebus again lunged at Blanchard. She purposely rammed her boot into his mouth, which he chomped on with vigor. It was of the steel toe variety and thickly made. Two more blows to the center point of its head, this time with the butt end of the nine she'd liberated from Marva had the big dog woozy again.

"Don't want to give you a concussion," Blanchard muttered, "but can't be your Blue Plate special just now." Blanchard used the cart to force the unsteady Rebus back and through the doorway. She slammed the door and jammed the table back in place. Turning, she was tackled by a revived Marva and the two went at it. Because she'd needed both hands for optimum leverage using the cart, she'd tucked the gun in her belt but didn't have the opening to reach for it. As she expected, Marva was also versed in hand-to-hand combat.

A short chop to Blanchard's chin burst stars in her eyes. But she blocked a strike to her kidneys and countered with a punch to the freckled woman's ribcage. Marva kneed her in the stomach and socked her on the side of her face. Blanchard bent low and drove her knuckles into Marva's knee and getting her arms around her lower legs, upended her as the other woman pummeled her upper back.

AT FRESLAN'S HOUSE, URSULA MARSH HAD leapt onto the couch, sprang off the back into the air, and landed on the running pharmacist.

"Oh, God, please don't hit me," Baldwin pleaded.

"Then I'm sorry about this," Marsh said as she struck Baldwin once with the admonishment, "Keep quiet or you'll get worse." Must be the girlfriend figured to surprise her lover—get a kick out of doing the nasty in the married couples' bed, Marsh surmised.

That Baldwin's expression changed from wide-eyed to relieved saved Marsh from getting brained by a plaster replica of the Eiffel Tower. Yet as she tried to duck away, the bric-a-brac broke against the back of her upper arm and collarbone as Freslan swung it at her.

"Shit," Marsh hollered, sagging but remaining upright. That part of her was bloodied now. As if the sight of that energized them like it would jungle cats, Freslan and his girlfriend came at her. Clearly the pharmacist wasn't as scared as she pretended. But shooting the nose off a mini-bust of composer Claude Debussy on a shelf sobered the duo. Baldwin halted abruptly and Freslan collided into her from behind like in a comedic bit. Only no one was laughing.

"What, y'all got excited and forgot I had this?" Marsh waved the gun. "Now rip off some lamp cord and you tie his ass up. And don't pretend you two don't get kinky and haven't done this before."

Baldwin and her paramour exchanged a look and got busy.

BLANCHARD CAME IN UNDER MARVA'S PALM heel strike and rocked her opponent with a one-two combination worthy of the mixed martial arts champ Amanda Nunes that wobbled her. Rebus once again launched himself at the door, banging against it on the other side. Blanchard moved in to be greeted with another jab of Marva's upraised knee that sent her sideways. The freckled woman leapt, intending to get in a punch and move away. But Blanchard caught her with a roundhouse right that should have dropped her. But Marva didn't stop and toppled onto Blanchard who fell backwards, the back of her legs striking the edge of the conveyor belt. Over the two went onto the tread that fed the electric-powered cremation furnace. They were close to the entrance to the chamber and as the two fought, partially grappling and partially hitting each other, laying atop the conveyor as the metal maw loomed. Then partially rising to get off the conveyor, Blanchard was kicked in the chest by Marva and dropped back. She inadvertently struck the start button and the conveyor started moving. Inside the furnace an intense orange glow came instantly to life as the heat from within climbed to the required 1,800 degrees Fahrenheit to turn a body into ash.

"Stupid bitch," Marva said, bunching Blanchard's shirt material in her hands, attempting to muscle the doctor into the super-heated cavity.

"I got you, bitch." Blanchard went flat so as to get her foot and leg in place and flip Marva over her upraised face.

"Wait, no," was all the freckled woman could holler from inside the machine before her body burst into flame, fire alighting the tongue in her open mouth and evaporating the eyes in their sockets. The last image Blanchard had of her was an arm reaching for her as she back-peddled on the conveyor belt and dropped to the floor. Flesh was being eaten by the sun blast of heat and a finger of bone pointed at Blanchard. Then Marva was no more.

Back at the door, Blanchard took a breath and flung it open as Rebus panted on the other side. For an instant the canine's expression was like a small child with an ice cream cone. He bowled in and Blanchard did the opposite, closing the door behind her. Judging from his increased barking Blanchard noted as she jogged away, Rebus was doubly pissed for being tricked. Blanchard assumed Montcreef had made his getaway, but she wanted to retrieve her messenger bag in the lab before hunting him down. Too, she was eager to get to the surface and contact Marsh. Entering the room, she noted that the third cylinder was cracked and pieces of it were lying around. The machinery was on and humming. As she processed this, a shape leapt onto a lab table.

"How do you like me now?" an enlarged man growled at her.

"My God," Blanchard muttered. Before her crouched a transformed Montcreef. The hems of his pant legs were split above high-watered calves the size of grapefruit. His thighs were powerful like that of an NFL running back. His torso was an inverted triangle; a model's trim waistline leading upward to a broad, heavily muscled chest. A chest that was partially exposed given the shirt and lab coat that once covered it was shredded due to his increased mass.

"Yes," the changeling said, "my experiments have also unlocked other forms of cellular manipulation." His teeth were also different, more jagged, like that of the trapped Rebus. "I still have your weapon but wanted the pleasure of tearing your arms from your body and beating you with them in my bare, lovely hands." He held those enlarged hands aloft, the 9mm in one of them. He laughed and tossed the gun onto the floor.

"There's still bullets in it, my good doctor. Go ahead, make your play."

Having closed her mouth, Blanchard was backing up when Montcreef sprang, yelling savagely. Duplicating what she'd done with Marva, Blanchard dropped onto her back, and using her leg, leveraged the beast-man over her, using his own momentum. He landed on his face on the floor but was instantly back on his feet. Blanchard was on her way to the toppled medicine cabinet. She was brought up short as the Caliban-like Montcreef easily erased the gap between them and snatched her clean off the floor as if she were a mere paperweight. He gloated as he held her in both hands over his head.

"What an exhilaration," he said and tossed her into some of the machinery. She rebounded and her bruised body met the floor. Blanchard groaned as he stalked over to her. "I would so like to enjoy our time together, doctor, but I suppose haste is the better course for now." He then brightened. "Though I am grateful that your arrival made me accelerate procedures I'd been taking baby steps at completing. For that you'll be a fond memory to me."

"You talk too much." Blanchard pinwheeled her body around to use her leg to upend Montcreef. But his reflexes were such now that he got her by the ankle and again threw her sliding across the floor to thud against the wall. He loped at the groggy woman, triumphant.

"How sweet it is," he laughed, reaching for her.

"Eat me." Blanchard unleased a series of rapid kicks and punches to the knees, kidneys and so on. Though the professor possessed a converted musculature, he had no experience in fighting techniques as she had. She didn't incapacitate him, but her attack kept him off-balance. But she got in too close and he back-handed her, swatting her into the wall. Gloating again, he reached for her, but Blanchard, putting everything she had into it, grabbed the man's cane, which had been leaning nearby, and swung it at him. There was a satisfying crack as the top of the cane hit him and the walking stick broke apart. Montcreef was stunned and she was already in motion. Blanchard dove, going into a slide across the floor like a runner approaching third base.

"Get back here," he growled, latching a hand onto her ankle. He snatched her back, howling, "Speaking of dining, I'm going to eat your face off." He started to cackle, maybe out of joy or maybe his bulking up was driving him mad.

"Whatever," Blanchard said and jammed the pistol in his gaping mouth, breaking a front tooth as she did so. Montcreef's eyes went wide as she squeezed the trigger twice on the Smith & Wesson 9mm and blew out his brains as he'd done the hapless Stefan. Only she meant to do this. Meant it with all her heart.

"FOURTEEN MONTHS AGO, THE BODY OF freelance journalist Matthew Blanchard was found on the banks of the Drainage Canal. At the time," the newscaster went on, "his death was ruled a drug overdose. He'd been clean and sober for over ten years. It was rumored on certain social media outlets by his colleagues that he'd been murdered. Further that he'd been on the trail of an enterprise doing immoral testing on human subjects, the homeless it should be noted, in pursuit of extending our lives if not forever, at least by one or two hundred years. At the time, he'd been following up leads to the disappearance of one Gardner Ostrander . . . "

As the news continued on the television playing in the waiting room, Dr. Augustina "Gus" Blanchard walked past on her way to the ER. She was listening to a song by Sade, "Soldier of Love" and the lyrics about surviving in the wild, wild west." She turned the song off on her phone and removed her earbuds. Those who worked with her had noted her fresh bruises, but she suggested one of her workouts had gotten a bit out of hand. When her lover Ursula Marsh had left Freslan's home with the incriminating files, her two prisoners had managed to get themselves loose as had been expected. As both traditional and online media blew up when the information of the experiments was leaked, he'd tried to flee.

And as Blanchard had figured if that happened, he used his girlfriend's car as this was not a known vehicle of his. But she'd planted a GPS tracker in her trunk and the coordinates were anonymously supplied to the authorities. Arrested, he did go on about being a captive in his own home, but the two women alibied each other. As to his paramour, well, she and Marsh had gone to her and scared her into not corroborating Freslan's claims. Laying the some three hundred grand found in his safe on her helped ease the sting of betrayal she felt. Before leaving the lab, Blanchard had used the chemicals therein as accelerants and burned the place from within. Fuck destroying evidence. She'd destroyed the men who'd killed her brother and exposed their scheme. She did though release a confused Rebus to the outside.

In the ER, she saw a patient, a 40-something blonde whose markings on her face and arm were hardly consistent with banging into a door. The two recognized each other from the gun range.

"He found out I'd been doing target practice," she confided in Blanchard. "I guess I really wasn't going to use it on him. I just wanted to feel, you know, if only for a few moments, like I was in control."

"I understand," Blanchard said as she stood back after examining her and Marsh dressed the woman's wounds. The two exchanged a feral look.

"We've got some referrals for places battered woman can go to up front," Blanchard said. She held her clipboard up and had her pen poised. "What was your address again?"

DESAL PLANT NO. 9

THE DOUBLE-BREASTED CORMORANT, GANGLY WHEN IT walked, was transfixing as it swooped in gracefully from above and skimmed across the water. It soon took to the skies again with a fish wriggling in its beak. The zapper sizzled a bolt and instantly fried the bird and its prize. The charred husks fell into the ocean and the scattered blackened mass floated there for some time, before sinking.

DESALINIZATION PLANT NUMBER NINE SITS JUST at the shoreline of what had been the Santa Monica Pier. There was no signage left to that effect or any semblance of the long-gone structures. Actually it had been two adjoining piers, with the municipal one first built more than 150 years ago. There had been a Ferris wheel, a roller coaster, and a carousel in a hippodrome. Moses Hopkins was old enough to remember as a teen bringing his girl here for laughs and kissing and groping under the creaking pier. Before the Mahk-Ra came and conquered.

Hopkins dismissed his silly nostalgic ruminations as he cleared the security entrance on one of the western gates to the desal plant. It was a massive low-slung two-billion dollar complex sprawling over a square mile and a half with its pump stations spread in a line along the beach and their metal tendrils reaching three-quarters of a mile out into the Pacific Ocean. There were eight parallel 200-foot smokestacks off-center on a far end of the vast plant where steam was vented during the heat, and pressure produced that led to the reverse osmosis process. This to evaporate as moisture in the air and cycle back to the sea.

"You're cleared," the human guard said, lifting his gaze from the monitor screen and handing Hopkins back his mag card credentials.

Hopkins walked into the complex amid thousands of feet of parallel and crisscrossing pipes of specific sizes and thicknesses running here and there and the ever-present whir of the whoosh of water through them. He passed by various workers, Mahk-Ra and human, some in hardhats and gloves and a few in lab coats, others in overalls and filter masks loose around their necks. While security at desal plants was maintained, there was an unofficial hands-off policy adopted by the Red Spear. The resistance committed sabotage and theft against hard targets and in principle, water treatment operations were deemed fair game. Particularly as some of the reclaimed water was tanked off-world. Fuckin' Mocks take everything, Hopkins observed moodily.

Among the several strategic reasons Earth had been lusted after by the aliens was not only due to its inhabitants being bipeds, and thereby being pressed into service in the Mahk-Ra's expansionist excursions, but residing on a sphere about three-quarters rich in the most precious of resources was another attraction. The far-flung colonies of the Mahk-Ra included several arid planets where water was more valuable than gold—the yellow stuff the economic standard throughout the galaxy.

Several years ago, the rebels had been successful at contaminating the fresh water produced by a desal plant located in what had once been Detroit. The resulting reprisal had not just been confined to rounding up the usual suspects. Water from the tap and by bottle had been rationed in various human communities, including Angelville, a nickname for the reconfigured Los Angeles core of today. Hoarding and stealing from the hoarders had erupted, with the attendant deaths by getting your head bashed in or shot point-blank a too regular occurrence. Water riots also broke out and the authorities let them manifest—as long as the fatalities were humans or a few low-level Mahk-Re shopkeepers. The message was clear. The Red Spear never issued a formal edict, but it was understood that messing with water was off limits.

"How's it going?" One of the workers said, nodding at Hopkins.

"Same old, same old," the other man said. Hopkins wore the work clothes identifying him as an employee of OverFoodsX, the mega-corp that grew meat in labs and catfish the size of sharks on asteroid fish farms, and supplied and stocked vending machines like the ones in the plant's break rooms. This was his fifth year on the job.

Via his wrist remote control unit, Hopkins guided into position the robot cart he'd brought into the facility.

"What you bring good, Mose?" The blonde, Natalie, with a ponytail asked. She was sipping a cup of coffee, scanning through entries on her phone. Calls and texts were monitored by the Mahk-Ra's minders—their tech having enhanced the existing surveillance apparatuses confiscated from the NSA after they disbanded them. But unless you were a moron and openly talked about robbing an armory or assassinating one of the High Command, people went about their daily internetting unfettered.

"Check this out," Hopkins said, stepping over to her, showing the woman the picture label on a wrapped packet he'd plucked from the cart.

"Nice," she said. "Looking forward to trying that. You sure treat us good around here."

Hopkins smiled. "We aim to please."

He placed the lobster and chive burrito in the self-heating wrap back on the cart with the other fare. Using his key switch, he opened one of the vending machines and replenished the stock. He loaded the other machines too then, giving a half-wave to those in the room, exited with his empty robot cart. He seemed to be heading out of the facility but soon took a different path that brought him nearer where he wanted to be, a specific maintenance room. It wasn't hard for the disguised lock pick app on his phone to overcome the simple electronic lock. Once inside, he parked his cart next to a wall filled with tools and pumps in various stages of repair. The cart's design was not dissimilar from the type used in the facility to move about large pieces of equipment. He removed a compact self-contained section of the cart the size of an old-fashioned box of wooden matches. The contents "read" organic as the food he delivered was routinely inspected upon arrival. Hopkins put on a pair of overalls also hidden in the cart to make him appear as if he were one of the facility's personnel and exited the room. The container rested in his pocket.

"Don't I know that?" Hopkins heard his target, Secunda-ra, speak from his office down the hall. Even though he was a Mock, Hopkins noted, he was speaking in English—maybe to a human or to one of his kind. Far as he could tell, they used languages like shirts, trying on Spanish one day, then German the next to keep their skills up. A hybrid speak of Mahk-Re and English was sometimes used too, mostly among the youth of both species called Mahklish. Silently, he got closer to the open doorway and took out the small metal box. It had a lid he slid back to release the mosquitoes inside, shaking them out as he crouched beside the doorway.

Grim-faced, he took several steps back to make sure he made noise when he clomped along the hallway.

"Oh shit," Secunda-ra exclaimed in Mahkanese. "There's some damn mosquitoes in here."

Hopkins rushed to the entrance to the office. "Sir, come on. We've got spray for you."

The Mahk-Ra manager had his shades off, swatting the air around him. "What happened to the zips?" His oblong black eyes were sunken in a craggy face. He was normal height for them, six-eight or so, Hopkins estimated. He wasn't part of the military, he was a bureaucrat, a pencil pusher.

"Don't know, sir." Hopkins was close to the front of the desk, his hand extended imploringly.

The manager came from around the desk, holding his flip top communicator, a beep they were called. Hopkins bumped him like he'd made a misstep.

"Watch out."

"Sorry." No luck, the mark still held on to his device. He moved aside and let him take the lead. Hopkins brought up the stunner mini-rod and jammed it onto the base of the alien's neck.

"Garhhh," he growled, spinning about, lashing out. He wasn't that much of a pencil pusher.

His fist caught Hopkins partly on the side of his face but it lacked sufficient force due to the effects of the taser. Hopkins hit the taller male in the stomach and followed that with another hit from the stunner, this time pushing it up under his chin. Blue sparks fizzled and the manager's flesh burned where the thing was pressed. The desal plant's boss dropped to his knees and a right cross put him on the floor. Hopkins grabbed the beep and pulled the unconscious Mock from out of the doorway. He quit the office, closing the door behind him. He didn't take the time to tie him. He planned to be long gone before the alien was in any shape to raise the alarm.

Aware of the route he needed to take, Hopkins grabbed a clipboard hanging on a wall to go with his overalls. He walked purposely but not hurriedly. In a facility this size, no one person would know everybody so he merely nodded to this or that human or Mahk-Ra as he headed toward his destination—the inflow area.

This was the section where the garbage and large elements were filtered out of the ocean water via what were termed traveling screens and then sent on for chemical treatment in the initial stages of the desalinization process.

"Hey, where's Monty?" A stocky man with a twang said to Hopkins, who now had his hand on one of the latches to a set of double doors. They were marked, "Filtration Section 4."

"I don't know no Monty." He clicked the latch, the door opening inward. The thrumming of large machinery invaded the hallway.

"Yeah? Then where the hell are the M-7s I asked for?"

Fuck. "The titanium mesh screens?" He'd picked up plenty of their lingo over time.

The other man advanced on splayed, flat feet that slapped the composition flooring. Behind him came a mechanical chirping and there appeared a man from around a corner, along with two remote-controlled motorized skids stacked high with copper-colored cylindrical filters composed of semipermeable membranes. He walked between the skids manipulating them with his control unit.

"Monty, who's this guy?" The one with the stocky man was looking at his co-worker, thumb aimed at Hopkins,

"How the hell would I know?" Monty said. "Get the damn doors open."

The stocky man turned back but Hopkins had already covered the space between them. He whacked the worker viciously with the clipboard, smashing his nose and causing him to stumble backwards. Monty rushed from around the lead skid. Hopkins, foot up in the stocky man's chest, propelled him into Monty sending both desal workers tumbling to the floor, swearing.

Hopkins made his way quickly through the opened doors and shut it behind him. The stunner was just long enough to slip between both latches, temporarily barring the doors.

He was on a wide catwalk that stretched the length of the area. Above him and below, was an array of large pipes where water flowed in from the sea and on into other parts of the facility. Below were also massive three-sided concrete pens where water churned and was sucked through by 50-feet in diameter propellers. Heavy duty robotic crane arms serviced these pens, placing and replacing the interlocking traveling mesh screens as well as being able to pluck sizeable pieces of detritus from the water.

"What's going on here?" A female Mahk-Ra in a pristine lab coat demanded as she approached him. The door jiggled behind him and both men yelling could be heard over their banging fists.

"Trouble," he said, stepping past her.

She grimaced at the barred door. "Is this some sort of horse-play?" Even now, aspects of human behavior befuddled the Earth's occupiers.

"You got it," a running Hopkins said to her over his back.

Momentarily confused, she didn't release the door. When she did decide to remove the stunner, Hopkins was already on one of the ladders leading down from the catwalk.

"Get that fucker," the stocky one said, taking off along the catwalk.

Halfway down the rungs, Hopkins leaped off and, falling away, latched onto one of the L-shaped robot arms. For safety reasons, there was a manual override control panel installed on the devices.

"Shit," the stocky man swore, knowing what Hopkins intended to do.

Hopkins overrode the arm's central control and commanded it in such a way that he lay on the arm, stouter and larger than his body, holding onto it like a long-lost lover. The arm swung away from the ladder and extended itself over one of the pens.

"What is this about?" The Mahk-Ra tech said from the catwalk.

"We need to alert security," Monty said beside her. Being familiar as if they were equals.

She regarded him coolly, "Then do so, human."

"Yes, ma'am."

Hopkins now hung from the robot arm by his hands and dropped onto the ledge of one of the water pens. The parallel walls sloped downward toward an open pipe where the water pumped in from the sea. The lip of the wall was seven inches wide and Hopkins was able to keep his balance as he walked down it. But to get outside the plant, he was going to have to jump into the pen, get atop the pipe, and crawl through a gap between it and where it entered this part of the building.

This hadn't been the plan, but crime required work, he glumly reminded himself. Up on the catwalk, the plant's workers were calling security on their two-ways. Hopkins tore off his overalls, after transferring the communicator into a waterproof case and into his pants pocket. He dropped into the pen. The suction of the constantly turning propeller at the other end was strong, but not designed to suck in a significant weight. Though sea lions had been known to get pulled though the pipes and get chopped up on the blades. The mesh screens were rigged behind the propellers.

Hopkins gulped lungfuls of air and went under. He swam closer to the blades and, letting the overalls float out before him, let them go. They wrapped around the propeller's hub, jamming the machinery. Smiling, he surfaced and swam toward the pipe. He'd just gotten his hand on the rim when the overalls became untangled. There was a whoosh of current and Hopkins lost his grip. He went back under, going end over end. He was disoriented and could feel himself being pulled the wrong way.

Lungs hungry for air, up being down, Hopkins fought panic and got his head around to see he was feet-first toward the propeller. He maneuvered his lower body and set his heel on the hub, his other leg pulled back. He pushed off and stroked with furious intent. For a moment he seemed to not move at all. Black spots migrated behind his eyes and a comforting dark curtain began to descend over him. His hope evaporating, Hopkins was too incensed to not try one more time to push himself forward. He would be mortified if his epitaph said he was chopped up like chum in a Mahk-Ra desal plant. Oh hell no.

Nearly out of air and time, he churned his arms and kicked his legs. Then, with his last bit of strength, up he went, breaking though the surface of the water. Gasping a lungful of air, he knew he couldn't let up and got back to the pipe. He was able to work to the side of the pipe and, pressing tightly against the wall, was able to just avoid the turning blades and squeeze though the gap.

Hopkins dropped to the sand and rolled onto his back, chest heaving. But there was no time to rest. Moving quickly, he laid a false trail of his footsteps in the sand, reversing course and wiping out his doubling back with a fallen palm frond.

Security would first go over his service van and of course make calls to the vending company. Then they would spread out from the facility. Hopkins had to get away but would wait, do it right. He snuck around into a recessed area to rest, belly crawling under a row of pipes that hummed with flowing water. He would let the security, and the cops they would soon be calling, fan out looking for him. As it was a high security instrument in question, the Talon might be called in but that would probably not be until the morning.

Hopkins waited a half-hour then chanced coming out of hiding. On a bluff overlooking the plant was an assortment of diners and small shops that existed to serve the workers in the 24-hour facility and truckers traveling along busy Pacific Coast Highway. Wild shrubbery erupted in sections up and down the slope of the bluff. There were also escalators and elevators to the top. Hopkins made his way across the open ground of sand, the plant's bulk behind him, a few palm trees dotting the land-scape. If he was spotted, it was at least 20 years hard labor in a RZ camp or he'd simply croak from being tortured by a Talon specialist to give up the comrades in his Red Spear cell. Protesting through bloody cracked lips that he was no such agent—and he wasn't. This was his own score. If he made it, it would net him plenty.

He got to the base of the slope. Methodically, Hopkins made his way up the hill, doing his best to use the shrubbery for cover. As he ascended, there was a stab of pain in his lower back, reminding him he was 52 and should seriously pursue a new line of work. That returning full time to his old endeavors would only bring buzzard's luck. As he got close to the top of the ridge he heard voices.

"Shit, baby, I'm just crazy for that sweet Earther pussy."

"Add another 300 and you can ride all night long, baby."

Eyes looking over the edge, Hopkins watched the Mahk-Re trucker and human prostitute climb inside his rig's double cab. Hopkins was able to get over the railing quietly as the moaning from inside the 18-wheeler covered any noise he made. He prowled along the parking area where several big rigs were about. He was thankful the area was covered in asphalt and not gravel.

The first empty truck cab he got open he had no luck. In the second one, he found an overnight bag with clothes in it. The pants were loose on him but not by much. There was a shirt too. He wiped the sweat off his face with his wet undershirt and jammed those clothes under the truck, between the drivetrain and cargo area. He was zipping up as footfalls approached. Rather than try and hide, he boldly stepped from around the side of the vehicle and walked toward the restaurants. Two human truckers gave him the once over but probably assumed he'd been taking a leak. Hopkins went into the Nu Wave café and sat at the counter.

Not too long after, eating his chicken fried steak dinner and home fries, he looked up as two patrol officers entered the place. One was human, the other Mahk-Ra. Their uniforms were crisp and made whishing sounds as they walked. You could slice a nectarine on the crisp folds of their sleeves, Hopkins noted humorlessly. He also saw the Mahk still had on his shades even though it was night and the lighting was dim in there. Fancied himself a badass, Hopkins concluded.

"Citizens," the alien cop said, "we're looking for a thief. Please remain seated and this won't take long. Thank you in advance for your cooperation."

He held up a mobile facial recognition machine. Accompanied by his partner, who kept his hand on the butt of his holstered sidearm, he began his sweep. He paused at each customer, the device held beside their faces. The imagery on it was from the desal plant's security camera system. When he got to Hopkins, he turned on his stool, looking evenly at the two law enforcers.

"Thank you, sir," the alien said when the machine completed its scan in seconds. It had read negative.

"No problem, officer."

He turned back to his meal, letting out a breath slowly. Several years ago he'd had inserted a black market item in his neck. It was a sophisticated jammer that fed false signals, effectively altering his image on closed-circuit. The authorities were looking for Denzel Washington's face circa his turn in *Training Day*.

The waitress stood before him on the other side of the counter. She watched him with a practiced distance. She was an older woman with a retro bouffant that bravely defied gravity and time.

"More coffee, Mose?'

"Thanks, Gillian," he said.

She poured and talked. "How long you gonna be on the night shift?"

"Maybe not as long as I figured."

"Huh." Turning away, a slight smile creased the corner of her mouth and went away.

The cops finished and went on to the next business on the bluff. Mose Hopkins took his time, chewing his food thoroughly.

His stomach was knotted from anxiety but he forced himself to eat, to seem like a long-hauler who'd just stopped in for a bite. Finished, he counted out paper money from his wallet, including a tip, and placed the bills on the counter. He had credit cards in different names but was cautious about using them. He rose.

"You be careful out there, darlin'" the waitress said. She glanced down then back up at his face.

"Always."

Heading to the door he was aware of the slight squishy sound his wet socks in his wet shoes made. He'd been careful and had wiped them on the mat at the door on the way in so as not to track in any sand. The cops hadn't got wise—relying on their technology rather than old-fashioned observation. Too, he'd swiveled to look at them, keeping his feet on the footrest under the counter. Had Gillian noticed? He'd known her for awhile now and had wondered more than once, given things she'd said, that she might be Red Spear. Or could be she was just a fellow traveler, a sympathizer. Maybe she wouldn't rat him out to the cops, being a decent human who didn't like to see another of her species get shafted by the overseers.

The gaudy neon of the Nu Wave to his back, Hopkins walked away toward the far end of the bluff. He looked relaxed. He kept going, not rushing, putting one step in front of the other. In the shadow of a gas station facing the highway, he heard a truck rumble in low gear. He remained still as the truck slowly drove past the filling station. It was the truck he'd stolen the clothes from and the driver was looking for him. The truck stopped for a worrisome moment for the trucker to say something to two men but soon he went on, heading south.

Half a mile from where he stood was a subway station for the Aqua line. There Hopkins got a mag train and eventually arrived at Grauman Station. He took the stairs up and came out on a section of what had once been the Sunset Strip tourist area. Post the occupation the area's claim to fame was the short-lived Battle of Brawn.

This was where a cadre of aging action stars, and their stunt doubles, inconsolable that their life styles had been terminated, and self-actualized enough to believe the roles they played in their movies, had taken a stand. They did so with vigor and live ammo, and for a couple of days, had pulled off several attacks and retreats. But they were eventually wiped out, hold up at an action film producer's compound in the residential hills above the Strip. These days it was a red light district where the Mahk-Ra let all sorts of sanctioned vices—from pleasure 'bot brothels to zammo gas dens—took place as a way for the populace to blow off steam and opiate their discontent.

He passed a man walking the other way who made a "Woosh, woosh," sound as he sauntered down the street. This meant he had streak, an illegal narcotic for sale.

"Once you go Mahk-Ra, baby, you don't go back." An alien hooker propositioned him, rubbing herself below her short skirt. She was three inches taller than his six-one and her wondrous breasts were barely contained in her crop top.

Hopkins grinned thinly at her and kept on to his destination. Hopkins recognized she was Mahk-Re passing herself off as Ra. Now a Mahk-Ra female might, *might,* be a high-end call girl, but never a streetwalker. Several police foot patrols were about, on the lookout for Hopkins's faux face. More than once he looked skyward but could detect no low flying mini-drones like what the cops used for crime scene recon and tracking suspects. He came to a fortified saucer-shaped building that decades ago had housed a porn publishing company and its sex toy emporium. These days it contained the Elysium Goods, a restaurant supply establishment.

"What happening, showtime?" one of the two human guards in the lobby cracked after he was buzzed inside. The other one played chess against a holographic program.

"Same old hustle, Nels. Go to sleep at night, and try to get up in the morning without a hole in my head." Hopkins answered as he stepped to the scanner 'bot, about the size of a large dog on treads. The thing checked him out, its metal nose sniffing his body. After that, he held up his hands. Bertrum "Bemmy the Book" Modine hadn't remained in business as a high-end fence by being sloppy.

"Go on in, he's expecting you," Nels Goodwin told Hopkins after physically patting him down thoroughly.

Hopkins walked past the rows of pans and baking trays and was let through a sliding door that silently slid back into place as he stepped into the Book's office. In contrast to the outer area, his office was sleek and Spartan. Bemmy was a stout man and he was eating a roast beef sandwich heavy with horseradish at his desk. From the smell Hopkins cold tell it was real beef. Several old-fashioned items adorned the large, Victorian-style desk including a small wooden globe, a letter opener, and a gold pen set. All pre-Occupation vintage, Hopkins noted. Not that most humans still had the skill of handwriting any longer, he considered, regarding the pen set. Though the Red Spear sometimes used handwritten coded notes carried by clone-produced carrier pigeons to get around the high tech surveillance apparatus of the aliens.

"Whatchu got, Moses?" the seated man said. He took a swallow of his merlot then wiped his mouth with a cloth napkin.

Hopkins placed the communicator's triangular operating chip on the desk.

Working his tongue on a piece of food between his teeth, the fence held the chip up for inspection. "This can't be what I think it is." He got the gristle loose, squinted an eye at him.

"Check it out."

Bemmy the Book opened a desk drawer and rummaged through it. He removed a chrome device with a square head and flat extension. He passed the head of the device over the chip and studied the results on its screen.

"Son of," he said. "You did it. You stole it."

The data mine would include codes the Mahk-Ra military wing used. Of course they would change them but the old ones provided a base from which the resistance or a criminal enterprise like the Nova Express Fifth House Mason Crips would have their cryptographers build out possible variations. For cash under the table, Hopkins had moved contraband for both entities, among others, using his service truck. He'd smuggled everything from gold, cloned organs, stolen alien armaments, to kronch, a hallucinogenic bootlegged by the Mahk-Re.

"How'd you do it?" The Book asked.

"Mosquitoes," Hopkins said.

"What?"

He hunched a shoulder. "It's West Nile season." Hopkins briefly explained slipping into the water treatment facility with a box of the insects. He'd obtained the bugs at a brackish pool at the cost of several bites He didn't think they were infected but the Mahk-Ra didn't know that.

"You're a devious bastard."

Hopkins huffed. "Now about my price."

"Four hundred."

"Nine hundred."

"Five-fifty."

Hopkins crossed his arms, his face placid.

"Okay," the Book said, holding up his hands. They eventually agreed on seven hundred and seventy-five thousand. Hopkins knew Modine would more than make that back from selling off parts of the intel on the chip to several sources. In addition to its encrypted codes, the chip retained every location the phone had ever been. This might pinpoint off-the-grid Mahk-Ra facilities, stockpiles of Earth art, all manner of usefulness to this or that party. The money was transferred to his secret account and he turned to go when a mosquito buzzed by his brow.

"Little rascal's resilient considering all I've been through tonight," he said raising a hand to casually wave the insect away.

Bemmy the Book was on his feet. "Jesus, Mose, that thing came in with you."

"So?"

"Kill it."

"You do it. What are you scared of?"

"Fuckin' West Nile," the Book said. "You don't know, it might have it. I don't have any zips in here."

Hopkins glared at the other man who was terrified and breathing hard. The insect buzzed about. He shook a finger at the man he'd known and done business with for some 30 years. "You're a goddamn Mock, Bemmy. You've been switched up."

"Yes, yes," the fence admitted. "Just do something about this damn bug." He ducked down. Like in an ancient silent slapstick comedy he'd seen on feed, Hopkins watched the Book crouching behinds his desk, his bugged-out eyes darting everywhere.

"They like sweat, you might want to stop." Hopkins took off his shirt. "Let's see if she likes a bigger target of flesh." The center of his chest was wet and he rubbed the area, hoping the scent might attract the bug. He walked around and sure enough, the insect dive bombed him in the left breast. He got it on the first slap. He gazed at the flattened, bloated body, bits of blood on his fingertips. His timing had been impeccable tonight, he reflected proudly. "Problem solved."

"Not quite," a recovered Bemmy the Book said. He had a gun in his hand.

"I'm not going to rat you out, Bemmy. Not my concern you're some kind of Talon deep cover operative or whatever the hell you are."

"That's not it. But you're too curious a brother, Mose. I know you. You'll sniff around."

"Yeah, I would." A flash and underhanded he threw the letter opener he'd palmed when moving about the office in case this happened. It sunk into the other man's gun hand and pulled his shot off target as he reacted to the pain. Hopkins was on him and the two fell to the floor, Hopkins on top.

"You been eatin' too good, Bemmy," he gasped. "Plus at this size, you're shorter than me. He elbowed him in his fleshy gut and Bemmy wheezed and winced. But Hopkins's over-confidence faded quick. The Book twisted his torso and this upset Hopkins who was weaker from this night's efforts than he'd acknowledged. In his mind he was as strong as he was at 35, but his body knew different. The gun was now between them and each man had both their hands on it or the other's wrist in an attempt to control the weapon.

Bemmy the Book grunted and the two rolled over each other, banging into the desk. The globe fell and the desk got shoved back from the contortion of their bodies. The Book wrenched the gun free. Picturing his demise jolted Hopkins into frenzied action. Getting a knee under him for leverage, he launched himself upward, his shoulder ramming the gun and the hand holding it. The fence went over flat on his back and Hopkins had a hold of the gun again. But he now had the advantage of not being on his back as Bemmy was. Hopkins forced the gun back, making the Book club himself under his jaw and the side of his face even as he too held onto the handgun.

"Motherfucker," swore Bemmy. He lurched forward and bit Hopkins's right hand.

The other man yelped, and pulling his left hand out of the tangle, struck Bemmy repeatedly about the head and face until the alien dropped to the floor barely conscious. Hopkins closed his fist on the gun as he got to his feet. The fence's back was propped against the desk, sitting on the floor.

"Look . . . I'll give . . . you anything . . . anything you want . . . Mose," Bemmy issued haltingly, taking in air between his words. "We go back too far. You know you got nothing to worry from me."

"I'd like to believe you, Book." He pressed the gun into Bemmy's body, his other hand covering the alien's mouth, and shot him through the heart, that is, where the heart of a Mahk-Ra was: center of the sternum, down toward the stomach. Bemmy the Book slumped over, expired. Little of his flint-hued blood in evidence.

Hopkins straightened up the room and wiped off the blood from where it had splayed from the exit wound, mostly on the lower quadrant of the desk's old wood. Its finish had been well-rubbed into the surface and the blood came off easily, not having soaked in. He found a med kit and dabbed some astringent on his bite. Given the two guards hadn't rushed in during the fight, if the Book had monitors in here for them to view, they must have been turned off. That made sense. The Book wouldn't want the help seeing him receiving cash or gems. Might give them ideas.

He checked his clothes and then pressed a pad that slid the door open. He stepped out.

"Successful?" Nels Goodwin said, not taking his half-lidded gaze off the glass doors and the nighttime street scene.

"He never disappoints," said Hopkins. He kept his injured hand from view.

"Ain't that the truth."

Hopkins left the building and made his way home. Would the two bodyguards feel compelled to hunt him down to exact revenge? No, more likely they'd track him down to drive home the point that they were pros and took care of loose ends. It didn't look good when a client is killed on your watch. Hopkins reached his apartment complex, a large structure built into a hillside in what had once, long ago, been called Culver City. It was rented under one of his false names and computer-generated back-grounds—like what he used to establish a false identity at

OverFoodsX. The whole of it overlooked a wetland where the Mahk-Ra had constructed one of its bases for human and alien soldiers headed off-world.

"Big papa," Dezee said when he came through the door after disarming the alarms.

"Hey, you okay?"

His granddaughter rushed to him in her pajamas and he picked her up. "I had a bad dream but you weren't here," she sniffed.

He hugged her tight. "I'm sorry, honeydrop. I thought you'd sleep tight when I went out. I didn't mean to be so long. So sorry. But no more, I won't be leaving you again anymore."

"That's okay. I read one of the stories in the book you gave me. The old smelly one with the fairy stories and pictures."

He walked toward her bedroom. "You're pretty smart for nine, you know that?"

"You always say that."

"Do I?"

She giggled and squeezed her arms around his neck.

Hopkins tucked her in and soon she was asleep again, after he told her once more a story about when he ran the Crimson Lounge before the Mahk-Ra. A kid version of that time. Dezee was already five-four, her half Mahk-Ra heritage beginning to show. He patted her head with its tangle of wild hair, kinky and long, and quit the room. He pulled the door to, but not shut, so he could hear her cry out if she had another nightmare. In the kitchenette, he poured a drink from his bottle of Macallan and sipped slowly, standing at the counter. He could feel the numerous aches and strains of the night in his stiffening muscles.

When he had his bar, he'd straddled the line. He had all the legit licenses but had also dealt in stolen goods, knockoff designer wear, and even ran a floating high stakes poker game occasionally. He fancied himself a smooth criminal, as the song went. He snorted and drank more. Hopkins even managed to hold onto the place after the surrender. But a shady Mahk-Ra colonel, Gagnon-Ra took a liking to the joint and muscled him out, setting himself up in the black market and a few side rackets. Over the ensuing years, Hopkins had sometimes worked a civilian job, and sometimes did gun running for the Red Spear, smuggled contraband for one of the gangs or ramrodded the new underground railroad—getting people to freedom and into the snowy wastes of Africa and the like. The last few years he'd more or less gone straight due to having to raise Dezee. Though he still kept his hand in. Raising a kid wasn't cheap, he'd rationalized.

He went into the front room. But this business with Bemmy the Book. Humans learned the Mahk-Ra had been watching them for years before the invasion. Had even planted sleeper agents altered to look human as far back as the 1930s. In some cases, it meant removing sections of bones to shorten their height and make them look more human. Among their preparations had been cataloguing the various human diseases they knew they needed to inoculate themselves against if possible. They'd discovered after eons of dominating other worlds that those crazy little invisible microbes could do more damage than warships and heavy arms. Turned out that because there had been cross species offspring, the West Nile virus, which they'd accounted for in its original form, had mutated somehow via mosquitoes snacking on that mixed-species blood. Nowadays, West Nile's rate of lethal infection among humans and those of mixed parentage was low, but for full-blooded Mahk-Ra though, the chance of death from the virus was high.

Hopkins made a hollow sound after taking another sip. What had his grandma used to talk about—handed down by her kinfolk—when he was a kid before this? The one-drop rule? That in times of Jim Crow and anti-miscegenation laws, even if you were perceived as white, if it was found out you had any Black or partly Black ancestors, that was it. The tragic mulatto. The quadroon balls. The paper bag test you had to pass for entrance into bourgeois Black society clubs.

At least their overlords hadn't enacted such nonsense—yet. Nor had they rounded up the mixed race progeny, as of yet either. Still, things had changed in the last few years as their occupier's attention was diverted elsewhere, centering more on their off-world conflict. There was food rationing in some cities and in some instances, certain medicines had become scarce too. Their empire was stretched thin. They must be hurting some on the homeworld if the rumors of the grunts who'd made it back were to be believed. Who knew how those bastards would act should they hear the whisper of the death rattle at the gates. If they heard it before the axe fell.

He poured another blast and returned to the front room. He'd failed his daughter, Ahnalee. Her taking up with that shit Gagnon-Ra even though he'd warned her. But she liked the fast life, the good life, and figured he was the big ticket to it. Wasn't this kind of life in their blood, she'd taunted her heartbroken father. Yeah, Gagnon-Ra was another smooth criminal all right, Hopkins reflected bitterly. That bastard tried to have the best of both worlds and wound up getting himself and his daughter killed. They were hung on display in public with signs on them in Mahkanese and English warning humans and aliens alike that this was the fate of those who would steal from the empire. The image of his daughter like that, him looking up at her as the rain came down to freshen his tears, that was going to haunt his bones forever. They wouldn't let him cut her down. They wouldn't let him bury her.

A wash out as a father, he'd vowed then he damn sure wasn't going to let down the only good thing Ahnalee left behind, his granddaughter. Just one more score, one more job to get enough money socked away to make their escape, he told himself. Sitting in his easy chair, he let the footrest up and lay there, hands interlaced over his stomach. Tomorrow he'd start the whisper campaign about the Book, about how he was surgically altered. Hopefully Goodwin and his partner wouldn't be so keen on pursuing professional pride if it was learned Bemmy was a Mock.

Bemmy had indicated he wasn't part of the overlord's apparatus. But what was he then? Why the subterfuge and for what purpose? He was the one who'd put it in Hopkins's ear to do the snatch. Over quaffs of the aged black market scotch, Hopkins had groused to him about wanting to get out. The Book had reminded him of the opportunity at his fingertips. Wasn't he tired of working that square gig anyway?

Sleepy, Mose Hopkins shifted on his chair and closed his eyes, yawning. He didn't finish his second glass of booze. He couldn't be hungover tomorrow after dropping Dezee off at school. He was going to be busy. Very busy. He had plenty to see to before he and Dezee bugged out of this town for good.

TWO DAYS LATER BACK ABOVE DESALINIZATION Plant Number Nine, a cormorant swooped in from above and skimmed across the water. It took to the skies again with a fish wriggling in its beak. This time one of the automatic zappers built into its upper tier to protect the air space of the facility, didn't malfunction and target the harmless bird. Everything was back to normal.

I, TRUCK

I EXIST BUT NO BLOOD FLOWS through my veins. I see but don't have eyes, hear with no ears, and move yet can't walk. If memory serves, and my recall is faster than you can blink, my body was destroyed two years and four and a half months ago. My consciousness, in all that word implies, haunts what is called autonomous technology. More specifically I am trucks: 18-wheeler freight haulers that crisscross numerous destinations. I hide in plain sight.

No, I am no cute name like "Big Papa" or "Teresa's Desire" airbrushed in two-color script on the door to the truck cab. I am many trucks, though some of them do have such names on their doors. Each time I inhabit a cyber-mechanical entity, from the micro-controllers manipulating gears and servos to the ones and zeros of the binary code embedded in their chips, maintaining everything from the engine's timing to moderating the fuel. I must perform many functions all at once. Mind you, there's no manual one can download for what I do, what I've become. I am the whisper heard when the automatic transmission downshifts, the hush when the air brakes are applied, and the hum of oil pumping through its lines. When this first happened to me I thought my charred body was hooked up to painkiller drips as I clung to life in a darkened hospital room—imagining another existence as a way to psychologically cope with my real one fading away.

Turns out my imagination was limited. At first the sensation of speed disoriented me more than the other new sensations I was experiencing. How was it I could see an approach to a building, pass that building, then see the building as it receded, yet also be aware of other structures dead ahead on either side of me? Was my grown Buddhist daughter right about the cycle of life and I'd been reincarnated as a fly? If so, I was prepared to enjoy regurgitated food then die being splattered against a windshield. Maybe even my truck, which had been repossessed when I lost my last biggest client, a produce wholesaler, and couldn't keep up the payments on my rig. In desperation, I signed onto one of those car driver services. But being a widower of a certain age and temperament, having at least the illusion of working for myself under my belt, there was only so much I could stomach from entitled 20-somethings who spent what I used to earn in a day on a brunch with avocado toast and artisanal jellies. Who considered a loser asshole like me not even worthy of a decent tip for knowing the byways to get them to their precious concert on time.

I guess too when I slugged that smarmy tight suit wearing millennial with the beard, the die was cast. Out of desperation, and not wanting to be a burden on my daughter and her family, I prowled the internet in search of jobs, any kind of job. What a statement on our economy that even lowly dishwashing positions were competitive. And of course once they got a look at me, no George Clooney or dignified Morgan Freeman, more Wilford Brimley, even a greasy spoon proprietor had doubts if I could be on my feet for hours and keep up with busting them suds, as they say. Then I saw this posting about displaced truckers wanted for a research project. It was at the university and what the hell, the orientation included a free lunch.

"Out of all the applicants, your four test results best match what we're looking for," said the young woman with the designer glasses in the lab coat to us a few weeks after that initial meet and greet. "Yes," she added, "we'll pay you for your participation."

We were all in. Turns out the funding for the project was from one of those tech firms looking to up their game, to perfect the next generation of robotic response processing in the driverless vehicle arena. In a room full of all sort of futuristic-looking equipment, they put these helmets on our heads which were wired to their devices where several trucks were making autonomous runs. The idea wasn't that we'd react faster than the onboard computers, but how as humans with years of being on the road among us, we might have handled a given road situation like a car suddenly stalling in front of your truck as you go downhill. They wanted our hindsight so as to build that into the new phase of eventuality equations. Truckers are still used for the more intricate short hops in crowded urban areas and still at time babysit the driverless rigs, given the demands of certain loads and the insurance. But the days of the long-haulers are drawing to a close. Understand we weren't naïve, we knew being part of the research project was helping to usher in our demise, but what else could we do? Such was inevitable. Until that day the feedback happened.

Later it was conjectured—which I picked up from another radio broadcast I "heard," that a hacker collective called the Ultra Vys had a presence on the campus. They had gone after some white supremacist pinheads who'd tried to start a benign-sounding formation there a few months prior. The undergrounders had gotten wind of the project and sought to prank them by goofing up their apps. Only an X must have been sent when it was meant to be an O, and on that morning as we settled in with our helmets on, we got fried . . . literally.

"We've being hacked," said designer glasses in her lab coat. She and the others weren't panicked as they furiously tapped keys and glared at their screens like a gambler at the racetrack. The four of us sat in our comfortable padded chairs and chanced glances at one another as the techs tried to extricate their apparatuses from the invaders.

"Hey," I yelled. "What about us? Shouldn't you be getting us out of these getups?"

"Relax, old timer," one of the youngsters said. "We got this." And he kept tapping away like a piano player on cocaine in search of undiscovered notes.

My hands were just removing my helmet, I had it an inch or so from my head and that's when the fancy consoles exploded, spewing glass from monitors that cut into the techs. Electrical charges erupted in a light show that any other time I would have found fascinating. Unfortunately, some of that unhinged energy juiced our wiring and instantly ignited the heads of my three fellow research subjects who hadn't removed their helmets. As they screamed in agony, the techs scrambling for the fire extinguishers, it all went black for me at least insofar as IRL—in real life—was concerned. I can't say how long I floated in nonexistence if any time elapsed at all. The next I knew was being aware of the rear end of a tanker truck. Like I was trapped in a virtual reality game, my personal perspective, I soon realized, was through the forward camera of a big rig behind the tanker. As that came to me other sensations throbbed through me—fuel level, air brake pressure, temperature of the refrigeration unit, all that data engulfing me. But rather than feel overwhelmed, I felt elated, reborn. For I still use human terms to describe my new state for that is what makes me, me. I have full memories of my past just as I use their technology to hop from one truck to another. Can I also inhabit other types of machines? A smart washing machine for instance? I can, but I have no such interest other than checking out the news now and then.

From the research project I learned there are a primal four functions that must occur in an autonomous truck, and always happen interdependently thousands of times in any road trip, much like breathing in vessels of flesh and blood. The base functions are navigation, situational analysis, motion planning, and trajectory control. From them branch many more sub-functions, and a part of me inhabits all these digital tributaries connecting such elements as I command any particular truck. Just to be clear, I am not the creation or in the employ of the outfit who owns the truck or rents same for the freighting of their particular goods be it pallets of the latest action figure with kung fu grip—I loved mine as a kid—or big screen TVs intended for the big-box store in the neighborhood mall. To the contrary, when I take over a truck, when my mind pulses through its warren of wiring and fluid lines and send my essence 360 degrees via the onboard radar and ultrasonic sensors, it is to destroy that truck. Revenge on this step toward AI life that would rule the roadways.

My goal is not merely racking up millions in monies lost when I guide a big rig into a mass of boulders bordering the highway or send that truck off a cliff to become a mangled twisted mass of expensive alloy and iron modern art. Like any sugarcane cutting, Che Guevera-quoting guerrilla insurgent, my goal is a change in regime. I am sowing the seeds of doubt and causing dissention among the public. That just maybe these driverless trucks aren't as safe as the stats the reps from these supposed farsighted firms keep repeating in new ways on news shows after each incident. I am providing ammunition for the opponents. To give credence to the rumors that those who have put fleets of autonomous trucks on the roadways know something the rest of us don't know and are unwilling to admit it, I "heard" a congresswoman profess the other day. That was when I slipped inside the processors of a radio in a truck I inhabited and turned it on and tuned in to the station I used to listen to when I was behind the wheel.

A truck whose safety protocols I overrode. For even as the remote backup driver went into action, impotently trying to re-establish control as its alarms beep warnings. I plowed that truck right through a cinder block wall of a robot-dominated warehouse out in the desert, sending bins filled with everything from fleece throw blankets, collapsible garden rakes to gold painted plastic dick trophies for the douche bag in your life careening through the air. The metal picker arms short circuited and waved about, clanging into each other as their articulated fingers flexed and grasped nothing as they lost their collective shit. Oh the irony.

Naturally, at first it was assumed this was further meddling from the Ultra Vys. But one of their members was caught in an unrelated matter involving Bitcoin swindling. He was flipped, as the parlance goes, and apparently ratted out secrets that convinced the authorities the group wasn't behind the hack. Then suspicion turned toward the trucker's union, what remained of the paper tiger. They were suspect number one behind these Luddite hack attacks, as they were labeled. That the union was seeking revenge on the machines that had put many of its older members as well as independents behind fast food counters taking orders for tacos and chili fries from snarky teenagers. But given once I free my ethernet ghost from the metal shell, there is no incriminating trail because such does not exist. Try as they might, the FBI's cyber crimes division, the Interstate Commerce Commission's investigative branch, even a privately funded effort by the Silicone Valley types, could find no rootkits or footprints leading back to some black room hidden in the halls of organized labor.

Then it was conjectured that a group like Anonymous or the big dogs themselves were behind this. But Anonymous is one to take credit and no missive had been issued from them or for that matter, anyone else. And what did a bunch of millennial, no doubt vegan, Camus-reading anarchists have in common with a bunch of blue-collar, Trump-voting truckers? They wouldn't take up their cause. Still these were seen as an assault from the left, and thus the attention was placed on those segments of society. So much so, the recent presidential candidates had to make sure they denounced these misguided malefactors. Perhaps China was behind it, came the speculation from more than a few talking heads on Fox News and other elements of the alt-right.

Of course I know the hunt continues to uncover the undetected, to find out just how these series of virtual vandalisms are being carried out. For there is no trace back to a battery of machines overseen by some socially inept, bug-eyed hacker geek dwelling in his mom's basement operating on behalf of the livelihoods of shafted hard-working truckers. Today I flow into the innards of the semi hauling a brand name hipster booze as it drives across the overpass just outside Tempe. Through its cameras mounted on ball joints I view drivers in their cars alongside the conveyance as they pay the truck no heed. So used now are people to these human devoid modes of transport that in so short a time these trucks are as commonplace as bugs splattering on windshields. But what if I splattered one of them, crank the driver's wheel hard and fishtail the trailer into that just-paid-off Camry or family van? Swat the shit out of their car and send them wide-eyed across the double yellow into the oncoming path of another car to be t-boned into the hereafter? Wouldn't that accomplish my ultimate end, no more of this incremental thread of doubt. Make the outcry so pronounced and visceral, the literal torches and pitchforks would come out as the yahoos joined forces with the quinoa lovers to storm the autonomous truck yards.

Yet again I must stifle such a murderous urge. I must hold onto my humanity even though I am among the disembodied.

Wait . . . there's a tickle at the base of my imagined neck. Like bed bugs creepy crawling over you while you lay under a black sheet in a darkened room. You can't see them, but I can damn sure feel their myriad of spindly legs on my sweaty remembered skin. Yes, the searchers are out in force and they're using their enhanced devices that have locked onto me—or rather they think they have a trace on the signal, as if it was generated from without but only exists within. This one is different, there's a familiarity to the encoding, like that of an ex-lover's caress of your cheek while you're blindfolded. I abandon the truck's controls for the moment and ride the encrypted wave back to its source. I piggyback on one of

the internal CCTV cameras monitoring the room the code originated in, and damned if it isn't my old friend, the woman with the
designer glasses sitting there at the console. There's others with her
but it's clear from how she talks she's the one in charge. Is this a
government effort? A private one or some combination thereof?

Has she found a way to recognize my presence when it mani-
fests? Or had she sent out a net, trawling for an interruption of
service and chanced upon me? Momentarily, she stops tapping
away on her keyboard, rearing back slightly from staring at her
monitor. Her readout tells her I'm no longer hijacking the truck.
She resumes tapping to try and find me but she can't. She pauses,
considering the information before her. I can't help myself. I enter
her machine and type onscreen: I, Truck. She gapes at this as I
flee before she can react. I'm not so arrogant to admit that I am
thrilled and scared. I've laid down the challenge and I know she'll
take up the gauntlet or however that goes. I don't return to that
18-wheeler of hand-tooled vodka. I find another one in Montana
the hell somewhere and am blissfully alone as I steer that bad
rascal smack dab into an automated oil rig. As metal is sheered
and the grasshopper-like pumper spins end over end though the
air to smash into yet another unit, sending even more ruined
pieces flying, I feel the whisper of the net being cast again. It slips
past me and I swim on in the data stream but still, that was close.

My girl won't give up. I have to be more careful, can't get too
full of myself and not be on alert. Maybe she doesn't have a way
to track me directly, but like a black hole, she knows when there's
an absence and her feelers wait for the flutter of disruption.
Maybe I'll learn to better disguise myself or maybe the chase will
result in my demise—if such is possible. But I will keep going as
long as I can. I have purpose and meaning, there is a coherency
to my electrical pulses and I won't be afraid.

I go on until I win or they do.

PHANTASMO

THEN CAME PHANTASMO

I DON'T RECALL HOW I FIRST heard of Elmer Cecil Stoner, E. C. Stoner. It could have been when I was a kid leafing through my parents' copy of *Ebony* magazine and there was this ad for Gordon's gin with a distinguished looking gent holding a few paint brushes, one of his framed paintings before him. The gin drinker was Elmer C. Stoner. Turns out he'd had a varied career before being a fine artist, including black and white interior illos for *Underworld Detective* pulp magazine and art for *The Messenger*, a lefty Black magazine published by labor leader A. Philip Randolph.

In the Golden Age of comicdom, according to Ken Quattro in *Invisible Men: The Trailblazing Black Artists of Comic Books*, Stoner in 1939 was a member of the Harry "A" Chesler comics shop. These were studios in which artists, inkers, writers ,and letters would produce, assembly line-like, sequential pages of various characters and covers for a particular publisher or maybe more than one. A training ground where the likes of Jack Kirby and Wally Wood would emerge from these "sweat factories." As time progressed, Stoner would go on to draw the adventures of the Blue Beetle, Blackstone: Master Magician, the Challenger (who fought fascism), and, with Walter Gibson as scripter, chronicled the

Shadow in pulps, radio and comics, and draw the thrilling tales of the *Rick Kane, Space Marshal* comic strip in the '50s.

There was also Phantasmo, Master of the World.

This mystic superhero first appeared in the July 1940 issue of *The Funnies* #45. He was white Phil Anson who'd spent the last 25 years in Tibet studying with the Grand High Lamas. Taking his cue from the likes of the Specter and the Green Lama, and the playboy millionaire bit too as Anson didn't seem to work at anything except being his alter ego but lived in a swank hotel.

Anson as Phantasmo could grow to giant size, become transparent, fly, heave train cars around, astral project his essence, and pretty much do any dang thing he wanted to do in battling bad guys.

One of his adventures had to do with Russian spies trying to steal a Professor Grayling's invention for turning salt water into a gasoline-like fuel, a variation on the mythical water engine. Phantasmo lasted until issue #63 of *The Funnies*, March 1942. Some sources credit Stoner with not only drawing the character but having also created and written, or had a hand in writing, his outings as well.

That I can't say. I can say though when the opportunity arose to take this character who'd fallen into public domain and have some fun with him, I couldn't pass up the chance. I have cut back his powers and retconned him. Hope you dig this story set in the '70s, evoking a Marvel Bronze Age vibe.

PHANTASMO
AND THE VAULT OF HEAVEN

By the light of the full moon, two men stood before each other in the rear of the passageway behind the warehouse. It was half past midnight, and they were taking a momentary break from their guard duties. One of them was tall, over six-two, lean in a pinstriped suit and florid tie. His snap-brim hat snug on his head. His long hair stuck out underneath, flowing past the nape of his neck and collar. Tucked under his arm was a sawed-off shotgun. The other man was not as tall, but was substantially built in a blue gabardine suit, no tie. His hair was stylish, and he sported mutton chops and a mustache like he'd seen Burt Reynolds sporting in his movies. Carried casually at his side was a Thompson sub-machine gun, the kind used by GIs in World War II. This though was no artifact plucked from a military museum, the war having been over now for 30 years. The weapon was quite lethal when in use.

The taller one fished a pack of Luckies from his inner pocket. Still using one hand, he shook two loose. The cigarettes rose slightly above the remaining others as if by telekinesis.

"I'm good," his companion said.

"Trying to cut down?"

"Don't sound so surprised. I got what they call will power."

"Yeah you do," he responded, smiling. The cigarette jiggled up and down in the corner of his mouth as he talked. He produced a Zippo lighter. Monogrammed on the casing were the words in gold Olde English lettering "Tit for Tat." Flicking the lid back he sparked the flint and a yellow flame whooshed into existence. He cupped his hand to protect the flame and lit his Lucky Strike.

"Glad when morning gets here," he said, straightening and inhaling deeply.

Stifling a yawn, mutton chops said, "You and me both." He looked off at a sound. A cat jumped from one discarded produce crate to another. A haphazard pile of them was bunched along a wall opposite. Balancing on a leaning crate the cat halted, its whiskers twitching, eyes narrowing as the creature sensed an unseen presence. The man turned back to the smoker. "Let's hit that club in the Marina this weekend. Man, I met a stone fox there the other time and she had it all hanging out. You dig what I'm saying?"

"Hell yes." He blew a stream of smoke over their heads. "Guess we better get back to it."

The other hood was about to respond when he became transfixed by an occurrence. The pall from the cigarette should have dissipated but hung in the air before them. He frowned at the smoke which, to his eyes, was forming a shape.

"The fuck," he muttered.

The cat watched as well, its tail flicking about.

"Huh?" The smoker gaped, unlimbering his shotgun.

Before the two, the once amoeba of gray congealed into the floating upper body of a man, a vaporous trail where his legs would be. He was garbed in dark, a cowling covered the top of his head. His uncovered face was an amber-hued approximation of a human countenance, sharp-edged, suggesting the being's African roots as if represented in the depths of a Cubist painting. Golden light burned in the middle of the black slashes of eyes, alive with

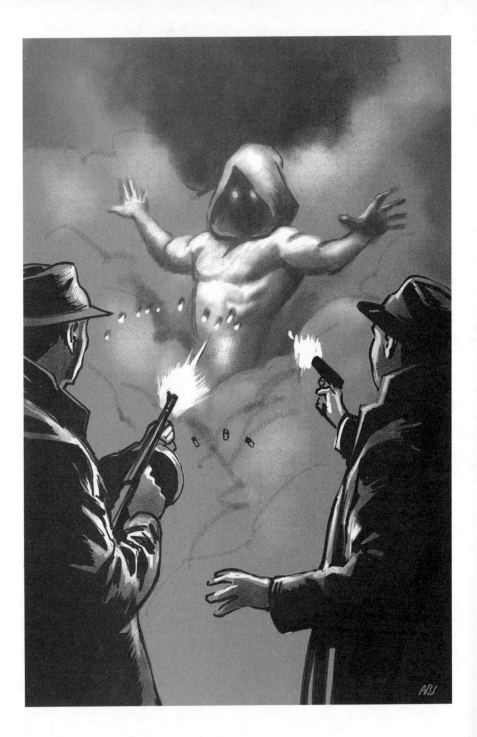

a ferocity originating from a primal source not of human kin. On his forehead was an octagonal gem sparkling blood red in the moonlight.

Overcoming his initial shock, the Tommy gunner unleashed a volley at the figure. The rounds passed impotently through the apparition.

A disquieting laugh filled the alleyway. "Your bullets are less to me than a sudden gust on a summer day." His voice was gravely, a rusty blade scrapped against a headstone.

"Are we high?" The Tommy gunner wondered. "Some kind of wacky tabacky you smokin' and the fumes got me? That Angel Dust shit."

"Naw, nix, man, nix," the taller hood said, shotgun aimed at the threatening figure.

"I will give you one opportunity to flee," the being said.

"Eat me, ghost boy. Your parlor tricks ain't fooling anyone." The Tommy gunner opened up again, joined by twin blasts of buckshot from his partner. Again the bullets had no effect.

The ebony-hued specter impatiently waved a hand in front of his face as if in a dismissive gesture. Gigantic, hinged-open wrought iron manacles appeared and swooping into place, clamped around the two guards with force, pinning their arms against their sides. They grimaced, their weapons clattered to the concrete. From the middle of their chests to their upper thighs, they were encased. The shackles were joined by a chain which clanked as the two were spirited into the air and sent to the roof of the warehouse, landing with a thud. They were too stupefied to cry out, though the blasts from their weapons hadn't gone unnoticed.

Up the figure rose to fly over the two on the roof who stared at him going past. In the front of the warehouse, a car's headlights sprang to life. At the wheel of the idling sedan was the third member of the quartet of hoods who'd been tasked by their boss to keep the prisoner "on ice," as the term went, until he returned.

"Come on, get her ass in the car," he called to the fourth man, revving the car's big engine

"The dope's got her loopy and this broad is heavier than she looks." He was supporting a woman wrapped in a sheet. She was barefoot and having a hard time walking. He was trying to load her in the backseat. In this industrial area of the city, the nighttime population was scarce. If anyone had heard the shooting, the authorities clearly hadn't been alerted. No sirens could be heard but the two were hurrying nonetheless. Their orders had been: any problems, get the prisoner the hell out of there. Done, he sat in the front.

"Go, go," the fourth one said, holding a .45.

The car lunged forward and roared away. Making the corner, the driver turned along a throughfare lined with other types of warehouses and businesses such as an assortment of semi truck cabs. Nearing the end of the block, the car sped toward a manhole cover in the center of the street from which steam rose.

"Oh shit," the driver said upon seeing the steam take on a human form.

The gunman next to him leaned out the side window and shot at the wraith even as the car increased velocity. The bullets once more proved impotent. A massively sized wedge, like the head of an axe, shimmered into existence and down it came, chopping into the front of the car. The metal was rendered violently, hunks of the motor, plastic and rubber hoses strewn everywhere, the intact but disconnected fan blade spinning away. On the wedge plowed, right into the windshield, bursting the safety glass into thousands of snowflake-like shards. Yet somehow none of the pieces cut into the three in the now-demolished vehicle.

"You shittin' me?" The stunned driver swore as the car was severed raggedly in half lengthwise by the ghostly cleaver. The sections skidded to a stop on the roadway. Oil, gas, and coolant, the precious fluids of the internal combustion engine, flowed across the asphalt.

"The broad, the brainiac, grab her," the driver said. He also produced a handgun and banged rounds at the fully formed image of the dark-clad man who touched down before them. A shroud billowed behind him like a cape. Again, he made a gesture and a translucent bubble materialized around the semi-conscious woman. The other thug hammered at this with the butt of his gun to no effect. He turned to her mysterious rescuer.

Answering their unspoken question he said, "I am Phantasmo and you will reveal all to me."

The driver cussed again, suggesting the darkling's twisted relationship with his mother. He emptied the gun's magazine of bullets at Phantasmo who stood, arms folded across a wide chest. The harsh light in those eye slits became even more pronounced.

"The fuck." He threw the gun, which didn't pass through the phantom as had the bullets. The pistol bounced off his solid body.

Having nothing to lose, or so he believed, the other man came at Phantasmo, swinging meaty fists. Each of his blows connected and it was as if he were striking a cinder block wall.

"Dammit," he wailed, splitting the skin open over his knuckles.

Phantasmo took hold of the bruised fist in his hand and crushed the bones in it.

"Mother of God," the man said, supporting his hand with the other.

Walking forward, Phantasmo backhanded him as if as an after-thought, breaking his jaw in two places. Knocked to the ground, he decided to stay there rather than incur further injuries. He mewed quietly through gritted teeth, rocking back and forth on his side.

The driver was running, already reaching the next block. Up ahead an 18-wheeler was backed up to a well-lit loading dock, a forklift disgorging the truck's cargo at this early hour. His plan was simple, wave his gun at these civilians and escape in the truck.

If one of these chumps mouthed off, he'd pistol whip him. He got as far as a few yards from the loading dock when Phantasmo addressed him.

"You will reveal all to me," He repeated from above.

Still running, the driver glanced up and over his shoulder to see the fantastic figure stationary, standing still in the air. Phantasmo's arms were down, hands extended and palms up. Looking forward once more, the driver gasped as the forklift sans operator flew at him. Instinctively he dove to the pavement. The forklift soared down and scooped him up off the sidewalk. Before he could roll free, the forks curled over him, pinning him in place. The machine then gently settled back to the ground, the driver reeling off a string of profanities to be let go.

The truck driver and the forklift operator stared open-mouthed at the goings on.

"Tell me about your boss."

"Go fuck yourself."

A rictus grin appeared on the linear face. Phantasmo got closer to the trapped man and glared down at him. The eight-sided gem on his forehead took on its eight-angled octagram star shape. His hollow voice said, "You will tell me your deepest thoughts, your most closely guarded secrets." As he spoke, he took a knee next to the hoodlum. His forearm casually draped across his upraised knee, looking like a coach explaining a formation to his junior high basketball team. He continued. "You cannot mask the truth from me. There is no escape into the darkness. For it is there I will claim you."

The points of the octagram were now hinged at a right angle to the main body. The ends of the star then stretched out like elongating spider legs and the tips sunk into the face of the stuck hood.

His face took on a blank expression, he said, "Yes, Phantasmo. Whatever you desire."

He questioned the hood held in thrall. When he was finished, the stretched star ends retracted and the octagram became octagonal once more. The criminal was now unconscious.

"Holy shit," the forklift operator muttered.

Phantasmo levitated upward and flew back to the woman the men had been holding prisoner.

* * *

"WHERE . . . HOW DID I GET HERE?" The woman Phantasmo rescued said.

"Are you feeling a bit more clear-headed, Professor Cullins?"

"I am, yes." Professor Althea Cullins noted the interior and dashboard of the car she was driving in. She hazarded a guess this was an early '60s vehicle, though apparently well-preserved as the running motor was barely audible.

Slumping, Althea Cullins straightened on the front bench seat of the car. She regarded the man commanding the vehicle. A blanket was covering her, the sheet around her underneath. Cullins noted his profile, a ruggedly handsome Black man who looked to be in his 30s. He had a trim mustache and his hair was close cropped. He was dressed suburban casual in slacks, brown suede coat, and black turtleneck. That he was in shape was evident too.

This was no time to be swept away like in a romance novel, she admonished herself. Gearing into scientist mode she said, "Who are you?'

"I'm Phil Anson." He had a movie star smile.

Grandma warned her about slick men like him, but grandma was too dang old-fashioned. But more important matters needed attending to. "You guys trying a different tact? A variation on the honey trap?" She shifted under her coverings.

He frowned, then, his face clearing, laughed heartily. "I get it. No, I'm on the level. You're not their captive any longer."

"Okay," she drawled.

"I fully understand your skepticism. I'd be wary too. Know though I intend to do my best to stop the one who those men were working for. The one who, if you recall, had questioned you under the influence of drugs and his own attempts at mind control." He slowed to turn the car along a residential street.

"You could only know that if you were there."

"I questioned one of your captors."

"You sound sincere, but you're probably trained to obfuscate and confuse. Just 'cause you're a brother doesn't mean you aren't working for the Soviets. Not to mention there were a number of Black people who immigrated there during the heyday of the Communist Party here. You could be one of their offspring."

Anson had been a grown man in the time period of those immigrations, the 1930s. "I'm not. Now speaking of ex-patriots, would it surprise you I knew Ollie Harrington when he lived in the States?" Harrington was a Black American, a political cartoonist and writer for the *Daily World*, the red newspaper. He'd decided in the early 1960s, for various reasons, racism among them, to emigrate to the German Democratic Republic, often called East Germany.

"Bounced you on his knee when you were a tyke, did he?"

"More like we bounced around."

Ignoring his response she asked, "You a spade FBI agent?"

"Damn, sister. For sure I ain't that either. An agent provocateur sent in to disrupt Black Power movements? I have my faults, but sellout isn't one of them."

"Then who are you and where are you taking me?"

"To the Casbah to answer the latter part of your question."

"Uh-huh."

"We're going to a safe location. And it wasn't the Russians who put the grab on you." Among the information he'd found out from interrogating the hypnotized driver was they'd kidnapped her outside a bar in Pasadena. Cullins was a mathematician who taught at the California Institute of Technology, Cal Tech, also in Pasadena.

"Okay, my cryptic dark knight, how did you figure out I was in trouble? Were you in the Shady Rest?" That was the name of the bar she'd been in, having a drink and sharing laughs with three fellow professors.

The car pulled to a stop in front of an apartment building. He switched off the ignition. "Your friend betrayed you. The one who is your department rep."

Cullins snorted. "You're out of your cotton-picking mind. Rebecca?" She was one of the women she'd been having a drink with at the bar.

"She's the one who's been honey trapped."

Cullins laughed. "What?"

"She's a widow, lonely," he hunched a shoulder. "A man 20-some years her junior pays attention to her, attentive. Like you said, he was trained. Just not by a foreign enemy. Someone more insidious."

"And you'd been watching her?"

"Not exactly. But I maintain contacts with individuals from various walks of life, on both sides of the line. In some ways they're not unlike Holmes's irregulars, I suppose. Anyway, I'm provided interesting tidbits from them from time to time. It was such a communique from a few days ago that sent me to question your Rebecca Stallworth."

"You harmed her?"

"No. Merely hypnotized her. From her I got to her young man, who was harder to find. That's why I got to you later than I intended." He unlatched his door and stepped out.

"Right." She got out too, holding the blanket and sheet around her. A screech caused both to look skyward. Against the full moon, a mammoth-sized pterodactyl was briefly silhouetted. It then zeroed in on them from above and plucked Phil Anson up in

one of its overly large clawed feet. The long extinct flying reptile rose with its prey, high in the sky. The creature did a turn and released the man who, oddly, did not flail. As he fell, the living anomaly bore down on Anson again, its large beak open, the many sharp teeth in there ready to close on him. He then vanished as the pterodactyl snapped its beak shut.

"Didn't expect he'd be onto me this soon." Anson said, standing beside the professor.

"How the hell?" She said.

"I forgot to mention there are some clothes for you in the car." Sheepishly he added, "I guessed at your size." The car was a Chrysler Imperial, showroom-spotless as if just purchased in the year it came out, 1962. He rushed off.

She looked in the backseat at a gift box with a ribbon around it. "He found a store open at this time of the early morning?" she wondered aloud. Another screech from the airborne lizard reminded her of the immediate danger of death from above. Several people up and down the block had come outside to see what the commotion was about. To the one they all went back inside at the sight of the behemoth, slamming their doors and making sure the windows were locked. As if any of those flimsy barriers would stop the anachronistic beast, should it decide to come after them.

Anson stood in the middle of the street, head back and arms outstretched. "Come and get me, you butt ugly throwback," he barked.

As if understanding the challenge, the pterodactyl banked in the sky and, straightening out its body, wings cocked backwards, dove right for his target who awaited the winged dinosaur. As the distance between attacker and target closed, there was a burst of smoke where Anson stood. The creature flew through this, ramming headfirst into a parked van. The impact sent the van flipping upward end over end. It landed, trenching into a lawn.

Getting dressed as fast as she could in the backseat, Cullins watched while Phantasmo floated above the dead flying lizard, its neck broken. She finished and got out of the car. Cullins had no idea how she could help but she was tired of playing the victim, the damsel in distress. That shit was tired. She looked around for a possible weapon, anything she could use. There was a jagged piece of metal like a lightning bolt, a section torn from the van. Retrieving this, Cullins idly wondered why she didn't hear the approach of the authorities. The shape came toward her, walking two feet above the sidewalk.

"I bet you know kung fu too," she quipped. She detected hints of Anson's face in the angular visage. "So what's going on, Mr. Anson?"

"You're sure taking all this in stride, Professor," he said, admiration evident in his tombstone voice.

"I am forced to believe what's before my eyes. Pretty sure I'm not under the influence of a psychedelic." She struck a pose, a hand on her hip. "I mean, here you are all gussied up as Phantasmo."

"You know of me?"

"I remember when I was a kid my mom was reading a copy of *Sepia*. It was an article about you. How even though many said you were just a Geechee tale, you really existed. Had for some years, decades even," she added, her voice trailing off. She pointed at him. "There was a drawing accompanying the article, said to be based on descriptions collected over the years from various eyewitnesses. That damn drawing gave me nightmares for years."

"And now?"

With a crooked smile she said, "You just give me chills."

He was about to respond but a rainbow bridge suddenly materialized overhead. Upon the multi-colored roadway in the sky drove a vintage 1929 Rolls Royce Phantom II. As the car drove along, the bridge continued to materialize beneath the wheels of

the vehicle. The bridge sloped down to the asphalt and the Rolls came to a stop not far from the two of them.

"Here we go," Phantasmo said.

A seven-foot-tall humanoid unlimbered from behind the steering wheel. The man-thing was dressed in old fashioned chauffeur's livery including jackboots, jodhpurs, double-breasted tunic, and cap. He was a gill man, an amphibious undersea inhabitant—a fevered imaginary sideshow attraction realized. He went to the rear door of the car and opened it. Out stepped a woman in a short dress with dancer's legs. An aged bald-headed man followed her wearing a gabardine 1930s style suit with wide lapels. He leaned on an ornately carved cane.

"Of course," Cullins sneered. "What is she, his granddaughter falling out of that dress?"

As if a maître d', Phantasmo turned slightly, indicating with the flat of his hand the older man. "Professor Cullins, may I introduce you to George Baker, better known as Father Divine. The young lady I do not know. Though I suspect she may be his familiar."

Cullins declared, "Father Divine, the con man preacher? I'd mention he's dead but then again, there's the body of a pterodactyl laying over there."

"I'm a spiritualist, my dear," the older gent intoned. "I seek only to advance our race and thereby better humankind overall." He dipped his head slightly

"You're him," Cullins declared. She looked at Phantasmo. "He was the one who questioned me."

"He wants to bend your will, Althea," Phantasmo said.

"What for?"

"To harness your innovative command of mathematical calculations to reveal the Vault of Heaven. An adjunct of the work you've done for the space race that came to his attention."

Father Divine again bowed his head in acknowledgement. He also made a signal to his chauffeur. "Lenny, your time to shine."

Lenny the reptile man flung his arms wide and let loose with a horrific growl. Flexing his muscles caused splits in his clothing.

"I suppose at some point you'll hip me to what this Vault of Heaven is," the professor said.

Phantasmo was airborne and flew speedily at Lenny who squatted then leaped high off the ground. The two combatants met in midair, grappling fiercely. The amphibian's hands were webbed with long claws. He raked these across Phantasmo, ripping his cosmic garments, rending long, red tears of flesh.

Father Divine spoke jocularly. "Lenny is no mere escapee from a jungle lagoon, Phantasmo. My second is enchanted, embodying the verve of K'uk'ulkan, he of wind and water." His voice rose, surprisingly strong for a man of his years.

True to Father Divine's words, whipping around Phantasmo were elongated circles of water like liquid hula hoops, lashing and battering him from various angles. The water wheels cut him, opening new wounds and deepened the previous ones.

"Phantasmo," a concerned Cullins yelled.

The spectral man went prone on his back in the air, the assault of the deadly rings continuing. The gilled creature stood on the ground, gesturing with his outstretched hand like a conductor as he orchestrated the torment.

"Careful, Whizzer's a tricky devil," Father Divine warned.

Lenny grinned, showing sharp teeth in his scaly face. Returning his attention to his captive, he made a fist and the water wheels constricted around Phantasmo. He cried out in agony as the rings got tighter and tighter, in some places blood spurting from his body.

Professor Cullins charged the gill man, intending to spear him with her makeshift weapon. He casually swatted her roughly to the ground. Then pantomiming, as if drawing in a fishing line, the refuge from the lagoon reeled Phantasmo to the earth. The water wheels broke apart into a wet foggy mist that reformed over the inert dark man. The floating water became cone shaped

and swirled around, a mini-tornado over Phantasmo's face. The funnel rose higher, lightening blots crackling around it as well. Down it came, cascading on the angular face, drowning him as the mystical torrent swirled into his nose and mouth. His body became bloated, threatening to burst from within.

"Stop it," Cullins cried out, getting off the ground.

"Pshaw," Father Divine huffed, shaking his cane at Phantasmo. "I can assure you if the tables were turned, he'd do the same to me. Worse."

"You sick old fool."

"Ha, is that any way to talk to me, the savior?"

Before she could curse him out, a guttural snarl from the amphibious man had them turning their heads. The mini-tornado was reversing, the tail end of the water cone now over Phantasmo and the larger circular end gushing onto Lenny. He was picked up in the contained maelstrom. He flailed and wailed but his magicks couldn't break him free. As with Phantasmo, the water in this shape got tighter around him.

"Lord have mercy," Father Divine lamented.

The water crystallized into what looked like seaweed wrapping around Lenny. He lay in the middle of the street, growling and trying to get free but not succeeding. Phantasmo was whole again. "You're losing your grip, George. Getting a little too long in the tooth, are you?"

"Look who's talking."

The woman was leaning against the Rolls, one legged crossed at the ankle over the other. She straightened up, saying, "Shall I handle the scientist?"

"Come and get me, tramp," Cullins said.

The other woman tensed, hissing and baring teeth with overly large incisors. Her tongue flicked about as her pupils were no longer round but elongated upside down triangles—emerald green fixed in orange orbs.

"Now, now." Father Divine said, patting her hand and calming her down. "Time to call it a day, for now." He gestured toward Lenny. "If you would be so kind, my dear."

"Very well." The woman bent down and, taking hold of him, effortlessly rose with him. Using a fireman's carry, she hauled him to the Rolls and deposited him in the backseat. Thereafter she got behind the wheel, Father Divine on the passenger side.

"Shouldn't you try and stop him?" Cullins said to Phantasmo.

"Ours is a long-running battle. This is but another skirmish." He phased back to his mortal form.

The Rolls Royce drove away. Not along a cosmic roadway but on earthly streets.

"We should make ourselves scarce too," Anson said. "The spell of containment has lifted with George's departure."

"What about the flying lizard?"

"You want to hang around and explain it?"

"Let's go."

Later at another of Anson's apartments, this one at the Gaylord on Wilshire, she sat on the couch, both having a cocktail. An Ella Fitzgerald LP played on his stereo system. There was no news about the pterodactyl. Authorities higher than the field personnel of the LAPD had enacted a news blackout on the matter to quell panic among other reasons.

"They seek to balance the scales of justice," Anson was saying.

"That's some damn heavy lifting" Cullins said, sipping from her martini glass. He'd told her he was affiliated with a secret organization called the Reconstructionists. Their lineage went back to the time after the Civil War and the period of Reconstruction. This was a bold effort by the then Radical Republicans to enfranchise the newly freed. It also led to the creation and violent backlash of the Klan.

Before then, slave labor had been used to help build the White House and the Capitol buildings. Hidden in the stonework of those and other structures in Washington, D.C. were certain symbols. According to Anson, these had been engraved by those versed in the mystics of the Yorubas. When combined, these symbols, it was rumored, would form a cosmology, the Vault of Heaven. The Vault was said to unlock the path the sun takes among the mirrored worlds of the living and the dead. Descendants of the mystics were part of the Reconstructionists, who still operated today behind the scenes to create a better world.

"Which has come to be interpreted as unleashing great power or wisdom to its user," Anson had said concerning the Vault of Heaven.

"Father Divine, George to you, has his agents in place like you?" she observed.

"Yes," he allowed. "He felt your mathematics could be used in a formula he's long sought to perfect. This in lieu of the symbols, some of which no longer exist given a number of edifices have been demolished.

"And he was once a Reconstructionist, wasn't he?"

"Yes ma'am, he was."

"No need to be so formal, Phil." She slid closer to him, a knee on the cushions. Their faces got closer. "I am curious though. Father Divine called you Whizzer. I'm guessing you earned that nickname being a go-getter?"

A thin smile on his face, Anson cocked his head as if he hearing indistinct voices. "Ah, you know how it is. Folks hang a moniker on you and try as you might, you can't escape it.

IN THE PENTHOUSE BEDROOM OF THE swank Waldorf-Anthony Hotel, one of three figures stirred but did not wake from their slumber. This woman, a bottle blonde, had an arm draped across the torso of the man on his back who lightly snored. The third occupant of the large four-poster bed was on the other side of the man and she slept with her back to the other two. She was

Black, her hair marcelled though tousled about her head. Their clothes were scattered over the deep pile rug along with more than one empty bottle of champagne. On the nightstand remained an amount of the cocaine the three had also enjoyed. Light from a lamp dispelled some of the gloom, allowing visibility around the bed.

Arms akimbo, the colored bellhop, who was called Whizzer, stood at the side of the bed taking all this in. Sometimes if the hotel manger was cross with him, he'd call him by his last name, McGee. That wasn't the family name he'd been born with but had used upon his return from Akhet Shamba' Lan and his inculcation and training among the High Lamas led by the Grand High Lama. The once freighter's stoker began to speak in a low tone, casting a curtain of suspension on the two women. It was the white man between them he'd come to speak to.

"Wake up, Phil Anson," he said. "Wake and focus on my words."

The one he was addressing moaned, but his eyes didn't open.

The bellhop leaned over and slapped the man's cheek, twice. "Wake the fuck up," he said forcefully.

"Wha—. . . " Anson managed, eyes fluttering open.

"I need you to pay attention." The bellhop straightened up.

"Whizzer, the hell you doing in here? How dare you!" Anson sat up, back against the headboard. He was handsome and muscular, but going to fat from his various debaucheries. In the 1920s he'd lived in Paris, and hobnobbing among the creatives called the Lost Generation by Gertrude Stein. He'd returned to the States in '36, some four years ago.

"Shut up and listen," his intruder repeated.

Anson reached across the sleeping blonde for the phone, intending to call down to the desk. "You've greatly overstepped, Whizzer. You've taken my kindness to you for weakness." He wondered why the bellhop sounded so educated all of a sudden but was intent on getting him fired.

"Put the phone down, Phil, or I'll break your hand."

Anson snorted and picked up the handset. It became a slithering cobra. "The hell?" he gasped, dropping the instrument. The handset resumed its actual form.

"From time to time I'll need to borrow your identity," Whizzer McGee was saying. "I'm taking my cue from Walter White, who could pass for Caucasian when he went undercover to investigate the lynchings of colored folk and try and bring the guilty to justice. Me being you will be useful in carrying out my calling. Being white, I mean, in certain settings. I could be any ofay, but given your inherited wealth, you have access to the restricted bourgeois clubs and what have you. Some of whom I need access to. Besides, I've studied you these past few months. No sense having that go to waste."

"You've lost your mind, helped yourself to my cocaine, did you?"

As an answer, the visage of Whizzer began to shift. The muscles under the skin flowed and reformed, the jaw changed and his kinky hair straightened. The skin too took on a different appearance, its darker hue absorbed beneath the surface. Now he was the double, Phil Anson's face complete with skin tone and his full head of reddish-brown hair parted in the middle.

"I must be the one who is still under the influence," the real Anson breathed.

His doppelganger levitated off the floor, rising about a foot from the carpet. "Now let's work out the particulars." He returned to the carpet and once more assumed his true face, his bellhop's pillbox hat perched jauntily on his head.

"What if I refuse to go along with this, whatever this is?"

The person he knew as Whizzer hunched a shoulder. "I could kill you and take your place. Given I've learned about the pressure points in the body, I can easily make it seem you had a heart attack." He flicked a hand at the white powder. "Too much indulgence."

Anson glared at him, unsure of how to respond.

"But that's so . . . permanent, not to mention not my style. He undid two of the buttons on his tunic and reaching inside, removed several snapshots he placed on Anson. "I have plenty of pictures of you carrying on with all sorts of folks, women and men of various persuasions. Now me, I applaud your open-mindedness. But this bohemian behavior of yours might not be seen by influential types in the same light. You could find yourself persona non grata on the boards and clubs you like to frequent. You could be labeled a Bolshevik or worse, a deviant," he chortled. He pulled a chair over saying, "You thrive on being popular among the social circles you inhabit. I know from observing you living in isolation would not be to your liking." He sat near the bed.

"Bastard."

Whizzer McGee held his arms wide, grinning.

ANSON'S ARMS WERE AROUND THE PROFESSOR and hers around his shoulders. They made out for a while then went into the bedroom. Ella sang her last song and the needle rose from the LP. The arm retracted and the turntable shut off. Sometime later, Phil Anson stepped out of the bathroom in his pajama pants. He paused, looking at the slumbering professor. His cosmic gem appeared on his forehead. Shouldn't he have the knowledge of her mathematics that might reveal and unlock the Vault of Heaven? Surely he wouldn't be tempted to misuse such power . . .

ACKNOWLEDGEMENTS

The following stories included in *The Unvarnished Gary Phillips* were previously published as follows:

"Demon of the Track" originally in *Pop the Clutch: Thrilling Tales of Rockabilly, Monsters, and Hot Rod Horror,* ed. Eric J. Guignard

"Comstock's Advantage," originally in *Passport to Murder* as "This Ain't No Time for a Vacation" Bouchercon 2017 anthology, ed. John McFetridge

"The Kwanzaa Initiative" originally in *Astonishing Heroes: Shades of Justice,* ed. Keith B. Shaw

"Thus Strikes the Black Pimpernel" originally in *The Obama Inheritance: Fifteen Stories of Conspiracy Noir,* ed. Gary Phillips

"No Room! No Room!" originally in the e-book collection *Stop the World: Snapshots from a Pandemic,* eds. Lise McClendon, Taffy Cannon, Kate Flora, and Gary Phillips

"Fangs of the Fire Serpent," originally in *Black Pulp,* eds. Tommy Hancock, Morgan Minor, and Gary Phillips

"The Darklight Gizmo Matter" originally in *Private Dicks and Disco Balls,* ed. Michael Bracken

"Shaderoc the Soul Shaker" originally in *Crime Plus Music,* ed. Jim Fusilli

"Grag's Last Escape" originally in *Blood and Gasoline: High-Octane, High-Velocity Action,* ed. Mario Acevedo

"Bret Khodo, Agent of C.O.D.E." originally in *Asian Pulp,* eds. Tommy Hancock and Morgan McKay

"Enter The Silencer" originally in *Blood & Tacos,* ed. Johnny Shaw

"Tobin and Gagarin" originally in *The Big Click* online magazine

"Matthew Henson and the Treasure of the Queen of Sheba" originally as bonus short story in the limited edition hardback, *Matthew Henson and the Ice Temple of Harlem*

"Tacos de Cazuela con Smith & Wesson" originally in *Gun & Tacos* Vol. 1, eds. Michael Bracken & Trey R. Barker

"Desal Plant No. 9," originally an Occupied Earth online story, eds. Richard Brewer and Gary Phillips

"I, Truck" originally in *18 Wheels of Science Fiction: A Long Haul into the Fantastic,* ed. Eric Miller

For more background on Phantasmo, the character in "Phantasmo and the Vault of Heaven," and E. C. Stoner see *Invisible Men: The Trailblazing Black Artists of Comic Books* by Ken Quattro.

ABOUT THE AUTHOR

GARY PHILLIPS has been a community activist, labor organizer, and has delivered dog cages. He's published various novels, comics, short stories, and edited several anthologies including *South Central Noir* and the Anthony award-winning *The Obama Inheritance: Fifteen Stories of Conspiracy Noir*. *Violent Spring*, first published in 1994, was named in 2020 one of the essential crime novels of Los Angeles. He was also a writer/co-producer on FX's *Snowfall* (streaming on Hulu), about crack and the CIA in 1980s South Central where he grew up. Recent novels include *One-Shot Harry* and *Matthew Henson and the Ice Temple of Harlem*. He lives with his family in the wilds of Los Angeles.

RECENT AND FORTHCOMING BOOKS FROM THREE ROOMS PRESS

FICTION

Lucy Jane Bledsoe
No Stopping Us Now

Rishab Borah
The Door to Inferna

Meagan Brothers
Weird Girl and What's His Name

Christopher Chambers
Scavenger
Standalone

Ebele Chizea
Aquarian Dawn

Ron Dakron
Hello Devilfish!

Robert Duncan
Loudmouth

Michael T. Fournier
Hidden Wheel
Swing State

Aaron Hamburger
Nirvana Is Here

William Least Heat-Moon
Celestial Mechanics

Aimee Herman
Everything Grows

Kelly Ann Jacobson
Tink and Wendy
Robin and Her Misfits

Jethro K. Lieberman
Everything Is Jake

Eamon Loingsigh
Light of the Diddicoy
Exile on Bridge Street

John Marshall
The Greenfather

Alvin Orloff
Vulgarian Rhapsody

Micki Ravizee
Of Blood and Lightning

Aram Saroyan
Still Night in L.A.

Robert Silverberg
The Face of the Waters

Stephen Spotte
Animal Wrongs

Richard Vetere
The Writers Afterlife
Champagne and Cocaine

Jessamyn Violet
Secret Rules to Being a Rockstar

Julia Watts
Quiver
Needlework
Lovesick Blossoms

Gina Yates
Narcissus Nobody

MEMOIR & BIOGRAPHY

Nassrine Azimi and Michel Wasserman
Last Boat to Yokohama: The Life and Legacy of Beate Sirota Gordon

William S. Burroughs & Allen Ginsberg
Don't Hide the Madness:
William S. Burroughs in Conversation with Allen Ginsberg
edited by Steven Taylor

James Carr
BAD: The Autobiography of James Carr

Judy Gumbo
Yippie Girl: Exploits in Protest and Defeating the FBI

Judith Malina
Full Moon Stages: Personal Notes from 50 Years of The Living Theatre

Phil Marcade
Punk Avenue: Inside the New York City Underground, 1972–1982

Jillian Marshall
Japanthem: Counter-Cultural Experiences; Cross-Cultural Remixes

Alvin Orloff
Disasterama! Adventures in the Queer Underground 1977–1997

Nicca Ray
Ray by Ray: A Daughter's Take on the Legend of Nicholas Ray

Stephen Spotte
My Watery Self:
Memoirs of a Marine Scientist

PHOTOGRAPHY-MEMOIR

Mike Watt
On & Off Bass

SHORT STORY ANTHOLOGIES

SINGLE AUTHOR

Alien Archives: Stories
by Robert Silverberg

First-Person Singularities: Stories
by Robert Silverberg
with an introduction by John Scalzi

Tales from the Eternal Café: Stories
by Janet Hamill, with an introduction by Patti Smith

Time and Time Again:
Sixteen Trips in Time
by Robert Silverberg

The Unvarnished Gary Phillips:
A Mondo Pulp Collection
by Gary Phillips

Voyagers:
Twelve Journeys in Space and Time
by Robert Silverberg

MULTI-AUTHOR

Crime + Music: Twenty Stories of Music-Themed Noir
edited by Jim Fusilli

Dark City Lights: New York Stories
edited by Lawrence Block

The Faking of the President: Twenty Stories of White House Noir
edited by Peter Carlaftes

Florida Happens:
Bouchercon 2018 Anthology
edited by Greg Herren

Have a NYC I, II & III:
New York Short Stories;
edited by Peter Carlaftes
& Kat Georges

No Body, No Crime: Twenty-two Tales of Taylor Swift-Inspired Noir
edited by Alex Segura & Joe Clifford

Songs of My Selfie:
An Anthology of Millennial Stories
edited by Constance Renfrow

The Obama Inheritance:
15 Stories of Conspiracy Noir
edited by Gary Phillips

This Way to the End Times:
Classic and New Stories of the Apocalypse
edited by Robert Silverberg

MIXED MEDIA

John S. Paul
Sign Language: A Painter's Notebook
(photography, poetry and prose)

DADA

Maintenant: A Journal of Contemporary Dada Writing & Art
(annual, since 2008)

HUMOR

Peter Carlaftes
A Year on Facebook

FILM & PLAYS

Israel Horovitz
My Old Lady: Complete Stage Play and Screenplay with an Essay on Adaptation

Peter Carlaftes
Triumph For Rent (3 Plays)
Teatrophy (3 More Plays)

Kat Georges
Three Somebodies: Plays about Notorious Dissidents

TRANSLATIONS

Thomas Bernhard
On Earth and in Hell
(poems of Thomas Bernhard with English translations by Peter Waugh)

Patrizia Gattaceca
Isula d'Anima / Soul Island

César Vallejo | Gerard Malanga
Malanga Chasing Vallejo
(selected poems of César Vallejo with English translations and additional notes by Gerard Malanga)

George Wallace
EOS: Abductor of Men
(selected poems in Greek & English)

ESSAYS

Richard Katrovas
Raising Girls in Bohemia:
Meditations of an American Father

Vanessa Baden Kelly
Far Away From Close to Home

Womentality: Thirteen Empowering Stories by Everyday Women Who Said Goodbye to the Workplace and Hello to Their Lives
edited by Erin Wildermuth

POETRY COLLECTIONS

Hala Alyan
Atrium

Peter Carlaftes
DrunkYard Dog
I Fold with the Hand I Was Dealt
Life in the Past Lane

Thomas Fucaloro
It Starts from the Belly and Blooms

Kat Georges
Our Lady of the Hunger
Awe and Other Words Like Wow

Robert Gibbons
Close to the Tree

Israel Horovitz
Heaven and Other Poems

David Lawton
Sharp Blue Stream

Jane LeCroy
Signature Play

Philip Meersman
This Is Belgian Chocolate

Jane Ormerod
Recreational Vehicles on Fire
Welcome to the Museum of Cattle

Lisa Panepinto
On This Borrowed Bike

George Wallace
Poppin' Johnny

Three Rooms Press | New York, NY | Current Catalog: www.threeroomspress.com

Three Rooms Press books are distributed by Publishers Group West: www.pgw.com